**Add to your Candace Irving Library**
**FOR FREE**

Sign up for my newsletter & get a free book, plus future exclusive content.

Details can be found at the end of
***Backblast*.**

# BACKBLAST

---

A US ARMY DETECTIVE REGAN CHASE THRILLER: DECEPTION POINT MILITARY THRILLER SERIES, BOOK 3

CANDACE IRVING

# PROLOGUE

*US Embassy Islamabad,*
*Pakistan*

Tonight he would enter Paradise.

The certainty that he would soon be freed of this barren, earthly existence caused the sweetest of serenities to flow through his body. He focused on the balm, using it to cleanse his thoughts and distance himself from the crowd pressing in. Unlike so many in whose footsteps he followed, he needed no promise of milk and honey to heed the holiest of calls. It was enough to know he was submitting to Allah's will.

And submit he would.

Soon.

He turned his sandals toward the platform beside the embassy gates, scanning the muted multitude of *shalwar kameez* that filled the darkened grounds, pleased the rougher-hewn fabric of his matching trousers and oversized tunic did not set him apart—much less trumpet the redemption beneath. The cool, sweat-laden air ripened with the stink of expectation and hope as the betrayer finally deigned to appear. Had his countrymen known how this night would end, they would surely have chosen to attend mosque for *Fajr* prayers rather than partake in this scripted farce.

Still, he felt no pity. No guilt.

Not when his people persisted in clinging to their shameless desire for peace with the infidel amid this rotted world. The moment he caught sight of the black beret and blue shirt of the Capital Territory policeman, he knew that the imam was right. Allah's will was here. Now. With him and within him.

He need do no more than heed it.

He pushed his way through the crowd, closer to the makeshift platform and the harlot standing upon it. The betrayer stood beside her. And then the betrayer was stepping up to the microphone, adjusting it before he raised those stained hands to silence the shouts of misplaced sympathy, disbelief and righteous discontent.

The clatter and clicks of countless cameras supplanted the quiet.

And then the lies began.

He ignored them, slowly but surely threading his way through the throng for most of that deceptively impassioned speech, all the while guided by that black beret—and Allah. Neither failed him.

The throng thickened as he continued his march, the earlier indignation and disbelief of his countrymen now all but mute as they absorbed the mounting lies that dripped from the microphone. Islam's hidden apostate held them firmly in his thrall.

But not for much longer.

The policeman turned and stiffened. He had been spotted, then.

It mattered not.

He ignored the policeman, turning instead to glimpse one of the Americans moving toward him as well. He slipped his hand into the sleeve of his *kameez*. Both the policeman and the American were nearly upon him now. Twice the gift. His fingers found their prize as the policeman and the American pushed closer.

They were too late.

He had already pressed the detonator—and smiled.

# 1

*Blanchfield Army Community Hospital*
*Fort Campbell, Kentucky*

With friends like hers, she didn't need enemies.

Cliché or not, the taunting refrain had been hammering through Regan's brain for the past ten minutes. Five more and she'd have the satisfaction of spitting that same refrain into one of her supposed best friends' faces. Regan held fast to the thought as she blew through the automatic glass doors that separated the post hospital's snow-covered parking lot from the emergency room within. Satisfaction set in early as she spotted the sparely populated patient lounge to her left.

*Excellent*. As head of Trauma, Gil should be free.

Regan dragged her black beret from her head and nodded to the Latina lieutenant manning the nurses' station. "Ma'am."

"Good morning, Chief. I didn't expect to see you unti—"

"This afternoon. I know." Regan jammed the beret beneath her left arm as she reached the counter. "Is Lieutenant Colonel Fourche with a patient?"

"No. He—"

Regan didn't bother waiting for the rest. She headed past the nurses' station and turned down the freshly waxed corridor that led to Gil's office. His door was closed, meaning he was still slugging down his morning gallon of coffee as he caught up on the previous night's cases. Regan offered Gil the single, sharp rap of warning he'd denied her before she shoved his door open.

"You *screwed* me."

Perhaps she should've waited long enough to hear the nurse out, because not one, but two startled faces greeted her opening.

The closely cropped blond mug behind the desk belonged to Gil. According to the ten-by-twelve-inch framed photo posted behind the nurses' station, the graying ebony mug belonged to Colonel Daniel J. Chilcote, Blanchfield Hospital's spanking new commanding officer.

*Great.*

Unfortunately, retreat was out of the question. The colonel's dark brown stare had already zeroed in on the paltry chief warrant officer two insignia velcroed to the center placket of her Army Combat Uniform before quickly shifting to take in the nametape above the right pocket of those same camouflaged ACUs.

Regan held her ground as the colonel stood. The man extended a slender surgeon's hand. His low chuckle bathed her nerves, reassuring her that she wasn't destined to end up on report before the morning was out.

"That was quite an entrance, Agent Chase. And definitely more personal information than I needed. That said—" The colonel's amusement faded, the distinct threads of professional curiosity assuming its place. "I've been eager to meet you. I understand I arrived at Campbell a mere hour after you were released from the hospital."

"Yes, sir." Gil had mentioned his new boss' arrival and

subsequent disappointment when he'd stopped by her apartment to check up on her that night. It seemed every neurologist, biological warfare expert and infectious disease specialist in the Army had been clamoring for a copy of her medical chart this past week, including Blanchfield's new head honcho.

The soldier who'd survived the unsurvivable.

Lucky her.

But at what cost?

Regan pushed the heartache aside as that eerily steady stare continued to size her up. If her pending showdown with Gil didn't pan out, she had a serious future as a lab rat.

Speaking of rats...

A swift glance at Gil assured Regan *he* had no illusions as to the cause of the fury that had fueled her entrance.

"Agent Chase, I don't suppose you'd mind if I—"

"Not at all, Colonel Chilcote." She kept her attention focused on the flush staining the base of Gil's neck. "I'd be thrilled to have a neurosurgeon of your caliber examine me. Perhaps you'd do me the honor of signing off on my readiness to return to duty when we've finished?"

A task her two-faced *friend* hadn't seen fit to accomplish.

"Absolutely. I'm about to head out for a meeting across post. Come to my office in say...two hours?"

"I'll be there." It wasn't as though she had anything else to do.

"Outstanding." The man nodded to Gil as he headed for the office door. "Dr. Fourche."

"Colonel."

Regan turned back to the desk as the door closed. Her triumph faded as she spotted Gil's frown; pissed or not, he still outranked her. "Sorry. I should've knocked—"

"Agreed."

"—but *you* should have warned me. At the very least. *Buddy*."

"I planned to. This afternoon. How'd you find out? You weren't scheduled to return to work until Monday."

Regan tossed her beret on the seat Chilcote had vacated and shed her ACU jacket. The digital camouflage followed her beret to the chair. "I stopped by CID for our morning brief. Figured I'd plow through the mountain of waiting paperwork, perhaps even put my name on the duty roster and catch the first case of the weekend. Let one of my fellow agents sleep in for a change. Imagine my surprise when my CO mentioned that my medical release form had failed to make its way across post."

Regan snatched Gil's spare Beetle Bailey coffee mug from the filing cabinet. His brows rose as she turned to thump the pea-green ceramic atop the calendar blotter on the desk—loudly.

"Surprise?"

"Okay, my fury." Which that stoic stare of his was causing to ratchet up again. "Where the hell do you get off insinuating I'm not fit for duty?"

"Because you're not."

She stalked so far forward, the edge of his desk cut into her thighs. "*Excuse me*? You told me two days ago that I'd passed my physical, lab work included. There is no psycho-toxin lingering in my body. Just a bazillion antibodies. In fact, one of your vampires drained a pint from my arm just yesterday to send to Fort Detrick so our biowarfare defense guys could study my astounding newfound immunity."

"True." Instead of elaborating, Gil turned to the filing cabinet to retrieve his massive thermos. Regan waited none-too-patiently as he charged the spare mug she'd plunked onto his desk with a generous portion of the steaming, black contents.

The moment the thermos resumed its post, she lit in. "So?"

His sigh filled the office. "Have a seat."

"No, thanks."

"Damn it, Rae. *Sit*."

Something in his voice forced her to scoop her beret and jacket out of the chair Chilcote had vacated. Gil pushed the spare mug to the edge of his blotter as she dumped her gear on the carpet and sat.

"Have some caffeine. You look like you could use it."

She didn't doubt it. Even if she hadn't caught sight of her admittedly haggard features in the mirror this morning, she felt the need for a piping hot pick-me-up deep in her bones. Unfortunately, ice-cold apprehension had just surpassed it.

Her blood was clean, wasn't it? Or had some lab tech at Detrick discovered otherwise?

Was that why Gil had refused to clear her for duty?

She dragged her air in deep, the burgeoning fear deeper. "Just say it."

To her horror, Gil abandoned the working side of his desk and snagged the spare patient chair along the wall. He dragged it to within a foot of hers and sank down into the seat. His proximity wasn't what scared her. It was the compassion simmering in that light blue stare. The same compassion that had simmered within nearly two weeks earlier as she'd crawled in and out of those godawful hallucinations for almost twenty-four hours, before she'd finally succumbed to coma.

"It's not your body that has me worried, Rae. It's your mind."

*Oh, Jesus.* First Art Valens dying, then John leaving—and now this. It couldn't get any worse.

Hallucinations.

Was that why—thirteen days after waking from his own coma—Sergeant Welch had yet to be released from the hospital? Had *his* hallucinations come back?

Was she next?

Regan swallowed hard. It didn't help. Acid still seared up her throat, and she was rapidly becoming too unhinged to care. "Gil...wh—what are you trying to say?"

"When was the last time you slept?"

Huh?

He reached for her hands. Warm, steady fingers closed over hers, squeezed.

She tugged them free. "Last night."

"Liar."

He was right. Damn him. The hallucinations might not have resumed yet, but the dreams had. The nightmares.

Who was she kidding? They'd never stopped.

Art's disembodied face floated before hers. It took several blinks before it faded. She stood, rounding the corner of Gil's desk, admittedly cowering behind his high-back leather chair as she dug her fingers into the padded shoulders for support. Anything to distance herself from that insidious compassion.

"I slept." Yesterday.

There. Close enough to the truth to be convincing, even for this man, who knew her better than most.

Gil nodded. "For how long?"

Long enough to watch Art's headstone drift into her dreams, coated with snow. Long enough to feel his wife's bottomless grief as it soaked into her neck. Long enough—as the dream twisted and morphed—to feel the desperately needed solid warmth of John's arms...until she woke and discovered that once again, John was gone.

"Rae?"

"Long enough, damn it. I slept *long enough*. Now will you please tell me what this is about? What did Detrick find?"

Confusion supplanted the compassion. Understanding followed. Finally, embarrassment. "I'm sorry I worried you. Chalk it up to my own running dearth of Zs. Except for the lingering tremor in your dominant hand, you're fine. There's no evidence of a medical relapse—absolutely none. But emotionally? You're at the edge, and you're teetering there with everything bottled up inside. I think that's why that tremor comes and goes. There's a good chance it's not so much physiological as psychological. And if you don't take steps now to deal with everything that's happened these past few weeks, there's a good chance it will get worse—especially if it's both."

Anger burned through the relief as Gil's words trailed off. "*That's* what this is about?" Her so-called mental state? "You still want me to break down and bawl like a two-year old?"

The compassion returned, suffocating the blue. "It just might help."

Since when? It hadn't the night they'd met just over a year ago when Gil had tried his best to stitch her insides back together after some sergeant jacked up on PCP had decided to rearrange them, causing her to miscarry and damned near die before all was said and done. And it certainly hadn't helped two decades earlier when Mommy Dearest had chosen to rearrange her own face with the working end of her dad's .38 backup revolver. "Trust me; tears don't accomplish squat."

"How 'bout talking?"

"We've talked."

"Wrong. I've talked. You haven't even given me the courtesy of listening. You just stare off and nod occasionally—like you're doing now."

She shoved the leather chair into the desk as the grief and the guilt finally broke free. "What do you want from me? You want me to say it? Fine. Art Valens is *dead*. Because *I* missed a clue."

"Bullshit!"

That reined her in—hard. Not the curse; Gil's ire. She'd never seen, much less heard him hit that level before. But then she'd never pushed their relationship quite so far. Case in point: her downright insubordinate entrance minutes before. Friendship or not, Gil was still a light colonel; she a warrant officer—

trapped in the nether region between commissioned officer and enlisted. Best she remember that.

She licked her lips. "Gil, I—"

He stood as well, looming over the opposite side of the desk. Over her. "*No*. You don't want to have a genuine conversation? Okay by me. I'll do the talking. Again. But this time, you are going to listen." He stalked around his desk, trapping her between his mahogany bookshelf and a framed pen-and-ink sketch of a skeleton hanging on the wall. "Yes, your old CID mentor and friend is dead, but *you* did not kill him. Nor are you responsible for Captain Mendoza's death or the six other soldiers from that Special Forces team who succumbed to that goddamned psycho-toxin. And it sure as hell isn't your fault that John Garrison was forced to abandon you in this very hospital three hours after you woke from your own coma to go Heaven knows where and do Heaven knows what. That *screw*—as you put it so succinctly—came compliments of Special Operations Command and the uppermost brass of the US Army."

He was right. About all of it.

Logically, she knew that.

So why did it feel so wrong? And why did she feel so utterly wrung out and hollow inside?

The tears Gil had been begging her to shed for six days burned at the corners of her eyes. Before she could stop them, they spilled over. No more than a handful. Apparently, it was enough. At least for him.

He cupped her cheek and smoothed the humiliation from her face—but that caused more to trickle down. She stared at the knot in Gil's throat as he swallowed. It jerked so firmly she feared he was suppressing his own ocean.

He cleared his throat. "I meant what I said when I signed your hospital release. You need time to heal. You're CID, for crying out loud. You wade though the worst of the crap our soldiers deal out on a daily basis. You need to take a minute to recoup before you dive back in. Preferably amid the peace and quiet of home."

He was so far off it wasn't funny. If she'd discovered anything this past week, it was that she needed the chaotic, consuming distraction of a new case like a junkie needed a fix. She'd also learned that there was no peace to be found, least of all at home.

Just the endless emptiness and constant recriminations.

"Gil, *please*. I need to go back to work."

"Rae—"

"No!" Damn it, this was not a case of doctor knew best. She twisted away until she'd retreated around the corner of his desk, poised to make her escape. "It doesn't matter. My hand hasn't shaken once this morning. You heard Chilcote. The man's drooling to get a crack at what's left of my brain. By the time we're done, he'll be so convinced I'm fit for duty, he'll be recommending I be assigned to the secretary of defense's personal staff."

"Wrong." Gil reached out to tap the phone on his desk. "One call, *Chief*. That's all it would take, and you know it."

"You'd do that to me? Tell your boss I have psyche issues?"

"If I have to."

White-hot silence pulsed between them. That goddamned, unrelenting compassion.

"One more week, Rae. That's all I'm asking. A week during which you talk—to me or someone else. A week during which you sleep. Every single night."

And if she didn't?

She didn't voice the counter challenge. She didn't need to; Gil's next words confirmed it.

"Or I go on the record regarding just how precarious your current mental state really is—whether or not your hand still twitches."

*Bastard.*

The silence returned. This time it filled the air for a full thirty-one seconds. She knew, because she watched the oversized, twenty-four-hour wall clock behind Gil's head tick them off, one by one.

A phone rang, shattering the quiet. But it wasn't the extension on Gil's desk. It was the cellphone in her ACU pocket. Grateful for the reprieve, Regan grabbed it.

"Agent Chase."

"You fit for duty or not?" *Colonel Hansen*. Her boss.

Regan stared at Gil and, God help her, she forced her lips to beg.

He held firm.

"Sir, I'm with Lieutenant Colonel Fourche now. He's experiencing...reservations."

"Hand him the phone."

Regan passed it to Gil, straining to listen as he greeted her CO. Unfortunately, she couldn't make out Hansen's side of the conversation. She did know Gil was not happy. Not with the initial information he was given and not with the ensuing discussion that he actively pushed on his end, abusing every embarrassing facet of the argument he'd just thrown in her face, plus a few. And, finally, Gil was anything but pleased with his own terse "Yes, sir. Understood" at the call's conclusion.

Gil severed the connection and passed the phone back.

Silence bunkered in once more, hardening down to depleted uranium as Gil turned to withdraw a form from the top drawer of his desk. He scratched out a few words, filled in her name and signed his at the bottom before handing the form over.

Bemusement set in as Regan deciphered his scrawl. *Fit for duty*. She jerked her chin up. Gil's seemingly blasé shrug was everything but.

"Seems I've been overruled—needs of the Army and all.

Congratulations, Chief. You're back on the roster. You won't be waiting for your next case, however. It's already here—but it's not new. You'll find out the rest when you get to CID. Now go; Colonel Hansen's waiting. And for God's sake, be careful."

He didn't have to tell her twice.

She left.

# 2

By the time Regan reached the building housing Fort Campbell's Criminal Investigation Division, her boss was nowhere to be found. Stranger still, the man occupying Colonel Hansen's office outranked her commanding officer by a hefty trio of silver stars.

Lieutenant General Thad Palisade.

Regan stared through the sliver of glass that ran down the length of the door. The general's wrought-iron back might be to her, the formal fitted coat and trousers of his Army Greens uncharacteristically crushed and creased from what had undoubtedly been a long and tedious flight, but it was him.

According to the duty sergeant out front, the current head of the US Army's Special Operations Command had returned to Kentucky...just to see her.

For a single, blinding moment, panic flooded her entire body.

*John.*

Palisade was the closest man John had to a father. If the general was here, hat literally in hand, and John was not, that meant—

Damn it. This was not a death notification. Nor was John missing-in-action. If he was, Gil would be here too...to pick up the pieces. But if John was still alive and kicking—wherever he was—that meant Palisade was here about her case.

The not-so-new one.

Regan blew out her relief and pushed the door all the way open. She closed it behind her as the general spun around, his weather-beaten ascetic features splitting into a warm, deep smile as he spotted her.

"What went wrong, sir?"

The smile evaporated as he tossed his hat on the desk. Like her, Palisade blew out his breath—and cut straight to the point. "Everything."

Shit.

Palisade waved his hand toward the pair of black vinyl armchairs and couch wedged into the corner of Hansen's office. "Have a seat. The file's on the table, waiting for you. I'll get the caffeine. Don't know about you, but I could use some."

Regan blinked back her shock as the man turned and headed for the door. A general running for his own joe? And a warrant officer's to boot?

This was bad.

Curiosity overtook her surprise as she reached the coffee table. The file was there, as promised. Regan doffed her beret and camouflaged jacket and dumped them in one of the armchairs, opening the four-inch-thick, brown accordion folder marked *Top Secret* and hauling it closer as she sank into the vinyl cushions of the other chair.

Confusion set in as she pulled out the folder's contents and flipped through the first two reports. It wasn't that she couldn't place them.

It was the contents of each.

More specifically, the summaries attached at the ends.

The first began with a slew of information that was already painfully familiar to her. Namely, that four short weeks ago, an Afghan Islamist by the name of Dr. Nabil Durrani had murdered seven pregnant Pakistani women in a cave located deep in the Hindu Kush—a cave that was also firmly located on the latter country's side of the Afghan-Pak border. The infants had been carved out from their mothers' wombs and left atop each to die. Except three of the babies had managed to survive their horrific entrance into the world. John, Captain Manuel Mendoza and Mendoza's Special Forces A-Team had breached that Pakistani cave in time to prep the three for an emergency chopper flight to Bagram Airbase. But only two had made it aboard. Another had taken a turn for the worse at Bagram and hadn't survived the night.

But one had.

Baby Doe #6. A girl. Not only had the tyke survived that chopper flight, a week and a half later she'd been flown on to Germany. She was currently thriving in Landstuhl's neonatal intensive care unit under the watchful eye of her biological father, Captain Mark McCord. Since McCord had been subsequently cleared of orchestrating the slaughter in that cave, the captain was now awaiting his separation from Special Forces and the Army so he could take his daughter back to the States.

A mere two weeks ago, the discovery that McCord had fathered a child with one of the Pakistani cave victims had turned their entire investigation on its head. But the information in the summaries of these two reports was even more startling.

They contained the respective DNA breakdowns for two *other* infants from that cave: Baby Doe #3 and Baby Doe #5.

They appeared identical.

But that was impossible...wasn't it?

Regan was in the middle of her own, systematic, visual comparison of the DNA breakdown when a Styrofoam cup of steaming black coffee materialized on the table beside the accordion folder.

"It's not a mistake, Chief."

She glanced up as the general scooped up her beret and jacket, tossing both to the couch as he claimed the chair beside her. "You're certain?"

"The lab guys ran the test three times. Of the seven babies Garrison and his men found in that cave, two of the boys were identical twins."

Regan leaned back in her chair, absorbing the implications.

Because, ultimately, the brutal murders in that cave had just been the beginning. The very nature of the deaths was part of a sick, two-pronged terror plot to provide one hell of a stressor to allow an unknown biological warfare agent to kick in, decimating Captain Mendoza's Special Forces team by sending the infected soldiers home to their loved ones in the States as violent, hallucinating human IEDs—while simultaneously framing Captain McCord's SF team to take the fall for the cave slaughter.

Nabil Durrani—the Afghan-born, so-called physician responsible for the depraved plot—had hoped to translate the resulting frame into a renewed burst of hatred for all things American within the Islamic world, and especially within Pakistan. For who would fail to avenge the death of innocent Muslim children?

But if two of those infants were twins...

Regan leaned forward, needing the caffeine the general had provided more than ever. She took several scalding sips before returning the Styrofoam cup to the table as she voiced the only possibility that made sense given everything else she'd uncovered while working the case. "One of the women was never pregnant. At least, not during the murders."

Palisade nodded. "Yes. By the time the medical examiner had

a chance to confirm that the mismatched mother from that cave showed signs of a late-term miscarriage and nothing more, you and the others had been kidnapped."

And then she'd been infected with the psycho-toxin. The moment she and John's men had taken down Durrani and his stooges in Afghanistan, she'd been medevacked back to the States where she'd succumbed to her own nasty bout of hallucinations—and, finally, coma. By the time she'd woken in the ICU across post, she was part of the crime. Durrani's latest victim. The case had been handed to someone else.

To whom, she still had no idea. Nor did it matter. Because, once again, the case belonged to her. That much she could see in the general's eyes.

Gil's parting words finally made sense.

As did her rapidly intensifying suspicion. "Do we know who she is? The woman with the mismatched twin?"

"No."

"What about the rest of the women?"

In lieu of answering, Palisade leaned forward. He dragged the accordion folder past her cup of coffee and flipped through the contents. He culled the crime scene close-ups of the victims' faces and splayed them across the coffee table. In each photo, the women's lashes were thrown wide, each vacant and glassy gaze offering testimony to the collective horror of their final seconds in that remote cave.

Regan pushed through her compassion as Palisade tapped the first picture. "Her name, you know."

She nodded. "Jameelah Khan." The local they'd discovered who'd once worked in the laundry on Bagram Airbase. Jameelah was also the mother of the massacre's sole surviving child...as well as the former, married lover of Captain McCord, the leader of the SF team framed for the murders. That Jameelah's child had been fathered by an American soldier had sealed McCord's fate—and his team's—in Durrani's eyes.

Palisade tapped a callused finger over five more crime scene photos. "We've identified these women as well. You were right—Durrani trolled for his victims while volunteering at the Malalie Maternity Hospital in Kabul. Agent Castile assumed lead on the case following your exposure to the psycho-toxin. Castile was able to uncover evidence that proves these women were also patients of Durrani at Malalie. Their names are now in the file."

Regan nodded. She leaned forward as well, tapping the final photograph. "And this one? Are we even close to identifying her?"

But she knew.

"No. And, yes, she's the woman who never carried a fetus to term. Miscarriage or not, there's no connection to Malalie. Not one Agent Castile has been able to unearth."

"What about Durrani? I assume he's been interrogated?"

Palisade nodded.

And, again, Regan knew. Nothing had come of those interrogations in the thirteen days they'd had the bastard in custody. There was something else in the general's stare. An odd, almost palpable mix of hesitation and anger.

"What's wrong?"

For a split second the anger intensified, then it was gone. Masked. "Durrani. He knows you survived the psycho-toxin. An interrogator let it slip."

For a moment she, too, was pissed.

How the hell did a trained interrogator just let something *slip*? Especially something as crucial as the survival of a detainee's intended, final victim?

That was information best held close to an interrogator's chest, deliberately tossing it out onto the table when, and only when, it was likely to yield maximum effect and gain. But from Palisade's expression, they'd gained absolutely nothing.

Then again—

Just like that, her fury fled. She could feel the tug of an honest-to-God grin curving her lips as she sat back in the chair. Her first in nearly a week. She allowed the grin to deepen as the thrust of the confrontation she and Durrani had shared in that darkened bathroom set in.

"I bet he's livid."

Palisade returned her grin and raised her a hearty chuckle. "Oh, that he is." A moment later, the man sobered.

His hesitation returned.

Regan suppressed a sigh. What was it with officers?

They just couldn't seem to impart what they perceived as negative news, at least not cleanly. "Sir, just spit it out."

Respect edged out the pique in the man's faded blue stare. Palisade's own, deeper sigh escaped. "Durrani wants to speak to you. In fact, he's demanding it."

Okay, not negative news. Not to her.

Still, there was no way the Army would let her meet with Durrani, alone or otherwise. Much as she craved a second face-to-face with the perverted shitbag, Gil was right. Durrani had murdered her fellow CID agent. And then the good doctor had injected her with that charming chimeral virus he'd gotten off the Russians—*personally*.

There was no way her CID chain of command or the lawyers in the Judge Advocate General's Corps would sanction a meeting.

Or would they?

Palisade shifted in his seat as Regan let the silence stretch out, waiting.

Watching.

And there it was. The evidence she sought had moved down the general's weathered features and into the slight but unmistakable clenching of his jaw. The man hadn't spilled everything he'd come to say.

Even better, just as surely as she was certain she needed to pursue the remainder of this case to retain the sanity Gil had so recently questioned, she knew what Palisade was withholding. "Durrani's refusing to talk to everyone else. Everyone but me."

The respect was back.

"Yes."

Regan clamped down on her excitement, forced herself to play it cool. Because she also knew full well that the objections and infuriating psychological assessment Gil had voiced on the phone to her commanding officer had been passed on to this man.

She could not afford to appear too eager, much less desperate. "What about Tamir Hachemi?"

The respect in Palisade's gaze deepened.

*Excellent.* Her tactic was sound. As was her suspicion regarding Durrani's sadistic man Friday.

"Hachemi clammed up."

No shock there. The Afghan translator had turned out to be nearly as cunning and verbally deft as Durrani. How else had she missed a working, state-of-the-art heater in an eighteen-year-old Nissan Urvan so battered and rusted a Sudanese junkyard would refuse it entrance? That pristine, perfectly functioning heater was the vital clue she'd missed. The one that'd led directly to Art Valens' death. The heater that had spewed the Russian-made anesthetic gas that had killed her fellow CID agent.

Gil was wrong; she should've caught that clue.

She wasn't about to miss another.

"What caused Hachemi to renege?" The last she'd heard, there'd been a deal on the table. The deal had been requested by Hachemi himself the moment the translator discovered that, due to the recent granting of his United States citizenship, he'd been officially classified as a traitor and was subsequently eligible for all dubious privileges said label entailed. Including, but by no means limited to, a sentence of hard labor and unusually spartan accommodations at the federal penitentiary at Fort Leavenworth—until his potential, pending execution.

Palisade shrugged. "We have no idea. One minute, Hachemi's claiming he has solid information regarding another terrorist—one we would be *very* interested in identifying—and the next, nothing."

Holy shit. Suddenly, the general's presence made sickening sense. "He's saying there's *another* traitor in our midst?"

"Yes. Only the claim is past tense now. Hachemi swears he made it up. Wants to take his chances at Leavenworth."

From the lock on Palisade's jaw, he didn't believe the translator's turnabout any more than she did.

Someone had gotten to the man.

Somewhere. Somehow.

Regan shot to her feet, executing a lightning about-face, stalking across her boss' drab carpet as she worked to contain the shock and growing rage. She spun around again. "Did Hachemi give up anything else before he clammed up? Is the soldier part of a larger terror cell? Has it been activated? Is he—"

Palisade held up his hand as he came to his feet. "We don't know. Any of it. But as you do know, the cave's existence—not to mention its precise location and contents—has yet to become public knowledge. The brass *and* the president would like to keep it that way, for a number of reasons. The least of which being that those women were Pakistani. The whole damned region is still a powder keg, especially now. That's the only reason the Pentagon agreed to let you back in the game."

*Durrani.* His demand to meet her.

The deviant doc had his own agenda; that was a given. She had a pretty good idea what that agenda involved, too. Either way, it didn't matter. Not to her.

And clearly, not to Palisade.

No wonder the general was here in the flesh. If there was even a chance this case wasn't yet over, the Army would use every asset at its disposal to ferret out the identity of that remaining traitor before the next catastrophe was scheduled to commence—including her.

"Sir, you think there's a chance they're connected, don't you? The identity of that woman—and the traitor."

The man's faded blue gaze strengthened. Sharpened. "Do you?"

"Yes."

"Agent Castile isn't so sure. He thinks it could just be a case of symmetry; so does the Islamist expert we brought in. Something about the number seven being sacred in the Muslim religion. And since Durrani tracked the pregnancies of six of the women at Malalie—"

Regan nodded. "They think he knew about the twins beforehand and needed another body for some mystical numeric portent."

"But you don't?"

"No." Castile was a solid agent, more than smart enough. But he was wrong on this. So was this Islamist "expert".

By the general's own briefing, no one had gotten Durrani to talk. Except her. She'd also bested the man physically. Granted, the tussle she and Durrani had shared had taken place thirteen days ago in the bathroom of a terror cell safe house in Charikar,

Afghanistan, but she'd managed to draw the doc out long enough to take him down.

It hadn't been easy. At the time, every muscle in Durrani's body had been meticulously and methodically honed.

His mind, even more so.

The conversation she and Durrani had shared then confirmed her instincts now. Palisade's too. There was more to that anomalous non-mother's presence in the cave than the need for numerical symmetry, mystically generated or otherwise.

Was she one hundred percent certain?

No.

But if there was a chance, however remote, that such a connection existed, she would be pursuing it. Especially if that chance afforded her another crack at the man responsible for injecting the psycho-toxin into not only herself, but an entire twelve-man SF team. More importantly, Durrani's coming interrogation with her could well lead to the identity of the final victim—and their unknown traitor. Because if Tamir Hachemi knew the traitor's identity, so did Durrani.

And, soon, so would she.

Her determination must have shown, because Palisade scooped up the classified papers. He returned them to the accordion folder, crossed the office and tucked it in her hands. "You'll need this. The latter half contains copies of the reports and forensic paperwork that came in after you were medevacked here. I'll have the remaining information forwarded to your email."

"When do I leave?" There was no way the Army would be packing up Durrani and shipping him to Fort Campbell, even if she was now key to this.

"Your C-141 takes off in less than an hour."

Barely enough time to head home and grab her duffel bag,

much less phone Gil and reassure him. To scratch out a message to prop up on the counter in case John returned to Fort Campbell and stopped by her duplex before she did. "I should go."

Palisade nodded crisply.

To Regan's surprise, he followed her to the couch, reaching for the now cold coffee he'd provided and dumping it in the lined trash bin as she donned her camouflaged jacket.

Just as well. She no longer needed caffeine. She had something far stronger coursing through her veins, snapping every cell in her body to life for the first time in over a week. Adrenaline.

She was collecting her beret when Palisade cleared his throat. Spoke. Softly, hoarsely. "*He's fine.*"

She froze. There was no doubt who *he* was.

John.

A hundred desperate questions burned through the adrenaline, each clamoring to commandeer her voice box first.

She knocked every one of them back, offering two quiet but heartfelt words in their stead. "Thank you."

Palisade nodded.

Even if the general had wanted to share the details of John's current, classified mission, he couldn't. Frankly, it was astounding that he'd offered as much as he had. And she refused to insult the both of them—and John—by pressing for more.

A phone rang. The general's.

He retrieved the phone from his pocket and glanced at the number on the screen. The area code was 202. Washington, DC. "Sorry, Chief. I need to take this—"

"Understood."

"—and you need to take these. Stuff 'em in your duffel. They might come in handy." His phone rang a second time as she stared at the slender, palm-sized box he'd tucked in her hand, bemused.

Dramamine?

Granted, she had a long flight ahead, perhaps two or three. But she didn't get airsick, and since they'd flown together before, Palisade knew that.

Just where the devil was Durrani being held anyway?

Unfortunately, it was too late to ask. The general had already pressed his phone to his ear and turned away.

She'd been dismissed.

# 3

She should've swallowed one of those pills.

Regan stared across the CH-53E's cavernous belly, zeroing in on the rectangular window opposite her flip-down seat. She searched in vain for a glimpse of land amid the distant, hazy horizon as each pulse of the helicopter's yawning seventy-nine-foot main rotor reverberated through her body. For the moment, her stomach was holding its own against the thunderous rhythm, despite the coffee and oversized chocolate muffin she'd consumed prior to liftoff.

But for how long would it last?

Though the muffin had served as her first meal since she'd left the States, consuming anything at all might have been a mistake—along with her decision to not interrupt General Palisade's phone call long enough to ascertain her present location.

The Arabian Sea.

Given the view through every one of the Super Stallion's windows, it contained a hell of a lot more water than she'd imagined. And for some sadistic reason, the pilot had been all but skimming the surface of said water for over an hour.

Shouldn't they have arrived by now?

Regan peeled back the grosgrain cover of her combat watch and noted the time. 0734. Seventeen hours in the air and a nine-hour time-zone change had added an entire day to her life. Gil would be thrilled. If only because during the initial leg of her flight, the C-141's droning engines had piggybacked onto the knowledge that she now had a case she needed to be rested for. The combination had finally seduced her into nodding off somewhere over the Atlantic. By the time she'd woken, they'd landed in Ramstein, Germany.

To her surprise, she'd logged another marathon, near-dreamless nap during the next leg to Al Dhafra Airbase in the United Arab Emirates.

There'd been no sleep on this final bird, however, dreamless or otherwise. Worse, the tang of the sea air laden with the stench of jet fuel had finally gotten to her. The meager contents of her belly had begun to slosh.

Regan turned toward the Super Stallion's cockpit and caught the crew chief's knowing grin. He tapped the dive watch strapped to his wrist and flashed a trio of fingers.

Three more minutes.

Hallelujah.

God willing, the churning in her belly would ease upon landing—though not likely. According to the classified orders she'd been handed after touching down in Al Dhafra, as well as the fascinating footnote from the crew chief still beaming at her, she was headed not for dry land, but the constant pitching and rolling of roughly twenty thousand tons of Navy steel.

The *USS Griffith.*

She'd worked with the Fleet before, had even been aboard a warship for almost a week to pursue a joint Army/Navy lead in an investigation a few years back, but this would be her first case aboard a ship currently at sea.

Curiosity clamored in from several fronts, the most pressing of which concerned Nabil Durrani and his hidden agenda. Because he did possess one. Even if she hadn't spent the better part of a night ferreting out the details of the twisted doctor's life, she'd know there was more to their pending confrontation than a congenial chat with his final, intended victim.

If she still even held that dubious honor.

After her conversation with General Palisade concerning Durrani's cohort, Tamir Hachemi, Regan was beginning to doubt her exalted status.

Why else involve the anomalous, murdered mystery woman?

Religious significance her ass. Durrani hadn't entered the terror game because of Allah. Allah was simply his excuse.

The proof was in the man himself.

Every action Dr. Durrani had taken over the past few months had been meticulously scripted, right down to the bloodstained shawl he'd used to cover Jameelah Khan's—and only Jameelah Khan's—face and torso. It was that act that had caused Regan to initially suspect that Captain McCord had simply murdered the other six women in the cave to throw investigators off track, only to display remorse—albeit unconsciously—at the last moment. Instead, it turned out Durrani had planted the shawl in an admittedly ingenious attempt to effect the ultimate misdirection.

A man that clever didn't toss in an extra victim to equate for the inclusion of twins, no matter when he'd learned of those twins' existence. No, Durrani had sought out and selected a woman carrying twins to mask the significance of an otherwise anomalous woman's identity for as long as possible.

But why?

And what, if any, connection did the mystery victim's identity have to their remaining traitor?

Regan was still pondering both questions when the crew chief caught her gaze. He flashed a thumbs up before directing her attention to the section of chopper window visible between the pilot and copilot as the men began flipping a series of switches in the cockpit's overhead. *There*—the *Griffith*.

The crew chief hadn't been exaggerating. The amphibious dock landing ship was massive. Even so, the *Griffith*'s flat-gray silhouette nearly blended in with the atmospheric haze and the increasingly angry waters of the Arabian Sea. The warship's jutting superstructure loomed impressively as they flew down the port side.

Her flight deck did not. Nor did that deck appear particularly stable as the helicopter swung a hundred eighty degrees around.

At least to this Army ground pounder.

Chopper pilots in general tended to impress the hell out of her. She'd seen them perform some amazing maneuvers at times, including an honest-to-God barrel roll. But to land a solid chunk of metal on the equally unforgiving deck of a ship violently riding the waves as the *Griffith* was currently doing?

Her stomach lurched at the thought. It lurched again as the flight deck disappeared beneath the belly of the bird.

Regan sucked in her breath as the Super Stallion's wheels rudely kissed those twenty thousand tons of Navy steel the crew chief had touted, releasing the air from her lungs only when she was certain the mechanical embrace had held. The pilot powered down the blades as several members of the *Griffith*'s crew converged on the chopper to lash it to the deck. The side door slid open and the crew chief bailed out, motioning for Regan to follow. She removed her ear protection and life vest and left both on the canvas seat before vaulting out onto the non-skid surface of the flight deck.

Another mistake.

The void deep in her inner ears instantly registered the brunt of the ship's motion as the *Griffith* rode out the waves beneath her combat boots, whipping the paltry contents of her belly into a full-blown roil.

"Agent Chase?"

She spun around. Yet another mistake. Regan fought to regain her equilibrium as an approaching naval officer tugged a pair of rabbit ears down around her neck.

No, not an officer, or even a chief warrant officer like herself —but an enlisted sailor. The center placket of the shorter woman's camouflaged working uniform sported an embroidered anchor, pegging the woman's rank equivalent to that of an Army sergeant first class. Confusing to some outside the military, since she and this Navy non-commissioned officer that she outranked were addressed by the same title: Chief.

The woman popped a salute, then stuck out her hand to offer a firm shake. "Master-at-Arms Chief Michelle Yrle. Welcome aboard. I'll be serving as your escort and right hand for the duration of your stay."

That wide smile would've been infectious if Regan's stomach hadn't chosen that moment to crank up the churn to a near-humiliating level. She forced a weak curve to her lips. "Glad to be here. Just need my gear, and I'm ready to get to work."

A glass of water wouldn't hurt either...so she could swallow the entire box of pills she'd stashed in her bag.

"Here you go, ma'am." The Super Stallion's crew chief held her tan duffel in one hand, her stainless-steel crime scene kit and black, nylon laptop bag in the other as she turned back to the bird—carefully.

"Thanks." Regan retrieved her crime scene gear and laptop, but her new right hand beat her to the tan duffel and pills.

Yrle tipped her cap of sleek raven curls toward the ship's lurching superstructure. "This way. I'll show you to your stateroom. It's got a small bath ensemble, so you can freshen up before we feed you to the head shark—er, captain."

"Wonderful." Forget the pills. Three steps across the rising, then dipping deck, and she'd decided on an immediate visit to the latrine.

"Dying to check out one of our heads, eh?"

Regan offered a limp smile as they moved up the port side of the ship. "That obvious?"

"You've got the proverbial green about your gills. Don't worry; it'll pass—one way or the other. For what it's worth, I prefer the 'other'. Once the genuflecting's over, I feel great. Until then, I do my best to keep my gaze fixed on the horizon." Yrle shrugged. "Either way, hang in there. We'll be riding smoother in about an hour—midway through our rendezvous and pending underway replenishment with the *Tippecanoe*. We're low on fuel and, hence, riding high. The current sea state's not helping either." A soft laugh floated between them as Yrle stopped beside an oval watertight door with a black 'Z' painted in the middle, inside a larger 'D'. "Welcome to the Arabian Sea in January, Soldier. The Navy part."

Another intimidating wave struck the bow of the *Griffith* and Regan wished herself anchored firmly on the Army portion as the ship rocked it out.

Her hundredth slow breath of the morning helped—until Chief Yrle swung the door open and waved her over the metal lip protruding up from the deck. The sloshing in her belly returned full force as she passed through the skin of the ship, intensifying as the chief led her down a claustrophobic corridor and up a skeletal ladder. As with the ship's exterior, everything inside was gray, albeit several shades lighter: the walls, the floor, even the ceiling—or bulkhead, deck and overhead, if she remembered correctly.

By the time they'd reached a succession of slim, darker gray doors that were lined up along both sides of the passageway like soldiers awaiting inspection, the acid in her stomach had breached the base of her throat.

*Shit.* "I gotta—"

"Step aside."

The chief had the door at the end unlocked and open in three seconds flat. Regan shot through the second, slimmer door just inside the stateroom and slammed it shut, her knees hitting the steel deck of the tiny bathroom in the nick of time. A solid minute of heaving commenced, ending only when the makeshift breakfast she'd consumed had completely reversed course along with a belly full of froth.

Eventually, she was down to dry heaves and then...nothing.

The chief was right. She felt fine now.

Better than she had in days, in fact.

She wasn't sure what she expected as she abandoned the bathroom, but it wasn't a pissed-off male in civilian clothes.

Except...that wasn't a civilian. Not with a twelve-round, .40 caliber SIG Sauer 229 holstered at the right hip of those black cargo pants and matching, long-sleeved polo. The six-foot, dark-haired and neatly bearded Arab wearing both was halfway into the narrow stateroom when Chief Yrle spotted him—and blanched.

"Agent Riyad. I thought you'd left along—"

"Obviously *not.*" The frown leveled on Yrle could've been chiseled from a block of Arctic ice. "If you'd performed your duties correctly this morning, *Chief*, I'd have been able to depart. But then, you know that, don't you?"

Yrle opened her mouth—and that was as far as she got. Riyad's right hand lashed out, connecting with the chief's left elbow and visibly clamping down as he propelled the woman out into the passageway. The stateroom door closed so quickly and firmly, there was no doubt in Regan's mind the barrier was meant for her, along with the mystery agent's unspoken order: *Stay put.*

She would.

For now.

She had no clue as to her counterpart's beef with the master-at-arms chief, let alone which combination of letters from the government's vast bowl of alphabet soup were attached to his name, nor did she care. She was here to see Durrani, and she had no intention of greeting that particular ass with the vestiges of her previous meal saturating her breath.

Regan turned away from the stateroom's door and its flanking drab, modular steel wall unit. Two steps away, a set of bunk beds abutted the opposite bulkhead. Like almost everything else she'd seen of the ship, their frames were painted a flat, haze gray.

Retrieving her shaving kit from the duffel Chief Yrle had dumped on the bottom bunk, she carted her toothbrush and paste to the tiny sink outside the shower and toilet area. Her teeth cleaned, she took the time to splash water over her face, then smooth several errant wisps of hair into the French braid she'd crafted and tucked under twenty-four hours earlier. The navy-blue suit she'd packed was bound to be wrinkled, so yesterday's camouflaged uniform would have to suffice.

Then again, it wouldn't hurt that ACUs were the last thing Durrani had seen her in...just before she'd taken the bastard down.

By the time Super Pissed-Off Agent shoved the stateroom's outer door inward again, she was more than ready to face the doctor.

But first, a few ground rules given this man's boorish behavior with the chief. She didn't care if he was the Islamist expert to whom General Palisade had referred. "They don't knock aboard ships?"

Riyad had the grace to flush. Barely. The slight tinge might've served to humanize the man, had his dark stare not settled on her smoothed braid and damp, unmade face—insolently. "Didn't realize you wanted to primp for the terrorist."

*Touché.*

Still, what was his problem? Yes, he'd probably heard the tail end of her heave session. So what? As if that hadn't happened on a ship before. Or did he have issues with breasts in general—or simply hers and Chief Yrle's in particular?

*Don't.* She was here to grill Durrani. Given this was a warship, the doc was probably housed somewhere down below in the bowels of the ship, most likely in the brig.

She tamped out a smile polite enough to get *this* jerk to take her there. "I take it I lost my escort?"

"Correct."

"Care to explain that moment you two shared?"

"Nope."

The hell with him. "Aren't you the welcoming committee?" And so chatty, too. Must be the salt air.

The man shrugged. "Don't believe you belong here."

She could respect that, albeit grudgingly. If *he* was here, he had to have read the entire case file—including her shift in roles from investigator to intended victim near the end. On the other hand, "Yet here I am. Perhaps you should take a moment to bring me up to date, *Agent* Riyad. Or should I head up to the bridge and see if I can't get the guy driving this boat to place a ship-to-shore call to USASOC? General Palisade appears to have left a few facts out of our briefing. For one, your rather uncooperative take on my presence."

That sparked a reaction. One moment those glowering eyes were murky brown and the next they were black. The Arctic ice had returned as well and, with Chief Yrle missing, it was directed solely at her.

Regan didn't bother attempting a thaw. Instead, she leaned into the metal stanchion supporting the upper bunk—to preserve her tenuous balance against the constant rocking of the ship if nothing else—and offered up her own insolent shrug.

Riyad stared her down.

For a good half-minute, the only sounds in the stateroom were their slow, steady breaths, along with the soft, rhythmic creaking of the shifting metal of the insulated pipes and exposed venting running through the overhead and along the bulkheads. The man was going to call her bluff. She was ninety-nine percent certain.

And then, "What do you want to know?"

*Everything*. Beginning with why he was still so pissed. But something told her the source of his mood was not on the table.

Table, hell. Before she fired her opening salvo, she had to deal with this constantly shifting deck. Her inner ears might've made the transition to shipboard life, but her sea legs had yet to make an appearance. She was in danger of falling flat on her face while simply standing.

Regan pulled away from the bunk beds, deliberately widening and squaring off her stance until her combat boots were planted well apart, as Riyad's were positioned. It worked. She had solid control over her balance, even as the deck continued to roll beneath her feet. It was time to extend that control to her case.

"Why is Dr. Durrani here, aboard a warship?"

Why put him in Navy custody at all?

Given the almost fanatical drawdown on current Gitmo detainees, she wouldn't have thought he'd end up there. But why not a black site prison in another country? A country that would look the other way during questioning...and provide local agents to direct any harsher verbal or physical Q&A sessions on US behalf.

Though that wasn't the way she operated, it had been known to happen.

Another one of Riyad's insolent shrugs greeted her query. "This is as good a place as any. In many ways, better."

Much as she hated to admit it, his half-assed response rang true. As interrogation venues went, this one was moveable, easily concealable, away from the preying vultures of the world's press and—as an absolute caveat—Durrani was separated from other terror detainees. Hell, if they wanted, they could weigh the bastard down when they were done and dump him overboard in the dead of night and no one would be the wiser—most significantly, the unnamed traitor she was now seeking.

Or was there more to it?

Was it possible that physical Q&A sessions involving Durrani were occurring even now—aboard United States sovereign property?

That, she found difficult to believe, much less stomach. "Exactly which agency are you with?"

"NCIS."

Naval Criminal Investigative Service: Army CID's Fleet counterpart. For the most part, the revelation tracked. This was a warship. But something had flickered in that murky stare when she'd pressed. Something that suggested there was more to this particular agent's presence aboard this unruly piece of iron than simple jurisdiction.

Please, God, *don't* let it involve the physical.

Before she could press the matter, the impression vanished. Riyad's foul mood had not.

She went with her gut. It had rarely steered her wrong. Even when she'd wanted it to. "What happened this morning?"

To her surprise, Riyad blinked.

Odd. She wouldn't have thought she'd be able to surprise him that easily. "The cause of your delay? The delay to which

Chief Yrle supposedly contributed? It has you pissed. Even now, with me."

"I'm not—"

"You are."

The silence returned. The overhead pipes and vents continued to creak, not quite filling it. "Doesn't matter."

But it did. She'd stake her next meal and a Gil-sized thermos of steaming black coffee on it. "Look, Agent Riyad, if we're going to work together—"

"We're not."

This time, the surprise was hers. "I beg your pardon?" They were both investigators. She had no idea whose authority had sent the NCIS agent here, but she'd been assigned to this ship and her old case via the very general in charge of the Army's Special Operations Command. She was not getting edged out without a fight.

And then she remembered. Of course. "You're leaving."

He'd said so himself.

Riyad surprised her again by shaking his head. "*Was*. As in, I am now remaining aboard the *Griffith* for the duration of this case. You, Agent Chase, are not."

She clamped down on her ire. "If this is some asinine version of an inter-service pissing contest—"

"It's not."

"Good. Because I'm not leaving." And not because it had taken her an entire day to get here. "I was told Durrani specifically request—"

"I don't care what you were told. And I could give a royal shit what Durrani wants. You, Agent Chase, are aboard this vessel for the sole purpose of getting that asshole to speak. That's it. Once Durrani opens his mouth, I step in—and you step *out*. Permanently. Have I made myself clear?"

It was her turn to blink. The hell with Durrani, what was *this* asshole's problem?

Before she could demand an explanation, the ship-wide, 1MC loudspeaker hanging in the overhead at the far end of her stateroom sparked to life.

*"Doctor Mantia, Special Agent Riyad, lay to the main deck conference room. I say again, Dr—"*

The remainder was lost amid the combined thunder of their boots as Riyad yanked the stateroom door open and vaulted out into the passageway with Regan all but welded to his heels. He shot her a tight glare as they reached the head of an angled ladder near the one she and Yrle had used earlier.

Regan ignored the glare, focusing instead on the stiff set of the NCIS agent's shoulders and the relentless pace of his boots as Riyad gave up trying to shake her off, double-timing down the metal steps and along the passageway with her still in dogged pursuit.

If something was happening that required this man's zealous attention, she would be tagging along to bear witness.

They were both thinking it. *Durrani.* What had happened to require the urgent need for a doctor?

God help her, she was beginning to reconsider the possibility of a Navy-sanctioned physical interrogation session.

She followed Riyad into a sparsely furnished conference room. One glance at the body lying on the blue speckled, linoleum-covered deck at the far end, and it appeared her worst fear had been spot on. There was a twelve-inch slick of scarlet blood beneath a man's dark hair, and the slick was spreading out, due at least in part to the life-saving actions of the Marines in the compartment. There were two—a corporal and a staff sergeant—both in camouflaged utilities.

Had one of them caused the injuries?

There was no way to tell from here.

She did know the Marines were doing everything in their current power to reverse their patient's condition. The staff sergeant had taken command of the torso, the heels of his palms braced together over the prone man's chest, steadily working to kick-start his heart. The corporal knelt on the linoleum beside the patient's head, attempting in vain to staunch the copious flow of blood frothing forth from a shattered nasal cavity in between three-round bursts of his own breath.

Both Marines had to be cognizant of the inherent biohazard in all that blood. Yet they'd refused to wait for protection.

That didn't surprise her. What did—what stunned her as she caught her first clear view of the patient's face—was his identity.

That wasn't Nabil Durrani lying on the deck, clinging to life.

It was his cohort, Tamir Hachemi.

# 4

Regan stared at the body of the Afghan translator who'd murdered her CID partner in a terror safe house in Charikar thirteen days earlier. Why was Tamir Hachemi even on the ship? Shouldn't he be stateside, well on his way to Leavenworth by now?

"*Gangway*!"

The owner of the deep, disembodied voice behind Regan didn't bother waiting for her to move. Instead, a pair of oversized paws clamped about her upper arms, physically hefting her up and carrying her three steps into the compartment before dropping her back down on her boots. Based on the camouflaged uniform and stethoscope hooked around the petty officer's neck as he passed, she assumed he was a corpsman. A shorter, wirier Navy lieutenant with matching camouflage and stethoscope—plus a bulging, stereotypical black bag—was a step behind.

To Regan's shock, Agent Riyad was not. The NCIS agent had spun around and was headed in the opposite direction—*out* of the space.

By the time Regan had refocused her attention on the crisis at hand, the ship's doc and hulking corpsman had converged on the translator's body, nudging the equally beefy pair of Marines out of the way as they took over CPR. The corpsman was at the translator's chest now, the doc at his head. Regan had learned enough from Gil to know the clear tubing Dr. Mantia retrieved from his bag would be used to intubate Hachemi. Once the doc had the translator's airway reestablished, the corpsman took over, working the attached airbag, steadily squeezing oxygen into Hachemi's lungs as the doc moved down to their remaining priority—Hachemi's heart.

From the frown darkening Mantia's face, it still wasn't beating.

Fortunately, another corpsman—this one a petite Filipina petty officer—chose that moment to barrel into the conference room and across the linoleum with a portable, suitcase-sized crash cart in tow.

Within moments, the doc had the defibrillator rigged and charged as the male corpsman parted the front of Hachemi's navy blue overalls in a single rip, exposing the translator's hairless chest. The doc brandished the paddles and, "Clear!"

A dull thud resounded through the compartment, followed by silence.

A good fifteen minutes and a steady slew of shocks followed with nothing in between but the ever-present creaking of metal and the near non-stop medical lingo that passed between Mantia and his assistants as the doc ordered a pharmacy of medication into the translator's veins. The doc finally reached out, staying the hand of the corpsman still steadily working the balloon. Mantia shook his head and sat back on his haunches, glancing past Regan's shoulder to meet Riyad's stare.

Until that moment, she hadn't realized the NCIS agent had rejoined them.

Resignation and defeat scored the doc's frown. "Time of death, zero seven fifty-eight. He's your responsibility now. Sorry."

The corpsman reached out to gather up the gear they'd used to try to resuscitate the translator.

"*Stop*." Regan jerked her chin toward the array of vials and expended syringes now littering the deck. "Leave everything exactly where it is."

At least until she'd photographed it.

She'd get started just as soon as everyone else cleared the room.

The doc nodded and stood. He glanced at his bag. "May I—"

"Yes." She pointed toward the defibrillator. "You can have that back, once I've arranged for disposition of the body."

Another nod. "I've got a ship-to-shore call to make. I'll return with a body bag."

Regan waited for the doc to clear the space. Both corpsmen filed out behind him, dejection in their every step. Hachemi might have been a traitor—and these sailors had undoubtedly known that—but it was always rough for medical personnel to lose the fight, no matter the patient. Especially when they'd invested so much of themselves in the effort.

Regan bristled as Riyad drew the Marine corporal aside. It was clear from his body language that the NCIS agent intended for her to remain ignorant of the contents of their chat. Before she could cross the compartment, Riyad ordered the corporal to the captain's cabin to brief the man.

Regan held her tongue as the kid complied. The corporal would return soon enough, and she could take his statement then.

She was itching to take Riyad's too. Where the heck had he disappeared to while the crisis was in full swing? More importantly, why?

Unwilling to grill him in front of the remaining Marine, Regan turned to study the compartment. As conference rooms went, it was unimpressive. Though there was plenty of room for the oversized U-shaped briefing table, most of the chairs were missing. The four that remained were skeletal metal numbers with unforgiving seats. The chairs were positioned in two separate groupings, with the first two facing her from the far side of the U at the head of the conference room. Both chairs appeared to have been thrown back from the table, as if their occupants had moved in haste.

The second two chairs were still mostly facing each other along the starboard bulkhead at one end of the U. Like the first pair, these chairs also appeared to have been thrown back from the opposite sides of the table. Despite the constant motion of the ship, two Styrofoam cups—one half full of black coffee, the other empty—sat on the table between the facing chairs.

*Good Cop/Bad Cop*?

If so, from the still glistening splatter of lightened coffee across the side of the table, as well as the upper right corner of the back of one of the chairs and a two-foot swath of deck nearest her boots, the time-honored interrogation technique had failed.

The evidence might mesh with Riyad's personality—especially bad cop—but he'd been below in the stateroom with her.

Chief Yrle was a possibility. The woman did carry a master-at-arms rating. She was, in effect, the warship's sheriff. But if Yrle had screwed up that morning as Riyad had so rudely asserted, would he have let the chief near one of the US government's most prized terror detainees?

Not likely.

That left the Marines as the most obvious choice.

Unfortunately, Riyad had sent the corporal on an errand. She hadn't gotten close enough to the kid before he'd left to note the possible splatter of coffee mixed in with any blood that could admittedly have also been transferred to the camouflaged fabric of his uniform as he'd performed CPR. It was the potential presence of high-velocity blood droplets on that same uniform—droplets that by their nature could only have been splattered during the translator's actual beating—that would seal the man's guilt.

Regan was about to turn to the Marine staff sergeant still awaiting orders beside the door to study his uniform when Riyad crossed the deck and crouched down beside the body. His left hand stretched out.

"What the hell do you think you're doing?"

His fingers paused as that frozen, murky stare settled on hers. "I was about to—"

"*Touch* the body before I've had a chance to photograph it? And without gloves?" Not on her watch. Jurisdiction be damned. "Agent Riyad, this compartment is now an active crime scene and that—" She pointed to the airbag. "—is evidence. It and everything else in this room must be handled and cataloged as such."

Ire torched the man's stare, cooking off the ice.

Regan ignored it—along with the grim satisfaction she caught pressing into the remaining Marine's lips. She had the distinct impression that, like Chief Yrle, the staff sergeant had recently tussled with Agent Riyad about something...and lost.

She let the insubordination go.

Unlike the man now rising to his feet, she was a steadfast student of the school of Praise in Public, Pummel in Private—unless it involved the prevention of evidence tampering. Speaking of which...unless they took serious steps and soon, that tampering was about to commence from an entirely new quarter.

Regan turned toward the frantic shuffle of boots outside the compartment. As she feared, a deep bellow followed.

"Captain's on Deck!"

The Head Rubbernecker had arrived. Right on time, too.

Soldier, Sailor, Marine, Airman or civilian, it never failed. Death fascinated them all. Whoever sat at the top of the food chain always wanted his own, unobstructed view of the kill, too, no matter how grisly. From the set of Riyad's jaw, even he knew the consequences of extraneous boots mucking up the scene.

"I'll go." She was Army. Nothing to lose.

Not in the long run.

Though to be honest, an Infantry or Artillery bird preening on the opposite side of that door wouldn't have changed her mind, let alone tempered her coming instructions.

Yet another reason why she'd turned down the Army's offer of a commission as a Military Police lieutenant following her coma. As a warrant, she could get away with her own particular brand of verbal murder during the course of an investigation. It was a perk she'd enjoyed to no end on occasion—and would again.

Not to mention, her strength lay in working investigations day in and day out, from the ground up, not overseeing them. The latter of which, as a Military Police officer, would become her lot in life.

To Regan's surprise, Riyad followed her out into the passageway, swiftly overtaking her to reach the captain first.

Evidently, Super Sleuth still didn't trust her.

"Sir, the translator's dead. Under the circumstances, I recommend Agent Chase be escorted to her quarters and removed from the ship—immediately."

Wow. She'd anticipated a bayonet to the back at some point today. But an open and preemptive slash right across the jugular? And in front of witnesses?

That took serious balls.

Riyad's appeared to be forged from the same steel that made up this rhythmically rocking ship.

Fortunately for her, the captain seemed to possess an iron

set of his own. He extended a hand toward her as he pointedly ignored Riyad's comment. The man's grip was warm, firm and—in light of the situation—surprisingly friendly. "Brad Armstrong. Welcome aboard the *Griffith*, Agent Chase. I've been hearing your name quite a bit these past weeks. Been wanting to meet the woman who took down the terror cell." The CO's stare shifted to the now closed conference room door just past her left shoulder, then came back. "Just wish it could've been under better circumstances."

"Thank you, sir."

He made no move toward the door. "What do you need?"

It seemed she'd misjudged the man. She couldn't be happier.

Riyad was not. "Sir, I—"

"*Don't* possess the experience to oversee a murder investigation." Armstrong turned to the NCIS agent, softening what amounted to Riyad's own public rebuke with what appeared to be a genuinely sympathetic shrug. "Sam, I know you're motivated. And I know this is serious. But you're FCI, not a detective. Agent Chase has worked countless death investigations. We both know we'll need her skills, *especially* now. Nor can we afford to let the scene deteriorate—especially with all this rocking and rolling—while we wait another day for someone else to get here."

Riyad opened his mouth again, closing it as the captain's hand came up to forestall follow-up argument.

"The decision's been made—at the Pentagon, no less. That's why I'm late. Just got off the horn. Agent Riyad, your concerns regarding Agent Chase's objectivity have been noted and negated at the highest levels—Army, Navy and beyond. She's got the lead on the translator's death. You're to assist. Understood?"

There was a swift undercurrent cutting through that last, though damned if she could discern its source.

But Riyad had.

He offered the captain a brusque nod.

If Armstrong recognized Riyad's lingering displeasure, he ignored it. The captain's answering nod encompassed them both. "Agent Chase, Agent Riyad, I'll be on the bridge should you need me. Keep me appraised."

She'd definitely misjudged the man. "Yes, sir."

Riyad stood fast as the captain left, his foul mood now directed solely upon her.

Regan forced herself to ignore it. "FCI?"

"Foreign Counterintelligence."

A spook? He was a goddamned *spook*? He wasn't the only one now pissed. And when she added on that he'd spent the bulk of the earlier crisis in the CO's cabin, whining about her?

Regan scoured her soul for patience. "You said you were with NCIS."

"I am."

Right. Some specialized Navy/FBI/CIA-ish/Homeland Security offshoot most likely. One look at the man's features was enough to confirm that, along with his last name: Riyad. "Sam" might be an American citizen, but a significant percentage of the blood flowing through his veins was of Saudi origin. "Just how long did you work crime scenes before you specialized?"

"Six months."

She pulled her breath in deep. "And in that time, how many death investigations did you pursue?"

"One."

"Let me guess—vehicular manslaughter."

To her bemusement, the same slight flush that had tinged Riyad's cheeks after he'd barged into her stateroom earlier returned.

*Jesus*. She'd been joking. But that flush wasn't. No wonder he'd made a grab for that airbag. The man wasn't incompetent—he was utterly and completely inexperienced.

And he wanted her gone?

Regan opened her mouth and promptly closed it as the remaining thread of patience she'd been clinging to snapped. She no longer trusted herself to stand here and talk to this so-called agent. Not until she'd had a chance to calm down and get a handle on exactly what lay on the floor of that conference room. She whirled around and headed across the ever-shifting deck, stopping beside the door as the corporal returned.

A swift perusal of the Marine's uniform allowed her to collect Corporal Vetter's name, but revealed no evidence of coffee or high-velocity blood splatter concealed amid the digital camouflage. Just the larger bloodstains marring the fabric at his knees, wrists and upper torso. The sort he'd have acquired during his zealous efforts at CPR.

Had Riyad been attempting *Good Cop/Bad Cop* after all, right before he'd confronted Chief Yrle in that stateroom?

She'd have been forced to consider the possibly after all, but for the fact that Riyad's black polo, cargo pants and boots weren't sporting coffee or high-velocity blood splatter either. And while the man's hands were callused and scarred in several spots, they were devoid of recent injury. Nor would he have had the time to change his clothes in between dragging Chief Yrle from the stateroom and returning to spar with her before the medical emergency had been passed over the loudspeaker.

Regan caught the corporal's waiting gaze. Captain Armstrong must have briefed him as to her status as lead case agent, because the Marine had automatically deferred, not to the spook she'd left behind, but her. "Corporal Vetter, head to the master-at-arms shack and have your uniform bagged for evidence. While you're there, please tell Chief Yrle I require her presence and a death scene kit. Have her stop by my stateroom. There's a stainless-steel suitcase on the lower bunk. I'll need both ASAP as well as a complete statement from you upon your return. I need to know exactly what transpired in that conference room before I arrived."

"Yes, ma'am."

She turned to the staff sergeant and carefully examined his uniform as well. As with the corporal, there was some evidence of larger bloodstains at the wrists and upper torso, but no coffee and no high-velocity splatter. The lack of the latter on both Marines told her all she needed to know. A third person had fled before her arrival.

She nodded to the senior Marine. "Staff Sergeant Brandt, I'll need your uniform bagged as well, though you can wait for the chief's supplies. Until then, position yourself outside this door. No one—and I mean *no one*—enters without my permission. This conference room is an active crime scene; I expect you to treat it as such."

"Yes, ma'am."

She spun back to Riyad as the staff sergeant took up his post. "Who's missing?"

The spook's jaw locked. Almost imperceptibly, but the tension was definitely there.

Why? Why would an FCI agent care *who*—

Regan instinctively shifted her attention as another door opened two yards down the passageway, on the opposite side. Curiosity sparked, then swelled as Chief Yrle stepped into the corridor—sans obvious signs of splattered coffee or blood—and immediately turned to reseal the dimly lit compartment she'd vacated...as if she too was attempting to conceal something. No, not something.

Someone.

For a single, blinding moment, Regan had caught a glimpse of a massive camouflaged form with a distinctive trio of two-inch shrapnel scars just beneath the edge of the man's roughly whiskered jaw, and then they were gone. As was he.

It didn't matter.

She'd already recognized their owner.

*John Garrison.* The recently reunited lover who'd been ordered from her bedside eight days ago, less than three hours after she'd woken from her coma in Fort Campbell's ICU. The same lover General Palisade had sworn was safe just yesterday morning.

But he wasn't.

Because John was here, aboard the *Griffith*. He had been since he'd left her hospital room. She was certain. Just as she knew that, deep down, John was the missing man she sought. The one whose uniform would reveal signs of coffee and the telltale evidence of Tamir Hachemi's splattered, high-velocity blood.

# 5

"Ma'am?"

Regan would never know how she managed to calmly turn and face Staff Sergeant Brandt as if her entire world hadn't imploded. Or perhaps she hadn't. The Marine took one look at her face and abandoned his post, closing the distance between them to comfort range as he reached out to grasp her arm.

"Agent Chase...are you okay?"

She nodded. Again, she could only hope her head had moved. It was difficult to be sure of anything after being ruthlessly drop-kicked out of the back of a C-141 at twenty thousand feet. Her scrambled brain was still flailing around, struggling to find the ripcord to a parachute that just wasn't there.

Or was it?

Regan pulled herself from the Marine's grasp and slowly turned around. She needn't have bothered. She was free-falling for the count—and her so-called partner on this case didn't care. If anything, she had the distinct impression Agent Riyad was looking forward to the splat. The glint in that murky ice confirmed it. Not only did Riyad know of her salacious history with John, the bastard had known John was aboard the *Griffith* well before she'd arrived.

And he'd said nothing.

Granted, neither had General Palisade. But that—she also realized—was because from what Palisade knew of the situation at the time, there shouldn't have been anything to tell. John was supposed to have left with Riyad via the Super Stallion that was still lashed to the ship's flight deck. If John had departed within minutes of her arrival as scheduled, there wouldn't have been a need for her to have knowledge of what was essentially a classified troop assignment.

But John hadn't left. And now, not only did the need to know exactly why John was aboard exist, it burned.

Regan sent her own blast of icy fury toward the man she now knew was no simple NCIS counterpart. "Agent Riyad, inside the conference room—*now*."

She didn't wait for Riyad to answer. Instead, she turned to the visibly nervous master-at-arms chief. Corporal Vetter had joined Chief Yrle, the crime scene kit Regan had requested from her stateroom in hand.

She retrieved her gear. "Thank you, Corporal. Post yourself at the end of the passageway and remain there until I exit the crime scene. Speak to no one else about this case—and I mean no one—unless I personally grant you leave to do so, understood?"

"Yes, ma'am."

"Good. Chief Yrle?"

"Yes, Agent?"

"Does Major Garrison know I'm aboard the *Griffith*?"

"No."

"Keep it that way. Wait until I've entered the conference room, then escort the major back to his stateroom and detain him there, in a complete communications blackout, until I arrive."

"Yes, ma'am."

The fact that John had been in isolation across the passageway since before she and Riyad had preceded the ship's medical personnel into the conference room confirmed her worst fears. It also explained Agent Riyad's subsequent disappearance while the ship's doctor and corpsmen were still desperately attempting to save the translator's life.

The bridge hadn't been Riyad's first stop during the crisis. That nearby compartment had.

It took every ounce of self-control Regan possessed to keep from crossing the corridor and entering that same compartment now. Much as she needed to speak to John—for her case as well as her sanity—she wouldn't. Not until she'd had time to examine the body at length. Gather her thoughts. Because whatever had gone down in that conference room, John had been at the center of it.

The nausea that had plagued her since the beginning of that hour-long chopper flight had returned—with a vengeance. And it had nothing to do with the ship.

Regan closed her mouth and pulled air in through her nose for several moments as she corralled her jangled nerves and forced them to settle. The *Griffith*'s relentless rocking didn't help.

Damn it, if John was involved in Hachemi's death, there had to have been extenuating circumstances. She knew the man. His strengths and his flaws. John Garrison might be a Special Forces soldier trained to kill with his bare hands, but he did so only in the defense of his country. And even then, only under direct orders and within the context of an officially sanctioned, albeit often classified, mission.

He was simply not capable of outright murder. Not even of a known terrorist.

Not even a terrorist whose crimes had led directly to the deaths of seven men under his command, several of their wives and very nearly her own.

She was certain.

But would her new, clearly reluctant partner be able to put his obvious bias aside long enough to entertain the possibility?

Regan turned back to the conference room. The door was still closed and Riyad was still standing beside it.

And she was still so much more than merely pissed over this entire situation—and his part in it.

"Agent Riyad, I issued a direct order. As case supervisor, I expect you to obey it. Immediately."

The fire in his stare threatened to melt the surrounding steel. But he turned.

Riyad shoved the door to the conference room open. If he'd hoped to stay her own ratcheting fury by waiting for her to precede him, he'd misjudged her.

The second he closed the door behind them and opened his mouth, she lit in. "Don't bother explaining. Just nod at the right spots and offer correction when required, understood?" From the grudging nod of respect as his mouth snapped shut, she knew he'd finally realized it was best not to cross her. "You and Major Garrison have been interrogating Dr. Durrani and Tamir Hachemi for nearly a week now, correct? In fact, you conducted the interrogations alone for several days before the major arrived aboard the *Griffith*—and got nowhere. That's why Major Garrison was ordered to leave Fort Campbell and was flown here to assist."

The slight flush she'd noticed twice before tinged the base of the spook's dusky neck. "Yes."

It made sense. Riyad's answer, his embarrassment and especially the motivation behind the mid-interrogation tasking shift. John had served with Tamir Hachemi on multiple missions during his tours in Afghanistan. The brass had clearly hoped the long-standing connection would serve to loosen the translator's tongue after Hachemi had arrived aboard the *Griffith* and clammed up.

But it hadn't.

Regan continued her assessment. "You were also the one who let the fact that I was still very much alive and recently cured of that goddamned psycho-toxin slip during one of those interrogation sessions, correct?"

"Yes."

The tinge faded, answering Regan's next question before she could voice it. The slip had not been accidental. It had been deliberate.

Her temper surged along with the bow of the ship, effectively supplanting any nausea. "Why?"

Riyad shrugged. "We weren't getting anywhere with the standard fare. I decided to change tactics." The flush might have faded, but the shadow in those eyes had returned and this one was not tinted with respect.

He was lying. The micro-expressions on his face confirmed it. Unfortunately, now was not the time to call him on it. Unlike this man, she needed more first.

"You speak fluent Arabic, possibly with an upper-crust Saudi accent, when you choose to use it, don't you?"

Another shadow flickered amid the murky black, and she could have sworn this one was personal.

"Agent Riyad?"

"*Yes.*"

And yet Durrani had still refused to open up. Interesting.

Or not. "Did you use Arabic with the doctor?"

Riyad nodded. "During our first few meetings, he refused to answer my English, Dari or Pashto. So I switched to Arabic."

*Ahhh.*

A third shadow slipped in, this one solidifying into pure curiosity—Riyad's—confirming what she'd suspected from the beginning. The spook was attempting to read her too; he had been since the moment she'd arrived aboard this ship. He just hadn't been as successful. It wasn't his fault. After all, she had her father's corrupt DNA, as well as the bastard's ability to lie convincingly, on her side. But the curiosity burning in that murky stare didn't concern her. It stemmed from the connection she'd made.

Why not? It wouldn't hurt to voice it.

It might even help.

"You miscalculated." Especially with the Arabic. Durrani got off on power. Everything she'd learned about the doc—from his official records, as well as their conversations when he'd had her isolated in the bathroom of that terror house—supported the assessment. The moment Durrani had heard what was clearly the real Royal Saudi deal from Riyad's lips, the Afghan son of a goatherd turned medical scholarship winner's own lips had been sealed. "Durrani will never open up to you. You won't even get him to speak if you're tucked silently in the corner of the same room."

The bastard would be too worried about being found out. Labeled as the lowborn that, deep down, Durrani feared he still was.

"You can't know that."

Oh, she could and she did. "I may look young, Agent Riyad, but I've been at this game a long time. Granted, I might not have a degree in psychology or whatever's stamped on that piece of sheepskin you've got hanging in your office. I don't need it." Not to become an Army warrant, and she sure as hell didn't need a four-year degree to grill the scum of the earth for a living. "Interrogations are in my blood."

Whether she wanted them to be or not. Her own father had

lied to the Washington, DC, Metropolitan Police Department for five years, and no one had figured it out. Not until it was too late.

From the fresh glint off that rapidly refreezing ice, this man knew the entire tawdry story too.

Then again, Riyad was a spook. She could only pray his loyalties weren't as divided as her dear ol' dad's had been.

Regan re-zeroed her attention, returning it to the opening comments Riyad had offered up in her stateroom. "Major Garrison was supposed to accompany you on that chopper flight you missed, correct?"

"Yes."

"Where were you headed, and why?" She didn't bother reminding him of the captain's directive in the passageway. According to Armstrong, the Pentagon had blessed her handling of the murder, meaning nothing related to this case was off limits—classified or not.

If Riyad's current frown was any judge, he was still ticked with the decision, too. But he complied.

"We'd decided to rendezvous at Bagram Airbase with a soldier detailed to one of Major Garrison's A-Teams, a Staff Sergeant Tulle. The three of us planned on dropping in on Hachemi's maternal uncle, the one who runs goats on the Afghan side of the mountain, near the cave where those women were murdered. No one outside the investigation knew for certain Dr. Durrani and Hachemi were arrested because we never released the information. Major Garrison felt he'd be able to abuse that fact. He and Staff Sergeant Tulle were to knock on the uncle's door under the guise that Hachemi went MIA during a military mission and that we feared he'd been kidnapped. We'd hoped to parlay that meeting into an introduction with another uncle who runs goats on the Pakistani side of the border —the one who actually owns that cave."

A solid plan. It might've worked, too. But only if the Afghan uncle wasn't in on the cave slaughter with the Pakistani one. Hell, the Afghan uncle might've clammed up even if he was innocent. He wouldn't even have to share Durrani's deep-seated inferiority complex. More than a few Afghans still despised Saudis for their crucial role in creating and funding the Taliban regime for so many years.

Regan turned away from Riyad to set her crime kit down beside the conference room's door, automatically glancing at the numbers on the lock. Her old mentor Art Valens had once confessed that he reset his tumble to one of several combinations every time he closed his kit, so he'd know if it'd been tampered with. With her thing for digits, she'd gone a step further, landing on a new random sequence each time she wrapped up a session.

Confident that no one had screwed with her kit while it had been stowed aboard the various aircraft she'd been in and out of that day—some of which she'd slept on—Regan opened the kit to withdraw two sets of paper booties and latex gloves, as well as a stack of numbered evidence markers. She hooked the stack of tented plastic in her right cargo pocket and handed a set of gloves and booties to Riyad as she stood.

Surprise lit his gaze, forcing a momentary thaw.

He'd obviously expected her to pull a tasking from his operational plan and relegate him to guarding this side of the door. He couldn't have been further from the truth. She might not respect, much less like the asshole, but she wanted him with her every step of the way on this investigation, two inches from her backside—or closer.

Who better to prove that she was, as Captain Armstrong had asserted, Impartiality Incarnate?

It was the only chance John had. All she could do was pray it was enough.

Regan slipped her booties over the soles of her tan combat

boots and donned her gloves before retrieving her digital camera and a fresh memory card. Riyad studied her intently as she snapped several overviews of the room.

She finally paused to sigh. "What?"

"I've got a question."

She turned away to snap a photo of the conference room door. It was still closed. "Fire away."

"Why did you order Chief Yrle to keep Major Garrison in the dark?"

She whirled back to Riyad, widening her stance to compensate for the sudden surging of the ship as well as the renewed sloshing in her belly.

Was it her imagination, or had the *Griffith* changed course?

"Because the CO was right. Not only do I know my job, Agent Riyad, I'm damned good at it. My investigation will reflect what happened in this compartment today. Nothing more, nothing less. No matter who is waiting to speak to me."

He clipped a nod. But the suspicion and disbelief were still there, in the subtle clenching of his neatly whiskered jaw. And something else.

Something she wasn't going to like.

She clamped down on her own jaw. "What?"

"You look like you could use another trip to the head."

He didn't pull any punches, did he? Not now, and not while Tamir Hachemi had been lying on the deck with those Marines, and then the doc and his corpsmen, still fighting for the translator's life. The proof was in Riyad's disappearing act.

The moment the spook had realized John had tangled with the translator and come out on the winning side, Riyad had run straight to the bridge to corner the ship's captain and whine about her impartiality.

Because of one simple purging.

What was it about men and nausea? As if there could be no

other reason for a woman to experience it. For example—a ship that, for some reason, truly did feel as though it was riding the waves higher and harder...or dealing with the even more unsettling discovery that the man she'd been unable to banish from her mind since the moment they'd met appeared to be guilty of murder?

Regan pushed the latter, truer, reason aside and concentrated on Riyad's. It was easier—for her and her case.

"Kill the euphemisms, Super Spy, and voice what's really on your mind...unless you don't have the nerve?"

The lock on Riyad's jaw tightened, but he said nothing.

"Well?"

He stepped closer. "*Are* you pregnant?"

"No." Nor was she likely to become so any time soon, and not without significant medical intervention and high-tech assistance. But there was no way she was telling him that. The status of her sole remaining ovary was none of this jerk's business.

But as much as she hated to admit it, her current relationship with John Garrison was. "How much do you know?"

Riyad's jaw relaxed a bit at the question, and he shrugged. "More than the rest of the world."

Meaning that, at the very least, he'd followed her humiliation in the news the year before.

Year, hell; it was going on sixteen months now.

It was also becoming clear that she'd never live that case down. Especially among her fellow agents—Army and otherwise.

Regan offered up her own shrug infused with an insouciance she'd never feel. Not about this. "I'm going to say this once, Agent Riyad, so listen closely. Yes, Major Garrison and I knew each other in Germany. And, yes, we met while I was undercover working a case to take down his houseguest before the sergeant could blow a certain Turkish general's remaining offspring to hell and back. Things got dicey—and, yes, we also crawled into bed together before he discovered I was CID. But then I crawled out of his bed before the main event—because it was my *job*. Lives were on the line, including those of innocent children. As I'm sure you know, Major Garrison was still pissed over my actions, even after he discovered why I'd been undercover. We parted ways and didn't meet up again until just over two weeks ago, after I arrived at Fort Campbell. We spent the next several days in and out of each other's company as we worked to figure out why the men on one of his A-Teams were alternately killing their wives, falling deathly ill or committing suicide. Just what sort of unprofessional relationship the major and I were supposed to have resumed in between our near constant visits to the hospital, the morgue and that Pakistani cave, I have no idea. Or perhaps you think the major slipped into my own ICU bed sometime during the three hours after I woke from my coma back at Fort Campbell and before he was shipped here?"

Dead silence filled the compartment as she finished. It was broken only by the ever-present creaking of metal and embarrassment.

Hers and his.

"I trust I've satisfied your curiosity—or at least soothed your concerns—about what is, or is *not*, inside my abdomen?"

This nod was stiff.

"Excellent. And is there anything else you'd like to know, or perhaps should share with me, before we get this show on the road?"

To her surprise, the man offered another nod before jerking his neatly groomed beard toward the body still lying on the deck just past the conference table. "You might as well know now; he did it. According to Corporal Vetter, the translator got in Major Garrison's face while Garrison was questioning him. Next thing

Vetter knew, the major had slammed Hachemi into the bulkhead, face first. Just one smack, but between Garrison's training and an inch of rolled steel, that was all it took. The Marines laid the body out on the deck and started CPR while Chief Yrle took Garrison into custody and escorted him out of the compartment. You know the rest."

She did.

She simply refused to buy that that was all there was to this. At least, not until she'd had a chance to examine the scene and question everyone involved—including John.

The pulse beating steadily at the base of the spook's jaw told her Riyad was of no such opinion. As far as Super Spy was concerned, John was guilty. End of case.

Worse, she had the distinct impression Riyad believed John meant to kill Hachemi, and had even planned it.

But why?

That was a question she wasn't prepared to press. Yet.

Regan nodded. "Message received. Now if it's all the same to you, *Agent*, I prefer to get my facts from the victim. Do us both a favor and stay out of my way. Don't approach the body without permission and do not, under any circumstances, touch so much as a speck of dust in this compartment—even when properly gloved—unless I give direct instruction. Understood?"

She didn't wait for confirmation, verbal or otherwise. She headed across the room, stopping to remove one of the numbered evidence markers she'd tucked in her cargo pocket. She set the marker on the floor beside the splattered coffee and snapped a photo before moving on to the four chairs in the room, the table and the two Styrofoam cups. Retrieving two more markers, Regan placed one beside the cup of cold coffee, the other near the upended cup.

The latter rolled several inches to the right atop the table, then to the left, repeating the pendular motion with each progressively more powerful surge of the ship. But for the lipped edges of the conference table, it would've hit the deck a while ago.

Had the *Griffith* changed course, then?

The speaker hanging from a corner of the overhead sparked to life. The piercing trill from a boatswain's pipe filled the compartment, followed by a disembodied voice briefing the crew on what appeared to be the imminent underway refueling Chief Yrle had mentioned upon Regan's arrival. The announcement ended with an admonishment that the smoking lamp was out throughout the ship.

Regan could only hope they relit that lamp soon. She might not be yearning for nicotine, but the resulting course change was playing havoc with her newfound equilibrium. At least her stomach was holding fast. That was something.

Given the bloodied and shattered features of her pending photographic subject—and who appeared to be responsible—it was everything.

To her horror, her right hand visibly shook for the first time in almost two days as she raised the camera to snap her opening shot of the body.

So much for her brag to Gil. And damn him for getting it right. Because there was no escaping the obvious. That tremor might be in her hand...but it was also in her head.

And it was back.

Fortunately, Riyad was behind her.

Regan waited for the tremor to pass, then raised the camera again. This time she managed to hold the camera steady and photograph the body. Intent on completing the task before her hand started shaking again, she adjusted the lens for a close-up, only to shift her attention as the door to the compartment opened behind her.

The ship's doc entered.

"Ready for the bag?"

"Not yet. But we are ready for you."

The doc nodded. Unlike Riyad, Lieutenant Mantia had been through the death drill at least once before, because he set the plastic body bag on the deck just inside the space. He also had his own booties and latex gloves in hand and paused to don both sets before he bent to retrieve the thermometer and several paper evidence bags from her kit. Regan snapped a succession of close-ups of the body as she waited for Mantia to reach her side. Riyad wisely remained at the table.

"Finished?"

She nodded. "Go for it, Doc."

They hunkered down together. Regan opened the largest of the evidence bags and waited as Mantia eased the O2 mask, balloon and tubing from Hachemi's face. She bagged the medical gear and labeled it as the doc inserted the thermometer into Hachemi's liver, waited for, then recorded the results.

"Done."

Fortunately, her hand remained steady. Regan quickly photographed the translator's battered face without the obscuring O2 mask—and bit down on her shock. If Corporal Vetter was correct and John had landed just one blow, it had been a doozy. Unfortunately, it had also been more than enough to kill him. Even she—sans four-year college and follow-on medical degree—knew that.

She tamped down on her dwindling hope. There was always a chance she was wrong. "Well, Doc?"

"It's as bad as it looks." He drew his gloved fingers alongside what was left of Hachemi's features. "The nose has been shattered. As have several teeth. I'm also fairly certain—" Mantia slipped his fingers lower and gently manipulated the coarsely bearded lower jaw. "You hear that crunch?"

"Yes."

"The chin feels as though it's been fractured too—right here, and clean through."

She resisted the urge to close her eyes and pray. "Recently?"

"Yes. However—" Mantia drew her attention to the three middle fingers of the translator's right hand. They were splinted. "These fractures are older by a good—"

"Two weeks."

Mantia nodded. "You have good instincts, Agent Chase."

Not instinct, memory. She'd been nearby when those three fingers had been broken, too. Again, by John.

At the time she'd been handcuffed to a sink in a darkened bathroom while John and half a dozen Special Forces soldiers and her two fellow CID agents had been fighting off the effects of the anesthetic gas that Hachemi had used to knock them out. John had recovered first. He'd methodically snapped those now-splinted digits one by one as Hachemi had refused to offer up her whereabouts and other intel.

Given that her mentor Art Valens had never regained consciousness, Hachemi had been lucky that she hadn't been the one asking questions.

Though if she had, they wouldn't be here now—with John's career, freedom and quite possibly his very life on the line.

"Cause of death?" *Riyad.*

Regan bit down on her tongue as the doc stiffened. Surprise furrowed Mantia's brow as he twisted around to focus on the spook leaning against the edge of the conference table. It appeared she should've added ill-timed queries to his "don'ts" list.

Riyad shrugged. "I won't hold you to it. I'm just looking for a best guess, given the injuries in front of you."

"Injuries can be misleading, Agent Riyad."

Mantia might have voiced the rebuke, but she was in complete agreement.

Riyad was not. The murky frost had returned, and this time it was blowing toward the doc.

Regan mirrored Mantia's movements as he came to his feet. There was no need. Not only did the doc have no need of backup, he'd definitely been through this drill before—complete with interfering, impatient rubberneckers—because he held firm.

"We'll wait, Agent Riyad. I received word that, in an effort to keep a lid on the situation as long possible, the Pentagon has decided against shipping the body to Bahrain. We'll be flying it to one of our aircraft carriers. A pathologist from Detrick has been rerouted to the carrier to conduct the postmortem. You may have your answer by tonight, possibly tomorrow."

The murky frost shifted as Mantia returned to the body. It settled on her. As with the stateroom door Riyad had shut in her face following her arrival, her fellow agent's message was clear. Riyad might not have more homicide investigations under his belt than he could count, but he was aware of basic procedure. He'd simply intended on lancing her hope.

Unfortunately, the evidence had beaten him to it.

She watched as Mantia manipulated the translator's head, examining the back. The skin was intact. The two-foot slick of blood beneath Hachemi's body had come from his shattered face. A shattered face that, according to Corporal Vetter, was the direct result of the single blow John had landed.

# 6

Three hours later, the horrifying reality of John's guilt was still ricocheting through Regan's brain, magnified by the plethora of evidence she'd meticulously identified, photographed and bagged inside that conference room.

Hair. Fiber. Fingerprints.

DNA from those two Styrofoam coffee cups.

The statement from the junior Marine.

She'd yet to interview Staff Sergeant Brandt and wouldn't for another hour at least, as he and Corporal Vetter were aboard the CH-53E, en route to the carrier with the translator's body. Once the medical examiner arrived, she and Riyad would rendezvous aboard the carrier for the postmortem. While she didn't as yet share Riyad's impression of the *Griffith*'s sheriff, she'd been reluctant to entrust the chain of custody of Hachemi's body to Chief Yrle until she knew more about the woman's dispute with the spook.

Not that it mattered. She doubted even Staff Sergeant Brandt's version of events would change the course of this investigation. How could it when each piece of the puzzle she'd managed to collect had already converged to form an increasingly painful image. And at its center?

John.

For that reason, and others Regan was loath to examine, she couldn't quite seem to reach out and clasp the taunting knob to the metal door six inches from her face.

"We going in or not?"

She refused to answer the query, let alone glance at the increasingly smug spook who'd voiced it. Instead, she filled her lungs with false courage, shoved the door open—and froze at the sight that greeted her.

John was seated six feet away, at the opposite curve of a small, laminated table, still clad in the camouflaged ACUs she'd noted earlier. With his dark head bowed, he was not so much staring at his hands as through them. He didn't look up as she regained her nerve and forced herself to step inside the compartment, nor did she prompt him. She took advantage of John's distraction, instead, as Riyad stepped in behind her and closed the door, instinctively cataloguing the palpable shame and regret crushing those once imposing shoulders. Crushing him.

And then, John raised his head and met her gaze.

For a split second, he stiffened. And then he blinked, absorbed her presence aboard the *Griffith* and in this particular compartment...and the implications inherent therein.

Resignation supplanted shock as John accepted those implications, deepening the lines at the corners of his eyes and bracketing his mouth as he stood. "Chief."

Regan returned his brief nod and matched his equally terse, distant tone. "Major."

First names and any intimacy they'd managed to rekindle were gone—firmly incarcerated back in that Fort Campbell ICU where she'd clawed her way out of a numbing coma and the agonizing hallucinations that had trapped her there. Through it all John had remained at her side, profound joy and a humbling relief filling those haggard and haunted gray eyes of his as she'd woken. Within minutes she'd succumbed to sleep, only to reawaken three hours later to discover that John had pulled another classified mission and was deploying yet again.

She hadn't spoken to him since.

Until now.

John scrubbed a hand through the several weeks' worth of unruly scruff darkening the lower portion of his face and jaw, then motioned for her to take the empty seat across from his. "Let's get this over with."

She nodded, painfully aware that he was attempting to make the coming interrogation easier—on her.

Regan set her crime scene kit on the dark blue couch that dominated the senior officer stateroom. Given the absence of bunk beds, not to mention the three-inch tail of linen hanging out from the far end, she assumed the vinyl sofa converted into an equally stiff and unwieldy rack. As with her quarters, a closed porthole, a modular-steel wall unit, a small sink and mirror, and a tiny latrine outfitted with a toilet and shower rounded out the furnishings.

Unless John possessed solid information that contradicted Corporal Vetter's statement, chances were good that he'd be spending the remainder of his days with half the space and a fraction of the amenities in this compartment—as he took up residence in the federal penitentiary at Fort Leavenworth.

Reality and regret weighed heavy on her shoulders and in her heart as she retrieved the interview folder she'd prepared from Agent Riyad before crossing the tiny space. She laid the folder on the table and removed the digital camera and voice recorder she'd tucked into her cargo pocket before claiming the chair John had indicated, leaving a now empty-handed Riyad to mark time behind her.

She'd lost her view of the spook's face, but she had a close-up of John's, and what she saw gave her pause.

The men were at odds. From the set of John's jaw as his stare flicked past her right shoulder, she'd wager they had been since before Hachemi's death.

But for how long...and why?

The question would have to wait, because another one had just been answered. She'd found the missing coffee from that upended cup. It was splashed across the front of John's ACUs, the majority of the dried splotches nearly blending in with the muted tans and greens of the digital camouflaged pattern. And there was more.

Blood.

The high-velocity splatter she'd been seeking marred the right side of John's face, specifically the upper half of his neck and the collar of his ACU blouse and tan T-shirt. Several dried rust-colored drops also stained the inner contours of his left index finger, thumb and wrist. That he hadn't attempted to compromise the DNA evidence via the stateroom's sink after Chief Yrle had unwittingly left him to his own devices both relieved and terrified Regan.

Years of experience forced her to add the stains to the evidence she'd collected in the conference room as she waved Riyad up to one of the remaining chairs. "Join us."

"I'm fine."

But she wasn't. Not with that distant tone in the spook's voice. And something else. Something she couldn't quite put her finger on.

"I insist."

Given the ominous vibes thrumming beneath the ever-present creaking of the metal pipes and venting running through the overheard, she wanted both men within visual range. It would help fine-tune her instincts. She swore Riyad knew it, too.

She turned back to John as Riyad finally shrugged and ambled forward. He ignored the empty chair on her right, posting his brooding form against the wall unit. Regan clicked on the voice recorder, running though the *who, what, when, why and where*, as well as the standard recitation of detainee rights, as she set the recorder on the table. She ended her spiel with an offer to delay the interview if John wanted legal counsel in attendance.

Professionally, she willed him to say no. Personally, she prayed he'd say yes.

He shook his head. "No, no lawyer."

From the corner of her eye, she watched Riyad stiffen, clearly taken aback by the decision.

She wasn't.

She prompted John regardless. "Are you certain?"

For a moment, the steel in those dark gray eyes softened. Remorse brimmed within. And then it was gone as he nodded firmly. "I want this done."

And he wanted her to do it.

He didn't say it. He didn't have to. And, damn it, she didn't want to feel it—and she sure as hell didn't want to feel like *this* while she was doing it.

But, like him, she had no choice.

She stitched her emotions together, zealously holding to career-honed habits as she opened the folder to withdraw the eight-by-ten inch glossy she'd printed in the *Griffith*'s admin office minutes earlier. She laid the photo on the table between them. Professional mixed with personal once more as she studied the trio of scars where shrapnel had torn through the left side of John's neck and jaw during his first foray into

Afghanistan's Hindu Kush mountains when he was still an enlisted combat engineer over a decade earlier.

The pulse point within jumped as John studied the close-up of Hachemi's shattered face. The oxygen balloon and tubing had been removed prior to the shot, allowing the full brunt of the damage and blood to shine though.

Damage John had inflicted.

Even without Corporal Vetter's statement, there'd have been no doubt in her mind. That flagging pulse removed it. Nor did she need to draw John's attention to the splatter of blood staining his left hand.

He'd beaten her to it, shifting his stare to the rusted spots. The trio of shrapnel scars tightened as his pulse continued to flag damningly from within. A good half a minute passed before he tore his attention from the blood to focus on her.

His voice, when it came, was hoarse and broken. Guilty. "Where should I start?"

Regan clamped down on the compassion—and more—churning through her, lest it leak into her own voice and reach the still looming, still coldly distant NCIS agent leaning against that wall unit. "At the beginning."

John nodded and cleared his throat. "The call I took after you woke in the ICU came from General Palisade. His brief consisted of the basics: Hachemi had reneged on the deal he'd made after you and Agent Castile formally arrested him in that terror safe house in Afghanistan. They'd brought Hachemi here aboard the *Griffith* for questioning. I was ordered to fly out ASAP to assist. It was hoped that, since Hachemi and I worked half a dozen ops together over the past few years, he might open up with me sitting across the table instead of a tag team of grunts and spooks he didn't know."

"Did he?"

"No. I wasn't surprised."

"Why not?"

John snapped his ire toward the wall unit. "Because that asshole insisted on fusing himself to my hide."

The asshole in question scowled.

John matched Riyad's grimace and turned back to her. "He's Saudi."

"I know."

"Then you've figured out the rest."

She had. She suspected Riyad had too, even before she'd thrown Saudi/Afghan history in his face in that conference room. The spook was just arrogant enough to believe he could cut through decades of well-earned religious and political prejudice. That prejudice, and especially the man's arrogance, also explained why Riyad had shown up in her stateroom hours earlier only to haul the master-at-arms chief out into the passageway for a dressing down without so much as a nod back at her.

"You convinced Chief Yrle to give you a shot at questioning Hachemi alone."

"I did. We had a good hour before the chopper was scheduled to touch down. Riyad was up to his holier-than-thou attitude in a ship-to-shore call with someone from the State Department. I figured, what the hell? Might as well give it one last go."

From the greeting Riyad had given Chief Yrle, by the time the NCIS agent had discovered John's rogue interrogation, it had been too late. The session had already begun. No wonder Riyad had been pissed. Much as Regan was loath to admit it, she'd have been livid too if someone—even John—had openly violated her case authority.

Then again, "Did you get anywhere?"

Despite Corporal Vetter's damning statement, or rather because if it, she was more than interested in John's take on the course and content of his final conversation with the translator.

John glanced down at the grisly crime scene photo before shaking his head. "Not at first. Hachemi was whining about his stomach being upset. That, and he kept rubbing at his neck. But as we talked, it hit me. Hachemi could give a rip about the Qur'an. He only has one to keep up appearances. And there was no way he was going to fall for the patriotic angle, timely naturalization to US citizen notwithstanding. So I changed tactics. I started in on that female doc at Bagram—you remember the one?"

"Yes." Soraya Medhi. Like Hachemi, Soraya's mother was of Afghan descent. Her father was Iranian. Unlike Hachemi, Soraya was born following her parents' emigration to the States. Twenty-six years later, she'd graduated from medical school and joined the US Army. Hachemi had run into her at Bagram's hospital five months ago and fallen for the woman—hard. Unfortunately for the translator, despite Soraya's recent breakup, she was still hung up on Captain McCord...the same Special Forces captain who'd been framed for the cave murders.

Regan reached for the voice recorder as the ship surged more forcefully than it had since the *Griffith* had completed her underway refueling, only to come in second to John's reflexes as he caught the recorder before it slid off the table.

He held it out, the disconcerting heat in his fingers warming hers as she accepted it.

Like her, John must have felt Riyad's interest sharpen as she set the recorder on the table. And, like her, John ignored that interest as he leaned back in his chair and resumed speaking.

"During his arrest, Hachemi had all but admitted he'd set McCord up to get him out of the way. Jihad was never part of the plan—not on his part. Hachemi figured that with Mac in prison for murder, Soraya would turn to him for comfort."

Regan leaned into the table as John's strategy became clear. "You lied to him."

"Flat out. I told him Mac and Soraya had reconciled. He didn't believe me at first, so I pulled a page from your book and improvised. I reminded him that Mac's kid was the only baby to survive that slaughter. With the biological mother dead and Mac no longer framed for murder and in danger of spending his remaining days on death row, he needed someone to care for his daughter. Especially since Mac had ten years to go 'til retirement. I said Soraya had volunteered for the job—that the wedding was in three weeks. Hachemi knew the woman was solidly US Army first; her ethnicity was a distant second. I told Hachemi that if he really loved Soraya, he'd give her a gift she'd actually appreciate: the name of the traitor he was withholding. For a good ten seconds, he waffled."

Regan couldn't help it. She smiled. As interrogation fiction went, it was good. From the way Riyad had straightened off the wall unit, even he was impressed.

For some reason, Corporal Vetter had left that part of the exchange out of his version of events, a version she'd elicited personally following her canvas of the crime scene. Perhaps the Marine didn't understand the significance of what John had managed to do. Because it was significant.

John had made it personal. At least for the translator. During an interrogation, that was everything.

The curve of the table cut into Regan's torso as she leaned even closer. "What happened?"

"He bit, just not the way I expected. Not only did he finally admit his involvement in the cave slaughter, he bragged about it. Claimed that while Durrani had sliced the women's throats, he was the one who'd cut the kids from their wombs. So I swallowed my disgust and shifted tactics again. This time, I nailed him on his incompetence. In light of his earlier waffling, I told him if he'd done his part right, Mac's kid would've died with the others. And once Mac discovered that Jameelah and his child were among the dead, Mac would've been so rattled, he might not have fought the charges against him—and you might not have realized it was all a set up. Not only would he and Durrani have escaped capture, Soraya would've been his for the taking."

"But?" Because there was one. Even if she hadn't shared a past with John, she'd have been able to hear it.

He shoved his hands through his hair before clapping them onto the table. "I miscalculated. I'm still not sure how. All I know is the man did another one-eighty. He admitted he'd lied after getting to the ship. He doubled down on his original story. He swore there was another traitor in our midst, but he still refused to ID him. So I played my last card. I told him that was our final meet. That I was leaving the ship when we were done. And then I told him he was leaving the ship too—for Pakistan. I said our side had agreed to turn him over, so their intel specialists could...question him. That's when he lost it. He tossed his coffee at me, then shot to his feet and got down in my face. He started yammering about that chimeral virus, claiming that, though Durrani had been the one to infect Mendoza's team, he was the one who'd targeted my men in the first place. The bastard wouldn't let up. He started chortling over my men's deaths like a hyena in heat. And then he started bragging that it was his idea to inject the contents of the last vial of that goddamned psycho-toxin into you so that Durrani would have it for the trip to Iran. That's when I just—"

Regan kept her torso fused to the curve of the table as John broke off. The trio of scars on his neck tightened as he swallowed hard. His account had converged back into the statement she'd taken from Corporal Vetter, right down to the maniacal laughter that had spewed from the translator's lips. She knew what was next.

She waited for John to finish it.

But he didn't. Couldn't.

That, too, was obvious. Even Riyad knew why, because though the spook had settled back against the wall unit, his entire body was on alert, waiting for the rest.

It didn't come.

John dropped his gaze. It landed on the photo lying on the table between them. His stare drifted from Hachemi's shattered features to the blood staining his hand. Lingered. She swore she could feel the remorse warring with the fury still consuming John's soul. Even Riyad must've felt it. Believed it.

Because the agent had pulled away from the wall unit once again, this time to quietly prompt John before she could. "Major?"

The ever-present creaking of metal filled the stateroom.

Regan ignored the fisting in her gut and offered her own prompt. "He bragged that it was his idea to infect me with the chimeral virus, and you just...?"

John's stare was colder than Riyad's had ever been when it finally sliced up, and it was beyond empty. "*I saw red*. To tell the truth, Rae, I still don't remember coming to my feet, nor do I remember taking that final step toward him. All I know is I reached through the rage to grab the back of his head and slam that laughing face into the bulkhead. Just once. At least, I think it was just once. I can't be sure. I just know if those Marines hadn't pulled me off him, I'd have bashed that son-of-a-bitch to a pulp."

John's scarred right hand came up to cover the crime scene photo and remained there as he sighed. "Hell, it looks like that's exactly what I did."

The hush returned. Terse breathing accompanied the creaks of the piping and vents, merging with the ever-present, distant drone of machinery. Even Riyad appeared loath to break the spell.

The satellite phone in his cargo pocket had no such reservations.

The phone shrilled a second time as Riyad retrieved it. "I need to take this."

She nodded briefly, then wondered why she'd bothered. The spook had already stepped out into the passageway and closed the door behind him, shutting her in with John.

Alone.

For a solid minute, neither of them moved, much less spoke. Every single, stark second was absolute torture. Through them all, John stared at the bloodstained hand still lying on the table beside the crime scene photo.

Suddenly, she couldn't handle it. Before she could stop herself, she broke protocol and reached out, ignoring the fresh tremor in her own hand as she sealed it to the crisscross of keloid ridges and valleys that covered the back of his.

His entire body flinched.

"John?"

He dragged his attention from the photo. But instead of focusing it on her, he stared at the voice recorder.

It was still on.

She hadn't forgotten. She simply didn't care. Or perhaps she cared too much. If she got pulled from this case, so what? The alternative was killing her. Just as John's grief over that single, instinctive blow was slowly killing him.

But he was right.

She reached out again, this time switching the recorder off before returning her hand to where it belonged. She threaded her fingers into his and squeezed firmly, attempting to impart the final vestiges of her hope before it evaporated. "John, I know you. Whatever happens during this investigation, whatever else we learn, I know you didn't mean to kill him. I plan on doing everything in my power to prove it."

There was no way—absolutely *none*—that she'd allow this man who'd sacrificed so much for his country to end his life where that so-called Army translator should be—on death row, waiting for someone to push a lethal injection into his veins.

To her dismay, John withdrew his hand from beneath hers and reached for the recorder she'd killed. He switched it back on.

His hand dropped into his lap, the stark truth of what had happened that morning locked in those dark gray eyes as he faced her full on.

For once she'd have given anything for John—a soldier of absolute, unshakable honor—to lie through his teeth.

But he didn't.

And she damned near died as John all but shoved that needle into his own arm as he took in her silent plea and slowly shook his head. "Agent Chase, I know you mean well. I appreciate it. But let me make one thing clear: I'm guilty. Not only did I kill Tamir Hachemi—in that moment, I wanted to."

# 7

Regan tracked the arc of her pen as it rolled back and forth across the metal flap she'd lowered from the wall unit to create the desk in her temporary quarters. While the waves hitting the *Griffith* were mild compared to those she'd experienced upon boarding, it didn't seem to matter. Her stomach had resumed its nauseating lurch—and it had nothing to do with the motion of her pen or the ship.

It had to do with John. His confession.

Those three damning words that had rasped past his lips. Agent Riyad might not understand their significance, but she did.

*I saw red.*

While they'd lain in bed together in Germany sixteen months ago, John had opened up a bit more about his childhood. That same, seemingly simple euphemism had served as the oft-repeated excuse from his father the morning after the bastard had gotten drunk and taken a belt, a branch, his fist or worse to John while he was growing up. He'd taken the beatings for twelve years, until the night his father had grabbed one bottle too many, only to have it jerked from his grip and smashed into the wall instead—by John. Fed up, and now tall enough to take on his father, he'd given the brute a choice. Hit him again, and the next time, John would hit back.

Hard.

The physical abuse had ended that night.

But the emotional?

For the next two decades John had lived with the deep-seated, insidious fear that his mother's prediction—and excuse—for taking his baby sister and leaving her five-year-old son to endure his father's vitriol and beatings alone would come to pass. That one day, some unknown and inescapable trigger would click deep within, and John too would *see red* and snap.

That day had finally come.

Whether the translator realized it or not, Tamir Hachemi had discovered it.

*She* was the trigger. The reason John had finally vaulted to his feet in that conference room and blindly vented the pain, horror and rage of the past few weeks—hell, the entire past decade—onto his once-trusted colleague.

Just one blow. But with those massive arms and combat-honed reflexes, that was all it had taken. The translator was dead. And unless she found exculpating evidence—and soon—John would be found guilty. Despite their past and her current feelings for the man, she'd be forced to support that verdict.

Christ, what a mess. A mess that, ultimately, lay at her feet. John would have been better off having never met her in that off-post bar back in Germany. But he had. Not only had she used his attraction, she'd ruthlessly exploited it. And now, he was trapped in a compartment a deck away, alone and tortured by what he'd done.

What he believed he'd finally become.

Because of her.

But she wasn't the only one at fault. The Army shouldered a

good deal of the responsibility too. Perhaps not as much as she did, but definitely more than John.

To the military, the mission was everything. And the way those missions were accomplished was through skills, to the extent that the military's entire branch and occupational specialty sub-structure was based upon them.

Need to blow up a critical bridge deep inside enemy lines? Task a Sapper team with soldiers who'd been weaned on rigging C4 and det cord since they were privates. Need to ferry an Army CID agent from a sensitive airstrip located on a patch of desert in the UAE to a US Navy warship while that ship was operating in the middle of the Arabian Sea? Task the pilot and crew of one of those mammoth Super Stallions currently strapped to the *Griffith*'s helo deck to fly to that airstrip and bring her here.

Why?

Because she was no more qualified to fly that monster than she could drop an entire bridge into a river in ten seconds flat—while the enemy was crossing it.

In fact, there were a hell of a lot of skills that were critical to the Army and its innumerable missions that she didn't possess and never would. But she was an interrogator. Which the Army knew full well, because it had spent years teaching her to sit across a table, identify the appropriate interrogation technique and slowly but steadily run it—and the detainee on the other side of the table—into the ground, until he or she coughed up whatever information Uncle Sam had deemed vital.

John, however, was *not* an interrogator.

Oh, he might get lucky. And there was always the chance that he'd be able to clear the goalpost by brainpower, patience and combat-honed instincts alone. But the risk was always there. The risk that those same combat-honed instincts could just as easily become triggered and blow up in John's face...as they had this morning.

Why?

John simply wasn't trained to do what he'd been ordered to do aboard this ship. It was the same rationale as to why a US Army infantryman, carrying a loaded M4, should never be slotted into a line of civilian police officers at the local county courthouse during a belligerent stateside demonstration. The average infantryman simply didn't possess the knowledge, skills and experience to perform the riot control mission effectively.

Again and again, history had confirmed that conquering armies made for lousy occupying forces and even lousier police. Peacekeeping just wasn't in their skill set. And professional fortitude and personal control only went so far.

That wasn't to say that John shouldn't be aboard the *Griffith*.

Quite the contrary. Once Hachemi had reversed course and clammed up, John should absolutely have been brought in. Just as someone from the *Griffith*'s audiovisual department should've rigged a camera to broadcast its signal beyond the steel bulkheads that formed that conference room. John should've been in the next compartment, watching the feed.

Assessing. Advising.

But he should never have been inside that compartment, let alone serving as the official face of the Army across the table. Because John was not CID; he was Special Forces. In that capacity, the Army had spent years teaching the man to execute two primary missions: kill, and teach others how to kill. Coldly, efficiently, effectively.

And in some singularly creative ways.

And then the Army had tasked John with honing those deadly skills, for over a decade—in combat, no less—until they'd become more than second nature.

They'd been branded into his flesh.

Muscle memory. The goal was to train a soldier to the point where he could draw on his skill set mere seconds from sleep...

or when his back was to the wall and he was fighting the renewed horror of the deaths of no less than seven of his soldiers, two of their wives and a young sergeant's unborn child. Not to mention seven Pakistani women and an equal number of infants in a cave deep within the Hindu Kush.

The idea was to push at a soldier under increasingly severe stress until his innate skills automatically surfaced and the soldier just...reacted.

As John had.

As General Palisade and the general's entire chain of command had to have *known* John would react. So, why on earth had Palisade and that chain risked it?

What else was going on?

And why did she increasingly suspect that Riyad was privy to it?

And if the NCIS agent was aware of it? Did she keep the real meaning behind that private *I saw red* explanation to herself? At least for now?

Or did she inform her newly assigned, so-called partner of the dark depth of John's belief in his own culpability? An NCIS spook who not only openly wanted her off this case so he could investigate it alone, but had done his damnedest to sabotage her initial assignment before she'd even stepped aboard the *Griffith*.

Regan was still struggling with the dilemma when the door to her stateroom reverberated with a solid, triple knock.

The knocks settled it.

If Riyad was on the other side, she confessed right now. If not, she waited. Bided her time. At least until she and Riyad linked up for the translator's autopsy.

She hadn't seen or heard from the spook since he'd walked out during her interview with John just over an hour ago. If Riyad was still on his sat phone, that was one heck of a call...the contents of which he didn't appear eager to share with her.

All the more reason to reconsider sharing the entire range of John's confession—now or later.

Damn it, *move*.

She reached for her pen, ignoring yet another traitorous tremor as it hijacked her hand at the last moment, causing her to knock the pen to the floor. She stood to retrieve the pen, then crossed the stateroom. Relief swamped her as she opened the door.

It wasn't Riyad.

It was Staff Sergeant Brandt. The Marine she'd yet to interview regarding Tamir Hachemi's death.

The staff sergeant's dark-blond, camouflaged bulk dominated the narrow passageway, somehow reminding her painfully of John as he shifted to attention. The man was even sporting a dimple, though Brandt's was smack in the middle of his chin.

"Good afternoon, Agent Chase. I just returned from escorting the translator's body to the *USS Ronald Reagan*. Chief Yrle said you needed my statement?"

That would explain the musical piping that had sounded from the ship-wide, 1MC loudspeaker box hanging in the overhead of her stateroom fifteen minutes earlier—and the terse "helo ops" announcement that had followed.

Regan nodded as she pulled the door wide. "Come on in, Staff Sergeant." She used her pen to point to the spare chair tucked along the bulkhead beside the sink as she returned to her makeshift desk and the pair of case folders burdening the upper right corner. "Grab that seat and drag it over."

The Marine complied, dwarfing the stateroom, and especially the second chair, as he moved it to within two feet of hers and sat. He reached for the right cargo pocket of his camouflaged trousers, then changed his mind before breaching the flap. The faint rectangular outline beneath had already given away its contents.

"If you need a smoke, feel free."

His brows lifted. "You don't mind?"

Honestly? She did. Plus, although the smoking lamp had been relit following the conclusion of the ship's underway refueling, she didn't know if that included permission to light up inside the skin of the ship.

But if not, she'd take the hit. Mainly because she wanted the staff sergeant relaxed, not preoccupied with an addiction. And since Brandt had been on duty and, hence, not allowed to smoke since the translator's interrogation had commenced five hours earlier, his nicotine craving had to be biting in hard about now.

"Go for it."

The Marine retrieved a pack of Pakistani cigarettes and held them out.

She shook her head and shoved her half-empty Styrofoam cup of coffee across the desk as he settled back to light up.

"Thanks, ma'am, but I've got something."

His hand returned to his cargo pocket, this time surfacing with what appeared to be a tin of mints. From the blackened and slightly warped inner base, the tin had served as a recycled ashtray for a while.

The Marine's lips twisted ruefully as he finished his first, deep drag and leaned forward to tap his ashes into the tin. "Been trying to quit for a couple weeks now—for the third time. This is number two for the day."

His next drag was deeper still, all but confirming that the earlier cigarette had been consumed well before John's final interview with Hachemi. Add on the translator's death, the bout of futile CPR, the subsequent forensic processing of the conference room, as well as the Marine's recent morbid escort duties, and that probably wouldn't be his last cigarette of the day.

Smoke clouded the stateroom's air as Regan retrieved the digital recorder she'd stowed inside her own cargo pocket following the conclusion of her interview with John. She activated the machine, its tiny green "on" light gleaming as she verbally tagged this latest interview session's time, place, participating personnel and subject matter, before setting the recorder on the desk.

She dragged her tablet and pen closer and waited for the Marine to finish.

Brandt finally balanced the dwindling cigarette over the edge of the tin and sighed. "Where should I start?"

"Anywhere you'd like." What someone chose to open with often revealed more than they realized. About her current case —and them.

But instead of choosing a spot, the staff sergeant leaned forward and snagged the cigarette. It didn't take the Commandant of the Corps to recognize the reluctance tightening the cords of Brandt's neck as he studied the glowing tip, much less understand the reason for it. *Semper Fidelis*: Always Faithful.

Like most Marines, Brandt appeared to take the Corps' motto seriously. A motto that, given a certain decades-long War on Terror, tended to encompass the remaining military branches. John might not be a jarhead, but he was a soldier. And he was Special Forces. Something this jarhead obviously respected.

Regan retrieved her lukewarm coffee and took a sip, giving the staff sergeant the time he needed to come to terms with what amounted to ratting out a fellow combat vet.

Another sigh filled the room, this one heavier than the first. "He's a good man."

Regan set her tepid coffee on the desk. "Major Garrison?"

"Yes."

Despite what had happened today, she thoroughly agreed

with the assessment. Still, there was something in that reluctant sigh. Something almost...personal.

Were the men more than fellow combat vets? "Did you cross paths with the major in Iraq?"

The staff sergeant blinked.

Regan glanced at Brandt's Marine Corps woodland utilities. By their nature, they were spartan compared to her ACUs. Although there was no war patch velcroed to the staff sergeant's right sleeve to reflect his seven-month tour in the Anbar Province when he was still a private, Vetter had mentioned it during their interview earlier.

And there was her personal knowledge. "Major Garrison led a number of missions in Anbar when he was a lieutenant." In fact, Anbar was where John's Humvee had been struck by an IED, resulting in the death of his first sergeant and the creation of the pair of thick, roping scars that tangled down the left side of John's neck and a good eight inches into his chest.

Surprise had invaded the Marine's dark blue eyes at the revelation. The reluctance to rat returned as well. Strengthened.

"It's all right, Staff Sergeant. I already know what happened. Major Garrison's own account dovetails into your corporal's. I just need to hear it from you."

Brandt held her stare for a good ten seconds, then sighed. He took one last drag on the now stunted cigarette and leaned forward to extinguish it. He left the crumpled butt in the tin, shaking his head as he sat back in his chair. "No. I've never run across the major before. And, yeah, he did it. Though I swear to God, he held out longer than I would have."

"The taunting?"

Another nod. This one was downright grim. "The bastard was in rare form this morning—and, trust me, I know. I've been stuck on this boat since they brought the two of them here."

Brandt knew about Durrani then, too.

Regan wasn't surprised. She simply retrieved her pen so she could make a note in her tablet to that effect before she continued. "So you were there for the earliest sessions that involved just Agent Riyad?"

"Yes. Not that anything came of them. I guess that's why they brought in the major—personal history, and all."

This time, Regan nodded. "Sometimes it gets things going."

"This was definitely one of those times. Just not sure it was a wise choice, at least not this morning."

"Why not?"

"'Cause they were both pushing at each other. Granted, the major was pushing harder, at least for a while. Not in a bad way, mind you. Just...smart."

"How so?"

"Hachemi wasn't feeling well. I don't think he'd slept well, either. He was rubbing at his neck, and he was sweaty and thirsty. At one point he admitted his head was pounding and that his stomach felt like shit. He was green about the gills—and the seas were rough this morning. But he'd refused the pills the doc offered, so it was his own damned fault. The major must've thought so too, 'cause he finally reamed the guy with it. Said ships weren't his thing either—but that, lucky for him, he was about to leave. But he figured he'd give the bastard one last shot at the most understanding ear he was gonna get. 'Cause the word had come down that we were gonna hand him over to the Pakistanis when all was said and done, and let them deal with him. And if that happened, that bastard was gonna wish he'd died with those women in that cave."

"Do you know if that was the truth?"

Given the focus of her interview with John in his stateroom earlier, she hadn't had a chance to ask him. But she suspected not. Not only had General Palisade not mentioned a Pakistani rendition back at Fort Campbell, Agent Riyad hadn't broached the subject either, earlier today aboard this ship or during that recent session with John.

Though, there was precedent for allowing the Pakistanis to take the lead. Most infamously, the Al Qaeda terror mastermind Ramzi Ahmed Yousef and the first attack on the Twin Towers in '93. Then again, Ramzi Yousef had been in Pakistan when he'd been hunted down and arrested by US Diplomatic Security Service agents. Nor had Ramzi been a recently minted naturalized American citizen.

Hachemi was—or had been until this morning.

Brandt shrugged. "I don't know. Like I said, I figured it was smart tactics. 'Cause let's face it, if the guy had ended up in ISI's custody, he would've wished he *had* died alongside those women."

True. Pakistan's Inter-Services Intelligence agents had no compunction with regard to full-blown torture. Once the ISI got going, they tended to make the Gestapo look like a gaggle of Girl Scouts. They had with Ramzi Yousef...and others.

Granted, the ISI wouldn't have gone so far as to kill Hachemi —but Brandt was right. Hachemi would've wished they had. For a very long, painful time.

As interview techniques went, it was impressive. But ultimately, "It didn't work, did it?"

"Oh, no, it worked. Just not the way the major hoped. The bastard believed him—and he was terrified shitless. It was like a switch went off. I think he decided right then and there to go out on his own terms. You know that phrase: suicide by cop? Only in this case, it was suicide by Special Forces. 'Cause from that moment on, that fucker got in the major's face and he would *not* let up. Tossed his coffee at him and started going off again on how he'd targeted the major's men personally, then he lit in on how he'd gutted those babies right out of their moms' bellies, while the women were still alive. He kept describing it, over and over—the screaming and the blood. And all the while, that bastard was cackling. Like it was the funniest thing he'd ever seen. And then he started in about you. Saying how it was his idea, not Durrani's, to put that shit in your veins. That he and Durrani knew you'd be dead by the time they got to Iran and they didn't care, because they'd planned on draining your blood outta you anyway, by the bucketload. And, hell, it was what a whore like you deserved. That's when—"

The Marine broke off, took a breath and...nothing. The solidarity had returned, this time with a vengeance.

"Staff Sergeant?"

He met her stare, held it—and refused to budge.

"Please continue." It wasn't a request.

"Damn it, you said you *knew*."

"I do. But you have to say it." She pointed to the digital recorder. "For the record."

Reluctant blue zeroed in on that gleaming dot of green as the Marine evaded her stare. He dragged his gaze back to hers on a heavy sigh. "Fine. *For the record*, that goddamned fucker was in his face—*laughing* about you dying and deserving it—and that's when he snapped."

"The major?"

Brandt reached up and slicked his palms over the naked skin above his ears, then scrubbed them through the island of cropped hair that formed the high of the ubiquitous Marine Corps high-and-tight cut. His fury ebbed as he dropped his hands to his lap. Resignation set in. "Yeah. The major. He grabbed the back of Hachemi's head and slammed his face into the bulkhead. Vetter and I shot to our feet and rounded the table to pull him off, but it was too late. One lousy crack, and it was over. Blood was pouring out of the bastard's face. By the time we got him laid out on the deck, he was shaking like he was having a seizure, and then his heart stopped. I'd barely bellowed for help when Chief Yrle vaulted into the compartment. She called the bridge and told them to pass the word for the ship's doc, then took custody of the major and escorted him out of the conference room while Vetter and I did CPR. You know the rest."

She did. She'd seen it for herself.

The Marine's fury might've ebbed as he finished his account, but his hate hadn't. A fresh wave consumed the blue as he captured her stare. "I swear to God, that fucker was begging for it. If I'd been in the major's boots, I'd have lost it a helluva lot sooner."

She believed him. Unfortunately, as extenuating circumstances went, belligerence and taunting didn't qualify, no matter how obscene. Not even in light of John's murdered men or those mutilated Pakistani women and children. Not even in light of her. Even without the confession she'd recorded, John would be found guilty.

There wasn't a blessed thing she could do about it.

"Agent Chase?"

Regan flinched as the Marine's fingers wrapped around her arm to squeeze gently. Until that moment, she hadn't realized she'd dragged the uppermost folder from the stack on her makeshift desk forward. She'd even opened it.

A color copy of John's current, official photo had spilled out with the motion of the ship, causing John to stare back.

The sounds of the *Griffith* filtered in. The creaking of the pipes and cables running along the overhead. The sudden heaviness in the lack of conversation between herself and the Marine to whom she should've been paying attention—but hadn't been.

She shoved the photo into the manila folder and faced the staff sergeant.

Blue eyes replaced gray. Compassion filled them. Pity.

*Christ.* Brandt knew about her past with John.

Even if Hachemi's whore comment had been a blanket insult

toward all women, she should've expected it. After all, Brandt had been entrusted with guarding two of the nation's deadliest terrorists. Not an easy gig to land. Not to mention, Marines took a lot of crap for supposedly carrying little more than rocks upstairs in lieu of smarts.

It wasn't true. But the majority of Marines she knew also tended to conceal just how clever they really were—especially from their enemies. Which in and of itself was brilliant. Because the subterfuge usually provided an immediate advantage.

Like the rest of the Corps, the staff sergeant seated two feet away was savvy enough to follow the news on a regular basis and smart enough to remember her face from when all hell had broken loose via an arrestee's lawyer and an international reporter, following her final undercover assignment for CID back in Germany.

Brandt didn't say a word about that assignment or John's role in it, much less the painfully personal fallout she and John had shared afterward. He didn't have to.

Somehow, that silent sympathy made it worse.

She swallowed hard and nodded.

He dropped his hand.

She purged her breath, the ache. Tried to, anyway. "Thank you for your time, Staff Sergeant. Your statement will be transcribed shortly. You'll need to stop by admin afterward to sign it. Meanwhile, get some rest."

From the lines etched in at the outer corners of his eyes, the Marine had been logging as few hours as she'd been lately.

And now this.

He reached out and closed the tin that had doubled as his ashtray, then leaned back to massage the cleft in his chin. "Will do—and thanks. It's been the longest damned month of my life."

Regan stiffened.

Month?

Just like that, the pinging and creaking of the surrounding metal magnified. The distant whir of machinery joined in, growing so loud that the added rhythm pounded through her ears, right along with the numbers. The numbers that, when compared, revealed a glaring inconsistency in her case's collective timelines.

Especially Brandt's.

John had been aboard the *Griffith* for eight days; Durrani and Hachemi had been on board for thirteen. And, yet, the Marine had been stressed for roughly thirty?

Was Brandt prone to hyperbole?

She suspected not. Not after the statement he'd shared. "Staff Sergeant...when did you and Corporal Vetter arrive aboard the *Griffith*—exactly?"

"December fifteenth."

Son of a *bitch*. He had been here for nearly a month.

And only a month.

She dropped her stare to that makeshift ashtray. The one that contained the remains of his cigarette. A Pakistani cigarette.

Bastard that he was, Riyad might be right about one thing. Perhaps she shouldn't be on this case. She'd been so rattled by what John had instinctively done to Hachemi in the midst of his overwhelming rage that she'd missed the clue that cigarette had offered, along with another.

What had Brandt said upon his arrival in this very compartment half an hour earlier? *I've been stuck on this boat since they brought the two of them here.*

Stuck.

As in, others had left. But Brandt—and Corporal Vetter—had not. Could not. Because they were still needed.

The Marine's hand found her arm again. "Agent Chase, are you okay?"

"Yes." But she wasn't. If what she suspected was true, Agent Riyad wouldn't be either. Not after she got ahold of him.

John's presence aboard this vessel wasn't the only secret the shifty spook had been clinging to since her arrival. And after she added all the evidence together, the sole explanation she could come up with for this latest lie of omission had the acid in her gut churning up so hard, she was in danger of losing the coffee she'd downed.

According to the crew chief on that Super Stallion she'd flown in on, the *Griffith* was an amphibious dock landing ship. As such, the ship should have a permanent Marine contingent stationed onboard. Which, also according to the crew chief, it did. Just not *this* Marine.

Regan stared at those spartan woodland utilities. Like the absentee war patch, there was no unit identifier velcroed to the staff sergeant's left sleeve. It didn't matter. Not only did she now know that Brandt and Corporal Vetter were not permanently stationed aboard the *Griffith*, she also now knew exactly from where the Marines had come.

US Embassy Islamabad.

Given everything else she'd discovered today, it made sense.

John and his men had entered that Pakistani cave on December fourteenth. At the time, they'd been operating on a tip, intent on capturing Osama bin Laden's number two, Ayman al-Zawahiri, who was still at large after all these years. But instead of locating Zawahiri, John's Special Forces team had discovered those murdered women and their dying babies—along with evidence suggesting that a fellow SF team had been responsible for the slaughter.

Days later, a diplomatic contingency from Islamabad, Kabul and the US State Department had come together. Their objective? Damage control. All parties concerned had been intent on keeping the world's press from learning about the murders before all the facts were in—albeit for each country's respective, geopolitical reasons.

She'd assumed those damage control sessions had taken place in Islamabad, Kabul or even Washington, DC. She was wrong. They'd taken place here, aboard the *Griffith*, something Riyad had known all along, but hadn't told her.

Yet another critical omission.

One that made no sense at all...unless she added in the rest.

Regan offered the Marine a smooth smile to soothe his concern...and conceal her deepening ire.

The smile worked. Brandt released her arm.

He lowered his hand, closing it over the tin.

She pushed through her anger as he returned the makeshift ashtray to his cargo pocket. "Staff Sergeant, when did Agent Riyad board this ship?"

The Marine's hand paused in mid tuck. "I don't understand. I thought you knew."

She did. She just needed confirmation.

What she got was another round of silence. And this time, it was Brandt's.

It confirmed the ugliest of suspicions. Especially since the Marine's hand was still halfway inside his cargo pocket, frozen. Brandt was wary of continuing—because he'd just figured out she wasn't quite as *in the know* as she was supposed to be.

There was only one reason for that trepidation.

Brandt was answering to Riyad. And she knew why.

Just as she'd finally figured out why Riyad had been lying to her since the moment she'd stepped aboard this vessel. Why he'd done everything in his power to sabotage her assignment before she'd even been brought aboard. And why the spook was so profoundly pissed with her—and especially John.

Not to mention why Riyad had done everything in his power

to prevent John from speaking one-on-one with the translator... and alone.

And why John's chain of command had risked everything by flying him here and seating him across the interrogation table from the terrorist who'd murdered his men. Hell, she now understood why the spook believed John had not only meant to kill Hachemi, but had even planned it.

As well as why Riyad himself had been sent here.

Tamir Hachemi had made his claim regarding yet another traitor in the military's midst before he and Durrani had been sent to the *Griffith*. While Hachemi and Durrani had still been in their respective holding cells at Bagram, in fact. Within the hour, both men had been on their way here.

Yes, the *Griffith* was a naval warship. And, yes, Riyad worked for the Navy.

But the jurisdiction for this case did not reside with the Navy. It resided within the Army and CID.

Yet, an NCIS agent had initially been tasked with completing the show she and two other Army CID agents had begun at Fort Campbell and in that Pakistani cave.

An NCIS agent whose skill set wasn't based in murder—but gathering intel and ferreting out traitors. An agent who believed he'd *found* that traitor.

But unlike Riyad, she built her cases on proof. "Staff Sergeant?"

"I'm sorry, ma'am, but I—"

"—arrived aboard the *Griffith* with Ambassador Linnet. You were tasked with overseeing security for the initial damage control sessions. Once Durrani and the translator were arrested and headed this way, the politicians departed, leaving you and Corporal Vetter to augment security for the coming interrogations and case wrap-up." She tossed another smooth smile into the mix as she glanced at the voice recorder on her desk. "I just need to confirm Agent Riyad's boarding date—for the record."

The Marine relaxed. Nodded. "Of course. Sorry. Like I said; it's been a long stint. Agent Riyad came aboard with the detainees, on the same flight from Al Dhafra."

Her smile slipped. Her control nearly followed. Because the timing of Riyad's arrival aboard the *Griffith* was even more revealing than the location of those damage control sessions—and utterly damning. For John.

At least in Riyad's eyes.

John hadn't been sent here because of his past with Tamir Hachemi. Hachemi was the excuse.

Did Palisade know? Or had the general been kept out of the loop, too?

A knock sounded on the opposite side of the stateroom's door.

Relief entered the Marine's stare as he stood, quickly stepping back so she could make her way across the tiny compartment. Just as well. She was finished with Brandt. It was time to track down another man. One she'd known for less than a day. If that one was lucky, he just might escape her presence with his head still attached.

She opened the door.

Riyad stood on the other side, that dark, neatly groomed, pretty-boy body part still attached.

For now.

She turned to the Marine. "That'll be all, Staff Sergeant. I'll let you know when your statement's ready to be signed."

"Thank you, ma'am." He escaped.

She glared at the remaining man still occupying the passageway. "Get inside. And close the goddamned door behind you."

If looks could kill, she'd have been buried at sea long before she and that Super Stallion had touched down on the *Griffith*'s flight deck this morning.

But he complied.

Smart move. Especially since she was still contemplating hauling the spook's sanctimonious ass out onto that flight deck and dumping it over the side—with the contents of her own SIG Sauer riddling it.

She folded her arms and locked them down to keep from reaching for that same SIG currently strapped to her right thigh. "So, Agent Riyad, when were you going to tell me that you've been investigating Major Garrison for treason?"

# 8

Regan met her so-called fellow agent's murky stare and held it, waiting for the answer. Not that she needed it. She'd worked it out all by herself.

She'd just wanted him to admit it.

"Agent Riyad, I'm waiting. When did you plan on telling me that you believe Garrison has turned traitor?"

The spook mirrored her stance, folding his own arms over his chest and locking them down. "Never."

"Congratulations. That's the first true statement that's come out of your mouth since I boarded this ship. Care to try for another?"

The man's stare grew murkier. "Brandt told you."

"Nope." But she now had confirmation that not only had the staff sergeant known about the treason investigation into John, he'd also been ordered to keep his mouth shut by the asshole squared off in front of her.

Based on that exchange of body language she'd witnessed, especially between Riyad and Brandt outside the conference room earlier, the staff sergeant hadn't been in sync with the order to keep his trap shut either, much less the rationale behind it.

Score one for the Marines—and those hidden smarts.

Not that she wanted those smarts, much less Brandt's integrity, questioned by this man. "Relax. No one said squat about your misguided suspicions. There was no need." She offered up her first genuine smile since she'd met the spook. It came out a smirk. "It turns out you're as good at concealing classified information as you are at fucking up critical interrogations with recently arrested terrorists *and* processing crime scenes. Now, I have another question for you. And, once again, you will cough up the truth." Or she'd pull it out of the man with her bare hands. "Does General Palisade know about this little side show you've got going on aboard this vessel?"

"Yes."

"And what is the general's position on the matter?" Though she'd figured that out on her own too.

The thin scar cutting down through the spook's left brow puckered as he scowled, marring that pretty-boy visage of his. "He was pissed."

Well, well. Yet another truth.

It seemed Riyad was capable of stringing three together, at least when cornered. She went for a fourth. "But he was overruled."

That one came in the form of a curt nod.

She scooped it up regardless and added it to the others. Quite the revealing picture was beginning to take shape. After all, Palisade might be a three-star general and in charge of the Army's Special Operations Command at Fort Bragg, but he and the entire Army Special Forces community were hard lined beneath the authority of the overall US Special Operations Command out of MacDill. And, lo and behold, at the moment USSOCOM was headed up by a Navy admiral.

"General Palisade drew a line in the sand, didn't he?" With Palisade on one side and Admiral Kettering on the other. "That's why I was flown here."

*She* was the concession, at least for Palisade's cooperation—and silence—regarding the spook's investigation into John.

Hell, Palisade had probably convinced his Navy boss that her presence was critical. That with her knowing John so well, along with her connection to both Durrani and Hachemi, she was their best bet at picking up on any clues the two Afghan terrorists might accidentally intimate regarding John.

Riyad was right. With Admiral Kettering covering his back, she'd have been removed from the *Griffith* the second her interview with Durrani was over. Only now, with the translator dead, both Riyad and the admiral were stuck with her.

It seemed nearly losing her life to that psycho-toxin had accomplished one thing. It had shoved her investigative skills above reproach.

At least with the spook's current boss.

Unfortunately, John's instinctive actions that morning had complicated everything and, quite possibly, condemned him. At least in the admiral's eyes. Not that this entire scenario hadn't been a quagmire from the start. "Let me guess; both you and Admiral Kettering believe Palisade was taken in by John—for years, possibly."

Could they really think Palisade was that stupid?

The spook's shrug was grudging at best. "The general's judgment has been clouded by his personal feelings for the major. As have yours."

At least Riyad hadn't branded a giant "T" on her forehead, too.

Yet.

As for Palisade and his feelings, she knew better. The general had proven he could keep one of his Chosen Ones out of the loop when necessary. Take those shadow duties Palisade had tasked Staff Sergeant Tulle with back at Fort Campbell.

Tulle hadn't been reporting back on her alone. Tulle had been reporting back on John's dealings with her too...*without* John's knowledge.

That was the real reason she still hadn't told John about Tulle shadowing her. She wasn't sure John's relationship with Palisade would survive the violation of his own trust.

Then again, depending on how the next few hours played out, she was no longer certain she wanted that trust to survive—at least on John's part.

As for the cloud-ability of her feelings, she had no illusions about John, much less about what John was and was not capable of. Frankly, she preferred it that way.

"What exactly do you think you have on the man?"

That thin scar rose along with the surrounding brow. "Garrison?"

"Yes, Garrison. Try and keep up, Agent. You just might learn something." And she might succeed in maintaining her tenuous hold on her temper.

That murky stare darkened again, this time all the way down to black, matching Riyad's polo, cargo pants and boots as he continued to look at her.

Judging, weighing. For the first time, wary too.

But most of all, the spook was livid.

Good.

She was pushing it deliberately. Pushing him.

She was also fairly certain Riyad had no idea as to why, at least not yet. She wanted the spook as pissed as Palisade would've been when he'd heard that John had been labeled a potential traitor. That anger would let more of the truth Riyad was holding onto so damned tightly leak out with his ire.

"Well? Where's your evidence? I assume you have something

against the major, most likely snatched up from a crime scene with yet another ungloved hand."

It worked.

The spook stepped closer, all but smoldering now. "What *don't* I have? Make that, *who*."

She kicked her own scarred brow upward. The one she'd earned back at Fort Campbell when she'd slammed through a glass slider alongside a suicidal soldier who'd murdered his wife and unborn child at the beginning of this twisted case. "Oh, do go on, Agent. Name names. Impress me with your deductive brilliance. If you can."

"Ertonç."

"The Turkish general?"

Riyad clipped a nod. "You remember him, don't you?"

Of course she did. The Ertonç case was how and when she and John had first met. Operating on a stateside interagency tip, she and a fellow CID agent had managed to save the life of General Ertonç's daughter in Hohenfels, Germany, with the critical assistance of one of her best friends, Mira Ellis—an NCIS agent she also very much admired and respected. Unlike the one in this stateroom.

The spook stepped even closer. "What do you really know about the general?"

It didn't matter what she knew about Ertonç, much less John's relationship with the man. What mattered was what Riyad believed John knew.

She held her silence. Waited for the spook to add more.

Given the mesmerizing tic that had taken up residence beneath the square of his lightly bearded jaw, he was chomping to add something.

That tic didn't disappoint. "General Ertonç is shady as shit. He has been for decades. And the major has been in the thick of some of the worst of that shit, right along with the guy."

Kabul.

The night John had invited her into his home for dinner, he'd freely admitted that Ertonç had had a reputation as an ass when the men had met years earlier in Afghanistan—not to mention Ertonç's rather tight relationship with a local Afghan warlord of shady repute.

So what?

"That's it? That's all you've got? Some Turkish general Garrison did a favor for almost a decade ago?" And another, sixteen months ago, in Germany. But since she didn't know if Riyad was cleared to be privy to that latest one, she left it off the list. "A favor, I might add, that the upper echelons of the Army not only knew about when Garrison was in Kabul, but had whole-heartedly approved—prior to the major bestowing it."

"And did the Army also approve of Garrison's relationship with Sergeant First Class LaCroix in advance of the sergeant plotting to blow up Ertonç's daughter, her husband, two children and half a city block in Vilseck, Germany?"

She shrugged. "If not, shame on the Army." Because while John had been juggling that latest sanctioned mission with regard to General Ertonç, he'd also been working his ass off to pull a valuable, hurting sergeant back into line *for* the Army.

While that intervention with LaCroix had ultimately turned out to be futile, no one else had even bothered to attempt it.

Arms still crossed, Riyad took another step toward her. He was inches away now, and even more pissed. "And the translator? Was Garrison working on behalf of the best interests of the Army when he vouched for Hachemi less than two weeks ago at a critical juncture in that cave case, *after* Hachemi and that bastard Durrani had hacked up those women? Was Garrison also working on behalf of the Army when he approved yet another mission with Hachemi to supposedly take down the doctor? A mission that saw Hachemi take the wheel of a van just before he ended up gassing a squad of Garrison's own soldiers and killing one of your fellow CID agents?"

"Yes, he was." And despite the loss of Art Valens' life and nearly her own, "Garrison got the job done too." And then some. "We were able to arrest Hachemi, save even more lives and prevent a political powder keg from exploding in the region."

One that would've obliterated the US military's reputation in Afghanistan, Pakistan and the entire world beyond.

Hell, it still might, if she couldn't push through Hachemi's death investigation in time to get her hide down to the ship's brig and pull the name of the real traitor out of Durrani before this spook got Admiral Kettering to change his mind about her and succeeded in having her removed from the *Griffith*.

As for John's relationship with Tamir Hachemi and General Ertonç, "Special Forces operate in the gray, Agent Riyad. Much like the SEALs in your own branch, as even you must be aware. SF seeks out, works with and—yes, befriends and maintains relationships with—some seriously crappy characters. Because that's part of their job. A job Major Garrison has proven that he excels at, despite the fact that he clearly doesn't know everything. Which, by the way, neither do you. So, unless—"

"What about McCord?"

"Mark McCord?" The captain of the SF team who had originally been framed for the murders in that cave.

"Yes. Yet another questionable association of the major's."

"How so?"

"McCord and Garrison are good friends. You may have found evidence that exonerated the captain, but the reason the frame worked as well as it did against him was because McCord was screwing a married local of Pakistani descent—in direct violation of US military policy. Both Admiral Kettering and the State Department are still dealing with the resulting hot potato, since the sole surviving baby from that cave massacre carries the captain's DNA."

"You're right about the DNA, but wrong about the rest. Garrison can't stand McCord."

Disbelief had that scarred brow scraping higher. "My source—"

"—is wrong. Granted, McCord saved Garrison's life. Twice. Both times, in combat. But that's it. There is no love lost between those men, and on either side. So if you think Garrison took out Hachemi this morning with deliberate intent, as some sort of premeditated payback for Hachemi killing the mother of McCord's child, think again. And dig a little deeper while you're at it. You'll be surprised to discover just how many soldiers who manage to work with someone in combat, stateside—or, heck, even on some warship at sea—are actually eager to see the backs of their so-called...partners."

He let the dig slide. But that brow and its owner were adamant about the rest. "McCord and Garrison are Special Forces. I don't think you understand how tight that bond is. And then there's what happened to you."

That was all true. It just didn't mean anything.

At least not what Riyad wanted it all to mean.

"Sorry to burst your bubble, but John Garrison wouldn't murder for me, any more than he would for McCord. Would he kill to defend me? You bet, and in a heartbeat. Believe it or not, Agent, he'd kill to defend you too. Even now. But murder? It's just not in the man's nature." She shook her head, seriously stumped. "As for the rest, you need to cycle back through your training course. Your logic sucks. You've offered two conflicting motives here: treason and loyalty. Not only is it impossible for both to be true, you don't have enough to support either one. 'Questionable associations', or not."

That last caused the man's brow and tic to react in tandem,

giving her serious pause. There was something else. Something the spook was actively refusing to put on the table. What on earth was it?

*Who* was it?

Because the *questionable association* currently searing through Riyad's brain went to the crux of why the agent really believed John had been turned.

And then, it was gone.

But that righteous fury wasn't.

And this batch was directed solely at her. "As you've surmised, you're here aboard this vessel against my wishes—and my instincts. So prove me wrong, Agent Chase. Do your job and wrap up the investigation into Hachemi's death. And while you're at it, keep your mouth shut about this conversation. Especially around Major Garrison. And that order's not mine; it comes directly from Admiral Kettering. Understood?"

"Absolutely." Nor did she have a problem with it. John had enough to worry about at the moment. Hell, so did she. "What about you?"

That scarred brow inched back up. "What about me?"

"You plan on doing your job? Because you haven't been. Not effectively. Or was that the plan all along?"

The spook lurched all the way in. The toes of their boots were actually touching.

She stood her ground.

"What the fuck are you getting at, woman?"

She ignored the "woman", especially since it served to tell her just how pissed he was. "Where were you this morning when that interview went down?"

"With the captain."

"Why? You were about to leave the ship. Anything you had to say to the captain should've been long since said. So why did you leave the major alone?"

"I'm not his goddamned keeper."

"Normally, no. But aboard this ship, for these past eight days, you were. You had one job. You were supposed to keep an eye on Garrison—no matter what. *Eight days*. That's how long you two spent in that conference room together. Most likely, morning, noon and all hours of the night. You had to have known that Garrison wanted one last crack at Hachemi—without you there, breathing down his neck."

After all, the spook had been sitting right next to John during those interrogations, soaking up the frustration even John wouldn't have been able to contain. Not since he'd entered that cave and found those women. And not with everything that had happened to his men and their wives after. Not with what had happened to her.

"You told Brandt about your true suspicions regarding the major's loyalties—and you ordered the staff sergeant to keep me in the dark. You also forbade Brandt from telling me that he'd originally come aboard the *Griffith* with that diplomatic contingent. You warned Corporal Vetter off too, at least about the latter." Otherwise, the embassy assignments would've come out in Vetter's statement too. "But you didn't tell Chief Yrle about your suspicions regarding the major. A much more senior sailor who, for all intents and purposes, is the sheriff aboard this ship. Why?"

"I—"

"Don't bother punting another lie my way. I already know the truth. That charming dressing down you gave the chief outside this very stateroom this morning was an act to cover your ass after the fact. You didn't tell Yrle because you *wanted* that final one-on-one between Garrison and Hachemi to go down." She'd wager the SIG strapped to her thigh that if she pressed Brandt under oath, the Marine would admit that the real reason he hadn't been as quick on his feet when Hachemi had hit that wall, was because he'd been busy scribbling down notes for the spook.

The spook who suddenly looked as though he'd swallowed a bucketful of seawater churned up by this ship. "That doesn't excuse what Garrison did."

"You're right. It doesn't." But it did condemn the man standing in front of her, right along with him.

At least John had admitted his culpability.

As for this man? The spook could choke on his for all she cared.

Because she'd identified his game, and she wasn't playing it. Not with her open death investigation, and not with her coming showdown with Durrani.

"You go ahead and deny your own responsibility all you want, Agent Riyad. It might even help you sleep better at night. But it's a fantasy, and deep down you know it. You glued yourself to Major Garrison's ass for over a week. And in the process you hindered the results our entire country needs. Garrison was in the wrong this morning. But so were you. If you'd let the major do what he came here to do—what he was *ordered* to do—he wouldn't have had to go in there alone. Even Chief Yrle could see it. And, no, I haven't spoken to her either. At least not yet. But she must have known or she wouldn't have believed the major needed to try one last time without you there, much less assisted and run interference for him. Major Garrison has to live with what he did—but so do you. If you hadn't obstructed this case day in and day out from the moment Garrison came aboard, he might've gotten results. Tamir Hachemi would still be alive—and we'd have the names of that blasted traitor. The *real* one."

She reached out and snagged the voice recorder she hadn't bothered to turn off when Brandt left. Nor did she have any intention of turning it off now.

Not until the spook left.

"Now, Agent Riyad, you are right about one thing. It's time for me to do my job. I'm headed down to the brig to interview Dr. Durrani. You are not invited. Not even to stop in to let me know the ship is sinking. Furthermore, you will not speak to Durrani again until I am finished with him. Have I made myself clear?"

His final nod was clipped.

Curt.

"Excellent. While I'm in the brig with that bastard, make yourself useful for a change. Get an update on the medical examiner's flight to that carrier, as well as the autopsy. If they've managed to move up the time, pass the info to Chief Yrle. *She* can inform me."

Like it or not, she had one more job to accomplish before she departed the *Griffith* for good.

Unless a miracle occurred during that autopsy and exculpating evidence came to light, she was going to have to charge John with murder.

# 9

By the time she'd reached the brig, Nabil Durrani was already seated at a small rectangular table in the center of an otherwise bare holding cell.

Tucking the folder she'd prepared in Chief Yrle's office beneath her arm, Regan paused just outside the cell to study that dark, sleek profile and the deceptive bastard that came with it. Yet another pretty boy. One who risked pissing her off a helluva lot more than the one she'd recently sparred with in her stateroom.

Then again, Riyad might be a grade-A asshole who still had her fantasizing about emptying her SIG into his backside, but at least the spook didn't cause her skin to crawl.

Not like this one did.

The *shalwar kameez* Durrani had been wearing when they'd last met was gone. The black silk pants and tunic had been replaced by a set of the sturdy, dark blue coveralls she'd seen on several of the *Griffith*'s sailors since her arrival. Durrani didn't appear fazed by the downgrade in attire or his spartan surroundings, much less the prospect of yet another grilling. If anything, the Afghan doc appeared excited, expectant even, as he watched Staff Sergeant Brandt use a set of steel cuffs to lock his wrists to the security bar, which ran parallel to the interrogation table, a few inches from its edge.

Durrani knew she was aboard the ship.

Had the Marine informed him?

Either way the element of surprise was gone.

She bit back her irritation and stepped over the bottom lip of metal at the base of the oval, watertight doorway as Brandt pocketed his cuff key.

Given everything Durrani had done, she'd have enjoyed shackling the bastard to the table herself.

No matter. Their coming chat wasn't about revenge. Hell, it wasn't even about those pregnant women who'd been slaughtered in that cave, much less the soldiers and wives who'd lost their lives to that demonic psychological warfare agent. Nor was it about her old mentor and fellow CID agent's death.

It was about the deaths she was here to prevent. The ones she suspected would put the doc's current toll of victims to shame if she couldn't discover the identity of that final, *not* pregnant woman in time to prevent the remainder of his plot from unfolding.

Regan focused on that need as she pushed everything else that had happened these past few weeks aside, including the events of this morning—and, yes, John too.

It was the only way she could do this.

She nodded to Brandt as he approached her. "I'll take it from here, Staff Sergeant. Go ahead and post yourself in the outer compartment with Corporal Vetter."

Instead of complying, Brandt stared at her.

For a moment, she thought the Marine was about to suggest that he remain inside the cell for whatever reason he could think of. In light of what had happened in the ship's conference room that morning—and that Brandt had been unable to prevent those events—she forgave the silent insubordination. But she did insist.

"I'll be fine. We both will."

"Yes, ma'am. I'll leave the door open, in case you need me."

She wouldn't. But she took pity on the Marine's nerves and nodded.

The moment Brandt cleared the lip of metal, she crossed the compartment and rounded the short end of the table to face the remaining occupant square on.

"Good evening, Agent Chase. How kind of you to visit."

The smooth smile that curved those downright sensual lips was identical to the one the doc had offered her back in the bathroom of his terror safe house in Charikar two short weeks ago. Only here, now, the effect was marred somewhat by the fresh bump high on his nose, as well as the fading yellow and green bruise surrounding it—and, of course, the three-inch crescent-shaped scar that rode along the ridge of bone that formed the man's left cheek. The scar that still bore stitches due to complications.

A bump, bruise and scar that she'd put there.

She smiled back. "Hello, Doctor. How could I resist? That was quite an invitation you extended via my chain of command. I understand you have something to say to me?"

He ignored her question as he tipped his head toward the empty chair opposite his. "Please, do have a seat. I would stand to assist as manners dictate, but—" The cuffs clicked against the steel bar suspended above his lap, momentarily overtaking the steady thrum of shifting metal that surrounded them as he lifted his wrists in lieu of explanation. "However, if my wearing these helps to put you at ease, who am I to protest?"

"Really, Doctor. If I remember correctly, the last time we spoke, I was wearing a pair of those and you weren't. Though not for long."

That irritating smile was slightly less smooth as she sat.

Regan set the folder she'd brought with her on the table and leaned forward, intent on forcing that smile to falter altogether as she tapped his bump. "Oh, look, I broke your nose. And that cut—" She *tsked* softly as she shifted her finger to trail the tip along the row of tidy stitches someone had reapplied well after she'd left this man lying face down on the floor of that bathroom with one of her filthy socks crammed into his mouth. "I'll have to talk to the ship's doc about getting these removed. Though really, you're bound to have a nasty scar due to the infection and restitching you suffered anyway." She offered a decidedly unrepentant shrug. "Sorry."

The man's smile managed to cling to his lips—barely. "If this is all the damage I suffer at the infidel's hand, I shall consider myself fortunate. After all, not all who enter your country's custody have fared so well, yes?"

Abu Ghraib?

If so, there was no need to try and shame her with an oblique allusion or even a direct reference to that heinous debacle. She had no illusions. Not all her fellow soldiers were as fair and honorable during the heat of battle as she'd like, much less in the quieter, more subdued moments before and after—especially during those moments that were well out of eye and earshot of the rest of the troops. It was why she had a job. Her own set of Army-honed, mission-oriented skills.

Unfortunately, the impetus of that remark hadn't been distant and sweeping. It was close and intimate.

Personal.

She was certain when that dark stare shifted across the compartment, toward the 1MC speaker hanging in the corner of the overhead.

"And how is my brother in Allah faring this evening?"

For a moment, she wondered if Brandt truly had spoken out of turn, or even Riyad or Corporal Vetter.

But, no, the bastard seated two feet away might be a mass murderer and a terrorist, but he wasn't an idiot.

Not only had Durrani graduated from Harvard medical school, he'd done so with honors, despite a rocky start during his undergrad years while he'd been fine-tuning his English. His later academic success wasn't surprising, since the man had also proven capable and cunning enough to steal a unit of blood donated by Captain McCord during a rare down moment at Bagram Airbase in Afghanistan months earlier. If another physician hadn't wondered about the absent plasma proteins in a forensics report, they might never have figured out that Durrani had frozen that stolen unit, only to thaw it out four weeks ago so he could plant McCord's blood inside that Pakistani cave during the murders.

Someone that clever could easily have heard the announcement that ordered Riyad and the ship's doctor to the conference room shortly after her arrival and put the rest together.

"Agent Chase?"

She paused in the middle of retrieving her voice recorder. "Hmm?"

"*Do* you require my assistance with Tamir? After all, I am a qualified physician."

Now that was debatable, wasn't it? Especially since a physician's leading dictate was *do no harm*. Something at which this so-called physician had failed.

Profoundly.

"Thank you, but no." She set the recorder on the table beside her folder. "Doctor Mantia and his assistants have everything in hand." She didn't bother adding that the latter had included a master-at-arms petty officer with a body bag. "I am glad that you're in the mood to be helpful, though. You see, I have a lingering mystery regarding that cave. One I'd appreciate your assistance in solving."

One of those sleek, dark brows rose.

She leaned forward to switch the recorder on, offering up the standard *who, what, when, why* and *where* as she sat back in her chair.

Initial legalities out of the way, she turned the manila folder around so he could view the contents as she opened it.

"Ah, you've brought pictures. I presume they pertain to this... mystery of yours?"

"They do." Regan tapped the uppermost one, suppressing the bile that churned up each and every time she viewed it and the succession of photos that followed. Namely, the close-ups of the slaughtered victims from that cave. "As you know, although Jameelah Khan was married to a man from Pakistan during the months that she worked at the laundry on Bagram Airbase, she was having an affair with Captain McCord. The child you sliced from her womb was his. As I'm sure you also know, Jameelah died as a result of the horror you inflicted on her. But her baby did not. She survived. The little girl will be heading to the States soon to live with her biological father, Captain McCord."

"Pity."

"That his child survived? Or that we discovered her parentage?"

"Both." Those dark eyes remained as cold and emotionless as they had in that safe house as Durrani stared at the grisly eight-by-ten glossy. But his mouth didn't. His lips curved into a distinct, shit-eating smirk that took every ounce of restraint she possessed to ignore as he leaned back in his metal chair and shrugged—as much as those steel cuffs would allow. "Of course, there was always the risk the latter would come out."

"Her parentage?"

"Yes."

"You're lying." She didn't need that sanctimonious smirk to know it either. It was the paternity itself. "After all, why go to the trouble of kidnapping Jameelah in the first place if you didn't want her daughter's true parentage to come out?"

Another shrug, and another smirk.

Good.

She wanted them. Needed them.

The more this man wallowed in his smug superiority, the greater the odds that she'd reach her goal before he caught onto it—and her. "I think Jameelah was crucial to your plans. It's the other women who weren't. After all, you simply reeled the remaining women in while you were making your rounds in Kabul when you volunteered at the Malalie Maternity Hospital. Once you identified a potential victim, you merely told her that you were worried about her baby. That she needed further tests. Tests her fundamentalist husband was likely to balk at. But not to worry—you would handle everything. At least, that's what one of my fellow CID agents discovered when he spoke with a nurse from Malalie." One who'd overheard Durrani with two of his victims. "The remaining women followed you out of the hospital to wherever you held them, before you drugged them and took them to that cave."

The proverbial lambs to the slaughter.

In their defense, why wouldn't they go? Durrani had been their doctor; they'd trusted him. And they'd paid with their lives.

Along with those of their children.

It took every shred of self-control she possessed to mask her rage as Regan lifted the photo of Jameelah from the folder to reveal the close-up of the woman beneath. This one was just as horrific as the first. "Zimal trusted you too. Along with Asali, Ilma, Yalina and Shaima."

With each new photo, that goddamned smirk deepened.

The bastard was getting off on the evidence of what he'd

already done—along with his strengthening belief that she had no clue regarding the rest.

Even better.

She laid the corresponding photos out along the table, then tapped the final one. This close-up was of the woman they'd yet to identify.

Regan waited.

The rhythmic creaking of the surrounding metal grew louder in the silence that followed.

Durrani finally broke it. "You have no name for that one, do you? This is your mystery."

"Correct. It seems this woman wasn't a patient at Malalie. What's even more interesting is that she wasn't pregnant either. At least, not when she was murdered."

"*Really*. You are certain of this?"

"Hmm." She moved her hand back to the beginning of the line, tapping the second photo more forcefully than she'd intended to mask the sudden tremble in her fingers. "Forensics has since proven that Zimal was carrying twins. You placed one of Zimal's babies—" Control over her fingers reestablished, Regan returned them to that final, horrific photo. "—on this woman's corpse. After you'd mutilated her, of course."

"Of course."

His voice was still smooth. Controlled. That smirk still infesting the man's dusky features. But he couldn't take his eyes off that final photo.

He was mesmerized.

Utterly.

She was right. That final victim's identity was crucial to whatever this bastard still had up his sleeve.

"Who is she, Doctor?" And was her identity also connected to the traitor Agent Riyad was really seeking?

That dark stare finally shifted. To her. It lingered on her face for several moments, then slid down her right arm. It stopped at her hand.

Narrowed. Assessed.

"You appear to be well, Agent Chase. Quite recovered from what must have been a difficult time in hospital...but you do have a slight tremor in your dominant hand. Of course, that tremor could be a simple manifestation of nerves over speaking with me. But given your general demeanor today and your self-assurance at our last meeting, I suspect not. Therefore, it must be related to your recent...illness. A lingering repercussion if you will. But is it permanent?"

*Shit.*

Then again, he'd changed the subject, not her. In doing so, he'd shown his own not-quite-steady hand. More importantly, he'd given her the confirmation she needed.

That woman *was* the key.

She smiled. "I am doing well. Thank you for noticing."

"Perhaps you would care to...satisfy my curiosity?"

"About my hand or the overall positive state of my health?"

"The latter first, please. You must admit, it is...unexpected."

Not to mention the reason she was here, aboard this ship.

He wasn't just curious; the man was consumed.

So much so, he'd played his best card to get her here. No surprise there. He'd injected an entire vial of that shit into her veins personally. She should be dead. And yet, as far as he could tell, here she was, sitting across from him, back in an American Army uniform with little more than a finger wiggle to show for it.

He might have schooled those smooth, dusky features, but he couldn't kill the fire that was finally warming up that stare, until it was all but smoldering.

He was dying to know *why*.

That same burning professional need to know had been this

man's downfall in Afghanistan, allowing her the time she'd needed to clear her head after she'd woken from that anesthetic gas and freed herself from those handcuffs. Only then, the twisted doc had been demanding to know why John and his fellow SF soldiers were still alive.

Why be surprised that he'd risk everything for an answer about her health now? Because that was what it was going to take for him to get those answers.

Everything.

She shrugged. "Actually, the current state of my health's not all that unexpected. No offense, but I've got an outstanding doctor of my own. He's quite the miracle worker." Even if Gil had spent the past week pissing her off. "As you said, I'm good to go... along with several of the other men you injected that chimera into."

That dark stare narrowed thoughtfully. "You mentioned Major Garrison's immunity in Charikar. And that of another... Sergeant Tulle."

"I did. Major Garrison and Staff Sergeant Tulle are immune to the chimera. But I'm not. Or, rather, I wasn't...along with several others."

That got his attention. "There are more survivors?" His fingers actually tightened to fists as he leaned all the way into the bar, just off the edge of the interrogation table. "How many survived? Did any succumb to coma? What course of treatment was administered to them while they were ill?"

She waved her hand. "Oh, I don't know the particulars, Doctor. I'm just a simple criminal investigator. The explanation was all medical mumbo jumbo to me when I woke in the ICU. Of course, I can give you the layman's version—which, granted, won't amount to much. Or, I can give my doctor permission to initiate a ship-to-shore call and share all the gory details of my case with you. Heck, I'll even toss in a copy of my recent medical records for your lengthy perusal...for a name." She reached out and gently tapped the final photo that still lay between them. "*Her* name. You tell me who this woman is and I'll grant you full access to the documentation detailing my bout with that chimera. Naturally, I'll need to clear the deal with my chain of command. But until then, I can offer up something else. Think of it as a good-faith swap."

Fire sparked within that stare once more as he straightened up from the steel bar. This glint was born of suspicion. "And what precisely do we...*swap*?"

"Oh, nothing too painful. Just another name." One that should be significantly easier for him to cough up. But one that would begin to break down his resistance and also provide her with a litmus test of sorts to verify his level of truthfulness. "You give me the name of the Russian operative who provided the chimera...and I'll tell you why the major and his staff sergeant were already immune back in Charikar."

The creaking of the ship returned full force, overtaking the silence that followed. Then again, it could have easily been a result of her nerves.

The Army needed this name too.

And she needed this first step from him...toward the potential for more.

The pipes and ductwork in the overhead grew louder, oddly enhanced by the sound of the watertight scuttle handle being spun open at the top of the ladder in the outer compartment. Boots clipped down the metal steps, though not as loudly as hers had when she'd arrived via a separate entrance earlier. Whoever that was, they were trying to be quiet.

Riyad?

If it was the spook, she didn't give a damn how stealthy his approach. If he stuck his face in here against her direct order and blew this moment—

"Agreed."

Relief swept in. It was twofold. Because of the answer—and the glimpse she'd caught of the form that rounded the bottom of the ladder.

That wasn't Riyad. It was Chief Yrle.

Even better, from the brief nod the woman tipped her way just fading into the shadows of the outer compartment, Yrle had news about the postmortem.

It was a go—and soon.

Regan shifted her full attention to the doctor. "Well?"

"Aleksi Skulachev. I believe he obtained the chimera from his father who works at Biopreparat, but that will be up to you to verify...somehow."

Oh, she'd manage just fine. Because not only had the deputy chief of the Russian biological warfare agency defected to the States back in '92, he was still hooked in through another Biopreparat scientist who was currently contemplating a permanent stateside change of scenery as well. Within hours of her passing that name to Palisade, they'd know if she could trust the rest of this bastard's answers.

"Thank you." She reached out to scoop up all but that final photo, tucking them into her manila folder as she stood.

The fists returned. "You cannot leave now!"

"I'm sorry, but I must. I have a meeting to attend." One where the guest of honor would be silent...and lying on a slab.

Durrani's snarl overtook the rhythmic creaking as he attempted to come to his feet as well—and failed. "I knew—"

"Relax, Doctor. I have every intention of holding to my side of the bargain. As for Major Garrison and Staff Sergeant Tulle, the men are alive today for two reasons. The first involves a vaccine that was developed by scientists at Fort Detrick to combat another nasty creation by Biopreparat. The second involves a preexisting immunity to a rather common childhood illness in my county, and I suspect yours."

"And you and the other soldiers who were not immune prior to your exposure?" Tension eased from the man's body as he sank back into his chair. "How were you treated?"

She retrieved the final photo as she shrugged. "Now you're getting into all the medical mumbo jumbo I mentioned. If you want a crack at the mumbo jumbo *and* my medical records—" She folded the photo lengthwise. Stepping around the table, she lifted the flap of the right upper pocket of the man's coveralls and tucked the photo within. "—you're going to have to cough up this woman's name. And you'd better be able to prove it. Now, if you don't mind, I really must leave." She had a flight to make.

An autopsy to attend.

One last chance to find something, *anything*, that would save John's life—or at the very least, mitigate his coming sentence.

Unfortunately, miracles were about as common in her world as a welcomed Christmas present from Santa Claus himself.

# 10

Regan stared across the belly of the CH-53E, focusing on the distant chunk of metal barely visible through the Super Stallion's portside window. To think, she was named after the same person as that aircraft carrier, the *USS Ronald Reagan*.

Irony didn't escape her.

But was it a good omen...or bad?

She'd lost count of the number of autopsies she'd attended over the years, but one thing was certain. Add them all together, and the result didn't come close to equaling the level of ice-cold dread she felt over this coming one.

How the hell was she going to do this—*and* remain impartial?

Unfortunately, she didn't have a choice. They were still in the middle of the Arabian Sea. There was no one else.

Not if she wanted the job done right.

She'd managed to distract herself from her chaotic and admittedly conflicting emotions during her interview with Durrani. But the reprieve had only lasted so long. Once she'd left the brig, the desperation had returned, and it was damned near debilitating now. Upon boarding the Super Stallion, she'd donned the hearing protection the crew chief had provided and promptly sunk into the nearest webbed seat to close her eyes and shut out the entire world as she allowed herself to wallow in the excoriating inevitability of where this helicopter was headed...and what she would be forced to do upon her return to the *Griffith*.

John.

He'd all but told her he was relieved the case was hers. He truly wanted her to be the one to record those damning witness statements, examine the crime scene, attend the translator's postmortem, fill in the charge sheet...and finally, formally, inform him of his present—and future—all-but-nonexistent rights and freedom.

It didn't help to have his blessing. Not one damned bit.

Nor did the stare from the sanctimonious spook seated across the belly of this bird help her simmering mood. It didn't matter that she was still focused on the growing wedge of Navy steel that now filled the window beside him. She could feel his glare, as she had during the entire flight. From the tension gripping the upper ridges of the NCIS agent's shoulders, Riyad still believed she didn't want him tagging along.

He couldn't be more wrong.

She welcomed his presence.

If by some miracle the medical examiner the Pentagon had sent found mitigating evidence during the autopsy, she wanted the spook there—heinous, inaccurate suspicions regarding John's loyalties intact. What better way for any potential mitigating evidence to stand up in court?

Regan caught the crew chief's wave. The Marine sergeant lowered his forearms and briefly crossed them. The Super Stallion was about to land.

She allowed Riyad's thumbs up to serve as joint acknowledgment.

She let the spook take the lead as the helicopter finally touched down on the carrier's deck too. Removing her hearing protection, she even passively followed Riyad out of the bird and allowed him to introduce the two of them to the waiting chief who'd been assigned to escort them. They headed across the flight deck, through a watertight door in the ship's superstructure and down a metal ladder and passageway until they'd reached the ship's medical department and the entrance to the operating room where the postmortem had evidently already begun.

But that was all the lead she was willing to allow.

Regan stepped up to retrieve her own paper booties, surgical mask and clear face shield from the black, twenty-something hospital corpsman within. "Thank you, Petty Officer. How far has the ME gotten?"

The woman handed over a pair of gloves as Regan finished donning her assigned booties and facial gear. "The body's already been weighed, photographed with and without clothes, washed and x-rayed. Also, blood and vitreous fluid have been drawn. Colonel Tarrington's about to make the first cut."

*Tarrington* was here?

Despite the circumstances, Regan smiled.

"You know the ME?" Riyad stared at her—and given the frown he'd covered with his mask, he wasn't nearly as thrilled by the turn of events as she was.

"I do." If the spook had spent any time at all adding to his paltry investigative experience, he'd have undoubtedly worked with the colonel too.

Niall Tarrington was one of the Joint Pathology Center's top coroners. Not only was the British-born, US Army colonel tasked with the government and military's diciest cases, he carried the latest portable versions of his profession's top gear wherever he was sent.

If there were answers to be had tonight, there was an excellent chance that Tarrington would be able to offer them, quite possibly on the spot.

Which could be good...or bad. For John.

Regan donned her mask and nodded her thanks as the corpsman opened the door to the OR for them.

As for Riyad, "The colonel and I met—"

"—in Iraq a few years back. Hip-deep in a heinous pit of local, long-dead bodies." The cool glare Tarrington shot over his wire-framed bifocals let them both know he'd been briefed on the spook's rather vocal feelings as to her position as lead investigator on this case. "So, Agent Riyad, does that mean you plan on crying conflict of interest and complaining about my attendance at this equally shitty shindig, too?"

The spook's dark stare flared, momentarily surpassing the ire in the colonel's. But he backed down. Shook his head. "No, sir."

"Good. And, for the record, that agent standing next to you is all about the truth, and always has been. So, relax." He tipped his crop of closely clipped gray toward the opposite side of the gurney. "Well, get up here. Let's get this finished. I would've waited to start, but I'm under the gun. I need to get to Bahrain before morning. I was on my way there to confirm a VIP suicide when I got diverted to this giant, bobbing boat. Though, I admit, it's not bobbing as badly as others I've been on."

*Amen* to that.

Her stomach was in full agreement as well. But for the constant thrum of vibrating machinery in her ears and beneath her boots, she might've been able to pretend she was back on dry land.

Regan headed up the translator's naked legs and torso as

ordered. Riyad followed. She came to a halt beside Hachemi's battered face as Tarrington offered up his full name and official title, then the NCIS agent's, into the voice recorder tucked up against the array of postmortem equipment filling the sterile tray table beside him.

That formality out of the way, he turned to the two of them, but focused on her. "There's a lot going on here. And some of it doesn't quite seem to match up—yet."

"How so?" Riyad, again.

Regan suppressed a wince as Tarrington's attention shifted to her right, then narrowed to let her fellow agent know he was less than impressed with the timing of his inquisitiveness.

"Let's get one thing clear right now, Agent Riyad. This is my postmortem. Unless I ask you a direct question, I talk—you listen. You save your comment and questions 'til the end. No exceptions. Understood?"

Riyad's nod was stiff.

"Excellent. Now, as I was saying, we've got lot going on here with Mr. Hachemi. I understand the man was knocked into a bulkhead by one of our very own, pissed-off snake eaters, correct?"

Another nod. This one was just as stiff...and hers.

She hadn't worked with Tarrington since she'd met John in Hohenfels, so she had no idea if the colonel had heard the gossip regarding her personal and professional past regarding the "snake eater" in question. Though the slight tinge of compassion in that light green stare suggested yes.

The tinge cleared as Tarrington shifted once more, this time toward a light box hanging from the bulkhead to his right. "The x-rays over there support that, along with the obvious bruising." He reached out to trace a gloved finger down the right side of the translator's chin. "Mr. Hachemi sustained a fracture here, in the mandible, along with several broken teeth." The gloved finger moved up to trace a shorter arc across discolored flesh at the bridge of the translator's nose. "And another here, at the tip of the nasal bone. However, despite the contusions around the orbital cavities, there's no damage to the bone beneath. Nor does the brain appear to have been impacted by the blow. Of course, I've yet to open the man up and look inside myself."

Something utterly unexpected infused her gut as that warm green stare found hers once more.

Hope.

It was a direct result of the gleaming intensity of that stare.

Something had hooked the colonel's curiosity—and it had nothing to do with the lack of visible damage to the translator's brain.

She was dying to prompt the man, but like Riyad, she'd learned to hold her tongue with this particular ME—in nearly identical circumstances. Granted, she'd been six years younger at the time and even more naive.

Though, really, was there an ME alive who tolerated, much less enjoyed, being grilled by a case investigator during an active autopsy? It so, she hadn't met them.

Her patience was rewarded as Tarrington drew his gloved index finger—and their attention—back to the translator's jaw. No, not jaw. Hachemi's lips.

What the—

"You see it, too. Don't you, Rae?"

She nodded.

"See what?" Riyad again.

She suppressed a wince. Would the man never learn?

But the colonel let it slide. "Rictus."

As the spook's brow furrowed, Tarrington tipped his head toward her.

She reached out to trail a finger above and around the translator's mouth, quickly extending the rest of her fingers along with it to conceal her latest tremor. Fortunately, it worked. "Hachemi's lips are pulled back, contracted into a grimace."

An eerie, slightly maniacal one at that.

"And that's significant?"

She shrugged. While she'd seen it before, the fresh glint she'd noted in Tarrington's eyes had already added the rictus to something else.

Something she hadn't noticed.

The colonel's nod confirmed it. "Look at his fingers...and his toes."

She did—and pulled in her breath.

Every single digit was curled down toward the surface of the gurney—*including* the three fingers John had snapped in Charikar. She'd seen that level of contraction before, in another deceased Afghan's remains, no less. During her first year with CID, a local contractor had suffered convulsions while on Bagram Airbase and died. At the time, the ME who'd been assigned the case had openly speculated as to the cause of death during the postmortem while citing that same rictus and convulsive grip. Toxicology tests had upheld the woman's instincts.

"*Tetanus.*"

Regan had murmured the word under her breath.

Tarrington nodded anyway. "Do you know if Mr. Hachemi's inoculations were up to date?"

"No." But she'd be looking into it, just as soon as this contractor's postmortem was complete.

While rare in the States, tetanus infections were decidedly more common in several parts of the world—including Afghanistan. Mostly because the bacterial spores that caused the deadly disease could be found around the globe, lurking in everyday dust, soil, feces and saliva. Of course, a simple inoculation along with a timely schedule of boosters could and did prevent the disease from developing. But the recipient had to reside in a country where the government and medical profession were dedicated to distributing tetanus vaccines to the masses.

Afghanistan still fell short on that end.

As a local Afghan translator, Hachemi would've been treated for any and all injuries he sustained on the job by military medical personnel in country—and even some injuries that hadn't been sustained on the job. But inoculations wouldn't have been included. For those, Tamir Hachemi would've had to see one of the many non-governmental organizations that provided preventative care to the local population.

If he'd received them. Since Hachemi hadn't even made it to the States yet to exercise his newly granted, naturalized-citizen status, the odds were slim.

And even if the translator had managed to get his initial tetanus inoculation and keep his boosters up to date, written records for any NGO-provided vaccines he had received might not exit. But if they did, she'd find them.

The ME pulled his instrument tray closer. "What about epilepsy? Do you know if Mr. Hachemi suffered from the condition?"

She shook her head at this new possibility, too.

As mitigating factors went, she preferred the first, and by far. But she'd take the potential reprieve offered by either one. "I do know that at least two of the witness statements I took this afternoon mention a final, seizure-like episode *after* the blow and just *before* the translator's heart stopped, while he was already laid out on the deck. Also, I don't know if it's significant, but both Corporal Vetter and Staff Sergeant Brandt stated that, during the interrogation, Hachemi claimed his head was pounding. He appeared to be sweating more than usual and thirsty, too. They also saw him rubbing at the back of his neck on and off. Major Garrison noted the rubbing as well."

The colonel's gaze warmed at the mention of John. The tinge returned.

Tarrington knew about their past, all right.

It just didn't matter. Not to her. As much as she liked the colonel as a person, she respected his vast store of medical knowledge and deductive skills so much more.

Tarrington could keep that compassion. She wanted his zeal.

She needed it.

If the ME felt the rictus and those contracted digits didn't match up with the presumed cause and manner of the translator's death—namely, the blow to his face— there was an excellent chance he was right. And that was definitely promising.

For John.

Tarrington followed up her burgeoning hope with another nod. "There's more. Whether it's significant or not, I don't yet know. Not only are his finger and toes contracted, but according to the intake report by the hospital corpsman who received the body aboard this carrier, Mr. Hachemi was also in full rigor upon his arrival."

Two hours after death?

"But—" The spook closed his mouth in the nick of time.

The professional curiosity burning through Tarrington must've put him in a singular mood, because he let the lapse slide with a dismissive sigh. "Yes, yes; the march of rigor tends to proceed at a slower pace. And, yes, I have also seen an equally accelerated pace following a simple gunshot. A rather creative bludgeoning too. Neither is it entirely unusual that Mr. Hachemi's body had also passed almost completely *out* of rigor by the time I opened the morgue drawer shortly after I arrived aboard this ship a mere hour and a half ago. As I said, mysteries clearly abound. Shall we open the man up and see what others we find —and, perhaps, solve them?"

This time, she and Riyad nodded in unison.

Tarrington failed to notice. The colonel had already retrieved a glistening scalpel from his instrument tray and leaned over the translator's chest to begin the initial leg of the Y incision at the crest of the man's right shoulder. Within moments, that enviably steady hand had carved the second leg and drawn the tail of the Y all the way down to the man's genitals. Skin and muscle layers peeled to the sides, Tarrington started in on the chest plate, carefully cutting through the ribs and pulling them away as one piece so that the inner organs could be examined in place.

She and Riyad watched in mutual silence as those steady hands poked, prodded, shifted and snipped. Regan caught the colonel's preoccupation with the translator's heart—along with the odd ballooning of blood that appeared to fill the sac surrounding it—but she was lost amid the stream of medical jargon that poured out of Tarrington's mouth and into the recorder.

The ME briefly paused his stream as he retrieved a syringe and filled it with blood taken directly from the heart, then resumed his steady professional spiel as he removed the organ from the body. Moving over to a separate workspace, the heart was weighed and then carefully dissected. Whatever the colonel saw as he sliced off tiny sections of tissue to send back to the lab appeared to give him pause.

Fortunately, the spook held onto his curiosity and maintained his silence alongside her.

Her silence and hope were tested as the ME moved on to the translator's lungs. Not by their removal and weighing, but by the following minute exam that took place out of her sight as the colonel painstakingly dissected the translator's pulmonary tissue, all the while remarking on the smattering of pinpoint hemorrhages within for the voice recorder.

She didn't know if Riyad understood the significance of those tiny hemorrhages, but she did. Asphyxia.

Yes, the damage that blow had caused to Hachemi's face could have easily interfered with his breathing and deprived the man of oxygen...but Tarrington hadn't mentioned a corresponding obstruction.

The liver was up—and out—next.

Dissection followed.

Was it her imagination, or was the colonel spending more time than he usually did with that organ? The number of samples he'd taken to ship back to the lab intrigued her too. She'd swear he'd taken twice as many as normal.

Just then, the ME's preoccupation with the liver folded back in to the memory of those pinpoint pulmonary hemorrhages. There, they joined up with the rictus he'd pointed out—along with the seizure Vetter and Brandt had mentioned.

The combination teased at something deep inside the recesses of her mind. She couldn't quite grasp the potential significance. But it was there.

She mentally reviewed the cases she'd worked.

No, the curious combination of organs and facts didn't dovetail into one of her investigations. Someone else's, then. But whose?

And *what* were the particulars?

The mystery dogged her for the next hour as the translator's remaining organs were removed, weighed and individually dissected as well.

With each successive removal, Regan was able to detach herself further and further from the reality that what lay in front of her had once been a man. Albeit a man who'd attempted to kill her and had succeeded in killing an unforgivable number of her fellow soldiers and their wives, but a man nonetheless.

She had no idea how many autopsies Riyad had attended in his career, but he appeared to be holding up well. The spook hadn't so much as batted an eye throughout the entire procedure...until the ME cut into the translator's scalp and began to fold his flesh inside out and down over his face.

The spook appeared distinctly queasy now.

Once the bone saw fired up, she wasn't feeling so hot herself. She hated that sound and the peculiar smell that always followed. The odor was more subtle than the stench of blood, bile, viscera and excrement that permeated the postmortems she'd attended, and not nearly as penetrating as the acrid stench of formaldehyde coming from the container that awaited the brain, but it always managed to get to her.

It was getting to Riyad too.

She noted the flagging tic that had taken up residence in the spook's right lower jaw as the power saw began carving a circular path through the top of the skull and murmured, "Not much longer now."

That earned her a sidelong scowl. A filthy one at that.

Fine by her.

She returned her attention to the ME as the colonel used his hammer to pop off the surreal circle of bone. The tension in Riyad's jaw ratcheted tighter as the protective meninges were carefully severed. By the time the brain had made it out of the skull and gently taken up residence in the waiting bath of formaldehyde designed to fix the organ so it, too, could be dissected and studied a week or two hence, she was tempted to nudge the spook back against the bulkhead. He was in danger of popping too—all over the translator. A split second later, Riyad stiffened and spun around to focus on the cabinets hanging behind them.

Smart move. Nor was there any shame in it. Hell, if this was his first autopsy, he'd held out longer than she had during hers—and better.

She'd had to leave the room.

The spook continued to face the cabinet as the colonel finished packaging and labeling his final tissue samples.

By the time Riyad had regained his composure and turned around to the gurney, the translator's skull, face and inner organs were all back where they belonged.

Mostly.

She and the spook continued to maintain their dual silence as the ME began to close the initial Y incision with a neat looping baseball stitch via that enviably steady hand. Still. Despite nearly two hours of constant, fine-motor work.

As the colonel finished tying off the thick thread, Riyad's jaw loosened and began to open.

She did the man a favor and pinched the thick, sinewy biceps beneath his polo sleeve hard enough to leave a bruise. Odd. For an intel guy, he was seriously buff.

He took the warning in stride—but obeyed.

She clamped down on her own impatience and swallowed it firmly as Tarrington finally retrieved the black rugged case that had been stashed on the deck at the starboard side of the OR since before they'd entered. The moment he hefted the case atop a waiting cart and cracked it open, the connection between that seizure, the rictus, those pinpoint lung hemorrhages, as well as the colonel's unusual fascination with the liver, locked in.

Hope outright exploded within.

Riyad stiffened. "Is that a—"

"*Shhh.*" But she nodded, even as she mentally crossed every single one of her un-contracted fingers and toes. Hell, her soul.

If she was right—if *Tarrington* was right—what she now

knew he suspected wasn't mitigating at all. It was outright exculpatory.

She also understood the fresh round of confusion burrowing in between her fellow agent's brows as he watched the ME fire up the specialized equipment within the case. After all, Riyad was a counterintelligence specialist. He was used to thinking in terms of terrorists. Bomb-making materials and explosive residue.

The microTLC that Tarrington had brought with him to the aircraft carrier was definitely used in the course of those types of investigations. The Thin Layer Chromatography system was often crucial to solving them. But it was capable of so much more. The portable gem had been designed to analyze forensic and environmental samples in the field, and even on the battle-field, in a variety of ways. The microTLC could detect explosives, illicit drugs, insecticides and pesticides from samples taken from a surface, liquid or solid.

In this case, liquid.

She watched as Tarrington switched on the microTLC's screen, retrieved one of the small plastic developing chambers and placed it in the waiting slot, then added the mobile phase. Next, he swabbed a sample from the blood he'd drawn from the translator's heart, added in the acetonitrile and began the agitation.

From there, the agonizing wait commenced as he nudged the sample through the remaining steps until, finally, it disappeared into the machine.

She tried to keep her hope in check as the minutes continued to tick out...and failed. Unlike Riyad, she knew the colonel wasn't looking for evidence of tetanus any more, or even epilepsy. He was looking for something else.

Something that could turn this entire case on its head.

Based on the sudden release of tension in the colonel's shoulders, he'd found it.

Unfortunately, she was too far away to read the confirmation on the microTLC's screen.

"What—"

She glared at Riyad, cutting him off once again. "I said, *shhh*." Tarrington wasn't ready to share, and she'd be damned if she'd allow the spook to jinx this.

Somehow, she found the patience to stand there beside Riyad, silent, as the colonel repeated the entire procedure with yet another sample. This one taken from the collection he'd removed from the translator's liver.

"Agents?"

*That* was their cue.

Relief flooded in as the ME turned to wave them over. The colonel's face and body were still set in impartial stone. But he was smiling inside.

It was in the gleam in his eyes.

She followed the spook around the gurney and stepped up to the microTLC's screen beside the men. And there it was. That lovely, exculpatory word.

*Strychnine.*

With it came the second tectonic shift in her day—as well as her current mission. Someone aboard the *Griffith* was guilty of murder, but it wasn't John.

Because Tamir Hachemi had been poisoned.

# 11

Regan dug her fingernails into her palms to keep from swaying as the relief blistered through her body, burning through the tension and the terror of the day.

She still couldn't quite believe it.

*Strychnine.*

She freely admitted that deep down, she'd been praying for a reprieve for John. The proverbial stay of execution. But what he'd received was so much more. That single word had granted John an honest-to-God *Get Out of Jail Free* card.

Of course, the container designed to preserve Tamir Hachemi's brain, along with the blood and tissue samples Colonel Tarrington had culled, still needed to be shipped to the Joint Pathology Center at Fort Detrick for a more detailed workup. But those ten tiny letters on the microTLC's screen were definitive.

Unless—

She turned to the ME. "Did you find anything else?"

The welcomed burn intensified as the colonel shook his head. "Nothing to contraindicate poisoning as cause of death.

And much to support it. Mr. Hachemi's pupils are still dilated; his mucus membranes are cyanotic."

"The pinpoint hemorrhages in the lungs?"

"Those, too." Tarrington nodded. "I also found star-shaped scarring in the tissue of the heart consistent with previous arrhythmia. Whether or not Mr. Hachemi or the US Army were aware of it, the man's heart was not healthy."

"So that seizure Corporal Vetter and Staff Sergeant Brandt reported to me—"

"Was not a seizure at all. It was the beginning of Mr. Hachemi's first convulsion, which unfortunately also led to the heart attack, that killed him. If Mr. Hachemi's heart had been healthy, he would have most likely suffered several more convulsions. With this particular compound, there tend to be two to four, on average. Unfortunately, given that no one would've been looking for the strychnine, I'm almost certain he would've died anyway. And those additional convulsions would have been excruciating."

"*Strychnine*?"

Riyad was still staring at the microTLC's screen, seemingly stuck on that beautiful, exonerating word. And his scowl had returned.

What the hell was wrong with the guy?

Give the dicey geopolitics of the case—not to mention that the White House, Islamabad and Kabul were bound to be read in on the autopsy report—he should've been as relieved as she was that John's actions hadn't led, or even contributed, to an Afghan translator's death. Especially *this* translator.

Instead, the spook was pissed.

Why?

Tarrington must have been wondering the same thing, because he'd begun frowning too. "Yes, Agent Riyad. Strychnine." The colonel retrieved the blood and tissue samples he'd finished testing and began to pack them up for transport. "Unfortunately, this is not the first case I've heard of in the military. The poison is obtained from *strychnos nux vomica* and related plants found in southern Asia and Australia, and is quite deadly. Death usually occurs within two hours of a fatal dose. Though strychnine was once available as cathartic pills, it has no true medicinal use. However, since the early sixteenth century, the compound has also been used to eradicate—"

"—rodents. I know." The spook had finally shifted his scowl from the screen to her. "What I don't understand, is how the hell it got on board a naval vessel. Especially since rat poison hasn't contained strychnine for decades."

An excellent question.

Unless they weren't looking for rat poison at all.

Regan had finally placed the case that had been dogging her brain since the beginning of the autopsy, quite possibly the same case to which Tarrington had referred. One of her instructors had shared the details during her CID course—ironically, the same instructor who'd become her mentor *and* one of Hachemi's many victims: Art Valens.

A decade earlier, Art had been tasked with investigating the death of a married sergeant in Bagram, Afghanistan. During the autopsy, the sergeant's body had displayed the same distinctive rictus and contracted digits as Hachemi's. The coroner had initially suspected rabies from one of the dogs that soldiers snuck onto the airbase.

It hadn't been rabies at all, but gopher bait.

Unbeknownst to the sergeant, the bait had been mixed in with the food his extracurricular girlfriend had been bringing to his quarters. But, according to Art, it had taken time and a hell of a lot of the stuff to kill the sergeant.

Not only had Hachemi been aboard the *Griffith* for the past fourteen days, he'd been in the brig the entire time.

Did the killer work in the galley?

But even if word about that cave massacre had leaked out and someone in the galley had decided to exchange his or her integrity for revenge, how would a sailor have gotten ahold of the poison?

Rats were one thing. Surely warships didn't have a reason to keep gopher bait lying around?

Then again, "It's possible the ship's rat poison was mislabeled at the factory. If so, the container might actually contain gopher bait. Or perhaps the bait was manufactured outside the States, in a country without stringent pesticide oversight."

As soon as she left the OR, she'd have someone from the carrier hail the *Griffith* via ship-to-ship comms. Chief Yrle could begin collecting up any bait the *Griffith* had aboard before she and Riyad even returned.

Naturally, Hachemi's cell would have to be searched too; Durrani's as well.

And soon.

Tarrington nodded. "It's also possible your suspect only intended to make Mr. Hachemi ill. The murder may have been accidental due to his heart."

Riyad ignored the ME's comment as he continued to scowl—at her. "That's what CID's nauseatingly feted agent is going to toss onto the table? A mislabeled carton?"

Regan ignored the feted agent crack as she shrugged. They had to start somewhere. And, frankly, she'd come across weirder over the past few years. Granted, Tarrington's possibility was by far the more likely scenario of the two. But until she had a chance to sit down and work out a timeline of who, besides those two Marine guards, even knew the translator had been coming aboard the *Griffith*—as well as who had access to strychnine—she was as stumped at the spook.

Except, Riyad wasn't stumped. Far from it. It was right there in that scowl.

He couldn't possibly still believe John was guilty of murder?

But his next words suggested yes. They were also directed not at her but at the ME. "The injuries to the translator's face—"

Tarrington's shake was swift and decisive. "Did *not* contribute to his death. Mr. Hachemi would've needed to have his jaw wired shut for six to eight weeks, and his nose set into place, but that's all. The poison caused his first convulsion, which in turn caused his heart attack. Without the strychnine in his system, the man would have lived."

There. Surely that was definitive enough?

But if anything, Riyad's scowl deepened, even as he continued to ignore her in favor of the ME. "Can we borrow the microTLC?"

Tarrington nodded. "Certainly. Not only is Agent Chase certified on its use, I don't anticipate needing it over the next twenty-four hours. Possibly longer. My suicide involves a handgun. If my needs change, I'll contact the *Griffith*."

The ME removed the disposable materials he'd used for the two tests he'd run and closed the case. He turned to pass the microTLC to her, only to be intercepted by Riyad.

Tarrington's brow rose as the spook brusquely thanked him for his time and turned to depart the compartment...with the case.

Wow. Riyad must've skipped military etiquette at his NCIS agent's course, because he'd been nothing short of an absolute jerk since they'd met. With everyone.

As for the microTLC, she didn't care who carted it to the *Griffith*. The only thing that concerned her was the tests she needed to run—and the results.

She offered the colonel a shrug and her own decidedly more

sincere appreciation for his time and expertise during the autopsy.

"You're welcome, Agent Chase. I'll forward my initial report to your email before I depart for Bahrain." With that, the ME resumed packing the samples he'd collected.

She'd been dismissed.

Regan departed the OR.

She hadn't expected Riyad to be waiting outside the door for her, and he wasn't. But neither had she expected to find him at the far side of the otherwise deserted patient ward, already unmasked and with one of those shipboard, sound-powered phones—powered by, well, sound—fused to his right ear and mouth. From the tension knotting up the muscles beneath that polo, not to mention his voice, the man's mood had yet to improve.

"Yes, Lieutenant. All of it. Every goddamned carton of bait you've got. Tell Chief Yrle I want it waiting in the master-at-arms shack before my return. No exceptions." He jammed the receiver home and spun around. Glared. "Well? You still got a problem with my investigative procedure?"

"Nope." Not on this. "It'll save time."

He blinked. The scowl faded—slightly. "You don't think the bait's mislabeled either, do you?"

She shook her head.

"Then why the hell—"

"It needs to be excluded." Might as well start there while she worked out the rest.

"Then how do you really think strychnine got onboard?"

This time, she offered a shrug—and the truth. "I have no idea. Yet." But she would. As mysteries went, they were dealing with a doozy of a locked-room scenario. Only in this case, the poison appeared to have been located on the outside of the door. Damned if she could figure out how it had been nudged across the proverbial threshold, let alone who was responsible for the nudging. "None of this makes sense."

On the one hand, they had Nabil Durrani.

As a physician, Durrani could've easily uncovered and chosen to abuse knowledge of his cohort's preexisting heart condition. Not only had Durrani been the brains behind that Afghan terror cell, the doc also had one hell of a motive to kill his bastard-in-arms. Namely, to shut Hachemi up before the translator could identify their unknown American traitor. But Durrani also had less access to strychnine than some unnamed, affronted shipboard sailor.

Hell, Durrani had had even less opportunity to actually poison Hachemi than the Marine guards.

In short, the Afghan doc would have to have found a like-minded marionette aboard a US naval warship willing *and* able to do his bidding.

A situation that appeared extremely unlikely.

As for Corporal Vetter and Staff Sergeant Brandt, either Marine could've tainted Hachemi's food as easily as one of the mess cooks, possibly more so, given that the Marines were bound to have been entrusted with said food without others present.

But Vetter and Brandt weren't just Marines. The corporal and staff sergeant currently served as US embassy security guards. As such, the men were considered the best of the best—for a lot of reasons. Not the least of which included loyalty, personal and professional restraint, and the proven ability to keep their mouths shut.

Both men would've known who they'd be guarding from the moment the assignment came down, but would either have shared that knowledge out of turn?

She suspected not.

Nor did the math add up. Both Vetter and Brandt had been

on board the *Griffith* for four weeks, since the fifteenth of December.

But the Marines weren't the only guests the *Griffith* had hosted lately. And a politician was a whole other animal. One more akin to a loose-lipped hyena than a silent, steadfast bulldog culled from the cream of the Corps.

"When did the diplomats board the ship? Where?" She'd assumed the *Griffith* had been at sea at the time, as it had been when she'd arrived.

Was she wrong?

Riyad must have anticipated the direction of her thoughts, because he shook his head. "The *Griffith* has been at sea since mid-November. She was taking part in a multi-national training exercise in the Indian Ocean when she was rerouted to the Arabian Sea to house the diplomats. All of them. The US ambassador and her staff, as well as the Pakistani and the Afghan contingents. Everyone arrived via the same Super Stallion that's waiting for us up on the *Reagan's* flight deck. The ship has been underway for nearly sixty days."

Damn.

While that underway timeline stunk for those sailors, it was even worse for this case.

But speaking of that CH-53E, "What about the pilot and the crew of the helicopter? Where did they drop off the diplomats once the geopolitical bitch-fest wrapped up?"

Odds were, the American ambassador and her staff, as well as the Pakistani and Afghan contingents, would have all been told that the translator and the doc were headed for deep interrogation aboard the same ship that the diplomats had just departed.

Given the current drawdown in the region, surely that gaggle of Afghan diplomats would've included at least one member of the Taliban, possibly more?

If so, would that Taliban have been as tight-lipped as the Marines?

Riyad removed his latex gloves and dumped them in the biowaste container beside him. "They left via the same UAE airstrip where they retrieved you. They all picked up the final legs of their respective US military hops from there."

"And Durrani and Hachemi? Were they picked up at the same place, at the same time? Or was there a delay between the diplomatic departures and the prisoner boardings?"

A delay during which someone on that chopper crew would also have known who they were now waiting on...and why.

The spook nodded. "Same strip. Same day. The crew was forced to wait at Al Dhafra for roughly three hours before the prisoners arrived."

"You're certain?"

This nod was firmer. "I was there. My orders put me on the same helo hop to the *Griffith* as the prisoners. I arrived at Al Dhafra before the helicopter touched down with the diplomats and the embassy guards. I watched them all disembark."

"What about the guards? Did either Vetter or Brandt—or any of the Super Stallion's crew—leave the apron during the wait?"

A third nod. "All of them. But no one left the terminal."

But who was to say one of them hadn't been met in, say, the latrine?

Still, three hours? A tight window to say the least. So tight, a potential perpetrator would have to have phoned a trusted contact ahead somehow, so that the poison would be waiting for him. On an airstrip in the middle of the desert in the UAE.

Damned difficult. But not impossible.

She'd noted tighter timing—and harsher, seemingly insurmountable odds—before. And when she added in that fact that the Marine guards and chopper crew had to have known who they were supposed to be picking up...

But it was still a damned dicey stretch.

Regan peeled off her gloves, surgical mask and shield, and deposited them into the same biowaste container where Riyad had dumped his gloves. "What about port calls? Has the *Griffith* pulled in anywhere since the translator and the doc reached the ship? Even briefly?"

"No." From the certainty in that frown, the spook had already considered that possibility as well, remote though it also was. The man might have the beginnings of a decent investigator, after all.

Though, at the moment, she'd prefer positive momentum in their case rather than in Riyad's professional skills. All they had perpetrator-wise were the Marine guards and the Super Stallion's crew—and a painfully narrow, three-hour window.

Hell, even *she* didn't qualify.

While General Palisade had informed her that Durrani and Hachemi were at the other end of her journey, her movements failed the clock test. Even if she'd brought the strychnine to the ship, based on the information Tarrington had relayed regarding the average, two-hour poison-onset window, Hachemi had ingested the compound long before she'd stepped off that chopper. That same two-hour onset window also excluded the CH-53E's pilot and crew.

And, according to Riyad, there'd been no other physical contact between the ship and the rest of the world. Unless the spook had missed something.

"What about mail? How do sailors get care packages while they're at sea?" Because according to Chief Yrle, the underway replenishment from that morning had included—

"Yes, the *Griffith* receives letters and packages, along with its fuel. But this morning's mail call was the only one the ship's had since I've been aboard."

And it had occurred after the translator's death.

Shit. They needed answers and now. A viable suspect. Before—

"What?"

Her deepening frustration must've shown. It definitely permeated her sigh. "At the moment how that poison got aboard is less important than who brought it...and does he or she have more?"

Confusion marred the man's pretty-boy brow.

"*Durrani.* Think about it, Agent Riyad. There's an excellent chance that whoever poisoned the translator is now targeting the doc." Despite Hachemi's initial dangling of a potential traitor's name, the doc was far more critical to their terror investigation than Hachemi had ever been. Because Durrani had *two* names in his possession.

And, now, she was seeking a third.

The unidentified woman from that cave, an unnamed traitor...and Tamir Hachemi's killer. At least two of those names were connected.

Why not all three?

If so, uncovering one of the names might well lead to both of the others.

The non-mother in the cave. She'd start with that unidentified Pakistani woman and move out from there.

Regan tipped her head toward the microTLC at Riyad's boots. "We need to get that to the *Griffith* and get the bait testing out of the way, so I can move on to the dregs of the coffee Hachemi tossed at Major Garrison in that conference room this morning. As soon as the dregs come up clean, we can have Garrison released from custody."

The scowl returned.

She ignored it. She didn't have time for the spook's bizarre suspicions regarding John. Not if she hoped to negotiate the name of that final victim from the doc before it was too late.

Because there was an outstanding chance that whoever had murdered Hachemi was already hard at work, putting the final touches on his plans for Durrani.

The clock was ticking, and in more ways than one.

The spook's scowl intensified. "No."

"Damn it, I need him." At the moment that need was also not only profound, but utterly professional—whether Riyad believed it or not. "Back in Charikar, Dr. Durrani was obsessed with Major Garrison and Staff Sergeant Tulle's immunity to that blasted psycho-toxin he shot into us. The doc wanted answers. So much so, I was able to use that obsession of his to buy time to free myself so I could take him down. With Garrison at my side, I can abuse that obsession again. Distract Durrani with it. And just maybe, I'll be able to get the name of the final victim from the cave—and, from there, the identity of the traitor as well as the name of Hachemi's killer."

Riyad shook his head. "Garrison stays in his quarters."

Unlike the scowl, that she couldn't ignore. "Are you telling me you honestly still believe the major did it? You were in that autopsy with me, *while* Tarrington logged his findings. You saw the initial tox results on the microTLC's screen."

Riyad didn't respond. He didn't need to. His answer was in that filthy scowl, just as it had been earlier in the OR.

Good Lord. Had the man slept through his entire investigator's course? "You do realize that you've managed to ascribe two separate *modi operandi* to the major in as many hours? Not only do they conflict, they suggest two distinct levels of intent on the part of our suspect."

"So?"

So, it didn't make sense. "If Garrison had poisoned Hachemi—and is thus guilty of first-degree, cool-and-calculated *premeditated* murder—why on earth would the major then opt for a second-degree, *spur-of-the-moment* utterly emotional killing by deliberately bashing the translator's face into that bulkhead less than two hours later?"

"Because the major was leaving the ship. Perhaps Garrison wanted it done by the time he disembarked so there would be no remaining risk to him should Hachemi survive the poison and give him up."

*Jesus*, the spook was stubborn. And with instincts so far off base it wasn't funny.

Not only were poison and bludgeoning a hundred eighty degrees out from each other, the timing was off—completely. "I told you this morning that Garrison was in the hospital with me in the ICU when he got that call from General Palisade. The major's flight to the UAE went wheels up twenty-five minutes later. He didn't even have a clean uniform on him. Garrison's XO had to head to the man's apartment, grab his "go" bag and bring it to the major's departing flight. You can contact Fort Campbell and check with Captain Ingle. How the hell was Garrison supposed to have obtained the strychnine in time to bring it aboard the ship?"

"You've already suggested the answer." Riyad reached down to retrieve the microTLC. "If the diplomats or crew of that Super Stallion could engineer the delivery of the poison to the terminal in Al Dhafra, why not Garrison? I've read the man's record. Garrison is resourceful and smart—and he's Special Forces. As such, he's proven himself more than adept at functioning under extreme conditions."

Riyad was right. John was an exceptionally proficient, quick thinker whose efforts produced results above and beyond his peers.

As for the man standing in front of her? The one gripping the handle of that case as though he was ready to fight her for it?

Sam Riyad was a bona fide idiot if he'd managed to miss the rest of what was in John's record.

She'd read John's file too after she'd been tasked with investigating his houseguest in Germany—*all* of it. John's enlisted and officer evaluations, the writeup for his Silver Star, as well as the Bronze Star with V device for valor, that he'd been awarded, not to mention the other countless medals and commendations that proved his character was above reproach.

But there was no point in wasting her time trying to convince the spook.

She'd simply run the test on residue from the cup of coffee Hachemi had partially consumed that morning, and then tossed at John in anger shortly before his death. The tox results would support her view of John's character, not Riyad's.

She held out her hand and waited for the spook to hand over the microTLC.

He simply stared. Make that, glared.

"Oh, for Christ's sake. I'm not planning on 'accidentally' tossing it out the back of the chopper while we're skimming the ocean." Though the verdict was still out on whether or not she intended to do the same with the spook.

And, Lord, was she tempted.

He finally extended his hand, relinquishing the case with a shrug. "I know you don't see it, but you will. There's no one else. The timing might be tight, but Garrison is the only one who knew Hachemi was on the ship before he ever came aboard."

The spook was wrong about that, too.

"Sorry, Agent Riyad, but there is someone else."

Someone her so-called partner had chosen to leave off his suspect list. Someone even she'd left out of her tally, at least her verbal one. Someone who was bound to have had at least as much warning regarding his own shipboard destination as John had been given before he'd left Fort Campbell. Someone who'd also known Hachemi was aboard that vessel, zealously guarding a traitor's name on the tip of his tongue. Someone who'd spent even longer aboard the *Griffith* than John, trying to get that name out of the recalcitrant translator.

Someone who, by the spook's own admission, had also had even more downtime in that terminal in Al Dhafra before he'd boarded the Super Stallion.

She doubted Riyad had even realized it.

She shook her head in disgust and turned, only to stop short as the spook grabbed her upper arm.

She jerked her arm from his grip as she spun around. "Touch me again and I *will* knock your ass out the back of that bird on our way to the *Griffith*."

And it wouldn't be an accident.

He stared down at her. "Who?"

"Just to be clear, Agent Riyad. Are you asking me—the 'nauseatingly feted' CID agent assigned to this case—if I have any inkling as to who else had the requisite means and opportunity to kill Tamir Hachemi?"

The glare turned Arctic. "Yes."

"*You.*"

# 12

The return flight to the *Griffith* was taking twice as long as the initial leg to the carrier, and it had nothing to do with the readout on Regan's watch.

It had to do with that glare. Riyad's glare.

The Arctic frost that he'd blown her way inside the *USS Ronald Reagan*'s patient ward had long since seared off. Fury simmered in its place, somehow spiking along with each rattle and rumble of the haze-gray helicopter that surrounded them.

It was ironic. She'd be the first to admit that she'd had issues with John when they'd met, due to the man's innate arrogance. But John had nothing on the overinflated ego squatting across the belly of this bird. The ego who'd spent the better part of their current chopper hop openly watching. Assessing.

Her...and the rugged plastic case tucked up against her boots.

She swore the spook actually believed her capable of plotting to render the microTLC inside useless. But that was crazy.

Wasn't it?

She caught the crew chief's wave. The Marine acknowledged

her nod with one of his own before crossing his forearms to signal the chopper's imminent landing.

Three raised fingers followed.

Three minutes to the *Griffith*'s flight deck.

Three minutes to waving goodbye to the asshole who was *still* scowling at her. Screw the man's co-investigator status. Chief Yrle could witness the tests on the rat bait that the woman had been ordered to collect up via the ship-to-ship call Riyad had instigated. And then, she and Yrle would move on to the dregs of that coffee.

She hadn't been exaggerating in the aircraft carrier's patient ward. If she hoped to pull off her coming showdown with Durrani, she needed the distraction John's added presence would provide. Especially since John would be conscious during this meeting. Something neither John nor Staff Sergeant Tulle had been back in Charikar.

The change in status just might prick the Afghan doc's own colossal ego deeply enough for her to get a name out of the bastard.

She was willing to start with any one of the three they were now after.

Unfortunately, it was nearing midnight. She suspected that Durrani had turned in hours ago, along with the bulk of the crew, after the ship had passed the word for taps. Even if Durrani was a night owl, there was no way she'd risk starting up an interrogation session at this hour. Doing so would send a dangerous message.

One of desperation.

The fact that she *was* desperate was immaterial. Until morning, patience reigned...however grudgingly executed, especially in her.

Oddly enough, her patience had been shored up by the

owner of that perpetual scowl. Upon boarding the CH-53E, Riyad had informed her that while he'd been on the ship-to-ship horn arranging for Chief Yrle to retrieve the rat bait, he'd also ordered an immediate search of the brig for any evidence of bait or pure strychnine.

For all his screwups, the decisions had been sound.

The reality of those decisions and their situation gnawed in as the Super Stallion's wheels finally embraced the *Griffith*'s flight deck, albeit heavily.

Regan removed her ear protection and life vest as the chopper's blades began to power down. She stowed the borrowed gear on the seat she'd vacated, then retrieved the rugged case at her feet before heading for the rear ramp of the bird.

Riyad followed.

Reality gnawed in harder as she stepped out onto the floodlit deck. What the hell. Riyad might not like her—and she definitely couldn't stand him—but they had a case to work. Several, increasingly complicated mysteries to solve. Three critical names to uncover. The quickest way to achieving all of those goals before Durrani's remaining cohorts succeeded in accomplishing whatever they were still plotting was bricked straight down the path of active, interagency cooperation.

Riyad was a spook. She might as well abuse that—and him.

And she knew just where to start.

It might be closing in on midnight aboard the *Griffith*, but it was barely 1400 back on the East Coast. Universities and medical offices would be open for hours yet. They could concentrate on the stateside ones until the others began opening up around the globe.

Regan swung around and caught that irritating stare through the chilly night mist that swirled in around them. "Look. Right now, we disagree on a number of issues. But there's a lot we do agree on." For one, the motive behind Hachemi's death. While she was willing to entertain other possibilities until they'd been ruled out, her gut was insisting that the translator had been killed for silence, not revenge. Someone wanted to shut him up, and permanently. Which meant Hachemi's murder was intrinsically connected to at least two of the names they were seeking. "You and I need each other. We each have knowledge and skills unique to ourselves. It's going to take all of those skills to work this investigation."

Was it her imagination, or had that ire cooled slightly? "And how do you suggest we begin, Agent Chase?"

"You work counter-intel, right? Usually?"

The simmer remained, but he nodded.

"So work it." She bent down to set the microTLC's case on the nonskid-coated deck, then straightened. "Concentrate on the non-mother. She's our best way in. For all Hachemi's boasts, Nabil Durrani was the real brains behind that cave massacre and the psycho-toxin infections. If Hachemi knew the name of the traitor, you can be damned sure Durrani knows it too. Unfortunately, the doc is not going to give it up. But he just might give up the name of the seventh woman in exchange for the access I offered him to my recent medical records. You weren't there when I questioned him earlier today, but I could see Durrani wavering over that offer. I could feel it."

She held up her hand as the spook's mouth opened.

"I know—your absence was on my orders." She lowered her hand. "But the fact remains: that man is tempted. Plus, he could not take his eyes off the photo of that final woman. Her identity is the key to whatever plans he and this unknown traitor still have." Her hand went up again. "Let's table the Garrison-guilt argument for a moment, okay? Consider these facts instead. The woman was not pregnant. And yet, she was cut open and given an infant to look as though she was while she was lying on the floor of that cave. Durrani took the time to find another woman with twins to complete the image. He had to have known it wouldn't last, that we'd eventually realize she wasn't pregnant at the time of the murders. But that obfuscation bought him time. Nearly two weeks now. That's where our priority needs to be—the identity of that woman. Because the clock is ticking, Agent Riyad, and the hands are not moving in our favor."

"You haven't yet shared precisely what you'd like me to do."

"What spooks do best. Human intel. We need your connections. One of my fellow CID agents, Nathan Castile, has been busting his hump doing legwork on both sides of the border since Garrison and his men discovered those cave victims. Castile's been able to prove that the six identified women all had prenatal visits with Durrani when he volunteered at Malalie Maternity in Kabul. The seventh doesn't appear to have been a patient, not that anyone there can recollect. We need someone with serious human intelligence contacts to comb through the other Afghan hospitals where Durrani worked, along with clinics and refugee camps—even his premed and med days at Harvard. Especially any extracurricular political or religious groups he may have joined while living in Boston, particularly those that have terror leanings. You'll understand that angle better than I or Agent Castile ever will. Our mystery woman may have been a fellow student Durrani met through one his classes or groups. They may even have had a relationship. Based on her dental work, she appears to have been upper class Pakistani. I need someone to coordinate with and direct Agent Castile's in-country searches. Someone who can reach out in fluent Dari, Pashto and Arabic to local laborers and medical professionals alike." If the spook spoke Urdu too, even better. If not, Nathan Castile did. "Our mystery woman's X-rays need to be run against *all* potential stateside, Afghan and Pakistani dental practices."

Riyad's brow rose pointedly as she finished. "And you? What

will you be working on while I'm crunching out message traffic to half the world tonight?"

She tipped her chin toward the case at her boots. "That. I'll start with the bait you had Chief Yrle gather up, then move on to testing the coffee I logged into evidence."

Naturally, she'd have Yrle by her side. She didn't need anyone questioning the impartiality of the results, including this man...whose scowl had returned.

What the devil had she done to incur suspicion now?

"Agent Chase?"

Regan spun around to find the master-at-arms chief in question standing three feet away with a sheet of paper in her left hand. She returned the chief's salute.

"Yes?"

"You have message traffic, ma'am. It's from USASOC."

"Thank you." Regan accepted the sheet of paper, tilting it so she could take advantage of the flood lamps that were still lighting up the flight deck as she scanned the block headers.

While the message was from USASOC, it wasn't from General Palisade. But it did concern the name Durrani had provided as his Russian bioweapons contact: Aleksi Skulachev, whose father supposedly worked at the Bioprepart facility. Regan kept scanning until she reached the body of the message.

Both Skulachevs checked out. Her deal with Durrani was a go.

*Yes.*

She was about to turn to share the message's content and subsequent mission directive with Riyad when she realized he'd deftly skirted around her while she was reading. The spook was already halfway across the flight deck, passing the V22 Osprey that was neatly nested up and chained to the deck off her left.

Within seconds, Riyad had reached the portside aft door in

the ship's superstructure. And locked within the fingers of his right hand?

The handle to the microTLC's case.

Son of a *bitch*. He really did not trust her with that thing.

She forced herself to let the irritation go. As a spook, Riyad wasn't signed off to run the tests. And with his reaction to Hachemi's brain being removed during the autopsy, she seriously doubted he'd logged time with the machine while assisting on a homicide case. Like it or not, he needed her skills, too.

But with the mood he'd left her in, she'd take her sweet time getting her ass down to the master-at-arms shack...while he waited.

"Ma'am? Is everything okay?"

Regan returned her attention to the chief. To the growing list of investigative chores that still needed to be checked off her list.

In light of those chores, she motioned Yrle toward the nested Osprey to create a bit of distance between the two of them and the sailors who'd begun lashing the Super Stallion to the flight deck. "Everything's fine." Or it would be. Just as soon as the answers on this case started outnumbering her questions. "Chief, did you manage to locate the ship's rat bait?"

"I did. We have two containers on board, both plastic, industrial tubs. According to the supply chief, the bait was manufactured in the United States and is in block form, not pellets. The main ingredient is bromadiolone. Since the containers were sealed, I simply logged them into evidence."

"Excellent."

She'd test the bait anyway, but the fact that it was US made, bromadiolone based and factory sealed all but foreshadowed the results.

As for the container that had actually held the strychnine that killed Tamir Hachemi, she suspected it had been of the glass-bottle variety and was long gone by now, most likely a hundred-plus nautical miles behind the *Griffith*'s frothing wake and permanently settled into its new home on the ocean floor.

Regan folded up the USASOC message traffic and tucked the resulting square into the right breast pocket on her camouflaged blouse.

"Chief, do you know if any of the diplomats made a round trip from the *Griffith* to any other ship after they were informed that Durrani and the translator were coming aboard?"

"I don't think so. I do know that today's the first day we've had flight ops since Major Garrison joined us. But I can check on the diplomats."

"Please do. While you're at it, I'd like to know if anyone received an official, physical pouch from their respective governments via air during the same time frame."

"Anyone? You want me to check on the communications of the Afghan and Pakistani diplomats too?"

Regan nodded. "Will that be problem?"

"No, ma'am. But the ops boss might want to speak to you about the request, possibly the XO too."

Fine by her. She'd simply direct the lieutenant in charge of operations and his executive officer toward the captain's cabin.

As for the remainder of her needs, checking those off her list was going to be a bit dicier—for the chief. As Army CID, she'd be leaving the *Griffith* as soon as she wrapped up her case. Yrle would be staying behind for the rest of the woman's shipboard rotation, to live and work with her fellow sailors...and ship's-company Marines.

Regan waved her hand toward the behemoth nesting in front of them, then the one behind. "I see two Ospreys on this flight deck in addition to the CH-53E. Major Garrison, his men and I arrested Durrani and his cohort in Charikar on December twenty-eighth. Find out if any of those birds have been in the air since then, including the CH-53E I don't see." She'd noted two Super Stallions upon her departure for the postmortem. The other CH-53E must still be in the air, since the *Griffith* didn't possess a hanger. "I want a list of the names of all the pilots and crew members who were aboard each flight. Especially those who flew to Al Dhafra. You and I will be searching their quarters first thing in the morning. When we're done, I'll need to interview each Marine pilot and crew member separately. You'll be there as well. I'll also need to reinterview Corporal Vetter and Staff Sergeant Brandt. We'll be searching the guards' quarters too. Naturally, you will keep all taskings, as well as our conversations, to yourself."

The woman nodded crisply. "Yes, ma'am."

"Did you get a chance to search both prisoner cells in the brig?"

"Yes. There was nothing suspicious in either of them. Just the usual items, along with the prayer rugs and the copies of the Qur'an that we provided upon their arrival."

Regan widened her stance to maintain her balance as the ship rode out a particularly daunting wave. She could hear the ship's bosun shouting behind them, egging on his sailors to hurry and finish securing the CH-53E she and Riyad had disembarked to the deck. Evidently they were in for rough weather tonight.

No surprise there. The clouds had turned ominous well before her return flight from the carrier. Even now, the surrounding mist had begun to thicken, threatening to coalesce into flat-out rain.

Hopefully, it would hold off. She'd prefer to finish this conversation outside earshot of the majority of the crew. "Who was with you?"

"Ma'am?"

"Corporal Vetter and Staff Sergeant Brandt. Was either Marine with you when you executed the brig searches?"

The chief was forced to adjust her physical stance as well—along with the obvious mental realization that the coming morning's activities weren't perfunctory. Not only were the quarters searches and interviews serious, one of them just might lead to a court-martial...for murder. "Vetter was in the brig. Brandt had just gone off watch. He looked exhausted. I know the staff sergeant was guarding the prisoners last night and then spent his scheduled rack time dealing with everything that had happened to the translator today. I told him to go straight to his rack and get some shut-eye. Do you need me to wake him up so you can speak to him?"

"No. It can wait 'til morning. Did Corporal Vetter appear interested in your search?"

"Not really. He did ask what I was looking for. But he accepted my 'random search' excuse readily enough."

"What about Durrani? Was he suspicious?"

"Yes, but he was certain the search was tied to your absence."

Shit. "Someone shared my destination with him—and the reason for it?"

"No. He's been asking for you, though. Well, insisting. That's the other reason I came out here to meet you. Durrani's been in rare form tonight. Brandt called up via the sound-powered phone shortly after you left the *Griffith* for the autopsy. He said Durrani wanted to speak with you—that he was ready to talk. You can hear the 1MC in the brig. Brandt thought that Durrani had figured out that helo ops meant someone had left the ship and was worried that it was you; that you weren't going to complete that bargain you made with him. I agreed—because Durrani's still in a tizzy. He had Vetter phone my office again, after they passed the word to prepare for your return helo ops."

"Let me guess; the doc still wants to see me."

"Not exactly. Now he's insisting on it. He actually ordered me to tell you he's ready to deal. I don't think you should trust him though."

She hadn't planned on it.

Still, "Why not?"

"He hurt someone tonight. One of the hospital corpsmen. It happened just after the strychnine search."

Now that was unexpected. Nor did it bode well.

"Is the corpsman okay?"

Yrle nodded. "She's fine. Just a bit rattled. Petty Officer Nguyen had accompanied Dr. Mantia down to the brig. They were originally scheduled to remove Durrani's second round of stitches this morning, but with everything that happened with the translator and then a mess cook's fall down a ladder, it kept getting pushed back. Mantia was about to start on Durrani when he got called away again. Someone in engineering thought he was having chest pains. It was indigestion. But, anyway, both Vetter and Brandt were still in the brig for the watch turnover, so Nguyen told Mantia that she felt comfortable enough doing the removal on her own. According to Nguyen, everything was fine for a while. Well, except for the fact that Durrani kept trying to flirt with her. She ignored his constant comments and was applying a cream to reduce scarring when Durrani just reared up and head butted her. He hit her so hard he gave her a black eye. Brandt and Vetter gathered her gear and got her out of there immediately, but she was still shaken when I took her statement."

"And Durrani? How was his mood?"

The chief snorted in disgust. "Oh, he had that smooth, shit-eating grin on his face that he gets when women are around. I took Vetter's and Brandt's statements, ordered the staff sergeant to his rack, and then I left."

That sealed it. Durrani definitely knew something was up.

And as usual, he was taking out his ire on the women around him.

Par for the doc's twisted version of Islam.

That black eye was payback for whatever Durrani believed they'd done to his cohort in crime earlier. No surprise there. The clues had been trickling down to the brig all day. And, unfortunately, Durrani was clever enough to collect them up and add them together. Hachemi had been missing since he'd been removed from the brig that morning. Even if Durrani had initially believed the man was ill and in sickbay, how many times had Durrani heard the word being passed for flight ops since he'd been brought aboard?

From what Yrle had inferred, not many. Other than John's, possibly none.

And now, at least three round-trip helicopter flights in one day? And she was at the center of two of them?

He knew—and he was worried.

Worried, hell. The man was genuinely terrified. In light of how prisoners were routinely "interrogated" in his neck of the woods, the doc had to be wondering what Hachemi had given up today...and if his remaining plans were about to implode.

It was why that corpsman was sporting a black eye. And why Durrani was openly showing his hand by insisting on seeing her.

And, hopefully, it was why she just might have the upper edge when she finally deigned to head down to the brig to speak to him.

But, first, she needed to secure the distracting presence of the biggest gun and largest caliber ammo that she could brandish.

She needed John.

It was time to get moving, anyway. The weather was getting worse.

Not only had she been forced to readjust her stance again, the mist was beginning to morph into a stiff, buffeting drizzle. The resulting droplets were soaking into her ACUs and the chief's Navy camouflage, puddling up and smoothing out the roughened, nonskid surface of the deck beneath them. A moment later, the flood lights cut out, suffusing the entire visible world in a cold, inky black.

"We should go inside."

"Yes, ma'am. Would you like to head to my office to examine the rat bait?"

What she wanted to do was go directly to John's quarters and let him know that he wasn't guilty of murder. But she wouldn't.

Instead, she'd do her job.

"Yes." It was time to fire up that microTLC the ME had loaned her. "I'll need you to serve as a witness while I test the bait, as well as the dregs of coffee from that cup in the conference room this morning."

And, *then* she'd see John.

No matter the results, or any new arguments the spook provided.

"Certainly." Yrle pointed toward the starboard side door in the *Griffith*'s superstructure. "This way."

They crossed the deck in darkness and silence. Once they'd passed through the skin of the ship, the chief led the way to her office.

Halfway there, Regan suspected that whoever was up on that bridge had ordered up a change in course, because the ship's rocking and rolling had eased a bit. The *Griffith* was also quieter than it had been when she'd left, though the lack of manmade sounds made the hum of machinery and subdued creaking of pipes that much more noticeable.

Still, the noise was calming, lulling. As was the red lighting of the dimly lit passageways they traversed.

By the time they reached the master-at-arms shack, the standard white lighting inside was almost too bright. But that wasn't what jarred her.

It was Riyad.

The spook stood with his back to her, flush with the waist-high counter, the microTLC kit already open in front of him. A collection of expended plastic developing chambers, stunted cotton swabs and tiny, acetonitrile-mixing baggies were strung out along the top of the counter to the spook's right—along with a turquoise-tinted brick of rat bait and the used coffee cup she'd signed into evidence.

And something else.

Was that John's ACU blouse? The one she'd also signed into evidence?

She stepped closer, spotting the flat-black embroidered, major's oak leaf cluster on the center placket—and more—before Riyad had a chance to turn around.

It was John's. The implications were downright stunning.

To her *case*.

She could make out the lash of dried coffee and the copious splatters of Hachemi's high-velocity blood across the breast pockets and collar of John's uniform. She'd also noted the three tiny squares of camouflaged fabric that were missing. Given the crisp edges, the fabric squares had been carefully cut out for testing. But the missing fabric wasn't anywhere near that dried lash of coffee.

They'd been taken from the generous splatter of blood. Blood that had already been tested aboard the carrier during that autopsy.

There was only one reason. One person. Someone an NCIS agent believed was capable of lying on behalf of the US Army. And it wasn't her.

Colonel Tarrington.

Riyad had been actively seeking proof that one of the military's leading and heretofore unimpeachable medical examiners had deliberately falsified evidence.

For John.

What the *hell* was going on?

# 13

By the time the NCIS agent turned around, Regan had instinctively drawn on her father's duplicitous DNA and masked her shock.

Riyad had not.

She spotted the spike of guilt that invaded the man's hardened features and opted for furious, proprietary...and downright dumb.

Leaving Chief Yrle to mark time at the door, Regan stalked up to the counter and jabbed her index finger into the spook's sinewy chest for good measure. "What the hell do you think you're doing? If your ineptitude has tainted my evidence, I'll have your badge pulled so fast they'll be hauling your ass off this boat by dawn—as a *civilian*."

It worked.

Oh, he was still pissed. At her, and at nearly getting caught in the act. Heck, he was unquestionably still livid with John, too. But the man had no idea she'd seen those distinctive, missing squares. From the way Riyad immediately swung back to the counter to smoothly fold the stained ACU blouse in on itself, effectively concealing his handwork as he returned the evidence to its bag, he was willing to do just about anything to keep it that way.

Once again, there was only one reason. He did not want her knowing he'd doubted Colonel Tarrington's impartiality. At least not yet.

But why?

And who, in addition to the spook, shared that doubt? Because someone did. And whoever it was, they were seriously high up on the food chain. Riyad's and hers.

General Palisade and USASOC?

Or Palisade's boss, Admiral Kettering, and USASOC's higher headquarters, USSOCOM?

At the very least, there was a parallel investigation going on. One to which she and Colonel Tarrington were not privy, much less John.

Another, even more insidious thought gave her pause.

Had the NCIS agent gone rogue? The one turning to face her with that familiar scowl leveled her way yet again?

It was possible. Based on the fine lines that had already begun to set in at the outer corners of the man's eyes, he had roughly ten years on her twenty-six. Riyad might be new to investigations, but he wasn't new to life. To temptation.

Disappointment.

*Christ*. She couldn't afford the distraction of an interagency face-off, let alone a less than forthcoming partner operating with his own hidden—and possibly nefarious—agenda. She had another critical confrontation to prepare for.

Her showdown with Durrani.

Despite the hour, it was to her advantage to keep the doc waiting on her for a bit longer. But if she waited too long, she'd blow that advantage.

And then where would her mission be?

Regan turned to the counter as Riyad retrieved the

remaining evidence bag he'd unsealed. He tucked the coffee cup inside and closed it, then obtained a fresh bag for the turquoise brick of bait he'd tested. He sealed that bag as well, then logged the rat bait into evidence, that dark displeasure of his deepening as he noted her deliberate scrutiny.

A weighted sigh filled the master-at-arms shack. His. "I do know what I'm doing, Agent Chase. With *our* evidence and the microTLC. You seem eager to forget that there are two professional investigators aboard this vessel, both capable of working this case."

The unwavering intensity in that stare, the rigid set of his jaw, not to mention the subtle bunching of muscle taxing the fabric of that long-sleeved polo as he leaned toward her. Together, they spoke volumes, and they were all communicating the same message.

He might still be pissed, but he wasn't lying.

Except, it didn't make sense. How had the spook even known how to turn that machine on, let alone prepare the samples and run the chromatography tests?

Yes, Riyad was NCIS. And, yes, the man had undoubtedly been exposed to the microTLC and other forensic equipment during his paltry forty-six days of Navy special agent training. But by his own admission, he'd also headed up only a single case before he'd arrived aboard the *Griffith*.

A traffic accident.

Regan studied both the fresh and expended supplies cluttering the counter. The latex gloves covering his hands. She had no idea where Riyad had actually gleaned his skills, but they were solid. And, tonight, he'd thoroughly abused them.

While she'd been up on the flight deck, conversing with Chief Yrle, Riyad had been down here, surreptitiously testing the ship's bait and that coffee.

Hachemi's high-velocity blood.

Even more telling, given the order of the forensic samples that were lined up beside the machine, he'd tested the blood *first*. He hadn't wanted to risk her arrival before he'd had a chance to compare his personal results to the ME's official findings.

Riyad had also methodically organized his test strips from the microTLC as though he'd done so countless times before. And next to those strips?

A scrawl-filled memo pad and a smartphone.

She'd bet her pending promotion to chief warrant officer three that he'd taken photos of the results with that phone. Recorded his own case notes. The ones on the upper sheet of that memo pad; the ones that had been written in *Arabic*.

Riyad was of Saudi descent. Had he written in a potential native tongue out of habit?

Or was there another reason? One that connected this man —not John—to the remaining prisoner in the *Griffith*'s brig?

The spook finally realized he'd left his notes in the open. Within moments the memo pad had been smoothly retrieved, closed and slipped into a pocket in his cargo pants.

A chill slithered down her spine as that scowl actively evaded hers.

She'd been furious with Riyad aboard the carrier when she'd informed him that he was her best suspect, but she hadn't been serious.

Was she wrong?

Her gut voted no. At least regarding the murder.

But something was definitely off about the man, and his actions. Everything from his anger with Chief Yrle over John's desire to conduct a one-on-one, former "comrade-in-arms" interrogation with the translator, to the spook's willingness to suspect one of Uncle Sam's preeminent medical examiners of tampering with evidence.

Unfortunately, she couldn't afford to press Riyad about any of it, much less those unusual notes and the missing squares of fabric.

Hell, she didn't even have a credible working theory to tie it all together.

Damn it, she needed to speak to John—about Nabil Durrani and her so-called partner...and *their* potential connection.

There was only one way to accomplish that tonight. "Well?"

One of those peeved, too-pretty brows rose. "Well, what?"

She jerked her chin to the evidence bag containing the cup from the conference room. "You tested the dregs from the coffee. What were your *professional* results?"

"Strychnine."

She nodded calmly, almost amused to find him attempting to discern her own micro-expressions. Almost. Unfortunately for the spook, her tainted genetics all but guaranteed that he'd only see what she wanted him to see.

And, right now, that wasn't the truth.

"You don't seem surprised, Agent Chase. Or disappointed."

She offered a shrug. A positive result had always been a possibility. As for her disappointment? Oh, it was there. But it was conflicted.

As was she.

In the short term, a negative result would've been preferable, since it would've allowed her to bring John into that brig to assist her with Durrani—and, yes, let him know sooner, rather than later, that he wasn't guilty of second-degree murder. A positive result was a bit more complicated. Mostly because she hadn't yet had a chance to establish how the coffee had made it into the conference room—and who'd had access to the cup before the translator had begun drinking from it.

But in the long term? The presence of poison in that cup was an absolute positive. Because she now had something to trace.

*If* the strychnine was truly there.

"Well?"

It was her turn to raise a brow.

"Does the result I found with the coffee affect your faith in the major?"

"Not in the slightest." But it would affect her actions.

After all, this man had provided the results. She no longer trusted his word any more than the spook had trusted Colonel Tarrington's. Hence, she'd be coming right back to this compartment along with Chief Yrle after her meeting with Durrani, so she could double check those "results".

She tipped her head toward the bagged evidence. "What about the major's ACU blouse?"

The spook's entire body tensed. The effect was subtle, but it was there. "What about it?"

"It was laid out on the counter when I arrived." She pointed toward the pair of scissors partially concealed behind a bucket of rat bait. The ones that were in danger of sliding off the counter with the next roll of the ship. "The remaining dregs in that cup were sparse to say the least. I assume you used those to cut off a sample of the coffee-stained fabric so you could test that as well."

"I did."

The hell with omission. Whatever Riyad's true tasking aboard this ship, he was willing to lie bald and outright to accomplish it.

But he hadn't inherited her father's ignoble skills.

Riyad might not have spotted her lies during their chat, but she'd just nailed his ass to the proverbial wall on another one of his. Not only had the tension in his body ratcheted that much tighter, it was now backed up by the flagging tic that had taken up residence at the outer right edge of his jaw.

She nudged another pointed brow upward. "And?"

"I confirmed strychnine."

"Well, then." She reached out and caught the scissors as they finally slid past the edge of the counter. "You repack the microTLC while Chief Yrle and I gather up the evidence and get it tucked back into the safe before it ends up on the deck."

Surprise entered those dark eyes at her seemingly easy acquiescence.

Wariness joined in.

But he did step forward, returning the unexpended chromatography testing supplies into the foam slots quickly, neatly... and absently.

Yeah, he had experience with the machine. A lot of experience.

And that was more than curious.

As the master-at-arms chief moved deeper into the compartment, Regan wondered how much the woman had read into what had just transpired during the confrontation she'd shared with the spook—and what the chief's conclusions had been. She suspected she'd find out soon enough. But for now, Yrle's bland expression as she accepted John's ACU blouse and the coffee cup before rounding the corner to re-stow the evidence in the safe revealed precisely...nothing.

Impressive.

Riyad had done himself a disservice by pissing the woman off this morning.

She wouldn't be making the same mistake.

Regan handed over the bait next. She was about to thank the chief when the sound-powered phone hanging from the bulkhead beside the safe buzzed.

The chief closed the safe and secured the lock before answering the phone. "Master-at-arms office, Chief Yrle speaking."

The creaking of the pipes and venting in the overhead took

up a pronounced chorus as the woman listened to whoever was on the other end of that line for several moments...as she frowned into the receiver.

"Hold on." Yrle turned all the way around to the counter and held out the phone. "Ma'am, it's Corporal Vetter. Durrani heard this last helo ops; he thinks you were on it. The prisoner's demanding to speak with you."

Demanding?

Regan stepped around the counter and accepted the phone.

Yep, demanding he was. In fact, that was a serious understatement. She could hear the bastard bellowing her name in the background while the receiver was still a good ten inches from her face.

"Hello, Corporal. I understand the prisoner is ready to talk."

Vetter's sedate southern drawl filled her right ear. "Evening, ma'am. You could say that. He's been asking to see you since two helo ops ago. Neither Brandt nor I confirmed that you left the ship, let alone returned, and the doc's been bellyaching rather loudly about that lack of confirmation ever since."

"Understood." She shifted her attention to Riyad and caught that murky, perpetual scowl of his as the man snapped the microTLC's case shut. "Corporal, I may have a few minutes to chat before I turn in. Why don't you go ahead and seat Dr. Durrani at the interview table in his cell while I run my errands? I do have a few things to take care of beforehand, though. It was a long flight." An even longer autopsy. "I could use a cup of joe. I'll be down...eventually."

She could practically feel the corporal's grin through the line. She could definitely hear it. "Yes, ma'am. I'll take care of that for you pronto. And...enjoy your coffee."

"I will." She might even bring a cup for the Marine.

Regan passed the phone back to Yrle.

The chief slotted the receiver home. "How long are you going to make him wait, shackled to the bar welded to that table?"

Regan rubbed the thin scar above her right temple. The one she'd earned during the wee hours of Christmas morning just over two weeks ago when this entire, twisted case had begun. When Durrani's first victim, Sergeant Blessing, had finally succumbed to the hallucinations brought on by that damned psycho-toxin and had unwittingly stabbed his beloved, pregnant wife, killing her and his unborn child.

What she wanted was to leave the bastard who was really responsible for that stabbing chained to that table for the rest of his unnatural life. But since the CO of this ship, as well as the upper echelons of the US Army, would eventually frown on that, "I am thirsty. And I did miss dinner. Do they have chow aboard this ship at night?"

The depth of Yrle's grin sufficed for both the chief and Vetter. "Yes, ma'am. In fact, midrats—midnight rations—are still being served in the enlisted galley. And the coffee's so strong, engineering's been rumored to run the emergency generator off it."

"Sounds perfect. Got everything secured in here?"

The chief nodded.

"Then, let's go."

Riyad's brows shot up. "Are you seriously headed down to the galley?"

She offered a shrug as both she and Yrle came to a halt beside the door. "Why not? I'm hungry." And she could definitely use a hit of that intriguing, Navy-enlisted-style caffeine—perhaps two. Not to mention, she could use a bit of time and distance from the asshole looming over her so she could collect her thoughts and plot her coming strategy before she went down to the brig to deal with the next one.

"What time *do* you plan on reaching the brig, Agent Chase?"

She met that familiar displeasure and held it as she considered Durrani's sparse, shipboard cell. The steel chair he was undoubtedly already seated within. The equally unyielding steel bar both wrists were now shackled to. "About an hour. Could be longer. Depends on what's on the menu. I am partial to omelets."

"Make it an hour. And I'll be joining you."

The hell he would. She wouldn't even risk having Yrle in that compartment while she laid her trap for Durrani, and she actually trusted the patiently waiting chief.

"Sorry, this is one-on-one. No backup required." Or desired.

Not unless the backup in question was on her personal, mission-tested, *I got your six covered* list. Which this man was decidedly not.

"On the carrier, you claimed you needed it. In fact, that's why you purportedly asked for the microTLC. Because you wanted Garrison in that compartment with you."

He really did not get this. Any of it.

Much less her.

Frustration finally seeped into her sigh. "Damn it, Riyad. Nothing I've done since I came aboard this ship has been about what *I* want. It's been about this case, and what it *needs*. The major has something to offer in that compartment tonight. Something Durrani wants—desperately. That bastard will do just about anything to satisfy his obsession about Major Garrison's supposedly 'natural' immunity to that psycho-toxin."

As for this spook, and what he had to offer?

Try thirteen wasted days of sitting across a table and getting precisely nowhere—while actively thwarting a plan from a seasoned colleague that just might've provided results if John had been able to put that plan into motion from the start.

But they'd never know now, would they?

"Garrison's not leaving his stateroom." Riyad jerked his chin toward the rugged case on the counter in front of him. "Not after the results I just got from that."

The filthy scowl had returned and, this time, it was carved into place.

The man simply refused to see past those bizarre blinders of his. Especially when it concerned John.

Well, she could be just as stubborn. Especially with a case at stake.

Those names.

Riyad might not be willing to let John out of his stateroom, but she had no intention of letting Riyad into that cell with Durrani. Not if the doc was even thinking about giving up the identity of the seventh victim from the floor of that cave.

Regan reached into her breast pocket and retrieved the message traffic that Yrle had brought topside with her earlier.

"You didn't stick around on the flight deck. It's going to be a long night. A longer chat." She passed the message over and waited for the spook to unfold it and read the tasking within. "I've been cleared to make the deal, Agent Riyad. My health records for that woman's name." And once Durrani gave up that first name—if she was patient enough, worked hard enough—she just might be able to crack through the bastard's resistance long enough to glean a second: Hachemi's murderer. And then maybe, just maybe, she could leverage those names for the third: that unknown traitor.

But it was going to take time. A lot of it.

No matter how desperate Durrani was, no matter how deep his obsession, tonight's showdown was going to be one for the record books. Because she was not leaving that brig until she had an honest-to-God lead to go on.

Then again, in light of those missing squares of fabric...if she did leave Riyad to his own devices tonight, what would he be doing while she was down in the brig?

And who would he be doing it for? USSOCOM and Admiral Kettering?

Or *himself*?

The spook refolded the paper and passed it back. "I can handle the wait."

But could she handle the fallout if the growing suspicion in her gut was correct? Could her case? Could her country?

Every single second she'd spent with the man bucked up against her sudden, unexpectedly profound need to keep him close.

"Fine. You can be in the brig, in listen-mode only. You will remain outside the doctor's cell at all times—and completely beyond his peripheral view. No exceptions. That bastard sees one hair on your Saudi-born head and I'll have Vetter toss your ass into the next cell until I'm finished. You can listen from there—with the door *locked*."

Those features were no longer smooth and pretty. Every one of them had turned clipped, cold and very ugly. "I'll meet you there."

Her answering nod was just as clipped, and even more determined.

Riyad might not be able to see Durrani tonight, but she would be watching him, from now until the moment her so-called partner left this ship.

Yes, like her, the NCIS agent had been flown to the *Griffith* to get that traitor's name out of Hachemi. But given everything she'd learned about the spook today—and, more importantly, everything she hadn't—she was now all but certain that Riyad had also been tasked with a second, even more critical mission.

Either that, or he was the traitor.

# 14

Eighty-seven minutes later, Regan opened the watertight door to the *Griffith*'s brig. Both Nabil Durrani and Special Agent Riyad were waiting for her as she stepped inside. The former sat shackled to the table inside his cell as per her instructions, his dark blue, coverall-clad back infused with a palpable air of serenity. The latter was pacing the far end of the brig's outer compartment and, based on the strength of that perpetual scowl, decidedly less at peace with himself, not to mention her.

But the spook was adhering to her orders. He was firmly out of the doc's line of sight.

Even better, once she entered the cell and walked around the table to commandeer the empty seat across from Durrani, Riyad would still be in hers.

"Evening, ma'am."

Regan nodded to the Marine as he stood. "Corporal Vetter."

Upon her arrival, the corporal had been seated at the duty desk. His posture had been—and still was—considerably more relaxed than even Durrani's. Given the possibility that the dregs from that cup of coffee might indeed contain traces of strychnine, she found that particularly telling. If Vetter had orchestrated the translator's poisoning, the corporal appeared to be neither afflicted with guilt, nor worried that he'd be caught.

She filed the information away as she turned to close the watertight door. Skirting the metal ladder that led up to the hatch in the overhead of the compartment, she approached the desk to hand the Marine the gift she'd brought.

"Why, thank you, ma'am." Vetter's cheeks turned ruddy as he accepted the coffee, matching the tint to the island of Marine Corps stubble topping his head.

He centered the melamine mug on the duty desk. Since the course change from earlier had ceased dampening the severity of the ship's rolls halfway through the midnight meal and copious supply of caffeine that she'd shared with Chief Yrle, she wasn't sure the placement was wise. But the cup, and its sloshing contents, held.

Riyad's temper, not so much.

The spook fairly seethed with annoyance. Unfortunately for him, the listen-only mode she'd stressed in the master-at-arms shack earlier involved his ears alone...not that fixed jaw and tightly compressed mouth.

She ignored both as she turned right and entered the occupied cell.

Durrani didn't bother looking up as she walked around the table to stand beside the empty chair. She knew full well the open Qur'an and that rapt, pious pose were for show. There was no way Vetter would've been shuttling in here every two minutes to turn the pages. And that was a task the doc had long since lost the ability to accomplish on his own. His wrists were neatly cuffed to the security bar suspended several inches above his lap and just past the edge of the table; the Qur'an wasn't. Due to the ship's motion, the book and its eye-straining print had inched all the way across the table.

Another good roll or two, and the Qur'an would be landing on her boots.

"Am I interrupting? I can always return tomorrow."

She knew his answer. As did he.

Still, the doc waited for several moments, then glanced up as if he'd just finished reading a lengthy passage and politely shook his head. "Not at all, Agent Chase. I have been biding my time and my patience with the words and wisdom of Allah."

Yeah, she doubted that.

Had that print been larger or the book closer, she still wouldn't have bought it. Not when this man had clearly managed to skip over most of the words in that tome. Particularly those pertaining to understanding, coexistence and peace.

"Would you like me to move the Qur'an to your rack?"

"No, but thank you."

She shifted her attention past Durrani's head, toward the entrance to the cell where Vetter was patiently marking time. Riyad had ceased pacing. He stood well behind the Marine and to his left, watching.

She ignored the spook in favor of the Marine. "Go ahead and enjoy your coffee, Corporal."

"Ma'am, I'm not sure if you're aware—"

"Of the incident earlier? I am. And I'll be fine. I can take care of myself, even when I'm the one who starts out cuffed." The placid glance she flicked across the table rivaled Durrani's. It landed on that three-inch pink scar. She'd assumed it would look better without the stitches. It didn't. He really should've waited until the corpsman had applied that cream before he'd taken out his temper on the woman. "Right, Doc?"

Durrani's smile held. Barely.

Vetter's deepened. "Yes, ma'am. I heard that about you." He tipped his head toward the duty desk as he backed out of the cell. "I'll be right here if you need me."

"Sure thing." But she wouldn't.

Nudging the Qur'an into a less precarious location, she set her manila folder on the table and seated herself in the only remaining chair. Since her favorite recorder was running low on power, she retrieved her phone and switched on her backup recording app, quickly running through the standard *who, what, when, where and why*.

The formalities out of the way, she leaned back, taking in the full measure of the remainder of those deceptively tranquil features seated across from her, just as their owner took in hers.

"I trust your meeting went well, Agent Chase."

"It did. Thank you."

"And your flights? Were they uneventful?"

She nudged a slight curve to her lips. "What makes you think I left the ship?"

"Please, I am not a stupid man."

True. But he was arrogant. And worried.

It was in his hands.

They'd been decidedly loose and relaxed during their previous meeting. They weren't now. Oh, his shackled wrists were resting on that steel bar lightly enough. But his palms were pressed a bit too closely together. His index fingers were also steepled toward her, with his remaining digits knitted up as if ready for prayers.

Except, Muslims didn't pray like that. Sunnis or Shias.

And their fingers generally weren't taut.

The doc was worried. About Hachemi. About the current state of the translator's potentially precarious health. About what his cohort had and hadn't given up today. And, more importantly, to whom Hachemi might or might not have not given it.

In light of everything that had happened aboard this ship since she'd arrived, and everything Durrani had to have overheard, she was fairly certain the man believed the CIA had finally been called in. That she'd taken his cohort to another ship to be "questioned". And since Durrani hadn't seen John or Agent Riyad all day either, he probably assumed the men were with the translator, assisting in his "questioning".

"So, where are your two friends this evening?"

And that confirmed it.

"Oh, here and there."

"And how is *my* friend?"

She shrugged. "He's been better."

She refined her assessment as the knit to those fingers tightened. Yeah, the doc was definitely worried. But not for his cohort. In fact, Durrani didn't give a damn about Hachemi. He was concerned for himself.

Durrani believed he was next.

She offered the bastard her first sincere smile of the day. "I understand you've been anxious to speak with me."

"I would not use the word *anxious*."

Yeah, she'd received the reports from Chief Yrle and Corporal Vetter. Heard the bellowing over that sound-powered phone herself. "I would."

He matched her shrug. "I have been...concerned about you."

"Concerned?" Now there was a first.

But he nodded solemnly. "Indeed. For many reasons."

Many?

Why not? She had the rest of the night.

She bit. "And those are?"

He tipped his head toward the manila folder. The one she'd tucked in front of her to keep it from sliding onto the deck. "How is your hand?"

For once the appendage in question complied with her will and remained motionless. Thank God. "It's fine."

"And the tremors?"

What the hell. He might be the devil incarnate, but he was also a Harvard-educated physician. It wasn't as though he wouldn't know. Plus, he'd been playing with that diabolical psycho-toxin for a while, recording his observations and his notes. The ones they'd found in that safe house in Charikar, and others they might not have.

"They come and go."

This nod was sage, compassionate even. So much so, she might've actually believed he felt the emotion behind it...had she not seen the photos of those pregnant women and their innocent babies in all their mutilated horror. Walked that cave where it had all gone down. Dodged those murky pools of frozen blood in the flesh...and in her current, all too crystal-clear nightly dreams.

The faux compassion strengthened. "It has not been long since your coma, Agent Chase. These things take time. You will heal."

She didn't doubt it.

Okay, she did doubt it. Particularly in the darkest, loneliest part of the night. Right around the time when she began to wonder if she'd be able to control those tremors long enough to pass her looming weapons qualification without one hijacking her grip and knocking her aim off at the last millisecond.

And if she *couldn't* control them?

Her undercover career had already been demolished. Thanks to Germany and Evan LaCroix, being an investigator was all she had left.

If she couldn't pass her quals, what would that do to the remainder of her career with CID? Any future livelihood?

The possibility of a real relationship with John?

Not only did she not have the answers. She wasn't even sure she wanted them. But there was no way she was confessing any of that to this asshole, let alone seeking medical advice from the man. For a career obliterating and potentially permanent neurological condition he'd caused, no less.

Even so, his reassurance wasn't what intrigued her. It was the effort behind his phony concern. The doc was genuinely attempting to connect with her.

Why?

What did he have up his sleeve? "You said many reasons. What else bothers you...on my behalf?"

"How well do you know the men with whom you work?"

Ah, so that was where this was headed. Divide and conquer. He planned on impugning her colleagues' integrity. Shaking her faith. It was a solid, time-tested tactic. But it wouldn't work. Not only was that tactic an Army CID agent's bread and butter, she knew John. Warts and all. Accepted them.

Riyad, however...

But while she admittedly knew the spook a fraction as well as she knew John and trusted him even less, her so-called partner still ranked above the bastard seated across from her. The one still gauging her micro-expressions and reactions just as closely as she was gauging his.

Durrani was definitely trying to get into her head, any way he could. And she was more than curious to see just how far the doc was willing—and able—to go.

*Know thy enemy, know thyself.*

Sun Tzu had been dead on with that one. Even if Durrani wasn't a proponent of ancient military philosophy, she suspected he'd taken the Chinese general's advice to heart years before. How else had the doc succeeded in decimating nearly all of Captain Mendoza's A-Team and slaughtering the women in that cave, and then nearly succeeded in blaming the entire, grisly crime on Captain McCord and his men?

Not that Durrani's implied offer wasn't tempting. If Agent Riyad had made it onto Durrani's radar before she, John and the rest of John's men had managed to take the doc down in Charikar, there was an outstanding chance Durrani had dirt on the spook. Unfortunately, anything Durrani placed on the table would, at the very least, be tainted by association and definitely suspect, especially since the man was clearly intent on trying to use it against her.

So...why had the spook tensed? And *why* was Riyad shifting closer to the entrance to the cell? It couldn't be in an attempt to hear better. Not with the recording app on her phone still ticking away, sucking up their conversation for posterity.

Good Lord, Riyad was in the doorway now. For a moment, she actually thought he was going to stalk all the way inside.

Evidently Corporal Vetter thought so too, because the Marine came to his feet and moved up to grip the spook's arm and pull him back.

Riyad jerked his head to his left. He stared at the Marine. Hard. For a split second, she suspected he was going to take the corporal down, right then and there. Even more startling, in that moment she had the distinct impression Riyad was more than capable of doing it. Despite the fact that the Marine had a good two inches and roughly forty pounds of honed muscle on the spook.

Just who the hell was he?

To her shock, the Marine backed down—and off.

Riyad remained in the doorway, once again utterly focused on the man within.

"Agent Chase?"

She snapped her attention back to the table and fused it on the lying, pretty boy seated across from her and not the one lurking just outside that door. Waiting.

For what?

"Is something amiss?"

It took every ounce of discipline she possessed to keep her

thoughts from seeping through as she shook her head. Smiled. "It's nothing."

"Are you certain?"

Not by a long shot. "Absolutely."

Was it her imagination, or had the ship's motion grown worse while she'd been watching the corporal and the spook square off? Even the creaking in the venting and pipes was more pronounced. The Qur'an slid into the upper edge of her folder, jamming in firmly enough that a folded-up sheet of paper jarred loose. It was now peeking out from between the pages at the back of the book.

Curious, she tugged the square free and unfolded it.

It was the photo of the seventh woman from the cave.

"I placed it there to keep it safe. After all, it is far too easy to lose that which is important to us, is it not? Especially equipment."

Equipment? This was an image. Of a murdered woman with someone else's child lying atop her violated abdomen, no less.

What on earth was he alluding to? Because he was definitely alluding to something. That word was not a missed attempt at a thought lost to translation. Nabil Durrani's store of English nouns was as vast as his overblown ego. Unless—

*Shit.*

Apprehension prickled up her spine. Had the doc heard Riyad earlier, before she'd arrived? Did Durrani suspect the spook of remaining in the outer compartment? Or was he simply hoping Riyad would review the recording on her phone later? Was that odd phrasing meant to convey something known only to the two of them?

If so, what?

She was about to expose Riyad and invite him into the cell, if only to study the interplay between the two men, when a powerful wave hit the ship, jolting the entire compartment upward, before causing it to plummet straight down, along with the table between them. The Qur'an went flying over the edge, landing with a thud on the deck beside the metal legs of her chair, along with the manila folder and her phone.

Regan grabbed the folder before the contents could spill out, then the phone and book. Fortunately, the recording app was still running. She set the phone and the Qur'an on top of the folder and laid all three on the table between them.

"I apologize." That tome might not be holy to her, but it was to a significant percentage of the world's population, including the monster seated across from her.

To her surprise, the monster shrugged. "All is well—and as Allah wills."

Whatever.

She wasn't impressed with his take on anything with respect to that book, any more than she'd been with her grandfather's rigid interpretation of the Bible, let alone how dear ol' papaw had used that interpretation as an excuse whenever he'd decided to take out his humiliation, anger and frustration on her backside.

Neither her grandfather, nor this man, was truly religious. Both simply used whoever was upstairs for their own rationalizations and ends.

"And how is your lover faring?"

Her stomach lurched—and it had nothing to do with the newfound rhythm of the ship.

Durrani didn't know she and John were involved, did he? Much less that John was still aboard the *Griffith* and confined to his quarters?

"Pardon?"

That irritatingly smooth smirk returned. "I was given to understand that you and Major Garrison had renewed your relationship. Am I incorrect?"

So he did know. But he was also fishing for more.

Neither was surprising.

Durrani had chosen two of John's captains and their respective A-Teams for his heinous plans. He would've been a fool to skip investigating John as well. And though the doc might be a monster, a fool he was not.

Sixteen months ago, the salacious relationship she and John shared in Hohenfels had made the international news. CID and all of Special Forces had been privy to details that even the media hadn't managed to ferret out. As an Afghan translator employed by the US Army at the time, Hachemi might have known some of her fellow agents, and Hachemi had definitely worked closely with SF. Hachemi would've eagerly shared any dirt he'd gleaned on John with Durrani as the men had plotted that two-pronged terror attack on those pregnant women and John's men.

And then there was her presence with John on that mission to flush out Durrani in Charikar. The bastard was simply connecting the dots.

Hoping she'd choke on them.

She matched that smooth twist with her own. "The major's fine."

"Excellent. I offer my congratulations on repairing an... unusual relationship. And my sympathies, of course. To have called you a whore in that parking lot. Well, a Mata Hari, but—" That twist of his finally shifted into a deep, disapproving frown. "—it was clear what he really meant, was it not? And so...humiliating. But you two have managed to work through your differences, yes? He trusts you in his bed now? This is good. Still, the major's mood has been dark this past week. Are you completely certain he has forgiven you?"

Okay, Hachemi could have shared a lot of the above. But not that name.

Mata Hari.

There'd been two people in that parking lot outside CID that night—John and herself. And John wouldn't have spoken about what transpired. Ever. She sure as hell hadn't told anyone, not even Mira or Gil. Which meant someone else had been there.

Watching John. Listening. Deliberately gathering intel on him.

*Sixteen months ago.*

The traitor she was after?

Riyad?

She had no idea. But two things were clear, and the second was even more chilling than the first. One, whoever had overheard the conversation in that parking lot had shared it damned near verbatim with Durrani. And two, given what she'd just learned, there was an excellent chance that Durrani and their unknown traitor had been plotting that cave massacre, the chimeral attack on John's men and whatever was still to come for a lot longer than anyone suspected.

But what Durrani failed to realize was that here, now, he'd tipped his hand. If she continued to play her cards right—and kept her own bent and battered aces out of sight—she just might be able to use the first mystery to solve the second in time to win the entire game.

She deepened her smile until she could feel it. "As I said, the major and I are fine, as is our relationship. Though I do appreciate the free shrink session."

"Ah, you have been checking up on me. Investigating my life."

No. But she'd read the reports during the flight to Al Dhafra from the agent who was. Nate Castile had included quite a bit of truly intriguing information.

"I admit, I was curious, Doctor. Especially with regard to your academic studies, given that chimera you injected into me.

Though I'm not sure I feel comfortable with your mental assessments." She held up a hand as his mouth opened. "I know, I know. You got your bachelors in psychology. But really? With those grades?" Her pointed *tsk, tsk* briefly overtook the rolling and creaking of the ship. "They weren't the best, now were they? It's a wonder they awarded you that degree at all, much less let you into medical school. You must have licked and polished the boots of just the right admissions administrator."

Lord knew, it wouldn't have been a woman's.

The smile evaporated. The thin line left behind was as acerbic and as pissed as Durrani now was. "Perhaps I would have fared better had I had you to study back then. For you, Agent Chase, are a truly fascinating subject. While I suspect there are several detectives within your army with police officers for fathers, how many have fathers who were so dishonest, they were murdered by a fellow policeman? And your mother?" This *tsking* was his and considerably louder than hers had been. "The shame of it. It is no wonder she committed suicide. In front of the family's final Christmas tree, no less. As a child of Allah, I sympathize with her. And you?" No *tsk* this time. Just the return of that chilly smile and his phony compassion. The latter of which was fairly oozing from the man now. "How *do* you bear the pain and the disgrace of both of them?"

Really? That was all he was going to lob at her?

While she wasn't thrilled with having this particular conversation with this particular man, let alone in this particular place with none other than the spook listening in, it wasn't nearly enough.

Not for what she needed.

She pushed forth a light shrug. "Oh, it's not as difficult as you'd think. And it does get easier with each case I work and every bastard I bag. Especially the intelligent ones and their equally challenging investigations, unlike you...and yours."

She waited for the explosion, but it didn't materialize. The faux serenity returned instead. Despite the creaking of pipes, the air nearly pulsed with it.

Impressive.

He followed it up with another one of those sage nods that would have made Freud himself proud. "Yes, that is understandable. Your passion for the difficult and the complicated. I suspect both are born of your childhood as well. The physical and emotional abuse from your grandfather. All those foster homes. Perhaps this is why you chose to repair your fractured relationship with the major, hmm? Your determination to see at least one through? But it won't work, I'm afraid. You are too damaged, Agent Chase. Profoundly defective, in fact. In your mind and in your body. " He paused with that, as if to assess how successful he'd been in landing those blows.

Considerably less than he believed.

Nor did she need this bastard ripping off the lifelong scabs that barely covered her innumerable insecurities so he could trowel in a fresh load of doubt.

It was already there.

And he'd made a mistake. A serious miscalculation.

She had no intention of letting him know. She needed him to continue. The more he said, the more he revealed...and the closer she would get.

To the most important of those names.

She pressed her lips together. Allowed her chin to tremble. Just barely.

It was enough.

He was certain he was getting to her. The fresh wave of oozing concern confirmed it, as did that soft, sympathetic sigh. "That man will never see you as an equal. Nor will a relationship with the major ever last. How can it? You put your career first, Agent Chase, and in doing so, you *killed* his child. Eventually, he will find someone else. Someone worthy. And he, too, will leave you. Deep down, you know this."

Mind fuck. She'd heard the term years ago.

This man defined it.

She had to give the doc credit. Psychologically speaking, he'd managed to make up for those less than stellar undergrad grades with bruising, real-world experience. Experience he'd honed and learned to inflict upon others. He was a damned site better at screwing with her head than she'd given him credit for. Though really, she shouldn't have been surprised. He'd had plenty of time to prepare for this round.

But where the *hell* had he gotten his intel?

Because it was solid. Extensive.

Even Riyad hadn't been able to unload as many armor-piercing rounds at her that afternoon in her stateroom. As much as she hated to admit it, this particular bastard had succeeded in piercing her painstakingly forged protective shell.

Her right hand had begun to shake.

She slipped it into her lap as nonchalantly as she could, but it was too late. Those dark eyes were fairly gleaming. Nor could he resist flaunting that shit-eating grin.

Bastard.

She met his glee with an insouciance she definitely didn't feel. "Thanks for the advice, Doc. I'll keep it in mind while I'm working on my intimate relationships in the years to come—and you're in prison, working on your own intimate relationship... with your eager brute of a cellmate." After all, even with that scar, he was so very pretty.

As for herself, Durrani might even be right, especially with regard to John.

Hell, he probably was.

It wasn't as though she hadn't already run through the

possible scenarios on her own—and come up with the same, inevitable outcome for her and John.

But she couldn't afford to worry about that now.

She shifted her phone and the copy of the Qur'an to the side of the table, willing both to remain in place and not hit the deck as she opened the manila folder. Bypassing the creased photo she'd left with Durrani earlier, she drew a fresh copy from the file and laid it on the table between them. As she reached out to re-stack the phone and the Qur'an on top of the folder, she caught sight of Riyad just past the doctor's head.

The spook's posture had relaxed.

Even more curious, he deliberately avoided her stare as he stepped back into the outer compartment. She couldn't see him anymore.

A moment later she realized why, as the quick-acting watertight door to the outer compartment groaned in ferric protest and opened. She caught Chief Yrle's soft apology for the interruption, followed by a pair of boots moving quietly toward the door. She could still see the Marine's left profile, so...Riyad's boots.

Several more moments, and she caught a second groan as the door closed.

Had something happened with John?

She forced herself to push the burning personal question aside and concentrate on the equally searing professional one in her hands. The question she might actually be able to answer before she left this cell. Regan turned the image of the seventh, desecrated victim from the cave around so that it faced her killer square on and gently tapped the woman's bloodied hair.

"Who is she?"

Those dark, rising brows feigned ignorance. "You tell me."

Both she and this monster knew full well that she still couldn't.

But she had learned a few inescapable truths about their mystery woman—truths that pertained to her killer. Truths that were rapidly coming into focus. Especially when Regan added up Durrani's polite, yet insolent behavior with herself today and back in Charikar; his sneering attitude at Bagram Airbase with his fellow Afghan-born and professional equal, Dr. Soraya Medhi; as well as the bastard's flirtatious, then violent behavior with the ship's female corpsman earlier that evening. Together, they added up to an intriguing—and damning—hypothesis. And, given Tamir Hachemi's motive for drawing Captain McCord in their heinous plot, one that was seriously ironic.

"You were in love with her."

Durrani's entire body flinched. A split second later, those dusky features flushed until they nearly matched the pink of his scar, then bled all the way down to a pasty gray.

*Pay dirt.*

Her smile grew, the one pinned to her lips and the other one. The one she'd kept tightly reigned in and stored deep in her gut. The one that had been fueling this conversation of theirs for the past half an hour. For all his airs, Nabil Durrani wasn't so different from the cohort he'd sneered upon after all, now was he?

But the real reason for both those growing smiles? His flinch. With the distinctive tell had come something truly promising.

A lead.

She had a decent chance at uncovering their mystery woman's identity now. Because somewhere—in the US, in Pakistan, or in Afghanistan—there would be a record or a witness of Nabil Durrani and this woman, interacting.

Given the nature of the photo, she also knew, "This woman rejected you. In fact, I suspect she not only wanted nothing to do with you, but she also went so far as to tell you to your face." With that level of violence against the woman, she must have.

"Why? Did you work with her, then harass her when she refused your overtures?"

No flinch this time. But the flush was back, and this time it surpassed the newborn pink in that scar.

Regan allowed her visible smile to stretch and deepen into an outright grin. "Thank you."

"I did not tell you her name."

And he wouldn't. That much had become obvious over the course of their conversation tonight. Specifically, his side of it. Not a single question from the doc since she'd entered the room regarding her newfound immunity to that chimera. There was only one explanation possible: this woman and her identity were too important.

Durrani had no intention of identifying her.

Ever.

Regan shrugged. "It doesn't matter. I'll figure out who she is soon enough. I'll begin with every doctor, nurse and lab tech you ever worked with, while a few of my associates start in on everyone you came in contact with before, during and after medical school—in Afghanistan, Pakistan and the States." She held up the photo. "Keep in mind, we have an infinite number of copies of this to bring with us, and to distribute if need be. In person, in the papers, online, and on TV. *Someone* will recognize her." Regan shook her head as she reached out to tap the cover of the Qur'an beside her. "And when they see all that blood and that baby, it won't matter which book they hold while they pray. They will come forward. And then, we'll know what you have planned next."

"That will take time."

She shook her head. "Not as much as you'd think. After all, we've got a lot of boots on the ground in the States and spread out among other countries, now that we've pulled them out of that hellhole you came from. Those boots are attached to hands that are ready, willing and able to carry copies of this picture around the globe. And as I said, as soon as we identify her, the battle will be over. We'll have won the war."

That got a response.

His fingers fused into a single, tightly knitted fist as he lunged as far forward as he could get. "*Never* will it be over! Not until *we* have won. Nor did you *pull out* of my country. You were chased out like the jackals you are, with your tails tucked between your legs as you scurried back to huddle up beside your cowardly president. No concessions were needed. If you think that with you gone we will forsake our brothers in Al Qaeda and elsewhere, you are mistaken. If you think we will accept the rule of the puppets you left behind in Kabul, you are doubly so. We will prevail, again and again. And unlike you, we are in no hurry. It is as it has been said: *you have the clocks, but we have the time*. All we needed to do was wait. And so we did. Soon enough, it will be truly over—everywhere. You will be forced from all lands where Allah smiles. You are, in fact, already defeated; you simply have not recognized it. This so-called democracy you tried to seed in my country and others has been strangled at birth. By the time you and your army recognize the noose, it will be too late. Until then, everything is as Allah wills, in Allah's time—as it should be."

With that, he jerked back in his chair, then fell forward over his hands with the motion of the ship. He landed so hard, his forehead smacked into the edge of the table, directly in front of the steel bar. The top of his head and his body jerked once, twice, then stilled.

"Doctor? Are you okay?" She snapped her stare to the doorway, but couldn't see Riyad. Nor had she heard the outer compartment's watertight door reopen. The Marine was still in front of his desk, standing guard. "Corporal! Get Dr. Mantia! *Now*."

She was dimly aware of Vetter yanking the sound-powered phone off its hook and barking into it as she vaulted up onto the table, her knees slamming into the manila folder. By the time she'd grabbed the doctor's shoulders to shove him up and away from her, Marine Corps camouflage was already thundering in on her left.

If Durrani had been poisoned—

Twin, thick jets of hot blood instantly drowned that possibility as they squirted up and out from two mangled holes at opposite sides of the man's neck, splashing across her forehead, over her cheeks and damned near into her eyes.

Instinct combined with relentless training and the time-tested reality of combat as she shoved her thumbs into Durrani's neck, digging in at his pulse points.

A fresh round of scarlet burst forth regardless, this time coating her jaw and neck as it arced down into her ACU top. She could feel the blood dripping beneath her tee shirt and soaking into her bra as she dug her thumbs in deeper. But Durrani's neck was also with slick with blood, forcing her to readjust her grip.

"Damn it, Doc, stop pulling away!"

The bastard just stared at her—and smiled. That blasted serenity had returned too, and it was directed solely at her.

"Vetter, get his cuffs." If he could get Durrani free and laid out on the deck, she could turn the physics of gravity and pressure into their favor.

The Marine worked as rapidly as he could, but the blood was still squirting out through those mangled holes with each beat of the man's heart. There was less and less force behind each jet, too. Less and less blood splashing into her neck and chest.

*Shit.*

She didn't need Colonel Tarrington's vaunted skills, much

less a formal autopsy, to confirm that Dr. Durrani had managed to shred both his carotids. The proof was in his blood. Most of it was outside the bastard's body now—coating her.

Slicking those damned cuffs.

Between slippery steel and the scarlet stain still spreading out over the rolling deck, it was impossible for the Marine to keep his grip.

What the hell had Durrani used to cut himself with anyway?

But, deep down, she knew. Just as she knew this entire, senseless fiasco was her fault. She should have made the connection sooner. Before the doc's lap had begun to fill with his own blood.

The cuffs finally clicked open and fell away. A split second later, half the ship's medical department barreled into the brig, and then the cell. Dr. Mantia and the beefy corpsman from the conference room that morning were in the lead.

Behind them, and coming up fast, a livid Riyad.

She ignored the spook and concentrated on the splatter of red now barely bubbling forth as Vetter worked around her hands, hooking his arms behind Durrani's neck and knees so he could lift and lay the man out into the ocean of his own blood. But she could tell—even before the *Griffith*'s physician reached her side and knelt to assess the situation, shook his head, resigned himself to the reality—it was too late.

The bastard beneath her thumbs had already given her his last fucking smile...and died.

# 15

"What the hell have you done, *woman*?"

Riyad.

Regan leaned back on the heels of her bloodstained boots and stared up at the NCIS agent, silent. Resigned. With everything that had happed, she couldn't even screw up anger over that slur. And that word, from this man, in that tone of voice?

"Woman" was definitely a slur.

At the moment, she just couldn't give a crap. Unfortunately, Vetter did.

The Marine jackknifed to his feet and stepped up into the spook's face. "Agent Chase didn't do a blessed thing, sir, except try and save the bastard. I saw it *all*."

Even Riyad backed down beneath that righteous fire. He took several paces to his left so he could level that scowl on her again. "How the fuck did Durrani even—"

"The scissors."

It took a moment for her quiet words to cut through Riyad's seething ire. Suspicion quickly followed. "What are you talking about? What scissors?"

The ones Petty Officer Nguyen probably hadn't even realized were missing because the corpsman had been so rattled by the black eye that Durrani had given her during the suture removal. The scissors Riyad would have known about if he'd stuck around up on the flight deck earlier instead of grabbing the microTLC out from under her and slinking down to the master-at-arms shack to fire it up all by himself.

She would've explained now, but Riyad had already turned away, executing a slow, three-hundred-sixty-degree, searching turn made even slower by the rolling deck and the slick ocean of red spreading further and further out around them.

The spook finally circled back to her, his standard filthy expression locked into place. "Unless they're beneath the body, there are no scissors."

Regan nodded toward the doc's coveralls. Vast swaths of the dark blue twill covering his torso, abdomen and thighs were darker still from all that wet, glistening blood. "Check his sleeves, up inside the cuffs."

Dr. Mantia passed a pair of sterile latex gloves to the spook.

Riyad accepted them, his stony stare rife with disbelief as he donned the protective gear. Hunkering down, he carefully tucked the fingers of his left hand beneath the cuffs crowning Durrani's right and fished around. His suspicion faded, though not completely, as he slowly slid a pair of Littauer suture removal scissors out from beneath the fabric.

Constructed of stainless-steel, they were roughly five inches in length, with the slightly parted blades taking up at most an inch, an inch and a half of that. A tiny—and in light of what had just happened—ominously scarlet-coated hook formed the tip of one end.

Several distinctly relieved sighs filled the compartment, momentarily competing with the creaking of the ship. None of them belonged to her.

Though the prints on those scissors would exonerate her, possibly even in Riyad's eyes, she knew better.

Tonight *had* been her fault.

If she hadn't been rejoicing in relief over that strychnine and what its presence meant for John—and, yes, if she hadn't also been in such a rush to clear him so she could bring John into this very cell and use him against the bastard now lying dead at her knees—she'd have given more thought to what Chief Yrle had said about how the suture removal incident had gone down.

Specifically, how Durrani had bashed his skull into the corpsman's eye.

The bastard hadn't been taking out his anger on Petty Officer Nguyen over her lack of interest in his flirting, much less his arrest back in Charikar and present incarceration aboard the *Griffith*—and pending lengthier incarceration elsewhere.

Nor had the Afghan doc been obsessed with any coming "physical" questioning. There was no reason. He'd already decided on his out.

His new, impromptu plan would get him out of any manmade prison and send him straight to Paradise for his first face-to-feet with Allah—seventy-two virgins and a river of milk and honey included, or not. Either way, Durrani had bided his time, waiting until the last possible moment, and then he'd distracted the corpsman with panic and pain. If the corpsman had discovered the scissors' absence in her kit, she probably assumed she'd dropped them as she'd hurried back to sickbay.

Durrani had then used the ensuing commotion to hide the scissors inside his sleeve. He'd been praying over that Qur'an, all right. Praying that no one would notice that the modest blades were missing and circle back to his cell before he was ready to use them.

That was why he'd begun demanding her presence before she'd even made it back aboard the *Griffith*. He'd planned on ripping through his carotids and bleeding out in front of her all along. One last *fuck you* to the States—and her.

And why her? Because he knew it would affect her more than most.

And it was.

She might be kneeling back on the heels of her boots, using the leg of the interrogation table for balance against the rolling ship as she stared into that smooth, pretty-boy face, somehow even smoother and prettier in death, but she was focused on another face, one that had also been covered in blood. A downright beautiful face with dark, glassy and sightless eyes that had looked so very much like Durrani's did now the last time she'd seen them. As she'd cried and begged their owner to stay with her.

*Don't leave her alone.*

"Agent Chase?"

The image evaporated.

Regan blinked up at the master-at-arm chief standing beside her. When had Yrle entered the cell? And was it her imagination, or had helo ops been called yet again?

Surely they weren't preparing to transport the body already?

She left those mysteries alone and settled for a simpler, more manageable query. "Yes?"

The woman extended a hand.

"Thank you." But she could stand on her own. To prove it, she tightened her grip on the edge of the table and used it for leverage as she stood. "I'm fine."

"No, ma'am, you're not. You're in shock. And you're covered in the deceased's blood."

She stared at her hands, her camouflaged sleeves and trousers. The chief was correct. She and her ACUs were saturated with blood. Evidence.

*Shit.*

She drew on more raw experience than any death investigator should ever want as she pulled herself together long enough to manage a nod. "Chief, please accompany me to my stateroom." She turned to the spook, grateful the ship's rolls had lessened in strength while she'd been dazed. Someone up on the bridge must've ordered another course change, possibly for that chopper. If they hadn't, shaky as her legs were, she'd have fallen flat on her face. "Agent Riyad, take charge of the scene. Have the duty master-at-arms meet the chief and me at my stateroom with a crime scene kit. The chief will photograph me and take my uniform into evidence. You do the same with Corporal Vetter."

As much as it burned to release the scene to the spook, she had no choice.

Despite her questions and suspicions about Riyad's loyalties, it wasn't as though she could work the coming investigation. Especially, as the chief had so forthrightly pointed out, with the deceased's blood still covering her. And there was the crucial matter of her part in that blood's current location.

To her surprise, Riyad nodded, but remained silent.

Then again, if the man was dirty, he was unquestionably looking forward to operating without her peering over his shoulder—as he'd done with that microTLC.

Fortunately, she had a plan for that too. "Chief?"

"Yes, ma'am?"

"Let's go."

Riyad and the ship's doctor stepped aside so she could pass.

She paused briefly beside the Marine to offer a quiet, "Thank you," for the corporal's assistance and support with Durrani... and Riyad's inexplicable, accusatory rage.

The corporal nodded, and she left.

It was a good thing the chief was accompanying her, because her brain was so rattled she wasn't sure she'd have made it through the maze of dimly lit passageways and ladders to reach her stateroom, now gently rolling ship or not. The red lighting was a boon though, since it effectively obscured the blood on her uniform and body.

But it was still there. She could feel it.

Pretty soon, she'd be forced to see it.

Watch it turn pink and circle down the drain, as it had when she'd taken that other, fateful shower when she was six.

If the bridge had ordered up a new course because of their latest helo ops, she prayed the *Griffith* stayed on it. Her gut was clenched tightly enough as it was. She was freezing now, too. And her hand was trembling. Badly.

Whether she wanted to admit it or not, Yrle was right.

She was in shock.

Fortunately, the duty master-at-arms had beaten them to her quarters.

Both the pretty Latina petty officer and the chief waited patiently as she fumbled past her sidearm and into her upper right ACU trouser pocket to locate the key to the stateroom's door. She could feel both women trying not to stare as she made her first, then second unsuccessful stab at the lock. Her third attempt failed as well, and so spectacularly that she was forced to bring in her left hand for backup and support.

The key seated on the fourth try...eventually.

Humiliation singed her cheeks as she led the way into the stateroom. Unable to handle the stark condemnation that the glare of bright, white light would bring, she bypassed the over-heard switch near the door. The desk flap was still down from her interview with Staff Sergeant Brandt, the bulk of her clothing and gear packed in the tan duffel she'd dumped on the lower of the bunkbeds upon her arrival that morning.

She reached into the void exposed by the desk flap and switched on the significantly softer, dimmer glow within.

It was still too much.

She could clearly see the blood staining her entire left hand as she tossed her keys onto the bottom mattress beside her duffel, then reached for her SIG Sauer.

Her pride took another knock as she attempted to slide the 9mm from its holster—and failed. She pulled her air and her determination in deep and tried again.

Relief seared in with her admittedly wobbly success.

The 9mm followed the keys to the mattress. By the time she'd managed to remove her holster and retrieve her CID credentials, and set those on the bed as well, the duty petty officer was heading out of the stateroom, the door closing behind her.

Chief Yrle moved up to the desk flap and readied her gloves and gear. She snapped several photos of Regan while she stood quietly beside the desk, fighting the urge to reach out and use the flap for support.

Photographic documentation complete, the chief tucked her phone in her pocket. "Would you like me to remove your boots?"

As awkward and embarrassing as that was bound to be, "Please."

She'd clearly taxed her hand and shredded nerves enough, because the former was now shaking so hard, the tremors had spread into her upper arm.

Regan sank into the chair she'd used to interview Brandt and Vetter and closed her eyes against the shame of it all as Yrle knelt to deal with the laces of her boots before removing both with a steady swiftness she envied. "Thank you, Chief."

The woman stood. Nodded.

Regan came to her feet and allowed Yrle to assist her in peeling away her ACU top and trousers, as well as the blood-stained tee shirt and bra beneath. She was left standing in her socks and underwear and trying to shield her scarlet-smeared breasts as the chief finished placing her clothing in separate evidence bags, then sealed them.

"Ma'am? Would you like me to remain for a bit? At least until you've showered?"

The request was gentle, and for once, the pity simmering within those soft green eyes didn't piss her off. Possibly because it was genuine and coming from another woman. But more likely, it was because she simply needed it.

Either way, Regan shook her head. Then wished she hadn't. The sharp motion had affected the roiling in her gut.

Damned if the spook wasn't right. She should've skipped dinner.

For a blinding moment, the coffee, eggs and toast appeared bent on returning from whence they'd come. Fortunately, the moment—and urge—passed.

"Thank you, but no. I need you bird-dogging Agent Riyad. Watch that man, Chief, every second. Tell him I ordered you to assist him. I need to know if anything unusual occurs during the investigation or with his procedures. *Anything.*"

The woman didn't bat an eye.

"You don't seem surprised."

"Nope."

"Why?" There. Nice and open ended. And with the tremors that had overtaken her entire arm and the numbness that had settled in everywhere else—including her sluggish brain—it was also all she could manage. But she needed an answer.

She needed to know if she could trust the chief.

"Ma'am, Agent Riyad's hiding something."

So Yrle felt it, too. More importantly, given that clear gaze and supporting micro-expressions, the chief was telling the truth.

"What?"

Frustration furrowed Yrle's brow. "I can't put my finger on it. But it's there. And it's big."

Agreed. But dare *she* risk doing so out loud?

Regan was prevented from making a decision when a round of quiet raps reverberated from the other side of the stateroom door.

A low voice penetrated the metal. "Agent Chase? Are you in there?"

*Mantia.*

She couldn't face another doctor. Not now. She doubted she'd have been able to face Gil tonight, let alone a physician who had the ear of the *Griffith*'s captain. Not with her entire arm haphazardly jolting under its own stubborn steam.

Worse, her father's DNA had failed her for the first time in a long time. The proof was in that fresh round of compassion swimming through those sharp green eyes.

The compassion and the green disappeared as the chief turned toward the tiny connected shower and toilet area, and stepped inside. A moment later, the shower's spray kicked in. The chief stepped out and headed across the short end of the stateroom, stopping behind the door's hinges and in front of Regan as she cracked the portal open just far enough for her to hook her short crop of inky curls and face through the opening. "She's fine, Doc. Just stepped in the shower. But I could use your help carrying a few things, if you don't mind. I need to get back to the scene."

"Absolutely. I must return, too. But I wanted to make sure I wasn't needed here."

"The agent's good to go. Just a sec, please." Yrle closed the door, pressing a silent index finger into her lips as she headed down the length of the stateroom. She paused beside the bunkbeds and unzipped the duffel. The woman evidently found what she was looking for—the shower kit—because she opened it as she stood, then traded the kit for the evidence bags she'd left on the desk.

Yrle returned to the door and passed the bagged clothing through to the doc, then went to the desk to retrieve the crime scene kit the duty master-at-arms had left behind. Kit in hand the chief caught Regan's eye and murmured, "You have my office and stateroom extensions. Please feel free to use them. Anytime."

"I will." But she wouldn't, and they both knew it. "Five, four, six, two. That's the passcode on my phone. You'll need it to access the voice recording from tonight's...session."

Those numbers would be used, however, which they both also knew.

The chief offered a crisp nod and left.

Cognizant of that running, potable water, a commodity that was surely in rationed supply aboard a warship, Regan retrieved her opened shower kit and headed for the small sink just outside the bathroom. With her hand and entire arm still quivering freely, she opted for dumping the contents directly into the sink and fishing out the bar of soap and her loofa rag, then glanced up into the mirror.

It was a mistake.

The chief hadn't been lying. She was covered in blood. It was in her hair, smeared across her forehead, her cheeks, her chin—all the way down her neck and over her shoulders and breasts. Hell, it was even on her lips and in the corner of her mouth.

*Durrani's blood.*

Her stomach lurched. Even now, the bastard was touching her.

Everywhere.

The shaking in her hand and arm grew worse. Hell, her entire body was quaking now. Violently. Even her teeth were chattering.

It seemed Yrle had been spot on with her first aid assessment, too. She was in definitely in shock. And it was getting worse.

Regan was certain as she grabbed her travel-sized bottle of shampoo with her normal hand and headed straight into the shower without testing the temperature.

Yet another mistake. The water was so hot she could feel it scalding her skin—and yet she was freezing. Somehow, she managed to release her braid from its confines and peel away her socks and underwear, then set about scrubbing every inch of her body with the loofa rag until her flesh was raw.

It didn't help.

She could see the final vestiges of the bastard's blood swirling down the shower's drain. Just as it had that day two decades ago. The day her mother had blown her own brains out with her dad's .38 backup revolver.

Durrani was right. Her mom had chosen to end her pain and misery in front of the towering fir that they'd finally decorated together that morning.

Throughout the years, she'd wondered if her mom had thought the location of her demise through. Surely, she had to have realized her six year old would find her there? Though even if the woman had realized it, Regan doubted her mother would've known that same six year old would also find her still alive, though barely—and be utterly, frantically, desperate to stop the flow of blood as she'd tried to put the pieces of her mother's face back together.

She'd failed then too.

She'd thought confronting and working John's first sergeant's suicide back at Fort Campbell had been bad. Tonight was far worse.

Regan leaned back against the wall of the shower as the memories shredded in once again. It wasn't enough to keep her already shaking legs from buckling completely. She slid down the wall and huddled into the corner, closing her eyes as she fought the renewed agony and horror of it all. She had no idea how long she sat there, cowering beneath that scalding spray, in the darkness of her own making, praying the water would heat up that much more and scorch away the layers of skin and the gnawing, empty pain that had overtaken her world, until there was nothing left to feel.

Nothing left of her.

But the water didn't get hotter. It vanished, instantly and completely.

Her unwelcome reprieve continued in the form of a pair of scarred, oversized hands attached to thick, muscular arms. Before she realized what was happening, they'd reached into the shower stall, wrapped themselves around her shaking body and lifted her up to set her on her feet.

*John*?

Either she was dreaming, or she'd finally lost it, because the mottled, roping scar crawling up the arm that supported her waist definitely belonged to the man she'd been missing for the past eight days. Hell, the past sixteen months.

She knew John wasn't really there. He couldn't be.

Not with Riyad calling the shots.

Crazy or not, she gave herself up to the fantasy of having the one man on this earth that she not only trusted, but needed, guide her out of the tiny bathroom before enveloping her shivering torso in the white terrycloth towel that'd been hanging from a ring beside the sink all day. All too quickly, John shifted the cloth and used it to dry her face and limbs. The towel fell away, and then her arms were being lifted and threaded through a tan uniform tee that, for some reason, fell midway down her thighs.

Not only was the tee too long, it was seriously baggy and it smelled like John.

He was definitely there, towering over her. As the numbing mist began to clear from her brain, she could make out that massive, naked torso, along with the dozen other thick, snaking scars where molten shrapnel and jagged metal had ripped through his flesh—as well as the five rounder, even more chilling, cicatrices created by the barrage of bullets that had nearly ended John's life the night his team's chopper had been shot down, then ambushed in Afghanistan eight years ago.

"What—"

"*Shhh.* Let me finish." He pressed his lips to her damp forehead, then turned her around, guiding her quaking fingers down to the edge of the sink for support before he retrieved the towel and used it to soak up the excess water from her hair. He plucked the wide-toothed comb from the nest of items in the sink next and carefully worked the tangles from the strands that hung more than halfway down her back.

Tangles dealt with, he tossed the comb into the sink and engulfed her shaking fingers in his steady grip as he led her to the bunkbeds. Once there, he shifted her duffel down onto the deck with his free hand. Clipping her sidearm, holster, keys and credentials from the lower mattress, he set those on the temporary desk, then turned to tug the sheet and blanket to the foot of the bunkbed.

"Hop in."

"I don't—"

The determination in his eyes intensified, deepening the gray as his hand came up to snag her chin. "Am I going to have to pull rank?" That deep dimpled fold she'd missed so very much slipped in amid his two weeks of unruly beard, softening the query.

But the determination held.

He followed up both with a gentle nod and gentler nudge toward the mattress. "In you go."

That stubbornness wasn't about to bend, and she didn't have the strength left to argue. Not after the barrage of memories that had pummeled in during her shower.

She crawled into the bed.

To her surprise and shamefully profound relief, John followed, carefully shifting her body over as he wedged his titanic frame in beside her, trousers, size-fifteen combat boots and all. He was using his body as he had in his driveway when his irate houseguest had shown up after dinner. Only here, now, he was deliberately shielding her from the ship and what had happened aboard it tonight...as best he could.

It was working.

Her back was to the outer bulkhead of the vessel, her face pressed up against his battered chest as he pulled her close, wrapping those solid, cocooning arms around her. All she could see was that endless expanse of muscle and those crisscrossing scars.

Damn, she'd missed them.

She closed her eyes and melted into his support. Given what they were and were not wearing, and more importantly, *where* they were, this should have felt wrong. But it didn't. If anything, it felt so very right it was terrifying. She was as human as the next soldier, female or not. She'd needed another before. But lately?

She'd needed *him*.

She had no idea how long she remained there, cradled against the length of his body, absorbing the soothing drum of his heart and the musky, lulling warmth of his skin. Eventually, the shards of ice that had begun to splinter into her bones before she'd even reached the stateroom began to thaw. The trembling eased. Even her arm relaxed.

Her fingers were still quivering off and on, but the tremors were subtle now. So much so, she could almost pretend they didn't exist.

Almost.

"You okay?"

The words rumbled against her forehead, cheeks and lips. She refused to open her eyes, but she did shake her head in answer as she resigned herself to the truth. She had no choice. She could lie to the entire world with ease, even lie to herself.

But not to this man. Never again.

"I fucked up."

"You did not."

She appreciated the support. But, yeah, she had.

More than she'd ever feared possible.

Nor had she needed that verbal accusation Agent Riyad had flung in her face when he'd vaulted into the brig, because she'd already internalized it.

John shifted, allowing just enough air between them so that he could hook his fingers beneath her chin and use them to gently force her to meet his stare.

The determination had returned. And it was darker and more firmly entrenched than before. "You did *not* do this. There was no way you could've known that bastard had those scissors. This is on Brandt and Vetter. And, trust me, they know it. Vetter's already taken responsibility. The corporal knew Durrani was getting his stitches out. But he was so focused on getting that rattled corpsman out of the cell after Durrani slammed into her, he didn't even think about scissors until he was laying the man's body out on the deck—just as that bastard of a doc intended."

Silence settled in as John finished.

She left it lying between them, punctuated by the rhythmic creaking of the piping and venting in the compartment.

"I mean it, Rae."

That much was clear by the insistent storm that had overtaken his stare. But how had John even found out about Durrani and those scissors? Hell, why was he even here, in her stateroom and not his? He hadn't left on his own, had he?

For a split second, trepidation reigned.

John shook his head. "Palisade."

Great, first Yrle, and now this man was reading her mind. Frankly, she preferred the former. Because there were far too many things she never wanted John to discover, much less from her.

Still, the panic eased.

"I assume the general came aboard during that last helo ops?" The one the bridge had called away while she'd been standing over Durrani's body, definitely more rattled than the suture-removing corpsman had been.

John nodded. "His plane had just touched down at Andrews Airbase when he got the word about what I'd done to Hachemi. Palisade had it refueled and a fresh pilot and crew brought onboard, and immediately took off for Al Dhafra. The ship sent their second Super Stallion out to grab him while you and Riyad were on the carrier for Hachemi's autopsy."

Hachemi's autopsy—

But John had not only read her mind again, he was already nodding. "*Strychnine*." Disgust filtered through the gray, blackening it as he shook his head. "Hell, I never denied wanting to shut that bastard up so badly that I snapped. I admit I intentionally cracked his face into that bulkhead. But poison? There is no way I'd feed anyone that cowardly shit. Palisade knows it, too. When he found out that Riyad still had me confined to quarters, he went ballistic. Ordered my release on the spot."

From there, John had headed directly here.

That was churning through the black clouds too. Along with the rest. John being told what Durrani had done in front of her tonight...and how he'd accomplished it. Thank God John hadn't arrived before she'd managed to scrub the blood from her face. She wasn't sure she could've handled his seeing her like that.

Though really, finding her on the floor of the shower, cowering in the corner, couldn't have been much better, could it? For either of them.

"You know...I've never killed a man before."

Oh, after nearly nine years in the Army, she'd seen plenty die. And as an MP and then CID, she'd dealt with the fallout of far too many additional deaths. She'd even shot two men over the years. But, somehow, she'd managed to never actually kill one.

Until tonight.

"Rae, that bastard killed himself. Even Riyad was forced to admit that Durrani intentionally committed suicide."

Part of her wanted to believe him, desperately. The rest just couldn't quite get there.

If a lie of omission was still a lie, surely failing to notice that a man was primed to slit his throat and bleed out in front of her —and had obtained the means to do it—was just as bad as wielding those scissors herself. Especially since she'd had the training and know-how to prevent it. And then there was that mood of Durrani's tonight.

From the moment she'd entered the cell and up until almost the very end, he'd been relaxed, content. Almost...happy. If she hadn't been so determined to a get a name—any one of those names—she'd have understood why in time to stop him.

Yeah, she'd killed him. And, deep down, she was left wondering if she'd wanted to.

John slid a finger beneath her chin and tipped it up. "*Stop*—and that is an order." But it wasn't from the major lying in her bed, holding her. It was from the man.

Before she could argue with either one, both had pulled her in again.

The arm beneath the right side of her head held her close. The hand attached to the other slid slowly up and down her spine. Soothing, comforting. Because he believed she needed it. The worst part was, she did.

She buried herself deeper into his chest, thoroughly embarrassed that she'd let her guard down so completely. That she'd let this man, of all men, see her as weak.

And then it sank in.

She was holding him, too, comforting him. When she felt his body quake, she knew exactly what had caused it—who.

Hachemi.

Less than an hour ago, John had discovered that he wasn't guilty of outright murdering the man. But the raw, deep-seated knowledge that he was truly capable of it would haunt him for the rest of his life. Because there was a profound difference between being willing to kill for your country and *wanting* to.

The line that separated the two was wide and dark, and distinct.

Even so, far too many civilians would never see it, much less understand it. But every single soldier did—especially the honorable ones.

Because they lived and worked squarely on top of it.

"We don't have a damned thing, Rae, do we?"

This time, she pulled away. Just far enough to smooth her palm over the unruly whiskers that shadowed the right side of his jaw. The trio of shrapnel scars that cut into the thicket at the edge and down into his neck tightened, causing the pulse point within to throb. Despite their current position and location, that uptick hadn't been caused by passion, but a deep, leaden resignation.

That, at least, she could soothe, and perhaps offer a bit more.

Something akin to hope.

"Actually, we do have something." And wouldn't Durrani have been horrified and livid to discover that she'd gotten it all from him?

John added to the slight distance between them so that he could focus on her face. His was wreathed in shock. "Are you telling me that you got a name?"

"No. But I did get the next best thing. Three *separate* avenues of investigation." Or culling clues, as Agent Castile would term them. First up, "The seventh woman from the cave. We already knew she was crucial to whatever's still scheduled to go down. Durrani's fixation on her—and the fact that he carefully tucked the photo I gave him of her earlier today in his Qur'an to keep it safe—proves it." For all the man's heinousness, Nabil Durrani wasn't some serial killer who'd been polishing a trophy, at least not in the traditionally morbid sense. "I developed a suspicion that there was a personal connection between the two. A suspicion Durrani confirmed when I tossed it in his face—and he visibly flinched. Not only did Durrani know the woman, he was in love with her. I'm also certain they worked together in some capacity."

She'd stake the future status of her hand tremors on it.

John nodded. "This is good. *Great*, in fact. Plus, we've already got Agent Castile working the medical clinics and relief organizations on both sides of the border."

"I know. But he's going to need a lot more help." Beginning with those boots on the ground with which she'd taunted Durrani. "They need to be armed with that photo from the cave; the one that shows the deceased baby. It'll help people talk." Especially those inclined to protect a radical Muslim at all costs. "Also, while there is a traitor mixed up in all this, Tamir Hachemi never had his or her name."

"Are you sure?"

Doubt had elbowed into his stare, knocking up against the relief.

She understood why.

As much as John was afraid to believe in Hachemi's ignorance, he desperately wanted to. It would mean his actions in that conference room this morning hadn't obliterated their final chance at obtaining that traitor's name. John had to be wondering—just as she had during the autopsy—that if Hachemi had experienced the full brunt of those agonizing, strychnine-induced convulsions and realized he was about to die, would he have had a come-to-Allah moment and given up that name?

Unfortunately, wallowing in what ifs wouldn't get them anywhere. Much less a blessed inkling of what was scheduled to go down...and when.

"Yeah, I'm sure. Hachemi did not know who the traitor is. Durrani's suicide proves it. The doc's imagination was working overtime today. He added my appearance on the ship this morning to the sudden spurt of subsequent helo ops and connected them to Hachemi's apparent disappearance, as well as my subsequent departure from the ship this evening for the autopsy. His result: CIA. Durrani believed Hachemi spent the day being interrogated—and tortured—aboard another, nearby vessel by a bunch of viciously determined spooks. Yet, he wasn't worried about what Hachemi may or may not have given up—because he knew the man had nothing to give up. Durrani also believed that he was next. And although Hachemi didn't know the traitor's name—"

"Durrani did."

"Exactly." But Hachemi had known something. Something worth killing for. Otherwise, why risk so much just to shut him up? Unfortunately, with Hachemi now dead, they might never know what the man had been privy too.

Just one more frustratingly, potentially critical mystery to solve.

Damn.

Regan arched her neck to work out a kink that had set in from holding her head aloft to meet John's gaze.

"Okay. Durrani was terrified *he'd* talk under torture, and he was willing to die to ensure he didn't. That's explains why he killed himself. But I'm not sure how knowing that helps us get the information we need." John brought his right hand up to her neck to rub the affected side for a few moments, then shifted his left arm to support her head better. Both helped more than her stretching had. "You mentioned three lines of investigation. If this is one of them, as near as I can tell, that bastard succeeded in killing it, along with himself."

That he had. But Durrani had left another clue on the table. Though this one was more than a bit humiliating. "Mata Hari."

John stilled, then blanched. He shook his head.

But she nodded. "Once I got him spun up, the doc lobbed a lot of crap in my face, including that name. He was also a bit... gleeful...as he accurately relayed why that name and the implication behind it were significant to me."

*Whore.*

Just over two weeks ago, when John had been on the psyche ward at Fort Campbell along with his remaining, chimeral-infected men, she'd assured him that she'd gotten over the tawdry insinuation he'd smeared her with that night in Hohenfels' CID parking lot. She'd lied.

She truly didn't care if the entire world spewed that word directly in her face.

But John? With him, even the implication managed to burn a hole through her confidence and her heart...every single time she thought about it.

She'd worked to mask the pain that had come with the

memory when they'd been back at Campbell on that psych ward. But here, now? Even before she caught the hurt reflecting back at her from John, she knew she'd already failed.

She was too raw to even try.

His fingers came up to smooth a damp strand of hair from her cheek. By the time he'd tucked it behind her ear, his fingers were trembling more than hers. "Hon—"

"Don't. Please. I don't want to talk about that right now. I just...can't."

It didn't matter that her voice had quavered at the end. His nod wasn't all that steady either.

"Okay, we'll table it. But we will come back to this. Soon."

Not if she could help it.

The heaviness in their sighs merged, underscored by the subdued creaking of the ship, the combined humming of all that machinery.

Somehow, the *Griffith* had become white noise on steroids.

"John...you know what this means, don't you?"

This sigh was sharper and curt enough to cut through any noise. "This plot's been in the works a helluva lot longer than we thought."

"Yup."

And for some reason, John was at the center of it.

As near as she could tell, the only person left who had an inkling as to *why* was the spook—and Riyad's mouth was locked up even more tightly than those of their two recently deceased prisoners had been, combined.

"Did Durrani give a clue as to who might've overheard that conversation?"

She shook her head. At the time, she and John had assumed they were alone. After all, it had been three in the morning. But the CID lot had also had police vehicles and half a dozen massive Humvees slotted in that night, offering plenty of cover.

And the section they'd been in had been dark. "I don't even know if he or she was Army." Hell, they ran Marines through the Joint Multination Readiness Center at Hohenfels, too. And there was the whole "multinational" aspect to consider.

Not to mention that during the week in question, the JMRC had been training roughly twenty-two hundred soldiers a day.

According to John's terse frown, all of the former had been tallied up by him, too. "Talk about a needle in a haystack."

And not only was the haystack camouflaged, so was the needle.

Fortunately, Durrani had slipped up more than once tonight. And this "culling clue" was a seriously revealing one.

"We have a leak."

John's frown deepened. "Who?"

"I don't know. But he or she knows me. Or, at least, my background. I'm guessing I attracted attention that night by extension when they saw me with you, because whoever was watching decided to go snooping. In the classified arena. A lot of the crap Durrani lobbed could only have come from my background investigation. How else would he have known about my mom's suicide—in front of the damned tree—and my dad's desire to walk on the dark side of the law while he was still employed by it?"

"*Jesus.*" John's frown had mutated into a dangerously filthy scowl that put every one of Riyad's to shame. "Even I didn't know some of that until you told me."

She nodded. Even with his Special Forces connections, John hadn't known the truth about her bastard of a father until he'd spotted her dad's old police badge on her coffee table and run the number through the internet the following day during a down moment at Bagram. John hadn't known the tawdry details of her mother's death at all, until she'd told him. How could he? Her mom had reverted the two of them to her maiden name shortly before she'd checked out in front of that Christmas tree.

The tree that John also hadn't known about.

Nor should anyone else in the Army—or any other branch of the military. Because she'd never shared that particular tidbit. "That's not all. Because of Durrani's arrest and then my coma, I didn't have a chance to follow up on something. But the night before we arrested Durrani, I interrogated Captain McCord."

"I know."

"But what you don't know is that McCord threw those three orange hairs in my face during the interview." Hairs that had been found in that cave. Hairs that belonged to one of McCord's men. Except, the soldier who'd grown those hairs had died two weeks before those women had been massacred. Like her, McCord believed the presence of those hairs in the cave proved that he and his men had been set up. While that was true...she'd never mentioned those hairs to McCord during their interview.

But someone had.

"Rae, I did not tell him about the hairs."

"I know that." She might've doubted John's integrity weeks ago, at the beginning of this investigation, but she didn't now. Nor would she again. Not after everything that'd happened since. And she sure as hell couldn't doubt John's integrity when he'd been willing to go to prison because he believed he'd killed Hachemi in anger.

"So, who told Mac? Do you know?"

She shook her head. "I have no idea. But if whoever leaked those hairs and the traitor are one and the same, we can track him or her through my BI."

Whoever had shared the contents of the background investigation that'd been run on her prior to the granting of her top secret clearance, had either pulled her BI and read it personally...or knew the person who had.

John scrubbed at the growth on his jaw as he blew out his breath. "What else did you get? Though I gotta say, that's a hell of a lot more than either I or your NCIS counterpart were able to ferret out, and we worked on those two bastards for a week."

And therein lay the rub. She still wasn't convinced that Riyad had wanted answers. Though his reaction tonight *had* gone a long way to refuting the suspicion.

If the spook was dirty, why had Riyad been so livid when he'd found Durrani dead in that cell tonight? He should've been relieved.

But he definitely hadn't been.

One thing was still certain, "Riyad thinks you're the traitor."

Of all the times for that dent of John's to carve into his cheek, this was not one she'd have figured was in the running. Then again, the smile it flanked was decidedly grim. "Yeah, I figured that out this past week. Would've said something to you earlier this morning but the man was standing right there. By the time he left to take that call, I figured I'd already tossed enough rotten meat onto your plate."

"Why would he even suspect you? For that matter, why would he risk entering that cell tonight when I was making progress with Durrani? Because he nearly did. Durrani pretended to make some offhand comment—but it was deliberate—about equipment, and Riyad almost vaulted through the door. I thought he was going to take Vetter down when the Marine moved in to stop him."

"Equipment?"

She nodded. "Possibly...lost equipment?"

John's hand made another pass through the unruly growth on his jaw. Anyone else might've deemed it identical to the first. It wasn't. There'd been a pause at the start. It had been almost infinitesimal. And, yet, that pause had reverberated through her gut like a bunker buster bomb going off deep inside a stateside hardened target.

John knew something. Something he was loath to share.

Even with her.

"John?"

Another pass though that unruly thicket.

The aftershocks multiplied. "You know why Riyad's got it out for you, don't you? And you know what Durrani meant by that comment. The two are tied together, aren't they?"

"I think so. I need to look into it first. Confirm a few things."

A few *classified* things. Otherwise, why not offer them up now, given everything that was going on?

"*Christ.*" That scarred hand made yet another pass, causing her gut to clamp down hard, because this pass had been followed up by an even more telling sigh. One that was almost a growl. "I need to get off this boat, Rae. Make a phone call in private, several in fact. Call in a few markers. Get some damned answers."

"And then?"

"And then I'll share. With you—and Palisade."

Another bunker buster dropped in, and this one exploded deeper still. If John hadn't even confided in the general yet, this was worse than she'd feared.

# 16

Her bed was moving.

No...rocking.

Regan kept her eyes closed, savoring the soothing motion as the fog of not nearly enough sleep ebbed, leaving behind a budding headache as well as the nagging need for caffeine that had caused it. She was still in her rack aboard the *Griffith*.

But John was not.

It had taken sixteen months, but she finally understood how he'd felt the night they'd slept together in Hohenfels. She'd heard his confusion and loss as he'd woken to an empty bed and called out for her...while she'd been sneaking out the back door.

Yes, she'd had an excellent reason for leaving then. And, yes, he'd had an equally solid reason as to why he'd slipped out of this metal cradle and her stateroom in the middle of the night. But that didn't make this cold emptiness any easier to bear.

Worse, she had all that remaining blood to confront.

The stains would've dried and would be set in by now, turning the tan leather of her combat boots a nauseating shade of rust. It was in the cracks and crevices of her sidearm too, along with her holster and her keys. Even her credentials had been embedded with Durrani's parting revenge.

Where she'd find the hydrogen peroxide to get it all out while trapped on a warship in the middle of the Arabian Sea, she had no idea.

Sickbay?

Not an option. Mantia would be there.

She'd successfully avoided the ship's doc last night, but only because of Chief Yrle's quick thinking and willingness to cover for her. She wouldn't be so lucky again. Not after the way her hand and forearm had begun to flail around like gasping fish out of water before she'd even left the brig. The doc would insist on examining her. Quite possibly, deem it necessary to shoot off an obligatory physician-to-physician assessment to Fort Campbell...and Gil.

If Mantia didn't opt instead to head directly to whichever stateroom Palisade had been assigned and rat out her decompensating psyche the moment the general woke.

What time *was* it?

Her alarm hadn't gone off. Regan felt for the wide, grosgrain band on her wrist. Her watch wasn't there. Confused, she opened her eyes.

Near pitch black greeted her.

John must've turned off the desk lamp prior to his departure. With the stateroom's porthole sealed shut, all she could make out on her wrist was the fact that her watch wasn't encircling it. Had she dumped that on her bed last night, too, and simply forgotten? Or had she taken it off in the shower and tossed it on the floor in front of the toilet, along with her socks?

Either way, it was just one more nauseating piece of gear to clean.

The only silver lining of the morning would be embedded in her clothes.

Since she'd had no idea of her destination when she'd packed for this trip back at Campbell, old habits had kicked in. She'd stuffed two additional sets of ACUs and two blue "CID" suits into her duffel, every one of them blessedly bloodstain free.

But the suits would need ironing. On a ship.

The camouflage won.

She was going to have to clean her boots anyway. God willing, she wouldn't have a follow-on meltdown in the process. Frankly, she didn't have the time. She had two Marine embassy guards, and a handful of chopper and Osprey pilots and their crews to interview. A murderer to find and a cave victim to identify. A traitor to locate.

A partner to investigate.

John wasn't the only one who desperately needed to get to a phone. One call to Mira Ellis and she'd have all the information she needed about Sam Riyad. Even if it took Mira trading in a few NCIS special agent markers of her own to get it.

Last night, shortly before John had pulled her back into his chest and gruffly ordered her to sleep, she'd told him about Riyad's end run around her planned chromatography tests on the coffee dregs with the microTLC Colonel Tarrington had loaned her—and especially how the disbelieving spook had rerun Tarrington's tests on the translator's blood with John's stained ACU top.

That hadn't seemed to surprise John either.

But he'd already asked for her patience while he conducted his own, unorthodox investigation into the spook, so she hadn't pressed it.

As for *her* investigations?

Regan swung her legs out of the bunk. The uniform tee John had removed from his torso last night so that he could use it to cover hers slid down to mid-thigh as she stood. With her eyes adjusted to the dark, she headed for the shadowy flap of steel that formed the stateroom's desk and reached into the void for the switch.

Her night vision evaporated on a flare of blinding white. She swung away from its source toward the chair John had shoved up against the end of the bunk as she willed her vision to readjust to the manmade light of day. It did. But as she spotted the boots on the deck, tucked between the chair's legs, and the nest of gear clustered together on its seat, she was forced to lean back into the wall unit for support.

It wasn't enough.

She slid all the way down the steel unit until her ass hit the gently rolling deck. Her vision blurred again as the tears welled up...and spilled over.

There she sat, for how long she did not know, absorbing the implications.

Sixteen months ago, between those torrid sessions in John's bed, he'd confessed that he'd rarely dated as a teenager and had stopped altogether at twenty after he'd discovered his sister was alive. Between caring for Beth, his commitment to the Army and getting his degree at night so he could get commissioned, he'd had very little spare time and even less desire to squander what he did have on anyone other than his sister. Once Beth had settled into college life, he'd dated a bit between deployments, but none of his relationships had gone well—especially his last.

His ex had ended things a year and a half earlier, at the eleventh hour on the eve of his deployment to Yemen, no less. When John had asked why, he'd discovered that he possessed a litany of selfish sins up to and including the fact that not only was he late for almost every date—the ones he didn't cancel outright—he'd never once marked a special occasion or anniversary. And he had *never* sent flowers.

Evidently his ex had finagled knowledge of the abuse he'd

suffered as a boy out of his sister and had decided that John just didn't have "normal" inside him.

In short, he was not, nor would he ever be, relationship material.

John had admitted the truth to Regan that night in his bed. He'd never thought about flowers, or cards and gifts. As for the other accusations his ex had tossed at him, she was right about those too. The job came first with him. It had to. His men's lives were on the line, his country's safety. He couldn't just drop what he was doing—especially when he was on a mission—to make a call or text.

Once his head was in the game, it stayed there. By the time he got back to camp, he was either writing up his after-action reports and too damned exhausted to do more than crash on a cot or a bedroll somewhere, or he was already prepping for the next push.

He'd thought his ex had understood.

But after that night, he'd gone over his paltry relationships in his head and had eventually admitted that maybe his ex was right. Maybe the way he'd grown up with his bastard of a father had scarred him. Permanently.

Hell, even when he was stateside, the gestures that women always seemed to want from him just...weren't inside him.

Regan hadn't argued with John then, nor could she argue with him now. Not until they'd had a chance to get to know each other better. John might be right. Flowers just might not be in his makeup. Ever. She had no problem with that. Wouldn't even miss them. Because as she stared at her keys, watch, boots, holster and sidearm—and, yes, even those CID credentials he still wasn't crazy about—she knew the gestures that were important to her were inside him. Several hours ago, her boots and her gear had been saturated with Nabil Durrani's blood...and now they weren't.

Every single item was spotless.

While she'd slept, John had gathered them up and taken them somewhere to eradicate every last trace of that monster, so she wouldn't have to. In the process he'd managed to burrow himself so deeply into her heart she suspected she'd never be able to get him out. The only question left was...did she want to?

Three light raps on her door offered a reprieve—from herself.

Unless they'd come from John.

"*Yes*?" Great. The tears had shredded her vocal cords.

"Sorry, ma'am. I didn't mean to wake you. I can come back."

*Yrle.*

She cleared her throat and tried again. "That's all right, Chief. I'm up. Just give me a minute to finish getting dressed."

Finish?

Regan glanced down at the baggy Army tee that clearly did not belong to her. She hadn't even begun to dress. What's more, with her face as blotchy as it was bound to be after that silent crying jag, normal voice or not, there'd be no doubt as to what she'd been doing in here.

She retrieved her watch first, glancing at the time as she wrapped the olive-drab grosgrain band around her wrist and velcroed it into place.

0713?

Good Lord. She didn't know if John had accidentally or deliberately killed her alarm while he'd been cleaning, but she'd overslept by nearly two hours.

She pulled herself together and swapped the man's rumpled uniform tee for one of her own and a fresh set of the ACUs in her duffel. She was dressed—boots, credentials, thigh-holstered sidearm included—in under two minutes. Making a beeline for the sink, she blew through another two as she collected the items within and shoved them in her hygiene kit so she could brush her teeth, wash her face and French braid her hair.

She was folding up the length of the latter and securing it at the nape of her neck with several pins as she reached the door.

Yrle stood on the opposite side, patiently holding Regan's iPhone.

"Morning, Chief."

"Good morning, ma'am." Yrle held out the phone. "Here you go."

Regan retrieved her electronic lifeline—at least on dry land and near accessible, abusable cellular towers—and noted the crevices around the black case. Like her boots and her gear, her phone was devoid of blood. "Thank you."

The chief shook her head. "It wasn't me. Major Garrison stopped by my office a few hours ago with your boots and sidearm. He took care of that too. But I hadn't yet had a chance to copy the audio file of the interview, so I held onto it after he left."

Regan nodded.

"Ma'am?"

A slight shiver scraped up Regan's spine as the chief glanced over her shoulder. "Yes?"

"Make sure you change your password...immediately."

The shiver intensified.

"Why?" But she knew.

*Riyad.*

Durrani must have hexed her DNA juju before he died, at least where this woman was concerned, because the chief nodded. Then rechecked her six. Satisfied that no one was behind her, listening, she swung back. "You asked me to watch for anything usual."

"And?"

"I caught him with your phone *after* I'd finished with the audio file."

The shiver morphed into an outright chill. "Do you know what he was looking at?"

"Yes, ma'am. He'd accessed one your text streams. The one between you...and Major Garrison. I was on the phone with Ops, arranging the flight for Durrani's autopsy, when he came into the shack. He saw me turn around before I hung up and quickly returned your phone to my desk, so I got curious. When he left, I typed in your password and the stream was still open. He hadn't had time to close it."

Why would he even look?

The moment John had departed the ICU back at Campbell, he'd gone into mission mode. She hadn't heard from him since.

Unlike his ex, she hadn't expected, or really wanted it. She'd known that whatever he'd been sent to do was serious or Palisade would never have pulled him from her hospital room three hours after she'd woken from that coma. Hence, she'd wanted John focused on whatever he'd needed to do. So he'd come back in one piece. Without any more scars on his body, or his soul, to show for it.

She'd even admitted to their comms drought with Agent Riyad yesterday, right in this stateroom.

Either the spook hadn't believed her...or Riyad had intentionally set out to search for the texts she'd saved on her phone. The texts John had sent sixteen months ago in Hohenfels, when she'd been using him to investigate his houseguest for plotting a terror attack...right around the time someone had also followed John to that CID parking lot.

The chill spread into an ice-cold void that settled low and heavy inside her. Dread began to seep in, filling it.

What the hell did John have on Riyad?

And what did Riyad believe he had on John?

And there was the personal violation against her—from a fellow agent and so-called current partner. Add on the standard creep factor and the invasion of privacy to the rest, and she was seriously pissed off.

But to rain down on Riyad would expose Yrle. Something she refused to do unless the situation became critical.

Regan nodded, carefully smoothing her facial features, despite her lingering ire and larger, looming concerns. "Thank you, Chief. We'll keep this between us."

Relief filled the woman's eyes. "Major Garrison asked me to pass a message along, too. He said you have a meeting with General Palisade in the ship's wardroom at 0800. If you'd like, we can head there now so you can eat breakfast first."

Regan glanced at her watch. She had almost forty minutes until that meeting.

More than enough time for what she needed to accomplish.

She shook her head, ignoring the dull throb that was already arguing with her coming counter proposal. Caffeine could wait. "Where are the guards?"

"Corporal Vetter just left for chow. Staff Sergeant Brandt's in sickbay."

"What's wrong with Brandt?" The Marine had seemed fine yesterday during their interview.

"The sea state got to him last night. You know what they say: the bigger they are, the harder they fall. He was so dehydrated from throwing up, he finally crawled into Medical early this morning. The doc still has him in one of their racks, hooked up to an IV. He should be good to go soon, especially since the seas have calmed considerably."

Hopefully, the doc would keep the staff sergeant connected to that IV for a bit longer. At least until she'd had a chance to snoop through the Marine's belongings—without Brandt in attendance. The corporal's, too.

Before John had ordered her to sleep last night, he'd told her the coffee Hachemi had consumed was already in the conference room when he'd arrived for their final interview. Which meant both guards were at the top of her suspect list, whether she wanted them there or not.

"Just a sec." Regan headed back into the stateroom to hook the fingers of her right hand around the handle of her crime scene kit. So far this morning, the digits appeared willing to cooperate with her brain. Accidental or not, she was thankful John had killed her alarm. The extra sleep had done her nerves a world of good.

Kit in hand, she closed the stateroom door behind her and locked it with considerably more finesse than she'd opened it with the night before.

"Let's go."

"Where to, ma'am?"

"Brandt's rack, then Vetter's." If the corporal had recently sat down to eat, there was more of a risk of the staff sergeant showing. Frankly, she'd prefer to keep both Marines ignorant of her activities and suspicions until the last possible moment.

Yrle nodded. "We put them up together in chief's country for security reasons. This way."

Regan followed the woman through the *Griffith*'s passageways, nodding a return greeting to half a dozen enlisted sailors and a butterbar ensign along the way.

Chief Yrle came to a halt beside a slim gray door and knocked once.

No response.

Selecting a key from the hefty ring attached to her waist, Yrle used it to unlock the door. She pushed it open, then hooked an arm inside to flip on the overhead lights. "After you, ma'am."

"Thank you." Regan preceded the woman inside.

The stateroom was nearly identical to hers, though slightly

smaller and with no private shower or latrine. The upper bunk had been neatly made up. The twisted sheets and blanket of the lower one, as well as the round metal trash can on the deck and tucked up near a mashed pillow, attested to its owner's nightlong ignoble activities.

As did the smell.

Though the tablespoon of water at the base of the gray can suggested it had been rinsed out via the stateroom's sink, the stench of vomit hung in the air.

No rush then.

And no wonder the quarters had been abandoned. She seriously doubted the staff sergeant who'd unwillingly created that odor or the corporal who'd been forced to endure it would be back anytime soon.

Regan set her crime kit on the deck and took a moment to reset the password on her phone before she opened her recording app. She stated her name and rank, as well as the chief's, and briefed the reason for her coming monologue as she and Yrle donned a pair of latex gloves. Beginning near the door, Regan described her activities for the recording as she began a systematic search of the metal wall unit, pausing to snap photos here and there along the way.

Unfortunately, she came up empty for contraband, let alone anything that looked as if it could have contained the poison that had been fed to Hachemi.

Uniforms, spare boots, laptop bags, duffels, as well as the carton of Pakistani smokes the staff sergeant appeared to prefer —they were all neatly stowed and devoid of strychnine.

She searched the bunkbeds next, hooking the toes of her boots up onto the metal edge of the lower rack so she could begin with the pristine upper one.

By the time Regan had climbed down, the corporal's bed was

in as much disarray as the staff sergeant's. It was also clean of contraband and suspect containers.

Her equally detailed search of the lower bunk revealed a curiosity...and a potential hiding spot. Two of the packs of Pakistani smokes that she'd come across during her canvass of the wall unit were half empty. So why was there a third pack of smokes tucked between the staff sergeant's mattress and the far bulkhead?

Regan brought the smokes with her as she climbed out of the nest of twisted sheets to stand beside the bed.

Chief Yrle frowned at the pack. "Brandt's smoking in bed?"

Based on the censure in the chief's voice, Regan assumed the activity was as advisable aboard ship as it was on dry land. Possibly less so. She opened the pack. All twenty cigarettes were accounted for. And, yet, this pack was heavier than the others. She tapped the smokes out into her gloved palm. All were less than half the length of the packaging...and there was a false bottom inside.

"Grab an evidence bag from my kit, please."

"Yes, ma'am."

Regan transferred the stunted smokes to the proffered bag, leaving Yrle to seal it as she carefully worked the false bottom free.

A small, dark blue bottle rolled out into her palm. She twisted off the lid and spotted traces of clear liquid in the tip of the attached eye dropper.

"*Strychnine*." Yrle's whisper filled the stateroom, stark with disappointment.

Given the stunted smokes and the hidden bottom?

"Yup."

Damn. She liked the burly Marine. But it appeared Brandt hadn't liked the translator. Possibly less than she and John had.

But premeditated murder?

Because that was precisely what this was shaping up to be.

Regan sighed as she closed the bottle. She snapped photos of the outside of the now empty pack of smokes and the bottle, then tucked both into the fresh evidence bag Yrle held up. She checked her watch.

0748.

Not enough time for the chromatography testing. Not unless she wanted to keep a general waiting. Something that, even during a murder/terror investigation, wasn't advisable. But she did have time for a few questions.

"Chief, did you get to know Staff Sergeant Brandt this past month?"

"Not really. Well, we did talk college football. We both have brothers who play, though mine's quite a bit younger than me."

"Same team?"

The woman snorted as she sealed the evidence bag. "Not even close. Brandt's a Longhorn fan. My brother's a Cornhusker."

A Cornhusker? Regan had no idea what that was, but a Longhorn? "Brandt's brother goes to UT—in Austin?"

Yrle nodded. "Is that important?"

It might well be. According the records she'd read on her flight to Bagram over two weeks ago, Captain McCord had received his commission from UT's Reserve Officer Training Corps program.

Coincidence?

Possibly. The University of Texas was a huge school. And the connection appeared to be solely through Brandt's younger brother...so far.

But if it panned out, Riyad might be right about the motive behind the poisoning after all; he'd just attributed it to the wrong soldier. During her interrogation of McCord at Bagram, the captain had begged her to slip him the name of the man who'd murdered the mother of his child. McCord had vowed to come back from hell to extract his revenge.

Surely a US warship in the Arabian Sea provided slightly easier access?

Except how would McCord—who was currently in Landstuhl, Germany, with his newborn daughter—have contacted the Marine, much less have gotten strychnine to the man?

Fortunately, with Brandt attached to an IV in sickbay, she'd be able to make her meeting with Palisade and still have time afterward to pull the staff sergeant's records and begin the search for another tie between him and McCord.

A tie strong enough to account for murder.

One thing was certain, the smell of vomit exculpated Brandt from lying about his nausea. Nor was the cause of that vomit poison, at least not with any self-induced strychnine Brandt might've had left over. While nausea was a potential symptom, there were too many others and all were more definitive.

And there was the timing.

If Brandt had ingested pure strychnine before he'd gone to sickbay, he wouldn't be ill right now, he'd be dead. At the very least, he'd be convulsing and about to be.

Yes, the possibility existed that Brandt had been set up. But, until she ruled it out, he was her leading contender—and nothing more.

A contender she'd sat two feet away from the day before while she'd interviewed him...and hadn't suspected a thing.

Of course, she hadn't known yet that there was anything *to* suspect, but still.

After that fiasco with Durrani, she was in no mood to cut anyone slack, least of all herself. The case was getting too damned dicey. And definitely more ominous.

Brandt was a Marine security guard, currently attached to one of the nation's critical embassies in the War on Terror. As such, the man should've been above reproach. Brandt sure as hell shouldn't have been up for murdering a terrorist on anyone's behalf, for any reason. Especially a terrorist who had yet to give up a critical name.

Unless, of course, Staff Sergeant Stephen Brandt *was* that name—and the terrorist she was after.

# 17

Regan stared at the evidence in Chief Yrle's hands as she absorbed the full implications of Brandt's possible guilt—and shifted her priorities accordingly.

She closed up her crime kit and reset the tumbler, then nodded to the sealed evidence bags. "Thank you for your assistance, Chief. Please take those to your office and finish logging them in. Then get them locked into the safe. I'll be down after my meeting with General Palisade to perform the chromatography tests. Under no circumstances is Agent Riyad to run them. Lock the microTLC up in the safe, if you have to. But first, contact Dr. Mantia directly and enlist his aid. I want Brandt kept in sickbay and in ignorance until I give the word that he's to be released."

"Yes, ma'am. Do you need an escort to the wardroom?"

Regan shook her head as she peeled off her gloves and shoved the expended latex in her upper right trouser pocket. She remembered the wardroom's tack number from the day before, along with the briefing Yrle had given her regarding how those numbers corresponded to the *Griffith*'s deck and frame numberings, effectively providing her brain with an interactive, three-dimensional map of the ship.

All she had to do was keep moving forward as the second number lowered in value, and then down, and she'd get there.

If not, "I'll ask someone if I get turned around."

But first, her stateroom.

Regan located her temporary quarters easily enough and stowed her kit within. She headed for the wardroom next and managed to arrive there unassisted as well. But as she reached for the handle of the door, however, she was forced to pause.

The tremors had returned. And they were visibly noticeable.

Really? *Now*? With a general on the other side of the door? The general in charge of USASOC, no less?

Even if she'd wanted to beat feet back up to her stateroom to try to massage the quivers into submission, it was too late. Someone had opened the door from the other side. An enlisted sailor stood amid the empty frame. Deeper inside, and to the young man's right, she could see Agent Riyad seated at the far side of the table. And, well, well, what do you know? He was glaring at her.

Another day, another scowl.

That spook could win the War on Terror single-handedly if he ever figured out how to weaponize them.

"Is that Agent Chase?" *Palisade*.

Great. She was trapped now.

"Yes, sir." She flashed a smile she didn't quite feel as the sailor stepped back so that she could enter the compartment, then turned toward her right.

The general was seated at the head of the long dining table, an empty seat to his right, then Riyad. A blond, ACU-clad male she didn't recognize and then John were slotted down the table on Palisade's left.

"Have a seat, Chief. There's one beside the major."

As embarrassing and heavy-handed as that comment and accompanying amused twinkle were, she was grateful for the suggestion. While both seats flanking the spook were open, she wouldn't have taken either one, general's orders or not.

Fortunately, John's military manners were more ingrained than his boss'. He settled for a sedate nod as she claimed the chair to his left.

"Coffee?"

She glanced across the table, bemused with Riyad's seemingly polite offer...until the man nodded toward the trio of white ceramic mugs turned upside down on the silver serving tray between them. The spook might've nodded toward the cups, but he was staring at her right arm.

"The coffee in the pot is hot, Agent Chase, and the cups are clean. Have at it."

Not an offer, then—but a dare.

Had the spook caught that fresh bout of tremors at the door?

The ones that were still quivering along her fingers. Fingers that were now firmly jammed into her lap.

Or was Riyad wondering if her hand was still shaking from last night?

Either way, John cut the agent off at the pass. He leaned forward and snagged a cup, deftly flipping it right-side up before he set it down on the table, directly in front of her. He extended that brawny arm again, this time for the pot. He filled her cup, leaving a good two inches of room lest the motion of the ship—or her hand—send the contents sloshing over the rim, then returned the pot to its slot on the tray.

"Agent Riyad?"

The spook was forced to shift his attention to the head of the table. "Yes, General?"

She took advantage of Riyad's distraction and whatever the general was saying to look directly into John's eyes. "Thank you."

Her quiet appreciation wasn't for the coffee, and they both knew it. She was referring to his predawn labors with her blood-stained boots and gear.

His answering nod was brief. The appearance of that slight, soul-warming slash, briefer still.

It was enough.

The tremors actually eased.

"Chief?" Palisade again. If he'd caught her exchange with John, much less had intentionally forced Riyad's attention away to allow for one, he didn't let on.

"Yes, sir?"

Palisade tipped his tight crop of silver toward the unknown male she now couldn't see at all. "My aide has an apology to make—to you. Captain Hoffman?"

His aide?

An apology?

She didn't know which surprised her more, the general's statement or that the captain had come to his feet. The latter was welcomed, however, since the captain had disappeared from her view the moment she'd sat down.

That titanic torso of John's was still blocking half the general's body and everything else at the far end the wardroom, too.

Hoffman cleared his throat as he focused on her. Flushed. "Yes, well, regarding those three orange hairs? Agent Chase, I'm the leak."

"Excuse me?"

The general's *aide* was the leak? According to the tab velcroed to the upper left sleeve of his ACUs, the man was Special Forces.

And he'd passed along classified information about a terror case? While the case was still open?

But the captain nodded. "During my previous tour, Captain McCord and I served together. He saved my hide a number of times. When I learned about those hairs, I believed I'd found a way to repay him. I just wanted to put his mind at ease. I shared the information with McCord when I was in Bagram on the general's behalf. I was wrong, and I apologize—to everyone involved in the investigation and especially to you. I understand that my lapse in judgement affected your interrogation with the captain, and could have affected the outcome of the case. I am sorry."

Wow.

Given the strength of that flush and the rigidity of his spine, she'd hate to have been in the room when Palisade had discovered that the leak had come from one of his own. She'd have lost a few inches of her own hide simply by being near the captain.

She offered Hoffman a clipped nod. Given her audience, there wasn't much else she could do. She was still pissed, but the information had solved at least one mystery on her list.

The captain resumed his seat and promptly disappeared behind John's bulk. She had a feeling it was intentional, too.

Palisade turned and murmured something to his aide. The captain came to his boots once more and swiftly departed the compartment, leaving her, John, the general and the spook behind. And then the general stood.

Regan assumed the purpose behind her attendance had been to listen to Hoffman's public mea culpa, and that with Palisade's looming stance, the meeting was now over...until the general caught her eye and nodded. To her utter surprise, Palisade was also blushing. Badly. "I'm your second leak, Chief."

"*Sir*?" Because if Hoffman had leaked the presence of those hairs, there was only one lapse of judgment left on the table. And this one was profoundly personal.

To her.

The general nodded again—and his flush darkened. "Your BI. When I tapped you to lead up both the cave investigation and the one into the SF deaths at Campbell, my decision met with some flak from the State Department contingent holed up here aboard the *Griffith*. There were...questions raised about your lineage. Some had also heard about your run-in with the major in Germany and, quite frankly, did not feel you were agent enough to support the weight of both investigations and our tenuous relationship with Pakistan. I disagreed. I'd already accessed your BI. Based on your background, I knew you were the perfect soldier for the job. I also knew you would not give up, and I needed State to know that. So I passed your BI along to certain folks."

Certain folks?

Hope began to trickle in. Which folks in particular?

Diplomats?

Because a diplomat who'd turned against his or her country would also qualify to be branded as a traitor...

Adrenaline joined the hope, surging along with the latest roll of the *Griffith*. She reached out to prevent her cup and the coffee within from surging out with it. She didn't care that Riyad watched, or that he saw her fingers quiver. Because *certain folks* would also make up a certain *list*. And the US Army general standing in front of her, humbling himself on her behalf, would know every single name on that list.

Every single suspect.

She smiled. "Thank you, sir—for the apology and the leak."

What was the humiliation of yet another public, town-square lashing compared to a solved case? A traitor thwarted, and a terror incident actively prevented.

At least this round hadn't made the nightly news.

"Chief?" She'd clearly confused the general.

From the nod John offered her, her sincerity hadn't baffled him. But then, she'd already discovered that John was well into mapping out how her brain worked, whether she was ready for the added intimacy or not.

"Yes, sir. I'm particularly grateful for the leak. If you'll provide a list of those you shared my BI with, we can use it as a starting point. If we assign an agent to meet with them face-to-face, we can winnow those names down until we have—"

"Just one. The bastard who passed your BI to Durrani."

"Yes, sir."

And *that* would give them their traitor.

"I'll scratch out the list as soon as we've finished here. If those initial names have shared your BI, and with whom, I do not currently know. But I will do all I can to assist in finding out." The determination faded from the man's eyes as the blue within turned solemn. "And I am truly sorry for the violation of privacy and trust."

"Thank you, sir."

To her relief, the general sat. For some reason, his regret had made her uncomfortable. Which caused her craving for the caffeine in front of her to bite in that much harder. She slid the cooling cup of coffee closer and lifted it to her lips.

The risk paid off. Her hand and fingers were steady enough.

She downed the contents of the cup as quickly as she dared, lest her nerves suffer a relapse.

Palisade nodded as Regan returned the cup to the table. "We'll consider the issue closed then. As for which agent will be doing the interviewing with the diplomats and their staff, that'll be up to you. Corporal Vetter witnessed your interview with Durrani. He saw Durrani smack his forehead onto the table so the bastard could rip into his own carotids before you launched yourself up onto that table to push him upright. Vetter also testified that you did your damnedest to save Durrani's life, even though the man was fighting you. Chief Yrle briefed me about the interview's audio file as well.

The contents back you up. While we all knew they would, it too was a necessary step, and now it's complete. Agent Chase, you are officially back in charge—of the case on this ship and the remaining questions that need answering regarding the unknown woman from the cave, as well as the traitor. Agent Riyad will assist you."

Agent Riyad was not happy with that.

Not only had the scowl returned, but lo and behold, it was leveled squarely on her as she went further out on that limb of chimeral tangled nerves, reaching for the pot of coffee with her still reasonably steady hand so she could refill her cup.

Captain Hoffman returned to the wardroom, slipping back into his seat to hand over a sheet of paper and converse quietly with the general. What was on that sheet, she had no idea, but from the general's frown the contents appeared serious.

She sat back, taking in the frown across from her. What the hell was the spook's problem this morning? He was acting as though he'd lost his best lead.

Did he honestly believe she was glad Durrani was dead?

Good Lord, the loss of potential intel alone was incalculable.

As she raised her cup, she caught a glimpse of John. He was shooting his own silent ire across the table. Which made the spook bristle. Visibly.

Riyad's scowl slid over to her right arm, then down.

She stiffened as John's left arm stretched out in response, casually coming to rest along the top of her chair. Except that arm was anything but blasé. The warning it carried was personal and professional—and very clear.

*Fuck with her, and you're fucking with me.*

What the devil had happened between these two men this morning? Because something had. And it had centered on her.

Had Palisade and his aide been privy to it? Was that why the general had made a point to seat her next to John? As some awkward show of support?

The humiliations just kept piling up.

And her arm. Riyad was *still* staring at it.

Worse, John refused to move his. With that annoyingly hefty major's oak leaf embroidered on his ACUs seriously outweighing the chief warrant officer two bar stitched to hers, she couldn't even jab her elbow in his ribs to get him to remove it. Not in front of witnesses, including a general.

She turned to glare at him. Not only did John ignore her, the arm stayed. As did that infuriating arrogance.

"Major?"

She and Riyad turned along with John to face his boss.

"Sir?"

"We need to wrap this meeting up. Much as I hate to admit it, this isn't the only shitshow on the planet today. Just got some new intel I need to act on."

"Yes, sir." John turned to her and nodded.

It appeared she had the floor.

She took advantage of the opportunity to eradicate at least one of her problems—that arm. She shoved her chair back, rudely dislodging it as she stood.

She didn't even bother glancing at John or Riyad as she turned to her left to walk around the back of her chair before she headed up the table. She drew her phone out of her cargo pocket as she reached the general's side and clicked it open to the slew of photos she'd taken in the stateroom that the Marine guards had shared.

Palisade nodded to the phone as she set it down in front of him. "What am I looking at?"

"Staff Sergeant Brandt's smokes. He's got several packs in his quarters. Chief Yrle and I searched the stateroom shortly before I came up here. I found this one tucked between the staff sergeant's mattress and the side of the ship." She reached down to slide her index finger across the screen to move to the next image. "This is a photo of what I discovered in the bottom of that pack. The cigarettes were all cut to make room for a false bottom. This bottle was inside. There's enough of the clear liquid left to test."

"*Fuck me.*"

It seemed the general's aide had serious issues keeping his mouth shut amid all sorts of circumstances and locations, because even his boss glared at him.

"Captain Hoffman, you're dismissed."

The man turned redder than the bottom of her shower had last night. But he stood and immediately evacuated the wardroom.

Palisade nodded to the now empty chair. "Have a seat."

Like the aide, she complied with the alacrity due a general's orders.

"All right, Chief. What's the game plan for this thread?"

"I'd like to pull his record, get my ducks in a row before I interview him. I have time. The staff sergeant's in sickbay at the moment. I tasked Chief Yrle with ensuring that he stayed there in ignorance until I give the word. Last night's seas hit him pretty hard. He's been there half the night plugged into an IV."

"Is he faking?"

With the stench she, Yrle and Vetter had been subjected to? "No."

Palisade nodded. "I'd like to see him."

She shook her head. "Sir, I'd rather you didn't."

"Explain."

"For one, we don't know if he's guilty. If he did do it, why keep evidence lying around? Regret? Perhaps. But Corporal Vetter also knows the staff sergeant from their embassy duties and is currently sharing Brandt's quarters aboard this ship. Also, even if Brandt did poison the translator, he may not be our traitor. Or Vetter for that matter. Hachemi's murder could just be a case of flat-out revenge. According to Chief Yrle, Staff Sergeant Brandt is prone to sharing about a younger brother who plays for the Longhorns. While Captain McCord received his ROTC commission from UT, that's something Vetter could have known —*or* share a connection with—as well. Frankly, I need more information about both men before I show my hand."

One of those steel gray brows lifted. "And if Brandt is guilty?"

"Then I definitely don't need you or your stars in the mix. It's just seasickness, sir. Nothing that should warrant a general's concern, an Army one at that. We'd risk alerting him as to the real reason behind my own...compassionate visit."

In short, let her do her damned job.

The one he'd flown to Campbell to personally ask her to do.

"Agreed. I'll skip the meet—for now."

"Thank you, sir."

"The major tells me you've already got a solid lead on identifying the seventh woman from the cave, too."

"Yes, sir. I believe she worked with Durrani—and that the doc had a sexual interest in her. Given his attitude toward women, especially those he worked with, that interest might stand out with his former co-workers. We bring along that photo of the woman from the cave, baby included, and someone may talk."

Palisade inclined his silver head once more. "Major Garrison briefed us on the bastard's interest in the woman. That's solid work there, Chief. The major also let us know that this damned plot goes further back than any of us suspected. Back to when you and he were in Germany, damned near a year and a half ago."

She caught the flash of compassion that briefly tinged the blue.

She wasn't surprised John had informed his boss and mentor about the exact nature of their conversation in that parking lot—and especially its significance. But the general hadn't drawn attention to Durrani's other comment. The one regarding equipment potentially lost by the spook.

Why?

Riyad had definitely attended John's meeting with Palisade then.

She was weighing the implications when the door to the wardroom blew open behind her. Too many combat tours had her and John on their collective feet and spinning around before Chief Yrle had made it all the way inside.

"Agent Chase, Doc wants you in Medical. Brandt woke a couple minutes ago and starting yelling for you. Then he had some sort of seizure. I think he—"

Regan never heard the rest. She was already barreling out of the compartment, her boots pounding along the deck as she headed for the door marked "Medical" that she'd noted in the corridor on her way to the meeting.

John was at her side, adding a surreal, déjà vu feel to the trip as they reached the door to sickbay and slammed through.

The scene inside cinched the feeling. And her clawing fear.

Make that terror.

The staff sergeant was lying on a gurney shoved into the middle of the aisle between two rows of patient racks stacked on either side like bunkbeds. Mantia and the beefy corpsman Regan had seen twice before—in that conference room and in the brig—were at Brandt's side. Only this time, the men weren't working on Hachemi or Durrani. Nor were they working on the Marine's sweat-drenched body.

Brandt was dead.

Worse, that telling, fetid odor that had all but oozed from the lungs and pores of every soldier who'd died from the chimera back at Fort Campbell hung in the air.

She took one look at John and knew he smelled it too.

Mantia looked up, the adrenaline from a full code still riding his damp, flushed features, along with the added grief of crashing down on the losing end. The man appeared...lost. "He's dead. Staff Sergeant Brandt was alive five minutes ago. He'd woken up from what we thought was another nightmare and looked straight at me and said, 'They're not real. Tell Agent Chase, they're not real.' And then he seized."

"Son of a bitch." *John.*

She nodded as the inescapable reality locked in. The psycho-toxin. Durrani hadn't injected all of that chimeral crap into her arm back in Charikar. There was more of the virus out there...and someone was using it.

As if to taunt them—as if that seizure, that sweat and that smell weren't enough, nearly those exact words Brandt had used had come from one of John's men, Sergeant Blessing, shortly before *he* had become the first one to die from the virus.

Regan threaded her fingers into John's and squeezed firmly as the doc continued to shake his head in disbelief.

"We lost him before you came through the door. It happened that quick. One minute he was dreaming, and the next, he was dead. There was nothing I could do."

Mantia was correct.

The only reason she and three of John's other soldiers had survived their own deadly dance with the chimera was because of Gil's brilliance and his access to Fort Detrick's vaccine for a virus that appeared to be related to the psycho-toxin, along with a dose of—of all things—the chicken pox vaccine. Neither of which would have been aboard a US warship operating in the middle of the Arabian Sea.

But as right as the doc was, he was also wrong.

Regan gave John's fingers one last squeeze and released them so she could step up to the gurney. To the utterly flabbergasted physician. "He wasn't dreaming, Doctor. Staff Sergeant Brandt was hallucinating. That's what he wanted me to know." Just as Brandt had wanted her to know what—and possibly *who*—had killed him.

Except he'd run out of time.

She could only pray that his mortal timing hadn't become theirs.

Regan retrieved her phone and located Gil's number. She held the phone up so that Mantia's corpsman could copy it down. "Contact Lieutenant Colonel Gilbert Fourche, US Army. Blanchfield Community Hospital, Fort Campbell, Kentucky. Dr. Fourche will be able to fill in the rest of the holes. At least the ones he's seen before. Dr. Fourche will also need tissue samples and blood from the staff sergeant." Lord knew they'd taken enough from her. "Fourche and several other doctors are still working on the virus that caused this. But, please, know that there's *nothing* you could've done."

As guilty as she felt for assuming the original seasick diagnosis was sound, she couldn't have prevented this either, even if she'd known differently. Heck, given that no one else had vomited to that extent, Brandt probably had been seasick, too. Which might have even masked his initial chimeral symptoms from himself. Either way, by the time the Marine had crawled into sickbay, he was already all but dead. The makeshift treatment Gil had cobbled together would never have reached the ship by now.

"Rae?"

She turned around to face John. He'd pulled himself together. But from the shadows darkening his tight, professional stare, she could tell that the same guilt was eating away at him too. And he'd known the Marine longer.

"This changes things."

"I know." She tipped her head toward the door, to where

Riyad and the general were standing. Waiting. "Let's go let him know."

John motioned for her to precede him across the rolling deck. Every cell in her body had been so focused on the journey here, and the horror of what they'd found when they arrived, she hadn't realized the sea state had picked up again.

She halted in front of Palisade, not even bothering to mask her expression. The general already knew that the news she was about to impart was devastating; she might as well let her face reflect it for a change. "I need to go Pakistan, sir. Today."

"Explain."

"I'll test the liquid in that bottle and dust it for prints, but I already know what they'll show." She'd bet every one of those iron birds up on the flight deck on it. "Staff Sergeant Brandt poisoned the translator."

"You found proof—here?" *Riyad.*

She nodded. It was in the air. It'd been in the air in the Marines' stateroom too, but the more nauseating stench of vomit had overridden it. "I've already provided Mantia with Dr. Fourche's number. We'll need the official, medical confirmation from them, but the sweat drenching the staff sergeant's body? The hallucinations Brandt himself confirmed seconds before he suffered the seizure that killed him—"

"That foul odor?"

This nod was for the general. "That, too."

"It's the goddamned psycho-toxin, isn't it, Chief?"

She nodded once more. "Yes, sir. But we've got a silver lining, General. Several, in fact. Staff Sergeant Brandt was an embassy security guard, so while I haven't had a chance to access his record yet, I can almost guarantee he wasn't suicidal or he'd never have passed the testing and been accepted into the program. That means someone injected the virus into him. Not only does the chimera need to be refrigerated, it also requires a significant stressor, mental or physical, to activate." Murdering Hachemi definitely qualified. "But the necessity of the stressor limits the timeframe of Brandt's exposure. Without an adequate stressor, the virus can linger for weeks, possibly months inside the body. Dormant. Dr. Fourche and his team have also since discovered that the virus peaks roughly one to two weeks after the introduction of the stressor—"

"But Hachemi was murdered yesterday." Riyad again. And he was taking on at least one annoying habit of the general's aide.

Speaking out of turn.

She smiled anyway. Sort of. "True. Which is why I suspect that Brandt didn't want to murder Hachemi." A suspicion that fit with the staff sergeant's general demeanor and personality, as well as the cross-branch loyalty toward John that Brandt had displayed during their interview. "But if Brandt was blackmailed into killing the translator against his will, that would do it." What better stressor to a man of honor? "And if the blackmail occurred while the Marine was in the hanger at Al Dhafra two weeks ago—"

"The timeframe fits."

Regan bit down on her tongue at this latest interruption. She had no choice. It had come from the general. "Yes, sir. It does."

Palisade ran his fingers around the crop of silver stubble atop his head. "So the staff sergeant wasn't infected aboard this ship."

"No, sir. I believe he was injected at Al Dhafra, albeit unwittingly." Just as she'd been. Though she'd mostly likely have been the easier of them to infect, since she'd been unconscious at the time.

Riyad opened his mouth again. This time, she cut him off with a swift shake. "I know, I know. I fell ill almost immediately. But I've been told that I was an outlier. Not only did Durrani inject the contents of an entire vial into me, I'd been unconscious for hours and already physically taxed because of the Russian gas Hachemi knocked us all out with while we were in his van. Plus, my physiology's different; I'm a woman. None of those factors apply here." She turned back to Palisade. "As for Brandt's infection, I doubt he even realized it occurred. It had to have been subtle or he would have come to sickbay upon his return, but I'll check with Dr. Mantia. Either way, whoever injected the staff sergeant is also most likely the traitor. He or she isn't with the Army though." Because they also knew that the traitor had read her BI and worked at the embassy.

"They're with State."

She offered up one last nod.

This one, the general returned. Grimly. "I'll make the arrangements—and I'll get you that list. Looks like you'll be interviewing those names personally. Meanwhile, get those tests on that bottle wrapped up ASAP. You're headed to Islamabad, Chief."

"Yes, sir."

God willing, she'd be able to tear through Staff Sergeant Brandt's life quickly and use whatever she found to locate their unknown traitor. Because there were several new questions burning through her brain. How many other vials of that chimera were still out there?

Who did their traitor plan on infecting next...and when?

Or had it already happened?

# 18

Thanks to Chief Yrle's connections in the *Griffith*'s laundry, Regan had been ready to disembark in under an hour, freshly pressed, dark blue suit already donned. Since the ship had moved into the northern part of the Arabian Sea to receive General Palisade's chopper the night before, it had taken a mere two hours to reach Al Dhafra. From there, it was an additional three to Islamabad via the US Air Force C-130 rumbling around her, most of which she'd spent in this webbed seat, reading everything she'd been able to download on Staff Sergeant Brandt while waiting at Al Dhafra.

Unfortunately, she'd finished skimming the material a while ago. With fifteen minutes of flight time left, she was officially bored.

But she wasn't alone. For the second time in two weeks, Palisade had sent her off to one of the 'Stans with a pair of bulked-out gorillas in tow. Although, this time, the general had added a sleeked-up ass into the mix.

Regan glanced across the belly of the cargo plane, returning the latest glare from said ass. Like her and the two gorillas flanking her, Riyad had swapped his shipboard attire for a ubiquitous white shirt and dark business suit. Also like her, the spook's sidearm was no doubt holstered neatly beneath the jacket of his suit.

She had no idea what Corporal Vetter and John had beneath their suits, but she suspected John was carrying considerably more than the rest of them put together.

She could only pray he wouldn't need it.

Once they touched down at the international airport in Islamabad, she and Vetter were headed for the embassy. John was not. He hadn't offered up his intended location, and she hadn't asked for it. Not given the nature of his mission. The only information he had offered had been a name. His. If she received a call over the next day or two from a Karl Goethe—pick up. That, combined with John's dark gray, hand-tailored suit, suggested he'd be going under via a CIA-related cover, most likely as a German executive.

It made sense. As a whole, Pakistanis were profoundly in love with all things German, up to and including—of all people—Hitler. While the majority of the world might consider Hitler a monster, a significant portion of Pakistanis didn't. There, many saw the *Führer* as the hero who'd freed them from British rule.

John would undoubtedly be leveraging his proficiency with the German language and that Pakistani love for the German people to his advantage.

But with whom?

Riyad had been right about one thing in her stateroom the day before. Over the years that he'd spent as Special Forces, John had operated on and around some exceptionally blurred lines on the globe, especially those along Afghanistan's porous south-eastern border with Pakistan. While doing so, John had made quite a few connections. And, yes, some of those connections were shady as hell.

Right now, those were precisely the sort they needed.

While Vetter returned to his guard duties in Islamabad and Riyad headed off to link up with Agent Castile at the US consulate in Peshawar to add his FCI skills, as well as his own proficiency with Dari, Pashto and Arabic, to Castile's knowledge of Urdu and the search for the seventh victim, John would be abusing every one of those connections of his that he'd deemed capable of getting them the information they needed.

Beginning with that Russian Bioprepart contact of Durrani's...and whoever else Aleksi Skulachev had been selling biological warfare agents to.

They might desperately need the intel John was after, and she might still be pissed over that chest-beating incident in the *Griffith*'s wardroom earlier that morning, but she was worried. About him. Who was she kidding? The idea that whoever had infected Brandt with the chimera was still out there scared the absolute shit out of her. How much more of that virus did their unnamed traitor have?

And what *else* was in his possession?

John might be immune to the chimera, but he wasn't immune to everything those Bioprepart monsters had created.

As the C-130 dropped noticeably in altitude, the sudden pressure in Regan's inner ears pushed her attention back to the mission. The cargo plane had begun its final approach to Islamabad International, where she was due to be met by an agent with the Diplomatic Security Service. From there, she and the DSS agent would head to the embassy so she could begin interviewing the State Department personnel who'd received her BI.

The only foreseeable complication—and, admittedly, it was a huge one—would be discerning if the initial seven recipients on the general's list had then turned around and shared her backgrounder with anyone else. If so, who? A dicey quest, to say the least, since anyone admitting to the affirmative would also be admitting that they'd passed on classified information without proper authorization.

A bit of a death knell for a diplomat's career.

Or it should be.

Minutes later, they were wheels down, cruising along the tarmac as the C-130's pilot headed for their pre-arranged parking slot on the military ramp near Pakistan's haphazard collection of older, Soviet-era aircraft.

Several more minutes passed before the bird stopped moving. Within moments, the C-130's giant turbofan engines had begun to power down.

By the time Regan had unbuckled and bypassed her half-full duffel to retrieve the small civilian suitcase Chief Yrle had procured from one of the *Griffith*'s generous sailors, Riyad had already hefted his civilian suitcase and was heading down the aft ramp. Regan shouldered her laptop case and grabbed her crime scene kit as well, before joining John and the corporal. She expected to catch up with Riyad out on the tarmac to exchange polite goodbyes, but the spook wasn't there.

As he had the night before up on the flight deck of the *Griffith*, Riyad had taken off across the tarmac—alone.

John slipped her suitcase from her right hand before she could stop him, then shouldered the black leather suit bag he'd had the foresight to bring to the ship. Since advertising US military status wasn't advisable in their host country at the moment, his own uniforms and duffel remained stowed in the plane alongside hers.

John swung his chin toward the spook's retreating back. "I need to make a few calls about that man, ASAP."

Amen to that.

"I'll phone Mira as soon as I get a moment alone, too." Only that call might be some hours from now, given that she could make out the silhouette of another man on the tarmac, and this one was passing Riyad and heading toward her.

Even better, that short, wiry build and sandy hair were distinctive enough to place.

"Scott?" She moved up the right side of the plane to set her crime kit and laptop down on the tarmac beside her suitcase and John's leather bag, then continued on toward the nose of the bird, eager to whittle away the remaining distance between an old friend and herself. "*You're* the DSS agent I've been assigned?" She glanced at John. "Scott and I went to MP school together; did our first tours over in Iraq with Agent Jelling." Though, granted, every time this guy had gotten roped into an IED/human-remains collections and cleanup, Scott had threatened to bail on the Army.

It looked as though he'd made good on that threat.

Though if Scott was with State's Diplomatic Security Service, he hadn't gotten very far, had he? Protecting embassies and their personnel was an equally rough gig.

In a lot of ways, far rougher.

"Good to see you, Prez. It's been too damned long." Scott grinned as he hauled her in for a wonderfully familiar hug. One that nearly crushed her ribs.

The man was definitely still in shape for the job.

He stuck out a hand to John. "Scott Walburn, DSS. Will you be needing a lift to the embassy, too?"

John's scarred hand engulfed Scott's significantly smoother one. "John Garrison, SF. Thanks, but I've got my own welcoming committee. He's right behind you."

Regan glanced past Scott's dark gray pinstripes to see yet another familiar face, similarly suited up and marking time, just beyond the edge of the tarmac.

Tulle.

The Nordic giant who'd shadowed her off the official books for Palisade back at Fort Campbell at the start of it all nodded to John, then her. She should've expected that John would be linking up with his staff sergeant. He and Tulle would have done so yesterday, had it not been for the situation with Hachemi.

John's staff sergeant remained at the edge of earshot, patiently waiting for his commander to wrap things up with them.

"Rae, you ready? I've got an embassy car and driver just off the tarmac."

She glanced at Scott, then tipped her head toward the plane. "I just need to get my gear and let Corporal Vetter know we're leaving."

As she and John headed back down the C-130's belly, she spotted Vetter conversing with a member of the security detail near the aft ramp. In light of the on-again/off-again relationship their country shared with the country that owned the tarmac beneath her shoes—and the reality that the relationship was currently tilted toward *off*—the detail would remain in place and on alert until she, John and Riyad returned to the plane that Palisade had left at their disposal, just in case.

Well, she and John. Lord only knew what the spook's plans were beyond hooking up with Castile, and whether or not he'd ever deign to share them. At least with her.

"Ready, Corporal?"

"Yes, ma'am. Just gotta grab my duffel. It's still inside."

She nodded as Vetter headed for the plane's rear ramp.

The tension had returned—inside her. She knew it was time to turn around and retrieve her own suitcase and gear. But for once, she didn't want to. Not yet. Not with the harsh reality of it all scraping back in and refusing to let go.

*John*. He was leaving too. The man was a minute, perhaps

two, from Tulle and that mystery bird of theirs, and wherever it was scheduled to land. The suits they'd both donned suggested that there wouldn't be a lot of backup. Not close by, anyway.

What if something went wrong?

"Rae?"

She forced herself to turn. John was staring down at her, intently. The way she'd worked very hard to not stare at him on that Super Stallion as they'd left the *Griffith* behind, then again during their brief wait at Al Dhafra and aboard the C-130 on the way here. The scruff that had taken over his jaw these past few weeks was still there. With his current mission, going barefaced wouldn't have been prudent. But he'd cleaned it up after he'd left sickbay. Trimmed his mustache and beard into something downright sleek and cultivated. The result was disturbingly touchable. Missable.

Along with the rest of him.

Damn it, what if he didn't make it back?

She was pushing through the fear, reminding herself of those who were waiting, as John reached into his suit jacket to pull a length of black silk from within.

A scarf?

Where on earth had he obtained that? When?

Her bemusement must've shown, because that distracting dent of his slipped in. "I bought it off a woman in Al Dhafra. You and Riyad were checking out the male latrines to see where Brandt might've been infected."

Unfortunately, they hadn't been successful in their quest. Unlike John.

"Surely you don't—"

But he nodded. Worse, he'd lifted the swath of silk and was carefully draping it over the top of her French braid, completely concealing it. He crossed the trailing ends beneath her chin and tucked them over her shoulders. "Wear the *dupatta* when you're not on the embassy compound. It'll deflect attention, help you blend in as just another expat. One with male ties."

He was correct. About all of it. But she still had an issue with the whole *cover up the woman* aspect of the thing. Ten seconds in, and she was already suffocating. Mentally, at least. She sighed. "I know. The mission's critical. I'll—"

He shook his head.

He wasn't debating the mission's importance, and she knew it. It was the rationale. The scarf, and the protection it offered, was personal...to him.

"Sir? Hate to push, but I got that lift fired up three birds over, burning through fuel."

That intense focus didn't shift. "Be right there, Tulle."

John held her gaze for another few seconds, then inclined his head. Turned.

She reached out without thinking, pressing her fingers into the sleeve of his dark gray suit, feeling the solid warmth beneath. The man.

He stopped, turned back. Waited.

Well, crap. She'd started this round. Now what?

"*Be careful.*"

He flashed that dent once more, and then he was gone.

She drew her breath and her nerves in deep and held them for several beats before releasing both. It helped. She bent down to retrieve her suitcase and gear. Scott was grinning like the proverbial village idiot as she returned to his side.

"Well, I'll be...the Prez finally found herself a First Man. Uncle Ronnie would be so proud." He added insult to injury as he chortled over his own sorry joke.

"Shut up."

When he refused, she swung the suitcase into his midsection, grinning herself at the sharp *oomphf* the blow produced.

Corporal Vetter joined them, his duffel and gear in hand.

She was still smiling as they followed Scott across the tarmac, taking Riyad's path instead of John's. Ten minutes later, she was sitting in the rear seat of a black, bullet-resistant Volvo with Scott and headed out of the airport and toward the embassy on the opposite side of the road than they would've been had they been driving in the States. Vetter was up front and catching up with the driver on what he'd missed while he was aboard the *Griffith*.

She was tempted to use the time to pump Scott for information as well.

The moment she'd spotted her old friend and his pinstripe suit on that tarmac, she'd realized she had an in with the embassy staff. A potential source of office gossip, and more, for the names on her list. Hence, she'd immediately accepted his offer of a late dinner. Unfortunately, she'd also since realized the odds that she'd discern anything actionable were not on her side.

It turned out Scott was temporarily assigned to the embassy. Not only was he nearly as new to DSS as Riyad was to NCIS, Scott had been snagged from his newbie DSS stateside posting to assist with an intricate and extensive human trafficking racket out of Islamabad because of his proficiency with Urdu. The arrests had gone down the day before. Once the wrap-up was finished, he'd be heading back to Arlington, Virginia.

Which, of course, was why Scott had been roped into his current chauffeur and Army-CID liaison duties. Still, the man was sharp. Though he wasn't working directly for the embassy's regional security officer, he had met the RSO on a number of occasions. Scott might've gleaned something these past two months that she in turn could glean—and use.

Either way, Vetter and the driver's presence would hamper their conversation. Scott wouldn't feel it prudent to dish on his fellow co-workers with others in earshot.

She'd need to tread carefully over dinner, too. Scott had been fed the same cover story that nearly everyone would receive: she was in Islamabad following up on the untimely death of Staff Sergeant Brandt while Brandt had been away from embassy grounds, nothing more. Only Vetter—by virtue of his personal involvement—and the ambassador—knew the truth...along with the embassy's hidden, terror-cell connection.

Regan settled for catching Scott up on the lives of several mutual friends, including Agent Jelling, as the Volvo turned onto Islamabad's Srinagar Highway and headed northeast toward the embassy. The endless, tree-filled expanse that bordered both sides of the road could've resembled the outskirts of any number of large cities in the mid-southern US, but for the daunting rugged peaks and slopes of the Margalla Hills that formed this section of the Himalayan foothills.

Scott was more impressed with her gossip. "Wow. I knew the guy wanted to join CID, but married? *Jelly*?"

She grinned. "Yep. And with a kid."

Jelly Jr. would be two in a few months. With all the numbers that tended to rattle around in her head, she still couldn't quite believe that one. And she'd presented Jelly with the box of hideously blue stogies he'd handed out on the big day.

"What about you, Rae?"

"Kids?" She shook her head firmly, before the memories could filter in, along with the ache that was still too raw to accept, much less discuss. "Nothing to see here."

"I don't know. That goodbye looked an awfully lot like *see you soon*."

She shrugged.

Really, what else could she do? Except pray her expression was as impassive as she needed it to be. For once, she wasn't quite sure.

"Prez?"

She finally located one of the deceiver's smiles and slotted it into place. "I'm just tired. Last night was a long one." One spent dealing with an utter bastard who'd thrown that same aching memory into her face, before he'd gone on to rip open his carotids in front of her.

Every time she closed her eyes, she could see that blood jetting out. Feel it. Probably would for the rest of her life, just as Durrani had intended.

Even if she'd wanted to confide in Scott, she couldn't. So she let it go and focused on the road.

Islamabad's Srinagar Highway and their shorter jaunt up the more crowded Khayaban-e-Suhrwardy had given way to the imposing gates of their embassy. Thirty-six acres filled with decidedly American buildings, the most impressive of which was that massive, seven-story, glass, concrete and steel embassy complex that had weighed in at a cool three quarters of a billion by the time it'd been inaugurated within the Diplomatic Enclave not too long ago—shortly after she, Jelly and Scott had met. In all, a decent sized bite of the Red, White and Blue smack in the middle of Pakistan.

Only, someone inside was not thrilled with that patriotic outlook.

Within minutes, the Volvo had cleared security and they were winding their way through the grounds of one of the largest US embassy compounds in the world. With its own commissary, post office, diplomatic staff residences and a three-story recreational building complete with an indoor pool, not to mention an on-site well water and waste treatment plant, Embassy Islamabad was essentially a self-contained city.

In light of where it was located, and that it was designed to accommodate a staff of twenty-five hundred, it needed to be.

"We're here."

The driver pulled up beside the striking seven-story chancery and stopped to let them out.

Vetter grabbed his gear from the trunk and Scott snagged her suitcase, leaving her to shoulder her laptop bag and retrieve her crime scene case.

She waved goodbye to the Marine and followed Scott into the marble and glass interior and through several more layers of security, until she'd gained yet another federal ID, this one to hang around her neck.

They finally reached a small, barebones, windowless room with a modest, faux wood-grained table and two chairs, one executive in nature.

Scott set the fabric suitcase Chief Yrle had procured down beside the door. "Sorry it's not classier, what with your lofty presidential status and all."

Regan laughed as she tucked her stainless-steel kit and laptop beside the suitcase. "This will do just fine."

That high-backed, padded chair was decidedly more luxurious than she usually got in the field. Especially on the battlefield.

She couldn't lie though. Right about now, a tiny coffee station would've been a godsend.

"So, what's the OPLAN, Detective?"

Regan removed her suit jacket and hung it from the shoulders of the nicer chair. "Find caffeine, then get started. I have a few folks I need to interview. Basically, those who were on the *Griffith* before I arrived." It was barely 1500 local time. If she was lucky, she'd be able to get through the leading contenders before the diplomats and staffers departed for home and dinner. "Of course, I also have Brandt's quarters."

"Absolutely. Once the RSO got word about the staff sergeant's death, Maddoc had Brandt's room sealed. He figured someone from the outside would want to take a peek—though I think he expected a Marine." Scott's sandy brows furrowed. "But interviews? Linnet told us the staff sergeant suffered some kind of seizure."

The ambassador had kept her word regarding the cover story, then.

Excellent. Regan could only pray Linnet had kept her trap shut regarding the untimely deaths of Hachemi and his scissor-wielding idol, as well. With some diplomats, you couldn't be sure. But the woman was serving as the president's face in a particularly tense part of the world. Clearly, Linnet was made of stern stuff.

She hoped.

"The ambassador's right, at least as far as we know." Regan removed the scarf John had purchased for her, then bent down to retrieve her computer bag. She set the scarf and the bag on the table in front of the executive chair and withdrew her laptop. "Seizure was the shipboard doc's initial assessment, though he wasn't sure what caused it. Probably something preexisting that the Marine Corps never noticed. We'll know more after the autopsy." That was true enough.

And she did need the confirmation that the autopsy would bring, along with the rerouted ship-to-shore consult with Gil that Dr. Mantia had scheduled.

As for the postmortem? For once luck had been on their side. Colonel Tarrington's chopper had been about to churn up its blades when the *Griffith*'s CO sent word to stand down. Her own ship-to-shore call from Tarrington regarding Brandt's autopsy results should be routing through her mobile phone before nightfall.

Either way, "A few observations and non-medical assessments on the staff sergeant's health by those who knew him best can't hurt." Especially since, while those staffers offered their assessments, she'd be making her own...on them. "You remember the drill. I was closest to the scene, so I was given the job. I'm just dotting the i's—"

"And crossing the t's." Scott hooked his hip onto the edge of her latest temporary desk and nodded. "I haven't been in long, but trust me, it's the same, mind-numbing bureaucracy with DSS. It's the other moments that make up for it—as with CID, I suspect. So, you'll need to grill me too? I've only been here two months and Brandt was gone for the second, but what little I know is up for grabs if you need it."

"I'll take you up on that." Just not for the reason she'd be grilling the others. Since Scott was on temporary orders, he wouldn't be intimately involved with the embassy compound's security, if at all. But he was still DSS, which meant he'd have a unique insight into Staff Sergeant Brandt and his duties. But, although she did need to find out what Scott knew about the Marine, right now what she needed more was what Scott knew about everyone else she'd be interviewing. "Do you have time now?"

The door pushed all the way open.

"No, Agent Walburn does *not*."

Scott straightened as the owner of that booming voice entered the room. She caught the glint in her former colleague's hazel eyes just before he turned.

Fascinating.

Regan studied the intruder, immediately placing the riot of short, salt and pepper curls topping those heavyset features. It would've been impossible not to. Their owner's mugshot had been slotted in at the very front of the background information she'd downloaded at Al Dhafra. This man was also the lead entry on Palisade's list: Warren Jeffers, Embassy Islamabad's deputy chief of mission. As DCM, Jeffers served as Ambassador

Linnet's replacement when the woman was not in country, and the ambassador's right hand when she was.

What Regan didn't know, was why Scott disliked Jeffers. Intensely.

Though Scott covered well. Had she not served with the man in Iraq, she might've even bought the respectful tip to Scott's sandy head.

"Rae, this is Warren Jeffers, the embassy's deputy chief of mission. Sir, Special Agent Regan Chase, US Army CID. She'd like to—"

"I know what the agent would like. I'll take it from here, Walburn. Nasim needs to speak with you. Now."

The glint returned as Scott caught her eye. "You still up for that late dinner? We can finish catching up after you grill me."

"Absolutely."

He slipped a hand into his suit jacket and withdrew a business card. "My number's on the front. Call me when you've had your fill." The glint flared, leaving no doubt as to whom Scott believed she was about to get her fill of.

She kept her expression bland as Scott departed.

If anything, the DCM's expression resembled Riyad's standard fare as Jeffers closed the door on his embassy colleague before turning back to her. "Let me be blunt, Agent Chase. I was not exaggerating. I know exactly why you're in Islamabad, and I am not happy about it. But what really pisses me off is your insinuation that someone on my staff is a traitor, up to and including *me*. And, yes, in case General Palisade failed to inform you, I was against your heading up the Fort Campbell murders and the cave investigation. Hell, I led the disgruntled pack. You weren't worth the risk. Not then, and not now. The ambassador agrees. So much so, she's in a meeting with our host country's president, informing him of the deaths of not one, but two terror suspects that his country had a right to interview when we were done with them. After all, that cave is located on *their* land."

Well, okay. Linnet definitely fell into the *can't keep her blessed mouth shut* category. As did the woman's metaphorical right hand.

Good to know.

And, yes, that cave was located on Pakistani land—as was a certain dusty compound that had once existed a mere seventy-five miles north of where she was now standing. A compound that had ironically also been located just outside Pakistan's version of West Point in Abbottabad. And, yet, no one—up to and including Pakistan's former president—had bothered to let *her* government know of the existence of said compound. Despite the fact that its infamous, now deceased, occupant—one Osama bin Laden—had led the terror strike that had taken the lives of nearly three thousand Americans on 9-11.

It appeared Pakistani diplomats were better at keeping secrets than her own.

Regan thought about masking her anger and surprise over the ambassador's loose lips, but decided to go with it. Even bumped the latter up several notches. She was intrigued enough to wind up the ambassador's right hand as far as she could. Heck, she'd even use her own literal right hand to do it. See what else Jeffers would reveal.

"Why so shocked, Agent?"

She lifted her fingers to smooth a wisp of hair off her temple and into her braid. For once, the resulting tremor was deliberate. "The ambassador had orders to remain silent."

The man's lips thinned as he spotted the quiver. Since they were on the fleshy side to begin with, it wasn't an attractive look. "She did. But here's the thing: at Embassy Islamabad, we don't work for the Army or the Pentagon. We work for the secretary of state—and the president. So if you need to bitch to someone, call one of them."

The mood she was in, she just might.

Especially since there was more of that chimera, and God only knew what else, floating around out there—and someone who worked for *this* asshole was bent on using it. But as much as she'd have loved tossing that hefty hind end of his into Leavenworth personally, she was all but certain the traitor wasn't Warren Jeffers.

He was too in her face. Nor was he concerned about drawing attention to himself. Whoever she was after was cooler, definitely more methodical. This man's temper could smack an intercontinental ballistic missile out of the sky all by itself when suitably pricked.

And there was the rest.

She'd been on the receiving end of territorial ass-rippings her entire career. But with this guy? There was too much rage leaking through. This almost felt...personal. Which was weird, since she hadn't had the displeasure of meeting him before.

"Is that all, sir?" Tirade or not, she was here to do a job.

"Actually, no. I also met with Dr. Durrani and Tamir Hachemi while I was aboard the ship. Privately. I don't give a crap what you think; that translator lied about this so-called traitor. He was trying to get a better deal. Hell, Hachemi all but admitted it to me. As for your fun-filled BI? Sweetheart, I knew all about your tawdry past before it landed in the *Griffith*'s conference room—because I knew your *father*. You're the brilliant detective; I'll leave it to you to figure out when and where. But I will tell you this: you're a chip off that old rancid block. And Hachemi's murder? I'm with Agent Riyad. John Garrison had a damned good reason to kill him. If you tried taking your blinders off and staring at the major with his clothes *on* for a change, you might just see that."

The hell with faking. She was stunned now. Her hand was shaking for real, too. Right along with the fury that was ripping through her gut.

She managed to round the latter up. Trap it there. But it was still roiling, threatening to spew forth. Jeffers could impugn her father all he wanted. The bastard deserved it. And at least she now understood why this had felt personal.

As for her? Jeffers could slime her to her face in front of the entire, snickering embassy for all she cared. She'd endured worse from at least three of her so-called loving foster "mothers" while growing up, especially her final one.

But she'd be damned if she'd let this man kick John to the dirt. Not after what John had given—and given up—for their country.

She stepped well into the DCM's personal space. The man had two inches on her five-eight, maybe three. It didn't matter. Her rage carried her right up to his level and a bit beyond. "It's a shame you've been channeling my NCIS counterpart, Mr. Jeffers. You should've picked someone more in tune with reality. Agent Riyad couldn't grasp the concept of motive if Ted Bundy himself had brought him along and offered up a blow-by-blow *while* good ol' Ted was selecting his victims and murdering them. And Riyad sure as hell doesn't understand what makes Garrison tick."

The surfeit of garlic Jeffers had consumed for lunch blasted right back into her, fueling his hot breath that much more. "Coming from you, that's amusing as hell. Because, unlike you, Riyad is more than some cut-rate Army *dick*. That man is a former Navy SEAL who's done more to track down terrorists and put them out of commission since 9-11 than you can hope to finger in a hundred careers. And if Garrison thinks he can slide into that slot alongside Riyad at Homeland Security, he's got another think coming. Especially after I finish sending my two cents up the chain."

*Riyad was a former SEAL?*

What the—

"Cat got your tongue there, Agent?"

Try every single lion on the Serengeti. But her instincts were roaring louder than all of them combined. And shredding though her suspicions with a lot more force.

If Sam Riyad was a former SEAL, *why* had he hidden it?

Because he had. With her, and with John.

Only, she was now almost certain the spook hadn't been as successful in deceiving John as he'd hoped.

She also knew why John had needed to get to a phone, and what he'd wanted to confirm. Part of it, at least. According to a number she'd come across while working a joint case shortly after she'd been tapped for CID, there were roughly twenty-five hundred SEALs on active duty. Special Forces had close to three times that.

Yes, there were joint training schools and missions. But as a rule, SEALs and SF tended to play in separate sandboxes when the day-to-day shit went down. Hence, while as a whole both communities were tight knit, they didn't know everyone.

A fact Riyad had depended on.

Something must've given the spook away. An unguarded comment, a suspiciously defining behavior. Possibly several. Whatever it was, it had caused John to suspect the man's professional lineage...and something else. Something so serious John had been loath to discuss it with her—*and* General Palisade—until he was certain.

But what?

And why did she have the feeling that whatever it was, it was also tied up with Riyad's irrational suspicions about John? Why else had the spook worked so hard to hide his former status from a current special operator?

"Agent?"

The sneer that blew in on that fresh wave of garlic hauled her back to the present. To her temporary office. She needed to get Jeffers out of there, so she could think. Make her own covert call—to Mira. Find out what the hell was going on.

As for the other revelation Jeffers had made, the one regarding John and a pending slot at Homeland, she'd take that up with the only man who mattered.

And he wasn't standing in front her.

Despite the garlic, she stepped that much closer to the one who was—and smiled, albeit grimly. "If Agent Riyad is so brilliant, how did he manage to miss the fact that Tamir Hachemi was poisoned by Staff Sergeant Brandt?"

"*What*?"

She nodded crisply, even as her eyes began to water from that odor. "Getting his face bashed into the bulkhead didn't kill the translator, strychnine did. That and *your* Marine."

Why not? The moment she and the others had reached Al Dhafra, Palisade had drawn her, John and Riyad aside before he'd departed to deal with whatever had been in that message traffic that his aide had brought into the *Griffith*'s wardroom that morning. Once again, the general had made it clear that she had absolute control and discretion over the release of information regarding her case. That hadn't pleased the spook, and would probably please Riyad's current cheerleader even less.

She didn't care what Riyad or Jeffers thought. It was what the ambassador did with the information that mattered. Linnet possessed loose lips, at least over this.

Why not use that to their advantage? What better way to let the Pakistanis know John hadn't been responsible for Hachemi's death?

They were going to need the Pakistani president's support, not rancor, if they hoped to identify the final victim from that cave and catch the traitor before he managed to infect someone else—and prevent whatever else Durrani's cohort had planned.

For once, Jeffers' fleshy lips appeared stuck in neutral. "I don't understand. Hachemi was poisoned? By *Brandt*?"

This second nod was even crisper, and more than a bit clipped. "Yes. Do try and keep up, sir. Brandt brought strychnine onto the *Griffith*. But he obtained it when you and the others returned via Al Dhafra. I need to know how, and from whom."

Jeffers swallowed hard as the implications ricocheted in. "We—my staff—we were the only ones who knew those two Marines were heading back to the *Griffith* after they picked up the prisoners."

"Exactly. But there's more. Brandt's seizure was caused by the chimera. He was infected at Al Dhafra too."

Either that tidbit hadn't been shared with Linnet or the woman had managed to keep something to herself, because Regan had succeeded in knocking the DCM back on his heels with something that carried a lot more punch than that smell.

The truth.

Jeffers was floored. Oh, the man tried to hide it. But that fixed stare, that tense jaw and that thick swallow? The gray that was slowly overtaking those meaty jowls as the blood slowly receded from the DCM's face?

Even this asshole had finally realized he had a traitor in his midst.

"Now, I have a question for you, Mr. Jeffers. Did either you or the ambassador share the details of my real mission with *anyone* else—American, Afghan, Pakistani or, hell, even Martian?" She wouldn't put any of it past either of them.

Color returned to those jowls, staining the generous flesh

redder than the deck had been in the *Griffith*'s brig the night before. "Yes."

"Who?"

"Just the regional security officer. And Maddoc won't talk. I guarantee it."

She was less than impressed with the assurance. Especially in light of the assurer's worship of Riyad. Still, she nodded. "Bring him in and press the point. No one else can know. Call me if you need backup."

Frankly, she wasn't sure Jeffers would have the balls to push it with the regional security officer. Look how quickly he'd folded with her.

Then again, clamping down on the embassy's senior Diplomatic Security Service agent didn't sit right with her either. Neither had lying to Maddoc and his DSS staff in the first place. Frankly, it was frustrating as hell to have as many counter-intel and investigatory assets as there were attached to this compound and not be able to use them. Much less confide in them. Receive time-tested wisdom and advice.

But during that out-brief at Al Dhafra, General Palisade—evidently with Admiral Kettering's support—had been firm. No DSS agent in Pakistan would be privy to the truth until every single one had been cleared and the traitor arrested.

She might hate keeping colleagues in the dark, but she understood why.

Especially on this.

Anyone who knew counterintelligence history would. All they had to do was look back to 2009 and the arrest of a Department of State employee with nearly thirty years in who'd been arrested and convicted of conspiring to provide classified US information to a foreign government. And there were more cases in other critical agencies. Certainly enough to give her pause, even without that chimera floating around out there.

As for Warren Jeffers, "Sir, I'd like to begin my interviews. I'll need to speak to every name on my list. I believe you have a copy." Not that Jeffers needed it. As he'd said, he'd been in the *Griffith*'s conference room when her BI had hit the table. "I'll be sure to let you know which one of your staffers is dirty—after I take the bastard down. Until then, *stay out of my way*."

She must have made her point, because the man nodded once, muttered something about her standing by for visitors, and left.

Regan slumped back into the edge of the table as the door opened, then closed behind him. The implications of everything the DCM had revealed continued to pummel though her brain. Her still trembling hand all but ached to retrieve her phone and punch in Mira's number. She wanted to demand that her friend drop everything, and pull up Riyad's file and read it to her word for word.

But she couldn't. Reality had set in.

She was stuck in this room until dinner, at least. And since she was in Pakistan, among a people known to eat markedly later than those in her own country, the meal might not occur for many hours. Until she made her escape, she'd have to remain on her guard. Assume that this room and potentially others within the compound were bugged. If so, there was no telling who might be listening on the other end.

Much less, if they were friendly.

With what she'd been forced to reveal to Jeffers to get him on her side and actively pursuing her goals, she prayed not. Nor could she risk revealing more, let alone to anyone else.

The thought dogged her through all four of her following interviews.

She had to give Jeffers credit. When he'd finally accepted reality, he'd moved heaven and earth to assist.

Unfortunately, nothing came from the DCM's efforts or hers.

Though Jeffers hadn't intended it, she'd discovered more in those ten minutes going at it with him than she had from all four of the staffers who'd shuttled through the chair on the opposite side of her makeshift desk. Even more frustrating, the two men that her gut had kept pinging on during her initial research on the flight from Al Dhafra to Islamabad hadn't shown. Couldn't.

According to a subsequent call from an almost apologetic Jeffers, both the embassy's senior political officer and the Pakistani Foreign Service National who'd accompanied the other staffers to the *Griffith* to transcribe the minutes and assist with translation were out for the remainder of the day. The political officer, Tom Crier, was in a meeting across the city, while Aamer Sadat had left the compound before Regan's C-130 had even touched down at Islamabad International.

Evidently Sadat's wife had phoned before lunch. The Sadats' three-month-old son had diabetes and had suffered an insulin reaction. Mrs. Sadat had taken the baby to hospital. The boy was still there, now in intensive care, along with his terrified parents. As excuses went, it was one Regan couldn't argue with.

Who'd want to?

Regan sighed as she closed her notes file on her computer. The lid of the laptop followed with a stronger snap. 1800 local time had just come and gone. Whether she liked it or not, it appeared she'd be meeting with Crier, Sadat and the embassy's loose-lipped ambassador in the morning.

Hope surged as her phone vibrated, only to sink as she caught the name in her caller ID. It wasn't Colonel Tarrington, or even John with news about whatever he and Tulle were up to. It was Gil.

"What's up, Doc?"

Despite the ten-hour time deficit on Gil's end, he laughed. Then again, it was 0800 back at Campbell. Gil was heavily and contentedly caffeinated by now. Unlike her. The first name on Palisade's list had arrived before she'd had a chance to locate the closest coffee pot. The caffeine-driven throb from this morning had returned.

"From what I hear, not you."

*Whoa*. What exactly had Gil heard? And from whom?

The possibilities sliced in. And all wielded the same double-edged sword: her hand. "I beg your pardon?"

"Garrison called."

Shit.

Stick to the case. And pray. "Did you give him the official assessment on Brandt? It's the chimera, isn't it?"

"Yeah, it is. And I told him. But that's not the only reason he phoned."

She wasn't sure what piqued her more. That John had spoken about her with Gil. Or that he hadn't bothered to let her know he'd planned on ratting her out.

Except her ire was already cooling, and rapidly...because she also realized what it would've cost John to reach out to Gil. To a man who less than three weeks earlier, John had believed she was not only involved with, but pregnant by. It didn't matter that he now knew differently. When John cared, he leaned toward jealousy—sharply. She'd known that from almost the moment they'd met. She'd even abused the knowledge out in that bar's parking lot to reel him in faster and tighter so she could get him to open up about his houseguest. She wasn't proud of her actions then, but she was of John's now.

John had known she needed to hear from Gil, so he'd arranged it. At his own emotional expense, and pride.

Her remaining ire eased out along with her breath. "What did you tell him?"

"The truth. That you're back at it too soon. That you need to get your butt home and get some serious rest." Gil's sigh mirrored hers. "But we both know that's not possible right now. So listen closely: you need to take your downtime whenever and wherever you can. And take it seriously. This stress? It's not helping. Neither did the stunt that bastard pulled on you last night. Garrison told me what Durrani said, what he did. I know you're rattled. Hell, anyone would be, and they don't share your past. But you'll get through this. Durrani won't. It's over for him. Don't let that bastard win. I meant it, Rae. The way your arm reacted? If you don't take it easy, you'll be risking a significant setback. Possibly one that's irreversible. And then where will you be?"

Lord, she hated when Gil was right. "I know."

Nor was she mad at him either. The contents of a soldier's medical record weren't sacrosanct like a civilian's were. The needs of the nation and the mission came first. Always. It was right there when you signed on the dotted line. Gil would've been obligated to talk no matter who'd called him from her chain of command with respect to her current mission. Frankly, they were both lucky it had been John.

Still, another sigh filled the line, overridden at the end as its owner's name was paged over the hospital's PA system. "Rae, I—"

"Gotta go."

"Yeah. Hang in there."

Before she could agree, he'd hung up.

She was left staring at those barren, windowless walls. They were driving her nuts. Her makeshift office was rapidly becoming her makeshift cell, trapping her with the other bombshell that Jeffers had lobbed her way earlier.

John had an open offer with Homeland Security. And he hadn't told her.

It hurt. More than she wanted to admit. Though, really, what had she expected? That he'd stick around for the long haul? John might've intimated as much when she'd woken from her coma. And he might've reiterated it silently last night aboard the *Griffith* when he'd held her in her rack. Hell, he'd even all but roared it in the wardroom this morning while he'd been staring down Riyad.

So why hadn't he told her about the offer?

They hadn't had a lot of time for privacy, but they'd found some.

Did he want the slot? More than he wanted her?

She could hear Durrani and his acidic filth filling her ear, eating away at her confidence. Damned if the man's voice didn't sound a lot like her final foster mother's at the moment. As much as she hated to admit it, both were right. She was damaged goods. Between her dad, her mom, her grandfather, fifteen different foster homes and her final, not-so-loving group facility, how could she be anything else?

Hell, even Mira, Jelly and Gil all added together had never been able to fill the gaping hole inside her. Worse, she'd donned a different mask with so many people for so many years, she wasn't sure who was really beneath it anymore.

How could John figure it out? Much less love who he found enough to want to stick around for the long haul? No one else had. Ever. She'd been told *eighteen times* that she wasn't worth it. Even the world's biggest moron would get that message. She didn't need Durrani or anyone else telling her that, eventually, John would do the same.

And then he'd leave. It was probably best that he do it now. While she still had the strength to let him go.

Screw this. Gil was right. She could *not* let that bastard get to her. Not even if John left the Army—and her—for good.

She retrieved her phone and called Scott. DSS agents were qualified to investigate embassy personnel overseas; he might as well assist. Even if he wouldn't know what he was really assisting with.

Not only had Scott pushed through his own work on the human trafficking sting, he'd already retrieved the keys to Staff Sergeant Brandt's quarters from the RSO's office and had been about to pick up the phone himself to call her.

"Grab your gear, Prez. I'll be there in five minutes to show you the way to the Marine House."

He made it in three.

Regan waited until she and Scott had entered the two-story barracks building and climbed the stairs to reach Brandt's room. "Do you know a Sam Riyad? He's NCIS."

Scott's snort was as sharp as the pocket knife he'd brandished to cut the seal on Brandt's door. "The Holy One?" He paused. Flushed. "Sorry. That's not Riyad's attitude, it's—"

"Jeffers'."

"Yep."

Curious and curiouser. "Why? What's Riyad done for the guy?" Or possibly the ambassador?

"He exists." Scott used the tip of his knife to sever the warning sticker that had been signed and adhered to the door's seam, then unlocked it. He pushed the door open and reached inside to flip on the light switch. "After you."

Regan preceded him into the room.

She set her laptop bag and crime scene kit on the staff sergeant's desk, then opened the lock on her kit. Retrieving two pairs of latex gloves from within, she passed the first to Scott and donned the second as she scanned the staff sergeant's quarters. They resembled nearly every barracks room she'd occupied while enlisted, along with those she'd tossed as an MP and more recently as CID. The layout consisted of a twin bed, a desk, a TV and a large, lockable wardrobe.

The latter intrigued her most, so she began there, severing Brandt's combination lock with the small bolt cutters in her kit as she nudged Scott for more on the spook. "Riyad exists? Surely there's more to it?"

"You do know the guy's a former SEAL, right?"

Oh, she did now. "Yeah, I heard that. So?"

"So, Jeffers is a wannabe." Scott shook his head as he snapped his second glove into place. He accepted the broken lock as she turned back to work her way through the staff sergeant's uniforms and personal items. "Nah, make that a woulda, shoulda, coulda been."

"What happened? Did Jeffers get accepted and blow out a shoulder halfway through the third month of Buds?"

"More like washed out. And it was nowhere near halfway. I heard the guy rang the bell by the end of the first day."

Yikes.

Granted, she doubted she'd have made it through an hour at Buds. She knew her strengths, just as she knew her limitations. But she'd never wanted to be a SEAL. Jeffers had. And he'd been forced to accept that he couldn't make the grade up close and personal. Despite that asshole behavior of his, she felt for the guy.

It also explained his hero worship. But there were operational drawbacks to willful blindness, whether Jeffers was willing to cop to it or not, especially with regard to Riyad. The DCM's judgment was clouded.

And that was *never* a good thing.

Not that she'd have shared the realization with Scott. Though from that glint she'd noted in his eye in her temporary office earlier, she was fairly certain she didn't need to.

Regan fell silent as she worked her way through the remainder of the wardrobe unit. There was nothing out of place. She closed the unit and crossed the room to toss the bed. Again, nothing. She hit the drawers in the desk next and came up empty once more. If the staff sergeant had been hiding something big enough to serve as blackmail leverage, there was no trace of it in his room. Except—

"Is that a picture frame?"

Blinds shifted and rattled softly against the window as Scott straightened up from the sill. "Where?"

She pointed to where he'd been standing beside the bed. Whatever that was, it was lying flat on the floor and tucked up underneath the bottom of the bed, near the head. As if Brandt had been staring at it while lying down, then slipped it beneath to keep it safe as he'd nodded off. She stepped forward and leaned down to retrieve it.

It was a frame. An electronic one.

Why wasn't it displayed on the desk?

Had Brandt been torturing himself with pictures of an ex?

She switched the frame on and clicked through the succession of photos that were stored within. There were nineteen—and all contained groupings of the same three people, with the occasional addition or substitution of Brandt.

She tapped the other male face she recognized. "That's Aamer Sadat, isn't it?" The Pakistani Foreign Service National who'd missed his interview with her an hour ago. "And I'm guessing this woman is Sadat's wife?"

Scott nodded. "Yeah, and that's a photo of their new kid." He shook his head as she cycled through the stored pictures once more. "A *lot* of photos of their kid."

Agreed. In fact, either the baby or the mother was in every single one. Usually both. Out of nineteen photos, Aamer Sadat was in nine shots, total. Regan stopped on one of the nine. Brandt was holding the infant. Mrs. Sadat was standing on Brandt's right with Mr. Sadat standing to his wife's right. Except Mrs. Sadat wasn't looking at her husband, but at Brandt. Brandt was also looking at her—and the glow that bathed the staff sergeant's face was more than friendly. It was reverent.

Blackmailable, even.

Along with the rest. Namely, the baby's chin. It was dimpled...like Brandt's. Aamer Sadat's chin was smooth, along with his wife's. But there was more. There were hints of Caucasian blood in the baby's features, too. Hints that Regan suspected would become more defined as the boy grew up. She was almost certain Aamer Sadat was not the baby's father.

And there was an excellent chance Brandt was.

# 19

It took every gene Regan had inherited from her own father to clamp down on the rush of adrenaline hitting her veins before it reached her face. The more she studied that photo, the more certain she became. The adrenaline had a right to be there. Those Caucasian hints in the baby's features were one thing. But that cleft in his chin? That was the clincher.

They usually were.

Dimples, in a cheek or the chin, were a dominant genetic trait.

She'd never ask—because John would detest admitting it—but there was an excellent chance his father had sported the same distracting dent that John did. Though for John's sake, she hoped not. As for Mrs. Sadat, with Brandt deceased, Regan suspected the woman would treasure that dimpled chin, along with the other features the boy had inherited from his father. But there was another crucial question burning through her brain regarding the baby and his mother.

Did Mrs. Sadat know her son was a cause of blackmail?

Because if Regan was right, someone had used this boy's true parentage to blackmail the staff sergeant into feeding Tamir Hachemi strychnine.

It was time to draft a second list. On this one? The names of those who might have known that Brandt was a father. Once she cross-referenced that list against the staffers who'd read her BI... she just might have their traitor.

The first of those names? DSS Senior Special Agent in Charge Charles Maddoc. There was simply no way a regional security officer could've missed a clue this huge. Not an RSO tapped to head up the protection of one of the nation's most vital diplomatic missions. Palisade's prudence regarding silence with diplomatic security had paid off.

And there was Warren Jeffers. While Marine guards at an embassy did answer to the DSS agent in charge of regional security, that DSS agent—and everyone beneath him or her—answered the deputy chief of mission. Hence, Jeffers, too, should have known. So why hadn't Jeffers said anything to her in her temporary office earlier? Especially once he'd supposedly come around regarding her true mission and the location of the traitor.

The obvious possibility chilled her to the bone.

Her instincts might've cleared Jeffers earlier, even while he'd been spewing his filth at her...but her instincts were not infallible. And neither was she.

She'd learned that the hard way.

"Holy *shit*."

Regan glanced up as Scott reached out to tap the photo queued up in the frame.

"That's Brandt's kid. It's gotta be."

"I'd say there's an excellent chance. Were there rumors?"

Scott shook his head. "None that I heard. But I answer to the RSO at the moment. I may be temporarily assigned, but I'd have had to inform Maddoc—and that would've killed Brandt's career. Could also be why she's been avoiding everyone."

"Mrs. Sadat?"

Scott nodded as Regan switched off the electronic frame and bagged it for evidence. "From what I heard, she visited the compound quite a bit while she was pregnant. But once she had the kid—*pffft*. A couple folks have remarked on it. Guess we now know why the visits dried up. I also heard Brandt had less than a month left on his tour. Could be that she was lying low. Maybe they figured once he left, no one would remember his face well enough to suspect the rest."

The rationale was sound. And Scott was right. If this had gotten out, it would've been a career ender for the staff sergeant, with potential Uniformed Code of Military Justice charges and stockade time on top.

If Charles Maddoc *wasn't* their traitor, could that have been a factor in the RSO keeping his mouth shut? If Maddoc had said something, he'd also have had to pull Brandt from his position as an active embassy guard, and charge him with adultery and conduct unbecoming, at the very least.

Only the RSO hadn't had direct access to her BI. He'd also remained behind here at the embassy compound to continue overseeing its security due to the potential flammable fallout from those diplomatic ass-covering sessions aboard the *Griffith*.

Jeffers claimed he'd revealed her true mission to Maddoc, but not the info in her BI. And that revelation regarding her mission had to have occurred today. There would have been no time for Maddoc to pull in favors to get a peek at her BI off the books and still share its contents with Durrani because Durrani was already dead.

Had Maddoc figured out the baby's potential parentage after Brandt had been sent to the *Griffith*? Was that why Maddoc was maintaining his silence? Because there was already enough crap being flung around the ship's conference room?

Maddoc would've known that Brandt had less than thirty days left on station. Had the RSO also hoped that with Brandt leaving, the potential shitstorm would be leaving with him?

Or was Maddoc simply ignorant of that dimple and its genetic implications?

Possibly. But someone else should have suspected something. Someone who *had* had access to her BI nearly three weeks ago.

Aamer Sadat.

Surely Mr. Sadat had noticed that cleft in his own son's chin? With how close they all appeared in those photos, he must have suspected a lot more. Had Sadat spotted an attraction between Brandt and his wife early on, even encouraged an affair as a way to get leverage over the Marine? There was only one way to find out.

And, at the moment, only one place.

Regan tucked the evidence bag with the electronic frame inside her kit and secured it. She had a feeling she'd be needing the photos for her coming chat.

"You done here?"

She slung her laptop over her shoulder and hefted her kit. "Yup."

"Great. I found this fantastic place my first week. It overlooks the entire—"

She shook her head. Dinner would have to wait. Along with her drumming need for caffeine. A need that was threatening to morph into pounding any minute now. "But I could use a lift—to whichever hospital admitted Baby Sadat this afternoon."

With his "son" in intensive care, even a traitor would want to keep up appearances.

And with all that stress floating around the room? What

better timing for an interrogation disguised as an impromptu sympathy visit?

"That'd be Shifa International." Scott peeled off his latex gloves and tucked them in his trouser pocket, before retrieving his keys. "It's not too far away from the embassy, or the restaurant I've got in mind. I can always drive you back to the compound and your complimentary flop slot for the night when we're done."

"Fantastic. I just need to stop by my temporary office and grab my scarf." She'd promised John she'd wear the *dupatta* while out and about, and a hospital visit with a follow-on dinner in town definitely qualified.

Nor did it escape her that she might come off as more approachable to both Sadats if her hair was covered when she dropped by. And there was that bottle of ibuprofen inside the ditty bag in her suitcase. Two of the capsules within would ease her growing headache and ward off the need for caffeine for a few hours, at least.

Ten minutes later, she was inside another black Volvo with her suitcase and gear locked in the trunk, two capsules duly swallowed and the *dupatta* concealing her French braid once again. This time she was in the front left passenger seat of the Volvo, watching the stark, almost desolate buildings of Islamabad proper pass by in the dark as Scott drove.

Within minutes they'd turned onto Srinagar Highway.

Scott glanced across the seat to her, then immediately shifted his attention forward to keep from colliding with a boxy Japanese number that tried to cut them off. "Sorry, still not quite used to driving on the left side of the road."

The box made a second attempt.

This time, Scott slowed and let it in. "So what's your assessment?"

"So far, it's not much different than the outskirts of a

southern city." Especially at night. Definitely not like Afghanistan or Iraq, and the places she'd been in both.

Scott shook his head. "Not the city. Jeffers."

As segues went, it couldn't have been more perfect if she'd tried. She laughed as she went with it. "Oh, he's a total bastard. He managed to toss Riyad's superior skills in my face within two minutes of meeting me. Hence, my interest in Jeffers at the Marine House."

"Yeah, that's him. To hear Jeffers tell it, he's the lifeblood of Embassy I. Has been since he held Tom Crier's slot when the new mission was inaugurated. The guy's a plank owner in the chancery—and he lets *everyone* know it. Jeffers saves his charm for the locals. Which is odd, if you ask me, with him being a career diplomat and all."

Agreed.

"I think his wife's gonna leave him."

*What*? Scott had been there two months. How'd he manage to glean that?

There was something in the set of Scott's jaw when he glanced her way that told her he was serious. Anger.

"What happened?" And why did she have the feeling that, like her, Scott had wanted to get away from the embassy so he too could talk—privately?

When he failed to curse at the next driver who flat-out cut them off, she realized he was truly upset about something.

"Scott?"

He kept his eyes on the road, which was prudent, as it was notably crowded. But he sighed. Heavily. "Bethany came to see me last week in confidence. She thinks Jeffers is having an affair. She asked if I could stick around a few days after I was scheduled to leave and follow her husband on the sly. Find proof for her to use in the divorce."

Yikes. This was big. And tricky. Yes, DSS investigated diplomats when needed. But for crimes against the country and other persons, not against the heart.

"And?"

"And I'm not convinced it is another woman. I mean, it could be. From what Bethany said, Jeffers is never in their residence when he should be, and when he is, he's preoccupied. She's says she's caught him on the phone late at night...in the guest bathroom with the door locked and the water running. When she pressed him, he lashed out, grabbed her arms so hard, he left bruises." Scott glanced over as he took the exit off the highway. "I saw them myself. Definitely compression fingermarks."

"Have you spoken to Jeffers about it?"

That earned her a snort. "The man's the fucking DCM. This is my first shot out in the real world of DSS—and he'll be signing off on my final assessment and making the recommendation on whether I get a second shot."

"You said you weren't convinced it was another woman. Why?"

Scott shrugged as he turned the Volvo into yet another street crowded with impatient, honking traffic. The scenery had shifted from shadowy stands of trees to sand-colored buildings, but she was too preoccupied now to study the signs in Urdu and English that covered them.

She stared at the left side of Scott's jaw instead.

It was tense.

"I've been watching him since Bethany came to me. The man is on edge. Seriously so. I doubt he's getting action from anyone, let alone a hot new number across town. Something is eating at that man, Rae. It has been since he and the ambassador returned from their week-long, off-site, hush-hush that they still won't discuss. That said, I watch the news. And there's the timing of it all. It doesn't take a genius to figure out you were involved with what went down with that A-Team over there, and most likely are still working the fallout. And, no, I am not asking for a confirmation. I may be new to DSS, but I've been around it and the military long enough to know when to stick my nose in, and when to keep it out. I just...thought you should know."

Regan nodded. "Thank you."

Scott let it drop with that, and so did she.

At least out loud. But that behavior Bethany Jeffers had described—potential extramarital activities and spousal abuse aside—it did mesh with a man who was trying to hide something...and was failing. Granted, Jeffers could simply be close to cracking over the political fallout from the cave murders and the psycho-toxin horror. Or, hell, any number of apocalyptic-level developments that top diplomats dealt with and were forced to keep secret, often on a daily basis.

But when she added on the fact that Jeffers might also be hiding knowledge of Brandt and Baby Sadat's dimpled chin...

*Were* her instincts off about the man?

She was still hashing though the connections and possibilities as they reached the hospital.

Regan took in the massive, modern and well-lit multi complex that appeared to crowd out more than an entire city block as Scott parked the Volvo. "Wow."

He laughed. "I know. It's a medical monster, isn't it? I swear, it feels even bigger inside."

And it did.

The Shifa was also a fascinating mix of modern and traditional. The dichotomy surrounded Regan as they entered and moved deeper through the corridors. Gleaming marble, stainless steel and glass were everywhere, along with an overabundance of men and women. The men were dressed in everything from executive suits and silk ties to the most modest of *shalwar kameezes*, complete with short, round *topi* skullcaps up high and callused, sandaled feet down low. The majority of the women were wrapped—often head to toe—in endless, wisping yards of bright blues, peacock greens and lush purples, as well as vibrant yellows, burgundies, oranges and reds, many with silver and gold threads stitched throughout. And right next to these women—at times even chatting with them—the coarser, drab drapes of the completely obscuring shuttlecock *burqa*.

But almost every single woman—sack-clothed, or gilded and silked—wore some version of the *dupatta* or a completely concealing veil.

John was right. She and her CID-blue suit did garner a few stares as they headed through the maze of corridors, but the somber *dupatta* attracted even more attention in the way of approving glances and nods, as well as the occasional outright smile.

Fortunately, the signs directing everyone were in Urdu and English. Within minutes, she and Scott had reached the waiting room outside the intensive care. She spotted Mrs. Sadat immediately. The woman was in her early-to-mid-twenties and dressed in gorgeous eggshell blue. The intricate silver floral design that edged her veil was delicate and stunning. The thickly lashed, caramel features within were more so.

Regan had no idea what the woman's husband was wearing. Mr. Sadat was nowhere to be seen. Hopefully, the man's tail had him firmly in sight.

If not, they were screwed.

Worse, Regan quickly discovered that his wife did not speak English. Odd. Not only had Inaya Sadat been married to a Pakistani Foreign Service National for several years, Staff Sergeant Brandt wasn't fluent in Urdu.

Had her husband translated?

Scott murmured something to the woman as he sat down a respectable seat away. Mrs. Sadat's response was equally soft.

He glanced up as the woman dropped her focus to her folded

hands. "I told her we came from the embassy to check on her family, see if they needed anything. The boy appears to be holding his own for the moment, and his blood sugar's stable, which is why her husband isn't here. He left the hospital to honor a scheduled appointment at their bank. She remained behind for their son."

"He didn't arrange for someone to sit with her?" Regan took in the woman's reddened eyes, the dried traces of tears on Mrs. Sadat's otherwise perfect cheeks. Biological father or not, abandoning the woman to her fears was cold.

Scott's sigh mirrored her thoughts. "Nope. And since she doesn't know when he'll be back—or if he's stopping anywhere afterward—I doubt we'll be able to explain away hanging around as long as it may take for him to return."

Double damn. "Does she know about Brandt?"

The woman glanced up at that name. Actually made eye contact with Regan. Spoke. In English. "Brandt?" Well, one, gently murmured word. The rest was a stream of still soft, but very rapid Urdu that Regan had no hope of translating.

She waited for the woman to finish.

Scott glanced over. "She wants to know when he's returning from his trip."

Oh, boy.

Not the best of ways to reveal this, much less the right time or place. But word regarding Brandt's unexpected death had been released that afternoon while the Sadats were here at the hospital. Mr. Sadat, wherever he was, was bound to learn of it soon. As much as she hated to push this woman while she was already distraught over her son, she had no choice. Mrs. Sadat was going to find out soon enough. She might as well offer it up now and catalogue the reaction.

They needed answers.

"Rae?"

She nodded. "Tell her."

He did.

Regan might not speak Urdu, but after three years as an Army MP and another five with CID, if she was fluent in anything at all, it was death notifications and grief. She could feel the news sear in on that sharp, swift gasp, watched as the subsequent denial shook the woman's veiled head until it coalesced and settled into quivering lips. Dark, reddened eyes turning redder still as they filled with a wave of fresh tears.

But that was it. They never spilled over.

And, then, they evaporated.

Less than half a minute later, Inaya Sadat sat there in her chair in the waiting room, staring at her hands once again. Silent. The quivering in those lips had long since ceased, her aura more subdued and remote now than it had been upon their arrival.

Gentle stoicism didn't begin to cover this woman.

The father of her child was dead, and this was it?

Suspicion prickled in.

Regan was about to suggest that Scott prod the woman with a few choice questions, when a slender, blond nurse interrupted. The lightly veiled British woman leaned down to whisper something in Mrs. Sadat's ears. A split second later, a high-pitched wail reverberated throughout the waiting room as Inaya stood and grabbed onto the nurse for support before both women half stumbled, half hurried across the room and through the door from whence the nurse had come.

Scott came to his feet as well. "Her son's taken a turn for the worse."

Regan nodded. She'd gathered that. But really? That was the reaction she'd expected over the notification of the staff sergeant's death.

Before she could share her suspicion with Scott, her phone rang. She glanced down at the caller ID.

Karl Goethe.

The wave of emotion Regan had expected to hit Inaya Sadat crashed into her instead. Riding the crest: relief so intense, it burned. She closed her eyes to absorb it, then glanced at Scott. "I need to take this."

She headed out into the corridor, turning so she had a view of all who passed as she accepted the call. "Yes?"

"We need to meet. Off embassy grounds. The Serena Hotel. Do you know it?"

"Yes." They'd passed the graceful, stone colossus on the drive here, though the hotel was closer to the embassy compound than the hospital. "I'm with Scott at Shifa International. Twenty, twenty-five minutes away. He can drop me."

"Good. You're Mrs. Goethe. I'll be waiting."

John severed the call.

As she headed back inside the crowded waiting room to inform Scott of the change in plans, she realized John hadn't given her a first name.

Then again, this was Pakistan. She didn't need one.

As far as any local at the hotel was concerned, she was simply Karl Goethe's woman, an extension of the German business*man*.

Scott took one look at her as she reached his side and sighed. "I've lost my dinner date, haven't I?"

"Sorry."

He shrugged and led the way out of the hospital.

Back at the car, Regan opted for the rear seat cater-cornered to the driver's in the front so she could still converse with Scott during the trip, yet appear to be the well-to-do, but modest expat upon her arrival at the hotel's manned entrance. Due to the influx of traffic on the roads, the drive took thirty minutes, during which Scott regaled her with his gustatory adventures around the city since he'd arrived. She tried to focus on their conversation, but dread had long since dripped through her relief at that call, coldly supplanting it. John had wanted to meet well away from the embassy.

Why?

She'd find out soon enough. Scott was already guiding the Volvo through the sculpted grounds of another dichotomous locale. Though the Serena appeared even sleeker and more impressive than the hospital they'd left, there was the whole veiled, two-steps-behind aspect of it all. Even here beneath the stone-covered entrance.

As promised, John was waiting beside the doorman as Scott pulled up.

He was wearing his dark gray suit from earlier in the day, though it was slightly wrinkled now. His leather suit bag was nowhere to be seen. With his Mrs. Goethe comment, she'd assumed they'd be having a secluded meal over china and crystal in a corner of the dining room. Had he checked them in instead?

What the hell had he learned?

He couldn't have gotten a name, could he?

Adrenaline and hope burned through the remaining dread so quickly, her nerves tightened. So much so, her fingers had taken up that irritating tremor before John had even stepped up to the rear passenger door to open it for her. His right hand engulfed the fingers of her still steady one as he assisted her in exiting the car...or not.

To the doorman, a passing local gentleman and probably even Scott, John appeared to be helping. What he'd really done was tuck something into her palm.

Two somethings.

Rings.

Regan turned into the side of the car for cover and donned the solitary diamond and accompanying gold band. Score one for Tulle. The staff sergeant must've been sent to purchase the rings while John had been in his meeting. Though slightly loose, both were an impressively decent fit for impromptu guesswork.

By the time John had retrieved her suitcase and gear, she'd gotten her confirmation. He had checked them in as man and wife.

She nodded her thanks to Scott before following meekly behind as John led the way into the hotel and across the echoing marble foyer. He stopped in front of a pair of stainless-steel elevator doors and pressed the *up* button. Unfortunately, by the time the set of doors on their right opened, she and John weren't the only ones to enter.

Conversation would have to wait until they'd reached their room.

Especially since the dark-suited Pakistani and the slight, equally somberly veiled companion standing behind him got off on their floor.

Though it grated, she followed well behind John again. But as he stopped in front of the door to the executive suite he'd apparently secured, another formal suit opened the door from within and motioned them inside. The man wearing this suit was as short, slender and ebony as Staff Sergeant Tulle's dominating Nordic bulk was not.

The unknown suit nodded as he hefted a nondescript stainless-steel case slightly larger than the one John had carried in for her. "All clear, man." The innate humor behind that follow-up grin was infectious. "Well...it is now."

Bugs.

Evidently John had called in a colleague to have the room swept for listening devices. And he'd found something. Not surprising. Executive suites tended to be occupied by executives.

Industrial espionage was as big a racket as the one in which she suspected John's colleague chose to partake. Not to mention clearing this room would be easier, and certainly less suspicious, than ordering a sweep of their own embassy.

"Thanks, Ty."

Ty?

Ty turned to her and nodded at the question evident in her raised brow. "Tyrell Bennet. I'm the Company man who's been dealing with the shadow requests you made via General Palisade this morning. Need any changes to the line up?"

She nodded. "Stay on Maddoc, Crier and Sadat. Contact Major Garrison or myself if anything seems off—and add Inaya Sadat to the list...along with Jeffers."

The man blinked at the final name, then inclined his head. "You got it."

"Thank you."

She headed deeper into the room to give John a few moments with Ty, since the man was primarily John's connection and not hers. The obvious rapport between them also suggested that John and Ty were friends, as well as occasional colleagues.

Since John had her suitcase and gear at his side, she settled for taking in her surroundings as she attempted to massage the tremors from her hand. The room was huge, with a king-sized bed anchoring the far end. A generous sitting area complete with a plush, maroon couch, two matching chairs and a gleaming coffee table anchored the opposite end of the room. A glass slider beyond led to a small balcony where a wicker table and two seats overlooked a bejeweled view of Islamabad at night. Back inside the room, at the middle, sat a decent-sized desk on one wall, with a mirror and dresser flanking the other, all carved from the same heavy expresso wood of the coffee table and that king-sized headboard.

Unable to massage the tremors into submission, Regan removed the scarf from her hair and dumped it on the desk. She headed for the connecting bath to splash water on her face, only to stop short as she heard the main door close. John had already set her suitcase and gear down beside the desk before she finished swinging back around.

He was staring down at her. Intently.

But not as he'd done on the tarmac before they'd parted that afternoon.

Worse, the longer this stare lasted, the more those three shrapnel scars that cut through the cultivated thicket on his jaw and down into the side of his neck tightened. The pulse point within was barely visible from this angle, but it was throbbing.

*Shit.*

"You have something." And it was bigger than big.

She stepped closer, meeting up with him in front of the desk.

John nodded. "Confirmation."

"Regarding your suspicion that Riyad's a former SEAL?"

His brow kicked up over that.

She wasn't insulted.

Mostly because the gleam that joined in let her know he was also impressed. He knew she hadn't had an inkling as to Riyad's credentials when they'd parted at the airport. Though she would've deserved that flare of respect more if she hadn't stumbled into the information while Jeffers had been spewing garlic and disgust in her face.

Silence crowded in, thickening the air between them.

When John didn't push through it, she knew this was worse than she'd feared. It was also clear from the regret that gradually replaced the respect that he was loath to pin whatever he'd discovered on a former fellow operator. Even a bastard like Riyad.

So she did it for him.

*Equipment*. "What went missing?"

John's sigh was heavy. Harsh. "An SDV."

"*A SEAL delivery vehicle*?" As in, one of the multimillion-dollar, covert submersibles that the teams use to infiltrate enemy ports and beaches?

"Yes." John turned to lean back into the desk, hooking the heels of his palms over the edge as he shook his head. "I don't have all the details. I put in the call to Palisade shortly before you arrived. I haven't heard back yet."

"What do you know?"

"It was a working prototype. It had new capabilities that the government does *not* want out there. I also know Riyad was on the mission when it disappeared. The SDV carries six men. Four are dead. Their bodies washed up. I'm not at liberty to pass on where."

That wasn't what bothered her. "With Riyad, that only accounts for five."

This nod was stunted. Beyond reluctant.

"Who's the missing man?"

"Senior Chief Zakaria Webber. His body never turned up—with the others...or elsewhere."

That, in and of itself, was not unusual. An SDV could be air dropped into open ocean or launched from a submarine or an amphibious warship. But without knowing where and from which platform this one had been launched, she had no idea how likely or unlikely it should've been for Webber's body to have washed up with the others.

But John knew. And the slight flattening in his lips, not to mention that jarring pulse point, told her the rest.

"You think he survived, don't you? Along with the SDV." And then Webber and that classified, multimillion-dollar prototype had gone off the grid.

Deliberately.

John's shrug was slight. The implications were not.

They were devastating.

They had a dirty SEAL out there. And there was the rather distinctive pronunciation that John had given to the man's name: Zakaria. It was either Arabic or Persian. No wonder John hadn't wanted to speculate until he'd found out more.

And, somehow, Sam Riyad was tied up in all this. "You know Webber, don't you?" Or rather, John had known him. And well.

With Riyad's almost fanatical zeal in trying to railroad John into murder charges over Hachemi, at the very least John had worked with Webber somewhere along the way. Had possibly been friends with the guy.

"Yeah, I know him—and, no, Webber and I are not friends."

She kept her brow from hiking in the nick of time. How had he figured out what she was thinking? She hadn't been deliberately altering or concealing her expressions; she hadn't needed to. Her speculation had been that deep. That private.

"I didn't—"

"Didn't have to. It's taken me a while, but I'm getting to where I can read you too." He reached out, traced the tip of one of those callused fingers along her brow, then tapped her nose as that crease cut in beside his smile, along with a healthy dose of the man's congenital arrogance. "I told you the truth when we met in that bar. I'm persistent. And when it comes to you, I am seriously motivated. Getting more so by the day."

She had no idea how to respond to that. Personally or professionally.

So she ignored it.

"The SDV? Do you think Webber sold it to the highest bidder?" Or was it stolen with a specific new owner in mind? Russia? China? Turkey?

*Iran*?

There was the inherent ethnicity in that first name. ...Or did Webber already have plans to use it himself?

John shook his head, his frustration finally spiking. "I don't know. Nor does my source."

His source. With what John had just brought to the table, that source was another SEAL. A SEAL who respected Riyad about as much as Riyad respected John.

A SEAL who had enough on Riyad that *he* was worried—or he wouldn't have confided in John.

She pulled her breath in deep and just said it. "And this source of yours...does he think Riyad is dirty, too?"

"Yes."

# 20

Regan tried to contain her shock as she stared at John.

It was impossible.

This was bigger than either of them had feared, and getting more complicated with each moment. One dirty SEAL was bad enough. But two, possibly working in tandem? One of whom—if Riyad was dirty—was now not only firmly embedded inside NCIS's foreign counter-intel division, but also had Admiral Kettering's ear?

Except... "What do *you* think?"

This shrug was as slight as John's earlier one; the implications it supported, just as heavy. "Jury's still out."

Yeah, with her too. Everything John had revealed actually pointed toward the spook not being dirty. But Riyad was still hiding something.

Damned if she could figure out what it was.

"There's more."

Despite all the possible ramifications that were swirling in, hope flared. John might be in the midst of slowly cataloguing her micro-expressions, but she already had a solid bead on pretty much all of his. "You got a name."

“Possibly.”

"Who?"

"The embassy's senior political officer."

"Tom Crier?"

"You seem surprised."

She was, and then again, she wasn't. "I don't know. I haven't had a chance to sit down with the man. He was away from the embassy this afternoon. But I did make some headway with two other potentials. But first, what did you get on Crier?"

And from whom?

"After we parted this afternoon, Tulle and I flew to Abbottabad. He took care of a few things, while I made some calls and hit up a few sources for information on that Russian name you got out of Durrani. I don't have anything on Aleksi Skulachev yet. But after I finished my calls, I had a face to face with another contact."

"From their military academy?"

"Yes." John loosened his tie and tugged the knot down a few inches. "Guy's a Pakistani army colonel who's also on the ISI's payroll...and Karl Goethe's. They—we—met a few years back when I was in Yemen. Since the coalition forces relied on German arms and tech, it was an easy enough cover to construct and maintain. I was able to get my foot in the door with the guy, and I've been able to keep it there. Basically, Goethe's with the German army and, naturally, the ISI doesn't know about Goethe."

Naturally.

The Inter-Services Intelligence was Pakistan's version of the CIA, Gestapo and KGB rolled into one. Not only did their interrogators consider waterboarding child's play, they saved their more horrifying techniques for those they perceived as traitors to Allah and the Pakistani state, which to the ISI were one and the same.

"Let me guess; the ISI's been tailing Crier." After all, Crier was the senior political officer at the American embassy in their capital city. She'd be shocked if they weren't following him—along with every other staffer in that compound. "What do they have on the man?"

"Crier's having an affair. According to the colonel, the ISI hasn't acted on the information yet. They were saving it for a rainy day."

"Who's the woman?"

"He doesn't know her name. Wasn't told. All he knows is she's a local. Does that mesh with what you've got?"

"Yes and no." According to her research, Crier and his wife recently celebrated fourteen years of connubial bliss. Seven longer than the purported itch. The fact that Mrs. Crier happened to be the cherished daughter of US Senator Jack Hawthorne may have helped to extend the timeframe.

After all, what would Senator Hawthorne—a ranking member of the Senate intelligence committee—do to Crier's future with the State Department if he found out?

"Rae?"

"It's solid blackmail material, yes. But I don't—" She shook her head. "Hang on. I've got something to show you." She reached down to retrieve her crime scene kit from beside the desk, only to come up empty as her fingers lost their grip midway up. The kit landed at her feet with a humiliating thump.

Her humiliation increased as John hooked one of those massive arms down and up, effortlessly sweeping the case onto the desk.

She stared at her hand as the tremor moved up into her arm. Within seconds, the entire limb was trembling. Not as badly as it had in her stateroom on the *Griffith* the night before when John had pulled her out of that shower, but it was noticeable.

Her conversation with Gil filtered in. His warning.

Was Gil right? Was she making it worse? Risking everything on what might well turn out to be her final assignment?

But if not her, here, dealing with this—who? She trusted John, and he was more than capable. But Riyad? All she had there was one seriously vague maybe.

But in her determination to see this through...what if her newfound shortcoming endangered the lives of others?

"*Stop*." She flinched as John's fingers found her chin, forcing it and her gaze up. "I mean it, Rae. You and your arm aren't dragging anyone down. You just need time."

Great. He *was* working his way through her expressions.

And that wasn't necessarily a good thing—let alone what was increasingly becoming an outright handicap.

What the hell. She offered John what he couldn't read in her face, because she was too terrified to let it that close to the surface. "That's what Gil keeps preaching. Time. Patience. For over a week now. Only it's not getting better; it's getting worse. And I—" She pulled her breath in deep and just said it. "I'm scheduled to re-qualify."

She didn't add that it was for her SIG Sauer. At the moment, it was the only qual at risk. The only one that mattered. This man, of all men, would know that.

"When?"

"Eight weeks." Sure, she could get it pushed back. But not indefinitely.

And doing so would invite questions. More of those damned neurological tests to which Gil and his ilk had already subjected her. Along with the very real potential for additional, follow-up tests that she just might be forced to take...as a civilian.

John stroked those enviably steady fingers of his along her cheek. "Then we have time."

"We?"

That dent flashed in. "You do know I'm SF?"

"Yeah, I heard that. So?"

"So, there are techniques. Ones I've trained more than few indigenous folks to use, along with our own troops—all of whose lives depended on success. So relax. Trust me. When we get home, we'll head to the range. I'll get you sorted in time."

What if he couldn't? Worse, what if she needed to fire her weapon before he even had a chance to try? Not on the practice range, but in the field. Here, in Pakistan.

While she was supposed to be protecting this man's back?

The answer to that question was slowly taking over her dreams and twisting them into nightmares.

His fingers found her chin again. They wouldn't let go. "Rae?"

She sighed, met that steady stare. "Fine."

She thought he was going to push it, but he didn't. He simply lowered his fingers and turned to tap her crime kit. "Now, what's in here?"

He waited patiently as she fumbled with the tiny tumbler dials on her kit's lock twice before she was able to open it. She tugged on a set of gloves and retrieved the electronic frame, removing it from its paper bag.

She switched the frame on and flipped through the photos until she reached the group shot that also showed the baby's face.

"I found the frame tucked underneath Brandt's bed. Take a look at this image of Brandt and the Sadats three, and tell me what you see."

John's low whistle said it all, as did the scarred hand that came up to rub his cheek—directly over the groove that slashed down into his now cultivated thicket.

"Yeah." She returned the frame to the bag, resealed and re-annotated it before securing it inside her case and resetting the tumbler. "But here's the thing. When Scott told Mrs. Sadat about Brandt's death, she was upset—but she wasn't devastated."

"You think it's Crier's kid?"

"I don't know." Yet. The photo she had of Crier hadn't contained a cleft chin. But it could've skipped a generation in his bloodline—or Inaya's. Along with the Type 1 diabetes the boy carried. That was hereditary too. Either way, "It's possible. I also know that Crier requested Brandt's presence on the *Griffith* detail. But if the request was significant, how?" Had Crier wanted Brandt away from Mrs. Sadat for some reason?

Were the men involved in a sex triangle? It wouldn't be the first time she'd come across one in her line of work. And a triangle was definitely grounds for blackmail.

Or had Aamer Sadat set out to use his wife to play the two off each other?

Because even if Crier was the father, that didn't mean that Brandt hadn't slept with the woman too. All she knew for certain was that Brandt had administered the poison that killed Tamir Hachemi. Brandt was definitely being blackmailed about something. Something big enough that he'd murder to keep it hidden.

But what?

Damn it, she needed more. Knowing who'd fathered that kid would get her closer to *why* Brandt had done it—and *who* had provided the strychnine at Al Dhafra.

"John—"

He held up a finger as his phone vibrated from within his suit jacket. "Just a sec." He retrieved his phone from an inner pocket and clicked into his text app. "It's from one of Ty's men. The guy just followed Aamer Sadat back to the hospital. Seems Sadat had stepped out to visit his banker. He took a call when he returned to his car, then stopped by his older brother's place on the way back to the hospital. Sadat's in the ICU now."

Inaya Sadat had been telling the truth then. At least about that.

Regan checked her watch as John texted his contact.

It was nearing 2100. The woman she met with tonight might've been willing to kick the memory of Brandt to the curb and quickly, but she was not leaving her baby. Inaya Sadat would be in that waiting room too.

Unfortunately, Regan couldn't risk dropping by twice in one night, let alone this late. It would kill the embassy-employee, compassionate visit excuse she and Scott had set up.

Much as she hated to admit it, other than reviewing the backgrounders and the case files, there wasn't a damned thing she could do to further her part in the investigation until the embassy reopened in the morning.

Hopefully Riyad and Agent Castile were having more luck in their search for the identity of the final victim from that cave.

If Riyad had even linked up with Castile as ordered.

She tucked her fingertips into the tripled-up braid at the nape of her neck, feeling around for the oversized bobby-pins that kept it in place. It took forever to get a decent enough grip to pull the first pin free. She was reaching for the second when John set his phone down and turned her around so that her back was to him.

"I can do it."

"Yes, you can." He located the three other pins and slipped them free with embarrassing ease, then removed the elastic band from the base of the braid and began unraveling it until her hair fell down her back. "But even you'd have trouble doing this."

This?

She bit back a groan as his fingers dug deeply into her hair, slowly, but firmly massaging the tension and worry of the day from her scalp, before those magic fingers and palms moved down to engulf her neck and shoulders. She had no idea how long she stood there, strangling her subsequent groans and sighs, but by the time he finished, she realized what he'd really accomplished and why.

The tremors were still there, but they were subtle now. Her arm had somehow relaxed right along with the muscles in her scalp, neck and shoulders.

Satisfaction gleamed down at her as she turned.

"They teach you that in the big bad snake-eater course too?"

He shook his head as he tugged at the knot on his loosened tie until it was completely free. "Internet. I looked it up today during a down moment." He tossed his tie on the desk and reached out to smooth several strands of hair from her cheek. "Now go take a shower. Or a bath. Either will help, too. I'll order dinner while you relax."

She shook her head.

"You're not hungry?"

Oh, she was hungry. And, as he slid those daunting arms from his suit jacket, then tossed it on the desk so he could remove his shoulder holster, she was getting hungrier by the second. Damn, this man looked good in a suit. ACUs, too.

But he looked even better naked.

His brow quirked questioningly as she continued to watch while he tossed his holster and the 9mm tucked inside onto the desk, before starting in on his backup firearms and concealed knives. The final nest of weapons could've outfitted a third-world junta.

She ignored the weapons and stepped closer, her intention clear.

Those proprietary hands she'd missed so damned much slid in around her waist, coming to rest at the small of her back as he eased her the rest of the way in.

"Rae? You sure you're ready for this?"

"Are you?"

His laugh was short and satisfyingly frustrated—for her.

"Honey, I've been ready since the moment I woke up in that bed in Germany and realized you weren't in it."

That earned the man a kiss. She pulled his head down as she stretched up.

"Wait. I need my bag."

His bag?

"Access to the internet isn't all I managed today. I've got condoms—"

"You don't need them." And she hoped to hell Tulle hadn't purchased those little gems along with the cover-story rock on her hand, or she'd never be able to face the staff sergeant again, much less look him in the eye.

But John was already reaching up to ease her hands from his neck. "I'm serious. I am not playing roulette with your life again. Ever."

He wouldn't be. "Gil gave me a shot a few days ago. I was annoyed that I'd started my period while I was stuck in the hospital. It was light, but still. Anyway, he reminded me that they'd likely stop if I got on the shots. And, well, there are other benefits." Benefits she'd already been thinking about with John back in her life.

Benefits that eagerly resumed as he guided her hands back up, so that she could link them behind his neck as he brought his forehead down to touch hers.

"So, no condoms...ever?"

"Nope." Just another birth control shot every three months. "Of course, if you really want—"

His swift kiss answered that one, but then he pulled away to finish removing his clothes. He probably intended for her to do likewise, and she did get her suit jacket and holster off. Even got her slacks unzipped. And that's when and where she got waylaid—standing there, watching him do the same.

He finished his mouthwatering striptease in under a minute.

Socks, shoes, slacks, shirt and underwear, they were all gone now. What was left was simply glorious. Even with that horrific collection of scars and occasional stretches of mottled flesh, the man's body could grace the cover of any muscle magazine.

And, yet, there was no vanity in him. Not about his body.

Like that scarf, those condoms and the nest of weapons on the desk—and even that paranoid habit he had of securing her seatbelt for her in cars—John's extreme physical conditioning was simply the embodiment of his personal, deep-seated motto.

*Control what you can; be prepared for the rest.*

His brow rose. "You plan on joining me?"

"Why?" Her brow mirrored his. "You did that so well, I thought you might want to put those particular skills to use again...over here with me."

Instead of answering, he stepped forward and let his hands and that smile do it for him. Her socks, shoes and slacks followed. But when his fingers slid down to her waist to begin unbuttoning her dress shirt, she flinched.

"*Hon*?"

He'd whispered it, because he knew. Even before her eyes began to burn. That flinch wasn't due to him. Or her shirt. It was what was beneath.

The scar.

Given the plethora of marks that crisscrossed his entire body, including the one that started at the left side of his torso and cut rudely all the way down and around his ass to end at the base of his calf, it was crazy to be worried about what he'd think. But the scar he was about to see, it didn't belong to him or even to her. It belonged to them.

He might've even seen it back at Campbell when she'd been unconscious in the ICU, and he definitely had to have seen it last night when he'd pulled her out of the shower on the *Griffith*. But she'd never shown it to him. Shared it.

Much less the pain.

Whether she was ready or not, she was sharing it now.

His fingers returned to her shirt, dwarfing the buttons as he released them from their holes one by one. It still amazed her how this man and these hands could be so nimble and gentle, but they were. And so was he as he opened her shirt and slid it down her shoulders. He turned to lay it over the rest of their clothes on the desk, then came back to peel away her bra and underwear just as slowly and gently.

Those too were carefully set aside.

And then he was smoothing those callused fingers down her abdomen. Tracing. Absorbing.

The more he touched, and the longer he stared, the more his eyes glistened.

By the time he'd lowered that enormous body down and settled onto his knees, they were spilling freely over his cheeks and onto her.

He kissed every inch of the scar, just as she'd kissed his many, many marks that night in Germany. When he finished, those powerful arms slid around her body, quaking softly as he pulled her close. She threaded her fingers into his hair and held him there for some time. How long, she couldn't be sure. Holding. Soothing.

And then his grip changed.

It became softer and lighter, and yet, somehow firmer. Determined.

Passion had gradually overtaken his sorrow, and he was intent on sharing that with her too. He slowly kissed his way up her curves, feeding the desire between them until it was alive and electric, and had begun to arc between them.

He gripped her waist and lifted her as he stood, his smoky murmur filling her ear. "Wrap your legs around me."

She laughed as she complied. She had to. It was what he'd

said that first time, as he'd pressed her into the wall. But there was no wall close by, and the bed was across the room.

"Now, you're just showing off."

"Not yet, baby." That gorgeous dent cut in. "But I will be."

His hands dug into her ass, anchoring her to him. Before she could draw her next breath, he was crossing the room and pressing her down onto the bed to make good on his promise. The man was relentless. He used those callused palms and nimble fingers along with his hungry mouth to drive her to the point of insanity—or, at the very least, to the point of begging. It wasn't until she was balanced on the razor's edge, desperate for him to take her over, that she realized he was deliberately withholding what she really wanted. What they both wanted.

She was so ready for him, she caved in and pleaded.

His smile widened as that damned dent deepened.

She reached down between them and got even. His hoarse, needy groan reverberated through her as his control finally splintered. He pushed in, shuddering as he filled her to the brim for a brief, blinding moment, before he took up a relentless pace that had them clinging to each other as they climbed higher and higher. All too quickly, she reached the ascent. But he was right there with her, wrapped tightly around her as they tipped over together, sealing her to him as they tumbled through the abyss.

She had no idea how long she lay in his arms afterward.

Worried that he was crushing her, he ignored her protest and rolled onto his back, taking her with him. She reached up, but that was all she could manage. The fingers of her right hand nestled in amid the cultivated thicket on his jaw, as boneless and placid as the rest of her. Worse, she could feel that ego of his swelling up, even before her fingers slipped into the dent already forming beneath them.

"You are such an arrogant *ass*."

The dent deepened as he laughed. "I didn't say anything."

"You're thinking it."

"How do you know? You're not even looking at my face."

"I would, but I still can't move, you jerk."

That colossal chest rumbled as he laughed harder. "Hey, I was just following orders. Military and medical. Fourche said you needed to de-stress." Those callused fingers left their home at the curve of her ass to come up and rasp lightly over hers.

Fingers that weren't trembling any more. At all.

She managed to move then. She lifted her head just far enough to take in what was fast becoming a permanent crease in his left cheek.

His twinkle joined in. "Mission accomplished."

She used those same fingertips to pinch the growth covering his jaw and tugged until he winced. "Like I said, you're an ass."

The twinkle faded. The crease disappeared as well. "Are you upset that I called him?"

Yes and no. Though right now, decidedly more no. But if John ever shared the details of this remedy with Gil, she'd kill him. Slowly.

"Rae?"

"At least the call was private...unlike this morning's display."

"Ah."

"Don't *ah* me. And, for the record, I can defend myself."

"Agreed."

"Then what the hell was that gorilla arm all about?"

The twinkle returned. "Gorilla arm?"

"The one that landed across the back of my chair and refused to move."

"*Gorilla*?" He appeared to be stuck on that word as he stared down at the limb in question as though offended—which they both knew full well he wasn't. He was too bloody arrogant. "You do know I can't help my size, right? It's mostly genetics."

"*John*—"

"Besides—" The twinkle took on a glow that put the north star to shame. "—a few minutes ago, I seem to remember you openly appreciating the size of a certain...appendage."

Okay, she had. And, yes, she planned on appreciating it again. Most likely before the night was out. But, "Not when that titanic ego of yours is in charge."

In front of a *general*, no less.

The twinkle evaporated, leaving that steady stare behind. His following nod was clipped. "It was necessary."

"Necessary?"

"Things were said."

She could just image what things were said, and by whom.

About whom.

John was clearly in no mood to repeat them. But he did offer up a shrug. "I was making sure he'd gotten my message."

Oh, they'd all gotten the message, including General Palisade. There'd been no missing it. But what had been the point? The things that were said were the same things John himself had said to her—or implied—in that parking lot in Hohenfels.

*Whore.*

Silence oozed in, saturating the air within the bed.

Suddenly, she wanted to escape his arms and slink off into the bathroom for that shower he'd suggested earlier. Scrub away the insecurity and ugliness that had begun to bubble up inside. If she could. But the second she started to move, his arms tightened.

His sigh was the only thing that slipped free. It filled the silence, easing it.

And her.

Still, she kept the left side of her face sealed to his chest, staring across the bed at the striped wallpaper, pretending a fascination she did not possess with those dark green lines.

"Love at first sight?" He shook his head. "As I'm sure you know, I'd hit thirty a few months before we met. I certainly didn't believe in fairy tales anymore, if I ever did. Not after the shit I've lived. Lust? Absolutely. But love?" Her cheek lifted along with the slab of muscle beneath as he shrugged. "And, yet, there it was. Though I freely admit, both those L's were there in equal parts, right from the start in that bar."

His fingers slid up her body and threaded themselves into her hair. He smoothed the strands past her shoulder and down her back, but he made no move to shift so that he could look into her eyes. Perhaps it was easier for him this way.

It was certainly easier for her. It allowed her to close her eyes and absorb his raw confession and just...listen.

"When you followed me into that parking lot, I was livid. I wanted you to hate me, so I could hate you. But it blew up in my face. I didn't hate you. I couldn't. Oh, I was still angry. And hurt. More than I've ever been in my life, before or since. And I've been in and out of combat for over a decade, so that's saying something. But I didn't stop caring. I couldn't."

She did move then. She raised her head just far enough to meet the stark truth in that gray, steady stare.

His firm nod followed. "I was already falling for you in that bar when you made me work so damned hard just to get your name. I fell deeper over dinner and then in my driveway. By the time you showed up the next night and starting talking me down from Stubbs' death, I'd hit bottom. I was completely in love before I got your bra off. Everything that happened after just sealed it. And then you walked into that interview room, and my world imploded. By the time I walked out, I truly believed you'd come over and slept with me to get to Evan. That you'd have slept with him as easily."

She started to protest but he shook his head.

"I know. I was wrong. About so damned many things. But

one thing's true. I really don't know how to make a relationship work. And the way I was raised? Baby, it wasn't pretty. But I took it because I was so desperate for that man to care. Until I woke up one day, and I just couldn't take it anymore—so I cut him out of my heart. I did the same thing with you, or I tried to. I wanted the pain to stop. And I couldn't risk crawling back for more. And, yeah, I would have. So I said the one thing I could think of to get you to hate me—and then I implied the rest of what I couldn't quite say. At the time, I needed you to despise me. And now...I am *terrified* I succeeded."

Lord, what was it about this man?

He was making her cry again. One moment, the tears were still trapped in her eyes, burning in at the corners, and the next, they were spilling over and coursing down her cheeks. His fingers came up again, this time to wipe the moisture away.

It didn't help. They both just got wetter.

"John—"

He pressed a damp finger to her lips as he shook his head, then lowered his hand to cup her shoulder, rubbing gently, as though he was afraid what he'd said and still had to say would cause the tremors to resurface. "It's okay. You don't have to respond. You just needed to know. I also know you're not ready. Given how you grew up, it's understandable. But I meant what I said in that bar and earlier tonight. It's never been more true than it is with you. I am patient and I am persistent. And, honey, I am so damned motivated when it comes to you, that you should probably run like hell and never look back. But if you don't hate me...if you can get past what I said, that's all I need for now. So, take your time. I am not going anywhere. Certainly not in my mind and in my heart. Yeah, the Army's bound to send my body off somewhere else soon enough. But, Rae, I'll keep coming back to you until I'm dead."

She pulled her breath in deep and tried not to shudder as

she let it out. Intense sex with this man was one thing. But intense emotions?

He was right. She wasn't ready.

She didn't know if she ever would be. If she even had it in her. And she certainly couldn't deal with it all right now, in the middle of this case.

She needed to *focus*.

So she did the only thing she could. She changed the subject. "Then...you're not taking that slot at Homeland?"

The sharp furrow that pinched through his brow wasn't powered by anger, but surprise. "Who told you about that?"

"Warren Jeffers. Well, 'threw it' would be more apt." In her face. "Jeffers worships at the Shrine of Riyad. I think he's furious that anyone would dare to equate you two."

"The man can rest easy. I already turned it down."

She struggled to escape John's arms so she could sit up and glare down at him. "*Homeland*? It's an amazing opportunity." Yes, he'd have to leave the Army. But, "Think of the effect you could have; the good you could do. Why would you even—"

"Are you getting out?"

Her?

"No." Unless her hand screwed up her career, she planned on putting in her full twenty. Thirty, if the swamp of rotting crap that went with her job didn't drag her under and suffocate her first.

"There you go." John folded those thick arms behind his head. "I told you. I'm staying put, and they absolutely know it."

Good Lord. "You told them why?"

"Damned straight I did. It was the only way they'd believe I was serious." He unfolded his right arm so he could brush his thumb across her chin. "Now stop frowning. Trust me; Palisade's thrilled. He was afraid I was going to take it. He knows I don't love him enough to stick around."

There was that word again.

John knew it too, because he unfolded his other arm and sat up with her. This time, he changed the subject. "It's almost twenty-two hundred. We've got just over an hour before the restaurant stops serving. Why don't you take that shower while I order?"

She appreciated the reprieve, but she shook her head. "You go ahead. I'll order. But I need to call Agent Castile first; see if Riyad ever linked up with him. If so, how it went." If they'd made any progress on identifying the final victim from the cave.

Though she was worried for another reason, too.

Nathan should've phoned her by now. Had something happened to the man? He was supposed to have spent the afternoon and evening with Riyad.

John reached out to tuck her hair behind her ear. "Okay. But make your call soon. Meanwhile, I'll make my shower last. I might still be in there when you've finished."

From the wink he shot her as he stood, he was counting on it.

She waited until he'd crossed the room and closed the bathroom door behind him before she abandoned the bed. She was too lazy to rifle through her suitcase, so she stopped at the desk and donned John's shirt as the shower turned on.

Last night, his tee had hit her mid-thigh. The white tails of his dress shirt skimmed the tops of her knees. She finished buttoning it and rolled up the cuffs, then retrieved her phone.

As much as she wanted to call Mira, she still couldn't. There was no way she'd risk putting the woman in the middle of the situation with Riyad and that missing SDV. Not after the rocky start—and near career-ending insinuations—that had caused Mira to switch her focus from a budding Navy career years earlier to join NCIS instead.

She could, however, enlist the aid of another good friend, this one Army CID.

Regan pulled up Agent Jelling's text stream on her phone and typed in her request—as well as a warning to pursue it *carefully*. Fortunately, Hohenfels was four hours behind Islamabad. Jelly was just sitting down to dinner, but if it worked for her, he'd be happy to head back to the office in a few hours and do his digital snooping while no one was around to glance over his shoulder.

Regan texted her sincere thanks and backed out of her text app.

She was about to hit Nathan Castile's number when several knocks reverberated from the opposite side of the hotel room's door.

Neither she nor John had ordered dinner, so who—

More knocks. These were louder, heavier. Seriously pissed.

And then, "Open the fucking door!"

*Riyad.*

How the devil had he found them?

*Why*?

# 21

The shower was still on. The cover noise from the running water had prevented John from hearing the knocking.

*Thank God.* Relief swept in as Regan quickly crossed the plush carpet of the hotel suite. Given the mood of the man behind that current round of pounding, John's absence was a definite plus. She thought about retrieving her 9mm as she passed the desk, but decided against its attendance as well. If her growing suspicions about the spook were correct, the SIG's open participation would only enflame the situation.

Unfortunately, the fourth round of pounding grew heavier still as she reached the door. Louder. Along with the outrage in Riyad's voice.

"Damn it, man. I said open—"

"Good evening, Sam." She scanned the hallway behind the spook. "What brings you to the Serena tonight—*alone*?"

Where the hell was Agent Castile? Because Nathan hadn't accompanied him.

Fortunately, there was no one else out there either.

Despite that racket in the hall, Mr. and Mrs. Goethe's cover identities just might remain intact. And, if she could get the spook inside and calmed down before John finished showering, she just might be able to get a handle on the rest of their case.

That noise from the shower would help.

She motioned the spook inside, swiftly closing the door behind him.

"Where the *hell* does Garrison get off—"

"*Lower your voice.*"

That scowl she'd become so familiar with finally shifted—to a sneer. "Why? Afraid lover boy will think—"

"—think what, asshole?" *John.*

Score one for cover noise, zero for her. The shower was still running, but of course, John was no longer inside it. Before she could blink, he'd crossed the remainder of the suite and swiftly inserted his body between hers and the spook's.

But that wasn't the worst of it.

John was buck naked. And every single inch of that scarred mountain of muscle was dripping with water and barely suppressed, ice-cold rage.

Could this get any worse?

Unfortunately, the spook's deepening sneer suggested yes. It swept down the dress shirt she'd put on, then slid over to the rumpled sheets of the bed across the suite, before returning to John. "Quite the cozy bolthole you two managed to scrounge up on Uncle Sam's dime—" The sneer snapped to her left hand, to the cover-story rings she'd donned and long since forgotten about. "—or should I say diamond?"

"You got a point to make, Riyad?"

"Yeah, you're on the job."

"Wrong. I was on the job—two hours ago. Unless the shit hits the fan between now and then, I will be again in another eight. Until then, this happens to be my downtime *and* hers. What she and I do during our mutual downtime is none of your goddamned business. Nor is how I spent *my* dimes—not the government's. So you can scurry back to the embassy compound and hole up there tonight, because I have no intention of paying for your bed."

"Damn it, Garrison—"

"*Goethe.* At the moment, the name is Karl *Goethe.*" He snapped his chin toward her as she stepped up beside him, hoping to calm the rumbling storm before it broke free. Though that wasn't looking likely. "This is Rachel Goethe. It's called a cover. Sometimes—while *on the job*—it's necessary. And when it is, we do our best to maintain it. Now, I know you've still got memories of live, tasty fish treats and all those bouncing beach-balls you've had to balance on your nose filling up that slippery head of yours, but try and gather up enough human brain cells to remember that, okay?"

The scowl had returned, only this time it was leveled on John. "You know."

"Buddy, I knew within two minutes of meeting you. What I didn't know was why you were so damned determined to hide it."

"Because you weren't *cleared* to know. And after that stunt you pulled today—"

"Stunt?" Crap. She should've kept her mouth shut.

At least until John had donned *something.*

Instead, he turned to her in all his still dripping glory, dragging out this entire ludicrous scenario as he casually crossed those obscenely hefty arms and shrugged. "He's still pissed because I lost his incompetent tail ten seconds into Abbottabad."

"That wasn't me."

John turned back to the spook. "Obviously—unless you managed to shrink a good four inches and bleach your hair down to dirty blond. Which brings me to my question of the night. How did you know I was here?"

"Kettering. He called Palisade. Then called me back."

"Well, well. You really are on first names with the Big Bubble. Congratulations. That'll do wonders for your new career. 'Course the way I also hear it, you've got your nose stuck so far up that man's ass, you've got permanent ring around the collar."

The spook's brow rose. That was it.

But so had John's.

Swiftly. Silently.

*Shit.*

She had about two seconds before this thing headed south—in a major way. Pun absolutely intended. "That's *enough.*" She stepped in between the men, shoving at John's damp chest as she glared up at him.

He didn't budge.

Neither did she. "I mean it, John. Knock off the gorilla warfare. And put some damned pants on, will you?"

She wasn't sure what had given the spook pause, but something had.

The scowl on his face had finally splintered apart and regrouped into open confusion. "I think you meant guerrilla."

John actually had the nerve to laugh. "Oh, no, she meant gorilla."

You bet she had. She stalked over to the desk to retrieve his trousers since he clearly couldn't be bothered, throwing them at him as she returned. "Now, put that appendage away, *Mr. Goethe.*"

The spook glanced down at John's shirt, her bare legs and feet beneath. "I'll...wait outside."

John's fury might have ratcheted down several clicks, but it was still there, spiking into his answering nod. "You do that."

The door closed behind Riyad with a solid snap.

She turned her back on her very own, chest-pounding silverback and headed for the desk to gather up her clothes. Bundle in hand, she turned again to march into the bathroom to get away from *him*, lest—

"Hon?"

She whirled around, staring up into that irritating twinkle that was once again warming the gray.

The twinkle took on a glow as that dent slowly folded in.

"*What*?"

His scarred paw came up. Dangling from the end—the scrap of white cotton she'd evidently dropped. Her underwear.

"Like I said—you're an *ass*." She snatched the scrap of cotton from his paw and spun around to stalk into the bathroom.

He was still laughing as she slammed the door.

Worse, everything that had been said while the spook had been in the room—and everything that hadn't—was still spinning through her brain as she thrust her hand into the shower to turn off the spray. It all continued to spin in as she dressed as quickly as she could. It was still spinning as she braided her hair and tucked it under, but when she reached out to switch on the faucet to splash water on her face, the diamond on her left hand winked up at her, finally forcing her to slow down and pause altogether.

To accept it.

She'd slipped in and out of so many identities, so many times, when she'd worked undercover, the rings hadn't even registered. She'd just put them on and immediately forgotten about them. But as she stared at the brilliant, mini explosions of blues that this oversized rock was throwing off every time light from the overhead fixtures hit it, she realized her mistake.

She should have looked at them.

Even without Riyad's dig and John's comeback, it would've been obvious. The diamond wasn't a fake. Nor had Tulle picked the rings up on behalf of the Army. John had. Somehow, he'd found a moment to slip into a jewelry store today and had purchased them with his own money. They might've needed the rings to complete their covers so they could compare notes in private and away from the embassy, but John had also been working a second, simultaneous mission this entire time—and it was extremely personal.

He had no intention of returning the rings for a refund. Let alone accepting them back from her.

So, now what?

*Focus*. Find out why Riyad was here—and if her budding suspicions about the former SEAL were correct. More importantly, if the two were connected.

She shored up her nerve as best she could and exited the bathroom.

John had obviously had a second shirt in his bag, because he was dressed and standing at the desk, secreting the final piece of his coup-level arsenal within his suit. She stepped up beside him and reached for her shoulder holster—only to find her right hand engulfed in his. He used her fingers to guide her around until she was facing him.

Those proprietary paws of his slipped into place at the small of her back, tugging her close as he bent down to capture her stare.

Her.

"Stop worrying. It'll all work out. Just...give it time. Meanwhile, I meant what I said. What we do when we're off the clock is nobody's business but ours. USASOC sent me here. You, too. I spent fifteen months wanting you back in my life. I'll be damned if I'll let anyone get in the way of us when we're not actively on the job. Anyone."

He was right. They might be Army, but they deserved a life.

She might not be ready for what he was really saying with that diamond, but she was ready for him. At the very least, she was ready to risk finding out.

"Rae?"

She slid her hand up around the back of his neck as she stretched up to press her lips to the growth on his cheek, then moved on to murmur in his ear. "Agreed."

His breath eased out as he released her. "I'll get the door."

She donned her shoulder holster, frowning as she automatically slid her SIG out, then in, to check it. Her fingers were trembling again.

Peachy.

She crossed her arms as Riyad entered the suite. The motion served two purposes. It hid her recalcitrant hand from John, and it also let the spook know she was still royally pissed at him. "Where's Nathan?"

"Near as I know, still at the consulate in Peshawar. Why?"

"Because you're supposed to be there, too. Assisting him."

"I was. I did." Riyad must've had as exhausting a day as John, because he finally scrubbed his hands over the dark growth on his jaw and sighed. "Look; Castile's fine, okay? He's a good man, and he has everything in hand. We sat down and reviewed his approach. I offered a few course corrections—but, all in all, it's solid. He's good to go. He will ID that woman from the cave. It's just going to take time. Boots on the ground."

John flicked his stare at the black leather dress shoes at the base of the spook's suit. "Those work as well as boots. Why aren't you assisting? As Palisade directed?"

"Because Riyad got a tip." That's why the spook had called Admiral Kettering and flown back from Peshawar.

From their expressions, her statement had surprised both men. John, because he had no idea what she was talking about, since she hadn't yet mentioned her budding suspicion, let alone her texted request to Jelly. And Riyad, because the spook knew exactly what she meant and was more than a bit bemused that she'd sussed it out.

Bully for her.

Her instincts might turn out to be off regarding Embassy Islamabad's deputy chief of mission, but they were dead on regarding the former SEAL that Warren Jeffers worshipped. At least about this.

All that rage Riyad had been channeling since she'd met him? His dogged suspicions regarding John, and his even more dogged determination to put him away for murder? Once John had filled her in on that SDV and the fiasco of a mission around it, she'd realized the rest. And then there was that wariness that was currently deepening Riyad's stare almost to black.

That was her proof.

"Senior Chief Zakaria Webber. You got a tip about him, didn't you, Agent Riyad? Today. You also knew Webber was dirty —*before* that final SDV mission went down." She held up a hand as the spook tensed and stepped toward her. Mostly because Riyad's instinctive movement had caused John to shift his body as well, so he could cut the spook off if need be. Physically. "Correction. You suspected it. I'm guessing whatever you had at the time on the senior chief wasn't solid enough to pull NCIS in."

Ironic really, since NCIS was precisely what Riyad had gotten out of the teams to become—solely so that he'd have the legal authority to track his nemesis down.

John took another step toward the spook. "She's right, isn't she?"

Riyad's nod was stiff. "He's been sighted. In Islamabad. Three hours ago."

John's laugh was short, and anything but amused. "And you really thought I'd be holed up here at the Serena with that bastard?"

The black stare narrowed. "Not here. But you haven't been here all day, have you? Much less on the grid, since you gave my guy the slip in Abbottabad."

"Well, I hate to be the bearer of unwelcome news, but I haven't seen hide nor hair of Webber for fourteen months—since the day I left Fort Bragg as a matter of fact. Don't believe me? Head down a few floors. Tulle's crashing here tonight too. He can vouch for today, at least. But for two personal stops, the staff sergeant's been with me since we boarded that bird at Islamabad International. And, hell, come to think of it, Tulle was watching the storefronts and guarding my back while I was inside during those personal stops, so I'm guessing he can account for those minutes too."

John took another step toward the spook, using his looming, gray-suited bulk to underscore what his voice hadn't. "How about you, Riyad?"

"What the fuck? I just told you where I was. I was in Pesh—"

John shook his head. "Not today. Sixteen months ago. September the second. Roughly zero three hundred in the morning. I was standing in the CID parking lot on Hohenfels, having a private conversation with Special Agent Chase. Where were you?"

"Stateside."

John glanced at her. "He telling the truth?"

As flattered as she was with his faith in her skills—not to mention his willingness to use them operationally—it wasn't that simple.

Like John and her, blood was still clipping through the spook's veins at an elevated pace, the man's adrenaline still surging. There were too many conflicting micro-expressions flitting through those dusky, pretty-boy features, the majority of which were still feeding off, and complicated by, emotions and thoughts left over from when Riyad had entered the room.

Fortunately, Jelly and his digital sleuthing skills were already on the job. Because there was also the reality that no investigator ever wanted to accept.

If someone truly believed what they were saying—suspected burglar or outright jihadi terrorist alike—it threw the whole game into the suspect's favor.

It was why she was even better at spinning bald-faced lies than she was at discerning them. All the shit she'd been through as a kid had merged with the fantasy escapes that had kept her sane, training her exceptionally well. In short, she was usually able to believe what she said. For as long as it took to say it, anyway.

As for Riyad?

She shrugged, and gave both men the unvarnished truth. "I don't know."

The satisfaction that curved those full lips gave her pause. John, too. Because he refused to back down, much less away from the spook.

"Don't look so smug, asshole. I'll check."

"Feel free. Meanwhile, speaking of locations, where'd you go in Abbottabad? Because I'm still not convinced you weren't hooking up with Webber. Hell, Tulle might have been there, too. The staff sergeant's usually glued to your ass when you're doing something off the books. Why were you both so determined to evade your tail?"

"Gee, I don't know. Think about it. What's in Abbottabad?"

"You've got a source in their army?"

"I do. And, no, I am not trusting you with his name. And I sure as hell wasn't about to let your bumbling associate crash our meeting."

"Then how do I know you're not lying about who you met?"

"As a matter of fact, that's exactly what I was doing in Abbottabad. Lying. Mostly about the fact that I'm not German, much less in their army. So, unless that incompetent shadow of yours is fluent or could've faked a damned good accent like Tulle—"

The spook brandished a conciliatory palm. "Okay. I get it. Did you learn anything from your contact?"

"Yeah, I did. And I already gave the intel to your *partner*. Now I want to know why you're so convinced I'm tight with that salt-water-soaked bastard. Because I didn't even hang out with Webber at Bragg. Hell, I was only there for eight weeks before I pinned on major and was sent to Campbell, most of which, he wasn't."

The conciliatory palm had curled into a fist; it pulsed with rage. "He *asked* for you."

"You're saying he officially requested that I work with him? That's why you've been so determined to believe I switched sides? Because of a request—and what we worked on together at Bragg?"

"Yes."

John glanced at her. "At the time, Webber and I were tasked with reviewing security contingencies and red teaming several that were already in place."

*Oh, Jesus.* She did not like where this was headed.

John nodded at the expression that he didn't need his new Rae-reading skills to discern, because she wasn't hiding it. "Yep. The contingencies we red teamed involved Embassy Islamabad." John pushed his focus back to Riyad. "Webber's sandbox-play-mate preferences are news to me. I never met the man before I walked into that office, and we definitely weren't buddies after. You've been tracking the son of a bitch for a while now. Do you know where he was on September the second?"

"On leave."

That earned Riyad a sigh. One devoid of even John's extended patience. "Where?"

Riyad shrugged. "No idea. He was off the grid then, too. You really think Webber was in that parking lot, listening to the two of you go at it?"

"Why not? Someone was. I don't have a clue as to why he might've been there in the first place, but if it was Webber, the man got a damned good look at me at my lowest point. Might even explain why the bastard kept trying to get me to hit the bars and strip clubs with him off Bragg. I finally had to get in his face and tell him I wasn't into that shit. He just smirked. I assumed he'd seen all the crap the networks had spread across the evening news. Now I'm thinking he had a front row seat to it all."

John shot her an apologetic glance. If Riyad hadn't been there, she knew he'd have followed it up with more. Because of Webber's obsession with John, Durrani had been able to get to her. And that bothered John. A lot.

She shook her head, silently absolving him.

Not only was it not John's fault, they had bigger issues than some rogue SEAL observing her dirty laundry. Or some Afghan bastard of a doc trying to strangle her with the clothesline from which it had all been hung.

Gil was right. Durrani was dead. No matter how and where the man had accomplished that death, he'd lost.

Nor did it matter where Webber had been a year ago September. The traitor was here, in Islamabad, now. There was only one reason. Whatever was about to go down, it was going to happen in Pakistan, quite possibly in its capital city.

Regan stepped closer to the spook. "Tom Crier, Warren Jeffers—do either of the men know Webber?" Especially the latter, given the DCM's SEAL-worship tendencies.

"Both." Riyad glanced at John. "After you left Fort Bragg, Webber headed overseas to go through the results of the security review in person. He lily-padded through several countries here in the Near East, but first up were the consulates at Peshawar, Karachi and Lahore. He wrapped up the Pakistani leg of his trip right here in Islamabad. Crier and Jeffers had recently taken over their slots, so yeah, they knew each other. And there's something you should know about Jeffers—"

"He drools over your type." Regan shrugged. "I got a face full of his spewing veneration of you this afternoon. It wasn't pretty." Had smelled even less so.

To her surprise, the spook flushed. Something told her he was even less comfortable with the DCM's worship than she'd been.

Riyad nodded. "Exactly. So who knows what Jeffers has done —or would do for Webber?"

That could be a problem. "DSS Agent Scott Walburn and I go back to MP school. Scott's been in Islamabad working on a human trafficking case. He confided something in me today. Seems Mrs. Jeffers has noted secretive behavior in her husband of late. Midnight phone calls in the bath and angry comebacks when he was caught—enough to leave bruises on her arms. She thinks the man's having an affair. But—"

"Could be something else. Someone." *Riyad.*

"Agreed." Possibly, even Webber. She raised a brow as she glanced at John.

Damned if the man's Rae-dar wasn't becoming fully tuned, because he already knew what she was asking: his Abbottabad colonel's intel on Crier.

John nodded.

She turned to the spook. "Major Garrison's source has dirt on the political officer too. Tom Crier's definitely having an affair. It's with a local. His source doesn't know who, but evidence I found in Brandt's quarters, a conversation I had with the woman, along with changes in her recent social behavior, suggests it might be Aamer Sadat's wife. Mr. Sadat's a Pakistani Foreign Service National. He and his wife, Inaya, have an infant currently in intensive care at Shifa International. The boy's a diabetic and they're attempting to stabilize him. Scott and I stopped by, but I wasn't able to speak with the husband. The wife's a curiosity. I'm almost positive her son was fathered by a Caucasian, but I have no idea yet if it was Crier or Brandt."

Or if the baby was someone else's son entirely.

Hell, she couldn't even be sure if the kid's parentage pertained to their terror case. At least not without further digging.

People weren't perfect, even those who tried. That was why some investigations were so mind-numbingly difficult. Oftentimes, rooting through people's personal and professional lives caused so much hidden garbage to float to the surface, it could be difficult to figure out what, if any of it, was related to the case at hand.

Regan adjusted her right hand, tucking her fingers deeper into the crook of her crossed arms to conceal the stubborn trembling. "As for Mr. Sadat, he was sent to the *Griffith* with the diplomats."

Riyad nodded. "I read the summaries of those sessions on the ship. If Crier or Brandt is the father, the Pakistani prime minister is going to shit bricks. And they won't be used to shore up goodwill toward US or our military. Iftikhar Bukhari has a serious problem with everything American—secular or Christian. Even Muslim. Bukhari has also got his eye on the presidency, so if you have to deal with him, watch him closely."

Good to know.

Surprising too, this newfound forthrightness of Riyad's. Then again, asshole or not, it appeared he was on their side, at least about this. No matter how the spook felt about her and John, the former SEAL in *him* had finally accepted that they were in this together. They didn't have to be friends, and probably never would be, but they did have to function as a cohesive unit if they planned on taking Webber down.

*Hooah* for the team concept.

The only problem was, while Senior Chief Webber was definitely a traitor to their nation and his former sailors on the teams, she wasn't convinced Webber was the traitor they were after. Yes, though Webber had officially been on the reservation a year ago September, he still could've been in that parking lot listening to her and John. And, yes, as a SEAL, Webber could've easily gotten ahold of her BI, especially if he'd done so while he'd been faking his loyalties.

If he'd really wanted to, John could've gotten her BI at any point this past year as well. He hadn't, because he had morals. Standards.

Something Webber had clearly lost, unless he'd been faking all along.

But what she suspected that Webber did have, was access to the traitor who was currently inside the embassy. How else would Webber have known to link up with Brandt at Al Dhafra to hand off the strychnine? The information that Brandt would be departing the ship and then returning with Durrani and Hachemi had to have come from those diplomats who'd been on the *Griffith* or from someone back at the embassy who was in the know. But who?

And there was Hachemi's murder, itself. Had the translator had a name after all?

Webber's?

As he had with John, had the translator and the dirty SEAL worked together in Afghanistan? Was that where and how Hachemi had been turned?

And why Hachemi had been marked for murder?

She was beginning to suspect so.

She glanced at Riyad. "What about DSS Agent Charles Maddoc? Do you know him?"

"The RSO? Only by name. But, yeah, he was in Pakistan when Webber came through on his security review. Maddoc was with the US consulate in Karachi then; arrived here sometime last year. Can't remember when."

"April seventh." Regan shrugged as the spook gave her an odd look. The date had been in the RSO's backgrounder. "I have a thing for numbers."

Scratch that; that wasn't surprise reverberating within the spook's fixed stare. It was shock, and not over her numerical recall skills.

It was John who voiced the cause. "That's the day the SDV mission went south, or damned close to it, isn't it?"

Riyad nodded. "My men died on the eleventh."

*His* men?

Oh, that explained so very much. The spook's constant, thrumming anger and obsession. Not to mention the bleak pain now swimming in the murky depths of his eyes.

It was the same pain she'd seen in John that night in Germany when he'd been mourning a fellow SF officer and friend who'd died from an IED earlier that day in Iraq, and again, as John had lost man after man to that psycho-toxin.

This time, she voiced the cause, so neither of them would have to: "You weren't just on that mission. You led it. You were in charge when those four SEALs died, and when Webber and that SDV went missing."

"Yes."

Ah, Christ. She did not want to feel for the spook. But she did. From the tension in John's jaw, the throbbing in that telltale pulse point of his, so did he.

Riyad managed to clear his throat first. "It's not a coincidence, is it?"

She shook her head. "Maybe, maybe not. Maddoc was already in Karachi. I'm assuming the transfer had been in the works for some time."

"Most likely."

But they were all thinking the rest. If Webber had followed John to that parking lot nearly sixteen months ago, the rogue SEAL could've recruited Maddoc even earlier, before the RSO had even been assigned to Karachi. If so, Maddoc could have *requested* his Karachi and Islamabad security assignments.

Given John's comment regarding Webber's repeated invitations to hit the bars and strip joints off Bragg, Webber had clearly attempted to recruit John. Why not Maddoc and others, as well? An ocean of booze, some male bonding, an abundance of tits and ass—it all went a long way to greasing the skids, if someone was ready and willing to slide off the rails. A conclusion Webber must've reached as he'd listened to their blowout in that parking lot.

"Why would Webber want to recruit me?"

It wasn't until she'd glanced up at John that she realized she'd fallen silent. But it hadn't mattered. John's Rae-dar was truly up to speed and working. This time he'd managed to read her mind.

She shrugged. "Your skills? Your contacts?" Until they had an inkling as to what Webber had planned in Pakistan and elsewhere, they couldn't be sure. "John—"

"Just a sec." He pulled his vibrating phone from his suit jacket. But as he turned away to answer it, Riyad's rang—and then hers.

*Shit.* A trio of simultaneous calls to a team like theirs was never a good thing.

As Riyad turned in the opposite direction from John to answer his, she headed for the desk to give them all space for their individual conversations.

Scott's name filled her screen.

She accepted the call and skipped the preliminaries. "What's wrong?"

"You got a TV in that room?"

"Yeah."

"Switch it on."

She turned toward the sitting area, but John had beaten her to the punch. He stood back from the TV so she and Riyad could watch from their respective corners of the suite. A mob of Pakistani men filled the screen. Most were dressed in the country's traditional *shalwar kameez*, and nearly all were crowding and pushing in on the main gates of the embassy compound she'd visited hours earlier.

A man nearest the gate had an American flag in hand. Two others appeared to be dousing it with gasoline. A fourth—a kid, really—brandished a lighter.

A split second later, Old Glory was engulfed in flames.

But that wasn't even the sight that turned her stomach.

It was the photos slotted in along the bottom of the screen. There were seven in all—each a graphic depiction of a woman who'd died in that cave. Worse, those seven photos hadn't been snapped by Durrani. They'd been taken by the US Army. Regan knew, because those exact photos were currently weighing down the classified accordion file in her possession—and ratcheting up her nightmares.

Son of a *bitch*. They had another leak.

But was it the same leak?

Because while those who'd had access to her BI would also have had access to those crime scene photos, there were others —in both the Afghan and Pakistani diplomatic contingents— that had only been granted access to the latter.

And what the hell was being said by that commentator?

She'd find out soon enough. John was listening intently to the accompanying narration. Evidently, she needed to add Urdu to the man's languages list. Though, really, with Urdu sharing forty percent of its vocabulary with two of his other proficiencies, Persian and Arabic, it would've been a natural acquisition for John.

She heard Scott shouting for someone to grab extra CS riot-control grenades before he refocused on their call. "All hell's broken loose, Prez. Someone called in a tip to the local news. Claims seven pregnant Pakistani women were murdered in a cave in the Hindu Kush by a US soldier—an SF captain by the name of Mark McCord. As you can see, the informant provided some seriously hellish photos of the carnage, as well as a DNA report proving that McCord's blood was found at the scene—on the women's bodies. I'm guessing this is connected to that psycho-toxin shit that hit the news a few weeks back. I remember McCord's name from that, though the commentator I heard hasn't made the connection—yet. I can only assume Staff Sergeant Brandt's death is somehow linked to that massacre, and that's why you're really here in Islamabad."

Regan glanced at the TV. Given the situation currently blowing up on the screen, not to mention in her, John's and Riyad's collective faces, she opted for honesty. To a point. "McCord's DNA was found in that cave—but the man was set up."

Unfortunately, the truth had a rabbi's chance in Tehran of being believed at this stage, didn't it?

Worse, with Durrani and Hachemi dead, they had no one to hold up as the real culprits. Sure, they could release the additional forensic reports that proved McCord's blood had been planted at the scene, but who would believe them now?

Not that raging mob.

Gil might be wrong after all. That Afghan bastard of a doc might have just won.

"Rae?" John had reached her side.

"Hang on a sec, Scott."

"That's all the time I got. Things are getting hot across the whole damned city. You'd best be getting back to the bunker. There's safety in numbers."

She killed her mic and turned to John. "Yes?"

"Ty's got good, bad and shitty news. The good—Tom Crier's en route to the embassy to assist. He's minutes out; Jeffers is already there. The bad—the Shifa was so crowded, Aamer Sadat managed to give his surveillance team the slip."

That was definitely bad. "And the shitty?"

"Ambassador Linnet had a function in town tonight. She's about eight blocks from here. The RSO's with her, along with a couple other men, heading back."

"Got it. Have Ty's men stay on Crier, Jeffers and Maddoc if at all possible." She clicked on her mic and resealed her phone to her ear. "Scott, contact the RSO. Tell Maddoc either Agent Riyad or Major Garrison will be heading his way to augment protection and assist in getting the ambassador safely back to the compound. The other one will be with me. I need to return to the hospital."

If she couldn't have Aamer Sadat's head on a platter tonight, she'd settle for his wife's. She had a feeling that, when pushed, Inaya would spill more anyway.

Unfortunately, she still needed a translator.

"Understood. Good luck, Prez."

"You, too." She was about to add a *stay safe*, but Scott had already hung up.

As had John and Riyad. Riyad was already pocketing his phone and heading for the door to the suite.

"John, where's Riyad go—"

"Down a few flights to pick up Tulle." John slung her laptop over his left shoulder, then grabbed her crime kit. He leveled a blistering frown on her when she tried to retrieve her kit from him. "Don't even. Your hand's been vibrating like an idling Humvee ever since Riyad walked back into the suite."

So much for hiding it from him.

She released her grip on the kit.

"As for Riyad and Tulle, they'll assist in getting Linnet to the embassy, where they'll remain. Riyad knows as much as I do about the plans Webber worked on, and a hell of a lot more about how Webber thinks and operates. I'll be escorting you to the hospital. Need anything from your suitcase?"

"No." Anything crucial was in her laptop bag or kit, including her extra ammo.

She did grab the scarf John had purchased at Al Dhafra and was truly grateful for his foresight as she wrapped the swath of black silk around her hair. Now was not the time to look western, much less American.

"We'll be back for our clothes." Her gear still in his left hand, John motioned her toward the door with his right. "I've got keys to the SUV Tulle rented. Riyad's got his own wheels. Let's go."

They did.

A teeth-gritting thirty minutes later, they'd bypassed a seething nighttime Islamabad via Srinagar Highway and were nearly at the hospital. Regan had spent the bulk of the journey on the phone with Agent Castile, letting him know about the latest leak regarding the crime scene photos and Captain McCord's DNA report. She tasked a member of Nathan's team with discerning its source, if at all possible. Meanwhile, she'd concentrate on breaking Inaya Sadat.

John was still on the phone with his own succession of contacts as she hung up. Unfortunately, nearly all of his conversations had been in Urdu or Arabic.

She had no idea what had been said.

John wrapped up his final call as he parked outside the Shifa. There'd been no point in asking him to let her out at the entrance. He would've refused on the grounds of her safety, and she needed his translation skills inside, anyway.

Since she'd visited mere hours earlier, she led the way.

Instead of finding a tearstained, but solemn Inaya Sadat in the waiting room, sheer chaos greeted them. As for Inaya, the veiled mother was sobbing uncontrollably and even more inconsolably just outside the door of the pediatric ICU. No less than three nurses and a doctor were trying to calm her.

Regan turned to John. "What happened?"

"Something's wrong with the boy. As near as I can make out, his temperature is dangerously high, and..." John cocked his head as if trying to concentrate on a single stream of rapid Urdu out of the many. "Convulsions. The baby just had a seizure."

Oh, Jesus. She possessed nearly as much knowledge of medicine as Urdu, but even she knew that was bad. The boy was barely two months, and—

"Why?"

John glanced down at her. "Why, what?"

"The baby's supposed to be here for diabetes. I don't know a lot about the condition, but there was a girl in one of my foster homes who had it. Seizures can occur. But that shouldn't be happening here in an ICU, while they're monitoring him."

Chills rippled in as Regan recalled the rest. Namely, the girl's insulin. The vials had been refrigerated.

Another vial flashed through her brain. This one had been stored in a locked refrigerator in the pharmacy at the Joint Craig Theatre Hospital on Bagram Airbase. Only that vial had been tampered with before John and Captain Mendoza's A-Team had returned to Bagram, leaving the vial with its original anthrax booster contents and—

"Rae, what—"

She sprinted for the door of the ICU. Not only was she certain John would follow, there was no time to explain. Nor did she have time for the heated stream of Urdu that came out of one nurse's mouth or the Arabic that came out of the doctor's, as she blew past both and straight into the ICU room, right up to the clear-plastic medical bassinet with "Sadat" written in Urdu and English on a card slotted in at the end.

Regan ignored everything but that sweet, innocent face as she leaned all the way over the side of the bassinet, until she was an inch away from those cherubic lips.

She inhaled deeply.

Her foster sister's breath had smelled sweet when her blood sugar levels were in the red. The boy's breath didn't smell sweet.

The air was distinctly...fetid.

"Fuck." The expletive had come from John. He was standing right beside her, leaning over the crib too.

She didn't have to ask if John had recognized that odor; the curse had confirmed it. Whoever they were after wasn't just a traitor, he was an utter monster.

One who'd deliberately infected an innocent baby with that psycho-toxin.

## 22

Regan caught John's tortured stare as she straightened and stepped back from the ICU bassinet to grip his arm. "You've got to convince the doctor that there's more going on here than just diabetes." Though she'd wager that the stress of the little guy's condition had activated that damned chimeral psycho-toxin. "Give him Gil's number. Gil speaks Arabic, too. Make sure the doc calls him—before you leave his side. Then meet me in the waiting room. I still need your help with the mother."

More so than ever.

As for Gil, he would need to arrange for an emergency shipment of his makeshift chimeral cure to be flown to Islamabad before the hour was out.

Even then, there was no telling if the boy would receive it in time.

They were dealing with a *baby* for Christ's sake. Who knew how that would affect the treatment? If that tiny, innocent body could even handle it.

Leaving John to his task, Regan spun around and headed into the waiting room to make sure Inaya Sadat didn't pull the same disappearing stunt that her husband had before John had a chance to assist her in grilling the woman.

She paused just inside the door to the ICU and retrieved a pair of sterile, purple nitrile gloves from the box atop a stainless-steel rolling table, then kept moving out to the nurses' station. There—with Inaya's eggshell-blue *shalwar kameez* and veil firmly in her sights—she stopped as she pocketed the gloves. Listened.

Studied.

The devastated woman was still sobbing amid the trio of nurses, but she was quieter now, calmer. And unquestionably not faking her grief.

Good. As much as it pained Regan to use that profound anguish against a young mother, she absolutely would. She had no choice. There was an excellent chance that whoever Inaya was sleeping with had infected that boy—including her husband.

*Especially* if Brandt was the father.

If Aamer Sadat was their traitor, he could've blackmailed Brandt into murdering Hachemi to prevent his name from crossing the translator's lips and then chosen to clean up his own life—and extracted the revenge of the cuckolded in the process—by taking out the child that wasn't his, as well as the boy's biological father.

Either way, she wouldn't rest until she caught the bastard capable of sentencing a baby to the hell she and John's men had endured weeks earlier. Most of those men were now dead. Of the lucky four who'd survived a full facing-off with that chimera, she'd been left with a dominant gun hand she could no longer trust to do her bidding. Staff Sergeant Hudson and Sergeant Welch were also dealing with issues surrounding fine motor coordination, as well as memory in Welch's case. Sergeant

Gutierrez was the only one who'd come through his bout relatively unscathed.

Even if the boy survived, what handicap would *he* be left to endure? And how much worse would it be because his brain wasn't fully developed yet?

And there was the traitor/terror angle to consider. If Riyad's rogue SEAL had been the one to infect that baby, Zakaria Webber had been slipping in and out of Islamabad for a lot longer than just today.

What else had Webber been doing while he was here?

"Rae?"

She turned to John, ignored the lingering frustration and fury still threaded within his dark gray eyes. "I need you to scare the shit out of that woman."

"*What*?"

"John, listen to me. We don't know who infected that boy in there, much less Staff Sergeant Brandt. Yes, given that both Brandt and the baby were infected, it's looking as though Brandt was the father, and that a guilty Aamer Sadat was getting revenge and cleaning house. But what if that's what we're meant to see? If your source is right, and Crier is seeing a local, that kid could just as easily be his."

If Tom Crier was the father *and* their traitor, what better way to obscure his trail? Crier could've just as easily gotten the chimera from Riyad's dirty SEAL. If she hadn't walked into that ICU and deliberately leaned over for a whiff, the boy would most likely have continued having seizures—confusing the hell out of his doctors—until he was dead, seemingly of complications from his diabetes.

And, once the boy was dead, no one would be looking to connect him to a father outside of Aamer Sadat.

Nor would this be the first case of infanticide that she'd come across in her time with CID. And as dastardly as this particular method would be—if it succeeded—it wouldn't even be the worst. She didn't have to tell John that either. After the hell his father had subjected him to growing up, it was a miracle John had survived long enough to grow into his body and take his survival into his own hands.

All that baby had was them. She needed to get to the bottom of this *now*. For so many reasons. And, frankly, she would use whatever she could to get there.

If that offended John, or tarnished her in his eyes, so be it.

"Just repeat what I say, no matter what. And remember—" She laid her hand on his arm, pressing into the hard layer of muscle to reach the surprisingly tender man hidden beneath. Whether John admitted it or not. "—*you* are not hurting her. It's me."

Nor would this be the first time.

That familiar gray stare studied her, much as she'd studied Inaya from across the room. Its owner finally nodded. "Okay. But you can't fool me. Not any longer. You don't like what you're about to do any more than those you're forced to do it to."

He was right.

But she wouldn't admit it. She couldn't afford to.

So she did the only thing she could. She ignored it. "We passed a consult room just outside this waiting area. It's empty. Tell Inaya I have news about her son's condition and that I'll speak with her in there. I'll be waiting."

There was no way a married woman in the Near East would admit to what they needed Inaya to admit to in a public waiting room, Muslim or not.

As John turned to fulfill her request, Regan headed for the consult room. Fortunately, it was unlocked. Unfortunately, there were only two black, plastic-and-metal chairs inside. The room was also more a claustrophobic booth.

It would have to do.

She scooted the shoulders of one of the chairs into the corner of the tiny room and placed the other facing it, in the center. When John opened the door, she motioned the petite, veiled woman inside toward the cornered chair, John to the other in the center of the room. Regan took in those wide, reddened eyes amid that delicate, silver-edged wisp of eggshell blue as she took up her spot, standing behind John.

Emotionally, Inaya Sadat was on the edge.

*Excellent.* It would help.

She and Mrs. Sadat waited as John leaned down to tuck her laptop on the floor beneath the metal legs of his chair. Evidently, he'd done this before, because he remained silent as he straightened, listening for her cue as to when and what to speak.

"Mrs. Sadat, my name is Special Agent Regan Chase. I lied to you when I stopped by the hospital earlier this evening with Agent Walburn. I wasn't here to offer my condolences. For that, I apologize. But there was an important reason for my lie. I'm investigating a case that involves soon-to-be mothers who were murdered in a cave in the Hindu Kush less than a month ago. Have you heard the news?"

Regan paused and waited for John. She could hear his deep voice, translating her words, but she didn't focus on it, or him. She stared over his imposing shoulders instead, completely focused on Inaya Sadat.

Black, white, European, Pakistani or Russian, it didn't matter. Micro-expressions were universal to humans, man or woman.

She needed to see this woman's.

Regan watched as the shock set in, caught the woman's slight nod, confirming that she'd heard of the murders, then continued. "Mrs. Sadat, I know what's wrong with your son. He's been infected with a new and very deadly virus. I recently survived the same virus. Your son's doctor is speaking to mine in the United States right now. I arranged that call. The cure will soon be on its way here. I'll be honest; I don't know if it will help. Your son is very young and his medical condition will most likely complicate his treatment. Now, I need something from you for my efforts. I need the truth." Even if it meant that she'd be getting it by implying that the boy's critical medical treatment was tied to his mother's willingness to answer questions from the strange Americans who'd brought her into this room.

The tactic might be heinous and brutal, and Regan might hate herself for it, but it was a time-proven producer of results. And with that mob closing in on the embassy and growing larger and more violent by the minute, it was more than necessary.

It was vital.

She waited until John paused his stream of gravelly Urdu, then drew in her breath and finished it. "I know your husband did not father your son. I'm not judging or condemning you—and there is no need for me to share your answer with anyone outside this room." At least, not at the moment. "But I must know; was Staff Sergeant Brandt the father?"

As John's gravelly Urdu filled the tiny room once again, Regan watched the horror, confusion and continued shock play out in the muscles in and around the woman's forehead, eyes and mouth.

Inaya's softer, insistent response followed.

"She swears Brandt's not the father. She also swears on the Qur'an that she never slept with him."

The micro-expressions in Inaya's face combined with the trembling tension in her hand as she reached out to grip John's scarred fingers and repeat her words. The woman was telling the truth. As if she'd realized what she'd done—that she'd touched yet another man who was not her husband—Inaya snatched her fingers from John's and knotted them tightly in her lap.

It didn't help. They were still shaking.

Regan knew the feeling.

It was the rest that confused her. If Inaya Sadat was telling the truth about her level of intimacy with Staff Sergeant Brandt, what had she missed during her initial canvass of that electronic photo? Regan anchored her palm against the wall of John's back, hoping to use the support to ratchet down the increase in her own tremors as she pulled the memory of the photo and its frame into the center of her mind.

There, she studied it. Considered the possibilities.

There was only one explanation left.

Brandt hadn't been staring at the woman on his right in that photo, he'd been gazing past her to the man on *her* right. The staff sergeant hadn't been having an affair with Inaya, he'd been having it with the woman's husband, Aamer Sadat.

"Tom Crier. He's your son's father, isn't he?" Lord, she hoped so. Because she'd just lobbed her last grenade. She was completely out of ammo, at least any that was capable of reaching their true target in time to take him down.

John's shoulder tensed beneath her hand, but he quickly translated.

This time there was no insistent denial. Just a fresh crop of very telling tears. They filled the woman's dark eyes, turning them darker and more luminous. And then, an ever-so-slight nod. The tears slipped free, filling the silence, drowning it out.

More tears followed.

"Do you need me to press her for a verbal yes?"

She shook her head, then realized John was still focused on his duties. He was staring at the sobbing woman in front of them, not up at her. "No. But I could—"

She stopped as the door opened.

Before Regan could turn around, Inaya jumped to her feet, slipping around a now standing John so that she could throw herself into the newcomer's arms.

Aamer Sadat.

It appeared Regan was going to get a crack at the woman's husband after all.

She swiftly catalogued the man's dark hair and eyes, full lips and neatly trimmed beard accenting all that dusky skin as he took the time to soothe his wife's tears before quietly conversing with her. Aamer's backgrounder photo had not done him justice. His wife might be gorgeous; this man was downright beautiful.

No wonder Brandt had fallen hard enough to risk his career.

Aamer also appeared to truly care for his wife. Though the soft pats to her back and gentle soothings of her cheek were decidedly brotherly, they were genuine. As much as Regan hated to admit it, Aamer's sincere affection for his wife provided even more leverage to use against him and his family.

She didn't argue when Aamer opened the door to the tiny room and sent his wife back to the ICU's waiting area.

Silence swirled in as the door closed, pulsing through the air with anticipation.

Regan could feel John standing behind her, supporting her personally and professionally, but ultimately leaving this new interview to her.

She waited patiently. From the gamut of emotions that had passed through Aamer's dusky features during that soothing session with his wife, Inaya had filled him in on everything that had happened since his latest departure from the hospital.

Frankly, she was curious which element Aamer would respond to first. His choice would reveal a hell of a lot, and set the tone for more.

"This treatment of yours. It is coming here soon?"

"Yes."

Relief flooded those same dusky features, cementing Regan's

instincts regarding the man and his priorities. "What do you want to know?"

Anything and everything that would help her find the bastard who'd infected that sweet baby lying in the ICU. Because that flood of relief had also confirmed that Aamer Sadat was *not* a traitor *or* Webber's contact at the embassy.

But if she was lucky, his answers would lead them to whoever was. "You and Staff Sergeant Brandt were lovers."

She could feel the slight tension behind her as the surprise rippled through John. But that was it. John remained standing where he was and quiet. She was grateful.

It allowed her to focus on Aamer's face and body language. *Aamer* had not been surprised by her comment.

Wary? Yes.

And, intriguingly, more than a bit relieved.

Or, perhaps, not so intriguing.

As huge as the risk to Aamer would be should his sexual orientation come out in any Muslim country, let alone this one, she understood the urge to shout it anyway. Or at least to whisper it. After all, she'd grown up with her own insidious secrets. Her own dual identity as she'd struggled with what she could share and, more importantly, what she couldn't with her closest friends...including now, as an adult, with Gil and Mira.

And, yes, even John.

As for Aamer, the man finally sighed. He nodded firmly. "Yes. We were in love. Neither Stephen nor I expected it. And with our careers, perhaps we should have resisted. But we did not. We could not. And now—" The man fisted his palms as though for support as he swallowed hard, then continued. "—he is dead."

"Do you know who killed him and why?"

"No. But Stephen feared this outcome. He called me."

"From Al Dhafra?"

"Yes. He told me I should be prepared. That things were not

as they seemed at the embassy. People were not as they seemed. He said that if something should happen to him, I was to take my wife and son and leave Pakistan. Disappear. He believed that soon it might not be safe here...for anyone. After you visited earlier, Inaya called me to tell me that Stephen was dead. I knew then that what he feared had come to pass. I begged Inaya to leave with me. I told her it would be safer for the boy if we left without him, appearing to abandon Danyal to my brother for a time. She told me she would consider my plans, so I went to my brother's house to begin to make the arrangements."

Not only did the micro-expressions in Aamer's face back up his words, so had his actions this evening. According to the intel John had received via Ty, Aamer had followed up his bank appointment with a visit to his brother's house. His *older* brother's house.

That relationship was everything to a Pakistani man.

Aamer's nod confirmed it. "Imran is the head of our family. I wanted him to understand why we would be disappearing, to assure him that it was not my choice...and ask that he and my sister care for my son in my stead and to find a way to send Danyal to us once he was well. My brother agreed. I left the hospital again a short while ago and returned to my brother's home to complete the arrangements and to sign the necessary papers so that he could make medical and financial decisions for my son."

Except Aamer was here, not finalizing those arrangements. Especially with the riots and the rest of Brandt's prediction playing out.

"Mr. Sadat, why did you return to the hospital?"

Aamer's palms came up as he sighed. "Danyal. Though I did not father him, he is my son. I thought I could do as Stephen requested. But while I trust my brother, I find I cannot go without Danyal. And, now, with this new illness that has befallen him, Inaya will not leave him either—and I cannot abandon her. You must understand; Inaya and I grew up in the same village. She knows what I am, yet she married me anyway. It is true; her family was poor, so they asked no questions. But she knew I must have a wife to have the job I wanted. She has been the best of companions. And so, when she fell in love, I did not stand in her way, just as she did not stand in mine. All I asked was that she be discreet and not leave me. Given her lover's career, and his family connections and obligations, she knew Crier would not want more than the affair. Danyal was a blessing both of us would have once her lover—and mine —moved on."

"Does anyone know about your wife and Tom Crier?"

"No." The man was adamant.

"How can you be so sure?"

"Because they met at our house. He always arrived to discuss 'embassy business' and I was always there in another room so that no one would ever suspect."

Aamer was right. It was a solid cover.

But not infallible.

If no one had figured out what was going on and Brandt wasn't being blackmailed over the boy's paternity, but because the man was gay...had Crier truly killed his own son to sanitize his trail? If so, surely Crier would have infected Aamer and Inaya along with the boy? Or was some other catastrophe due to befall Danyal's parents? But, if so, why not wait and include the boy?

Damn it. This case still made no sense.

Yet.

"Mr. Sadat, Staff Sergeant Brandt killed a prisoner in his charge. Brandt deliberately murdered him. With poison."

Shock stiffened Aamer's entire body. He stepped toward her,

stopping short as she sensed John's form shifting slightly—decisively—behind her.

Aamer shook his head. "*No*. He would not do this. Yes, Stephen was a soldier, but he was the gentlest of men. He *could* not—"

"The man Brandt killed was responsible for the slaughter of those pregnant women in that cave in the Hindu Kush. The one on the news tonight. Captain McCord did not kill those women or their babies, an Afghan translator did. And not only did Brandt murder the translator, he did it while he was aboard the ship—*after* he spoke to you from Al Dhafra. I found his prints on a vial containing the remaining poison. A vial that was hidden in a doctored pack of Pakistani cigarettes that also bore only his prints."

Aamer stepped backward at that. Staggered really, until his spine hit the wall.

Regan was half afraid the man was so dumbfounded he was going slide all the way down.

He didn't. But Aamer did use the wall for support as he nodded. "To avenge what I saw on the news? That, Stephen might want to kill for. But I still cannot believe he would."

"What if he was being blackmailed—about his relationship with you?"

If the Marine Corps had learned of the staff sergeant's secrets, Brandt would've been court-martialed. Not because he was gay, but for a host of other violations under the Uniformed Code of Military Justice, including the fact that indulging in an affair with a married Pakistani Foreign Service National had left Brandt open for blackmail while he was serving as a Marine Security Guard at a critical US embassy. Blackmail which, by extension, had risked the security of that embassy *and* his nation.

Also, while Brandt might not have been willing to murder to

save his own career, gentle man or not, she suspected he'd have done it in a heartbeat to save Aamer. Because his lover's career hadn't just been on the line, but his life. The traitor wouldn't even have had to threaten to kill Aamer; the bastard could've simply let it be known to Brandt that he'd leak the truth regarding Aamer's sexual orientation and stand back to let the righteous wolves descend to carry out the so-called will of Allah.

Then again, given what they were dealing with—and that an infant had been targeted, too—the traitor had probably just threatened to kill Aamer outright.

"Mr. Sadat? *Do* you think he was being blackmailed? You told me that Tom Crier and your wife were careful. That no one knew about them. But you also told me that Crier met your wife at your house. Did Crier know about you and Brandt?"

To her surprise, Aamer's eyes filled up with tears, much like his wife's. "I do not know. I pray not. But...it is possible."

And there was something else. *Someone* else. She was certain of it. Someone this man believed capable of blackmailing his lover into murder.

"Who?"

Those dark eyes blinked. "I did not say—"

"No. But you're thinking it." Because *she* was thinking it too.

There was a reason no one in Staff Sergeant Brandt's chain of command had thought to compare that baby's dimpled chin with his.

"Mr. Sadat, *who* knew Brandt was gay?"

"Warren Jeffers. Stephen could not abide the man. He refused to tell me why, but I believe Jeffers knew Stephen was gay. And Jeffers? That man, he is so polite to everyone outside the embassy, but he is ugliness itself inside. Jeffers would abuse such information. I know it."

So did she. Hell, she'd had firsthand experience with Jeffers' abuse that afternoon. Why else had he slugged her with that tidbit about working with her dear old dirty dad? A man like that was willing to use anything to further his own goals.

But what were those goals, damn it?

John's phone pinged behind her.

She tensed, waiting for hers to go off. It didn't. She was still breathing out her relief when she heard John click off his phone and then,

"Rae?"

*Shit.* It was time to go. "Okay. Just a second."

She pulled the purple nitrile gloves she'd taken from the ICU from her pocket. "Mr. Sadat, do you or your wife have your son's insulin vial handy?"

"Here, at the hospital?"

"Yes."

He shook his head. "My wife was panicked when she left. There was no time to check. And when she arrived here, no need. But I think Inaya had just opened a new one yesterday. The empty one has already been discarded. Why?"

"It doesn't matter." She returned the gloves to her pocket. There was no sense in admitting what she suspected. If the boy did survive the chimera, she'd only be giving his parents nightmares about his medication—and what might really be inside it—for the rest of their lives. She glanced at the door. "You can go. But don't go far."

"I will not. For all you have done and are doing, I swear it. I will be here."

Of that she was certain. Only because she was about to have Ty double the man's shadow, and this time, she wanted those involved posted within tackling distance.

Aamer bowed his head toward her, then John, and left.

The second the door closed, John was at her side, her laptop already slung over his left shoulder, keeping his right—and *his* dominant gun hand—free as he motioned her toward the door.

"That was Tulle. The ambassador has returned to the embassy, but the protests are spreading. If we want to slip in the back gate unnoticed—"

"We need to go now."

John didn't even take the time to nod. He simply opened the door and shepherded her through.

As with their trip to the Shifa, the drive to the embassy was burdened with calls. Again, John's were in Urdu and Arabic with men she didn't know. Hers were in English, the opening one to a man she knew very well and trusted even more: Gil.

With Gil's call came a sliver of hope for the Sadats' baby. Gil had already arranged for an emergency flight to Pakistan to transport the chimeral cure he'd used to treat her and John's surviving men. It would be airborne within the hour, in Islamabad less than sixteen hours later.

God willing, it would be soon enough.

As for John and herself, they arrived at the embassy within forty minutes of departing the Shifa and managed to slip inside relatively unnoticed. Both Riyad and Staff Sergeant Tulle were waiting for them at the entrance to the chancery.

From the tension in the spook's and the staff sergeant's features, each had news.

And neither set was good.

John opened one of the glass double doors and ushered her inside to the silvery marble foyer. There, he finally relinquished her laptop and crime kit with a murmured, "I'll find you," then peeled off to head deeper into the chancery with Tulle. Most likely to assist with the compound's security once he'd received the latest update.

The update she'd be getting from Riyad.

Midnight had come and gone well over an hour ago. With her grip once again becoming questionable at best due to the inherent exhaustion of yet another night of stunted sleep, Regan tipped her head toward the carpeted waiting area to the right. Just off the echoing marble and its gleaming grand piano. "Over there."

Fortunately, Riyad followed.

She dumped her laptop and crime kit on one of the plush chairs and stretched out her recalcitrant hand as she turned back to the spook. "What's wrong?"

The scowl she'd become so familiar with was still firmly in place, but for once, it wasn't directed at her. "We got that ID you wanted."

The seventh woman from the cave?

"Oh, thank God."

Riyad shook his head. "I'd wait on that praise. Plus, you should know, we didn't make the ID. The victim's father recognized her from the collection of leaked photos that are still being slapped up on all the local news stations."

Oh, shit. That particular close-up was the one she'd ordered the boots on the ground to have in hand—for the necessary shock value. But that was a shock she'd never intended. Not that any of the other leaked photos were less horrific.

Especially to each victim's family.

"Who is—was—she?"

"Asma Chaudhry Jafari. Chief Justice Harun Chaudhry's youngest child and only daughter—and, from what I understand, the apple of his and his wife's eye."

Their victim's father was the chief justice of Pakistan's Supreme Court?

Oh, this was bad. Very, very bad.

And, hell, even Riyad could read her expressions now. Because he was nodding. "You were right. She's the key."

Wrong. That poor mutilated woman was the log that was going to fuel the fires of hate and discontent that were already sweeping the city, and keep them raging for who knew how long. How the hell were they going to put this one out?

"Wait—did you say, cherished daughter?"

"Yeah."

"Then how is it that mom and dad didn't even know she was missing?" Asma Chaudhry had been murdered four weeks ago. Granted, her own upbringing had been utterly shitty, but if Asma's hadn't been, shouldn't the woman's mother or father have noticed her absence at some point over these past weeks?

Especially with this country's extended, and very tight-knit, family structure?

And then it hit her.

"She's a traveling nurse, or—" Given those pregnant victims, "—a midwife." How else had Durrani lured her away from her job, prior to murdering her? Asma might not have trusted Durrani as dating material, but he was a doctor. She'd have believed the bastard when he claimed he had patients who needed her. Either way, "The woman was working in the Federally Administered Tribal Areas, wasn't she?"

Directly across the border from Afghanistan, and near enough to that cave. Where Pakistani villages were few and far between. With even fewer amenities.

Phones.

Riyad nodded. And was that actually a glint of respect in the man's eyes? For her? "That's a damned good guess."

"Not a guess." She'd earned that insight during her hellish final session with Durrani in the *Griffith*'s brig. "How did Asma and Durrani meet? Do we know?"

"Not yet. But she did get her nursing degree in Boston, so Agent Castile will begin there. She worked in Islamabad until she married a local doctor, Ejaz Jafari. They were in a car accident about two years ago. Ejaz was killed and she miscarried their son. She went back to work afterward. But there's more. It's about her father, the chief justice—and the prime minister. There's been a power struggle going on this past month in this country and it's more serious than outsiders think."

That was news to her. But then, this past month she'd been up to her neck in the cave investigation and then in a coma.

She knew Chaudhry by name, but only because of the news he'd made a year ago, not a month ago. And, of course, there was the reason for her instant recall after all these months. An element had hit a personal hot button. "I just remember the older news. Last year Chaudhry became a national hero when he outed a longtime, trusted clerk of the courts who was passing information to the Indian government." And the hot-button reason she still remembered it out of all the other news that month? "The clerk-turned-mole, he's related to Pakistan's prime minister, isn't he?"

"Yes. Though the clerk is now in prison, serving a life sentence...and is also now Iftikhar Bukhari's *former* son-in-law."

She nodded. She wouldn't admit it out loud to Riyad, but asshole or not, she actually felt for Bukhari. She definitely related to the personal and political shitstorm the prime minister had undoubtedly endured as a result.

"I assume the news I missed while I was working the cave murders and in a coma is related?"

"It is. I'm not sure if you know, but Chaudhry's been one of our country's biggest supporters over here. More so than Pakistan's president and especially Prime Minister Bukhari, who still regularly takes to the floor of their parliament to bitch about how we violated their country's sovereign borders to take out Bin Laden without letting them know—while completely ignoring the fact that the powers that be in this country knew damned well the fucker was here the entire time. But Chaudhry's take is more balanced. Even leans a bit toward us. Possibly because the man got one of his degrees at Yale, and then sent at least two of his kids back to the States for theirs."

The first half she'd known, but not the part about Yale and his kids.

Regan tucked the insight away as Riyad shrugged. "Anyway, love for Chaudhry still runs exceptionally high on the Pakistani streets, and of course, Bukhari can't stand him. But now their military is on Chaudhry's ass, too. The chief justice made a ruling last month against the army, then followed it up with a major televised interview. Chaudhry's never been a fan of military rule. During the interview, he laid out why. Made a damned good case for why both coups and military rule have actually been detrimental to the world as a whole and to his country in particular. Chaudhry's of the mindset that Pakistan must be an Islamic democracy, but that the country's strength lies in *both* elements; that while he does believe in a strong military, it should remain in the wings within their country and *out* of the internal power structure. His arguments are being discussed openly in the media and on the street—and ordinary Pakistanis are beginning to agree with him."

"Is that it?" Though, frankly, that was a heck of a lot.

"Nope. There's one more thing. Chaudhry's eldest son? Ironically, he's a colonel in their army...and he's currently assigned to the country's nuclear weapons' arsenal."

Well, shit.

Didn't that just complicate things?

As for Chaudhry, the chief justice was a hit-and-run accident or home gas heater explosion away from the grave. With the country's prime minster *and* the army gunning for his hide, even with his son's connections at the arsenal, the only thing that had protected the chief justice this long had to have been his connection to the common man. If the army did kill him, there was a real risk that they'd end up elevating the man's status posthumously. And in doing so, would be giving credence to Chaudhry's arguments, since everyone would know who'd killed him and why.

But, now, with his daughter dead?

And his colonel of a son quite possibly arguing against democracy and for vengeance upon those who'd mutilated his baby sister?

Riyad's suit jacket vibrated. He reached in and retrieved his phone, only to glance at the screen before returning it to his inner pocket. "You know what this all means, don't you?"

Yeah, she knew. "Basically, we've got a Pakistani army general who wants to be president and a prime minster willing to help him out for a share of the pie, topped off by a moderate sitting president without the political oomph to fight off Prime Minister Bukhari or the army. And, of course, the only one with that political oomph has just discovered that his cherished only daughter was supposedly murdered by American soldiers."

In other words, they had a recipe for the very thing Chaudhry had argued against. A coup.

At the very least, Bukhari and the army might have effectively killed Chaudhry's pro-American sentiment and—without the apple of his eye around to boost it up—quite possibly his spirit too, especially given how Asma had died. Hell, Regan wouldn't be surprised if the man retired from the bench to grieve with his wife in private.

A win-win for Bukhari and his G3-rifle-wielding thugs.

With those riots spreading out around the embassy and, eventually, the city and the country, all the army had to do was wait a bit longer and they could take the presidency for themselves, installing their current commanding general in the job, or they could pretend to hand power over to their current political lapdog and puppet, Bukhari. Again, a win-win.

Either scenario spelled disaster for future US-Pakistani relations, not to mention Pakistan's support for any current and upcoming joint anti-terror efforts.

"I need to speak to him."

"*Chaudhry*?"

She'd finally succeeded in stunning the spook.

Good. She had a few more surprises up her sleeve, if she could get her recalcitrant hand to cooperate. Yeah, it was after 0130 local time, but she doubted very many folks were sleeping in the city tonight, much less the chief justice and his wife.

Not with the image both of Asma's parents now had reverberating around inside their heads and their hearts.

"Yes, Chaudhry. And I'd like to speak to his wife, as well." Not so much so she could make an appeal to the mother, though she'd definitely do that, but because she owed the woman and her husband a personal apology over that photo.

Hell, she owed an apology to all the victims' families. Not only should those photos have never been leaked, the images within were ones that loved ones should never have to carry around for the rest of their lives.

She ought to know. She had one hell of a final, horrific view of her mom lurking in the recesses of her own mind...always.

Regan rubbed at the vibrating fingers of her right hand, hoping the self-massage would work as well as John's deeper one, but it didn't. "If the ambassador can't arrange it, I can put in a call to Palisade—or you can hit up your buddy, the Big Bubble. I'm sure both men have our president on speed dial."

And *he* should be able to arrange it.

To her surprise, Riyad nodded swiftly and decisively. "I'll speak to the ambassador. If she can't make it happen, I'll see what Kettering can do."

"Fine. I'd like—"

"Uh...Agent Riyad?" *Jeffers*.

And just like that, the scowl was back.

The spook wasn't kidding. He really did not like Warren Jeffers, much less the man's sycophantic attitude.

She could see the tinge of disgust coating Riyad's latest frown as he turned toward the DCM's downright timid approach across the foyer. "Yes?"

"The ambassador's looking for you."

"Was. I left her side fifteen minutes ago. Unless this request is new?"

"Oh, no. Sorry. I'll just—"

Regan stepped forward, before the man could complete his almost comical tail tuck and instinctive about-face. "Mr. Jeffers?"

The man froze. In honor of her presence, Riyad's nearly perpetual scowl had shifted, now appearing on the DCM's meaty features. "Yes?"

"I need to see Mr. Crier. Now." She hadn't had a chance to discuss the latest with Riyad, so she shot him an open glance instead. One that promised dirt, if he'd but back her up.

To her relief, the spook clipped a nod in return. "Right. As a matter of fact, we both need to see Crier." Riyad nodded to the DCM, tapping into a surprisingly effective store of charm she'd yet to see from the man. "Mr. Jeffers, if you would be so kind as to escort Agent Chase to Crier's office? He told the ambassador he'd be holed up there until further notice." Riyad turned to her and leveled a brief, but stunning smile on her in place of his standard-issue frown. "I'll join you shortly, Regan. Just as soon as I've taken care of that matter we discussed."

*Chaudhry.*

She returned the spook's smile with more than a touch of pure camaraderie, if only to piss Jeffers off, as she gathered up her laptop and stainless-steel kit. "I'll see you there. Good luck." She allowed her smile to drip away as she headed for the DCM and his thatch of wilted peppery curls and wrinkled suit. "Shall we?"

The DCM's annoyance at having to do her bidding echoed with each peeved step along the silvery marble flooring as they crossed the foyer. It continued to serve as the only communication between them as Jeffers led her past the inner security, as well as darkened office after darkened office, until they'd reached the chancery's political section.

She paused to set her crime kit down on the secretary's outer desk as Jeffers grudgingly continued on toward a closed, inner door, presumably to knock.

A split second before his thick knuckles connected with the slab of wood, a sharp retort reverberated from within.

*Gunshot.*

Regan dumped her laptop and vaulted toward the DCM, drawing her SIG with her right hand as she knocked the man's entire body down and away from the wooden door with her left. "*Call security—and stay down*!"

She needn't have whispered—much less slowly cracked the door open so she could case the inner room. Her first, brief glance inside told her all she needed to know.

There was no lingering threat to Jeffers or herself.

Or Tom Crier for that matter.

Not anymore.

The man was seated behind his desk, his navy-blue suited shoulders braced against the back of an executive chair. His green eyes were open, his blond head tipped toward his left shoulder with his jaw split jarringly apart. Half hung freely at a surreal, mutilated angle she'd seen once before. Just after midnight on Christmas Day.

When she was six years old.

All things considered, the man looked remarkably similar to that final image she carried of her mother...but for one notable exception.

Tom Crier was already dead.

# 23

"Agent Chase? Are you okay?"

Regan was dimly aware of the spook touching her sleeve. She ignored the sensation, and him, fighting the inexplicable fog that had closed in as she stared at the scarlet and gray splattered across the desk she couldn't recall moving in front of.

The fog. It wasn't surrounding the desk.

It was inside her.

It took several torturous moments before she was able to push her way through. To accept where she was—in the present, not the past. At the chancery at Embassy Islamabad, Pakistan, not on the ground floor of a skinny, brick townhouse in desperate need of remodeling on the outskirts of Washington, DC.

How long since she'd heard that retort?

"Agent Chase?"

Damn it, *focus.*

She drew her breath in deep, gathering up her jangled nerves as she forced her equally jangled hand to slip her SIG back inside the jacket of her suit and into the waiting slot in her shoulder holster. Only then did she risk turning around to face the open door. Jeffers was nowhere to be seen. Three Marines stood in the middle of the outer office, waiting instructions. Corporal Vetter's familiar, uniformed form loomed among them. But that was it.

"*Regan*?" Riyad again. His voice was sharp this time, determined.

Knowing.

Worse, those dark eyes of his were brimming with genuine compassion as she swung around toward the desk and the spook waiting patiently beside it, and her.

"*Can* you do this?"

She knew what he was asking. Admitting.

They didn't have time for him to play catch-up cop, and Riyad knew it. Not with that unruly mob still swelling outside the gates.

There might be a slew of diplomatic security agents currently swarming in and around the buildings and grounds of the embassy, but every single one was actively attempting to keep that smoldering powder keg from exploding.

This investigation was up to her. Despite the fact that the physical fallout to the victim in front of her was identical to the horror she'd been attempting to banish from her brain for the past twenty years.

*Focus. Work the case in front of you.*

*Now.*

She drew her breath in deep once more, this time purging the lingering remnants of past horrors with it. Mostly. "I'm fine." But her hand definitely wasn't. "My kit. It's in the outer office. Would you—"

"Absolutely." He turned on his boot heels and left, leaving her with that goddamned mess in front of her.

And it was a mess.

Like her mother, the embassy's senior political officer had pressed the working end of a pistol beneath the base of his chin, only to shift his hand at the last moment, sending the round exploding up at a slight angle, through his jawbone, nasal cavity and forehead, blowing the top of his skull into the ceiling of the room. Bits of brain, blood and bone had then rudely rained down around him. In her mother's case, her shoulders and lap... and, of course, the recently decorated Christmas tree behind her.

Tom Crier's flesh and fluid, and bits of brain and bone, had ended up on the shoulders of his dark blue suit and in his lap as well...along with a sheet of previously plain, white paper with two words scrawled amid the center.

*Forgive me.*

"Agent Chase?"

She drew in her breath and turned to find Riyad behind her, brandishing her crime kit. She thought about ordering him to remove the polite kid gloves he'd inexplicably brought into the room with him, but what the hell. His eggshells attitude might be grating, but overall it was a welcome change from his disdain when they'd performed a similar activity in the *Griffith*'s conference room two days earlier.

Not trusting the fingers of her rattling hand, she reached out with her left and spun the barrels on her crime kit's waiting combination lock. Once inside the stainless-steel case, she withdrew a pair of latex gloves and booties, then motioned for Riyad to do the same. Protective gear donned, she retrieved her camera and automatically began her photographic sweep of the scene while the spook moved across the office to set her opened kit down on the modest, wood-grained conference table.

Other than that body and what definitely appeared to be a suicide note, nothing appeared amiss.

She tipped her head toward Embassy Islamabad's now

former political officer. "He was having an affair with Inaya Sadat—with her husband's knowledge and permission. Crier fathered her baby."

"You're sure?"

As sure as she could be without paternity test results in hand. "Brandt and Aamer Sadat were lovers. Major Garrison and I got verbal confessions from both Sadats at the Shifa this evening." Something neither would ever have invented with their religion and Pakistani citizenship, since both risked death with the admissions. "Also, their son, Danyal, does have diabetes, but that's not why he's in the ICU. Someone infected the boy with the chimera. I could smell it on his breath. Dr. Fourche is already consulting and arranging to have the cure flown in later today."

"Holy *fuck*. A baby?"

"Yep."

The spook extended a gloved finger toward the desk. "Hence, the bastard's note."

She nodded. "It would seem so." Then again, appearances could be deceiving. She'd learned that lesson the hard way... several times.

*Forgive me.*

For fathering a child outside of his marriage? Or for infecting that child with a deadly virus to cover it up? Or had Thomas Crier been alluding to the investigation he'd come to suspect she was really here in Islamabad to pursue? The one involving their nation's latest, and perhaps deadliest-to-date, traitor?

Regan pondered the questions as she wrapped up her close-up photos of the victim and his immediate surroundings. She'd taken no photos of the weapon Crier had used, though, because she'd yet to spot it.

Had it bounced beneath the desk?

She reached out to grasp the left arm of the executive chair. The leather monstrosity did possess wheels, but with her recalcitrant hand, there was no way she was going to risk losing control of the chair and accidentally spinning their victim out onto the floor. "I'm done photographing the body. Can you help—"

"Let go. I've got it."

The spook's filthy frown returned when she failed to obey, though this one resembled John's when she'd tried to take her kit from him as they were leaving the Serena hotel earlier tonight, rather than the others Riyad had been bestowing upon her since her arrival aboard the *Griffith*.

She released the arm of the chair and let Riyad roll Crier's body several feet back.

And there was the gun.

Crier's right hand had hit his thigh following the 9mm's retort, sending the Glock he'd used to blow his brains out skittering underneath the desk.

She crouched down and took the requisite photos, then reached down to retrieve the Glock. "Can you grab an evidence—"

"Right here."

"Thanks." She slipped the 9mm into the paper bag already open in Riyad's hands.

He filled out the evidence label, but left the bag unsealed as she'd yet to dust the Glock for prints. The label finished, he walked the bag across the office to lay it on the conference table beside her stainless-steel case.

"I've got a gunshot residue test kit in the second drawer—"

"Got it."

Damn. The man might make a decent investigative colleague after all. He'd even spent his time while she was photographing the scene splaying her kit wide on the table so he could root thought its contents and set out items he thought she might need. She turned back to Crier's body as the spook reached her side. Ignoring that glassy, vacant stare as best she could, she accepted the GSR swab for the lab's sample. She used her steady hand to dab the swab down the victim's right index finger and along the inner webbing, then up to the tip of his thumb.

Fortunately, that vacant gaze was green, not blue. And while the rest of those misshapen features were baby-faced, they were definitely male.

It helped.

She finished dabbing Crier's right hand and moved onto his left as Riyad took care of packaging up the initial samples. Once both hands had been dabbed for the lab's definitive test, she retrieved the small square of white cotton, swiping the entire inner webbing of Crier's right hand once more with the material.

This second round of swabbing was for herself.

She set the square of cotton into the plexiglass developing chamber, then accepted the dropper from Riyad and popped the ampule within. Once the square was soaked with the testing solution, she sealed the plexiglass box and handed it to Riyad so he could set it on the conference table along with the rest of the materials she'd expended.

And now, the wait.

Within five minutes, they'd have the results.

Though really, given that she and Jeffers had been outside the office when the Glock had gone off and that no one but Crier had been inside when she'd entered, the pending results of their GSR field test were significantly less of a mystery than the contents of the man's imposing executive desk.

Riyad returned to her side. "Now what?"

She pointed toward the column of drawers on either side. "We search." Unfortunately, the drawers were locked. Had her hand been cooperating, it would have been easy enough to pick the main lock. But they didn't have time. Not with that mob outside the gates, swelling even now, as her watch closed in on 0230. "There's a small crowbar at the bottom of my kit."

Moments later, the spook returned with the iron bar and performed the destructive honors.

She pointed toward the far column of drawers as he turned to lay the crowbar on the windowsill behind them. "You take the right side; I'll take the left."

"Will do."

They searched in silence for several minutes, sifting through a mind-numbing amount of bureaucratic paperwork until she hit the bottom of the lowest drawer in her assigned column —literally.

Odd. Her trembling hand continued to smack into the base of the drawer with a steady rhythm—but both the sound and the feel were off.

Riyad shifted his suit-clad bulk to her side. "What's wrong?"

"I think we've got a false bottom." Was this why Crier had created one in that pack of Pakistani smokes? Because he'd used one to conceal something else?

The spook turned to the window, then back, crowbar in hand. "Step aside."

The bar went into the drawer. A solid pop filled the air around the desk. Regan reached in with her steadier hand and lifted the damage piece of wood.

Definitely a false bottom.

A tantalizing, smooth brown envelope lay in the space beneath.

She pulled the envelope out with her right hand. Riyad waited patiently as she worked the stiff brass brad on the reverse so she could lift the crisp flap and tip the significantly less crisp contents out into her waiting palm.

She sucked in her breath as she skimmed the header of the upper sheet.

Her colleague wasn't nearly as polite. "Holy *fuck*."

The spook appeared fond of that phrase. But in this case—as Regan continued to flip through the papers beneath the upper sheet—she couldn't argue with it.

"Ah, shit." *John*.

She glanced across her latest crime scene to find the man's dark gray suit filling the doorway of the office. John hadn't been kidding.

He had found her.

Though clearly not where and how he'd hoped.

John's glower strengthened as he strode into the room, pausing at her side to take in the corpse still seated in the executive chair several feet away. His glower turned downright caustic as it moved on to the visible rattling of her arm.

He was about to say something about one or the other, when his gaze fell to the papers in her hand. "Is that—"

"The security review for Embassy Islamabad?" She reached into her pocket and retrieved the purple nitrile gloves she'd taken from the Shifa's ICU earlier that evening, passing them over. "You tell me. Is this as bad as Riyad and I think it is?"

John donned the gloves and accepted the sheaf of papers.

The curse that escaped as he flipped through the stack was filthier than Riyad's had been. "Yeah. These are the plans Webber and I worked on. And *these*—" John held up the smaller, stapled sheaf that had been tucked beneath. "—are copies of my personal notes concerning our contingency plans for securing Pakistan's nuclear arsenal."

Oh, Jesus.

Both Chaudhry and his son were definitely targets. Even if they weren't, she couldn't take the chance that Webber didn't have Colonel Chaudhry in his sights as well as the chief justice's.

But was Webber simply trying to foment hate and discontent for the US within the colonel's mind and heart? Or was there something else going on? Something truly horrific, as suggested by the presence of John's notes?

If so, how the hell did they stop it?

John caught her glance. "Rae, you've got a visitor."

At the embassy?

Other than Palisade, Kettering and select members of the embassy staff, no one outside their team even knew she was in the city.

She glanced at her watch. It had taken her and Riyad longer than she'd thought to process the scene. All she had left was to test the Glock, and the envelope and papers for prints—and arrange for the disposition of Crier's body pending autopsy. "Who wants to see me at 0258 in the morning?"

"Chief Justice Harun Chaudhry and his wife are waiting in a conference room one floor down. I was near the back gate when their car pulled up. I called the ambassador, then escorted them inside and got them comfortable. Justice Chaudhry seems to think you're expecting them. He also said that he and his wife have seen the news, and now they want to hear what really happened to their daughter—from you."

She turned to Riyad.

He shrugged. "You told me to call Kettering. I called."

Yes, but she'd fully expected to go to Chaudhry. The man was here—at this hour? And with what was going on outside? And he'd brought his wife along? Then again, it wasn't as if the woman—or her husband—would be able to sleep. Nor was the unruly mob outside the gates a danger to the Chaudhrys.

At least, not yet.

Regan shoved Crier's hidden envelope at John so he could tuck the incendiary evidence back inside. If that was even possible—even *with* steady hands.

She headed for the wood-grained conference table and the plexiglass box containing the GSR field test results to give herself something to do while her brain continued to work through the latest developments.

As for the chemical one inside the plexiglass, that development was downright anticlimactic. The brown specks now staining the square of white cotton proved that Thomas Crier had indeed taken his own life in this very room, leaving the rest of them to clean up his personal and professionally traitorous *shit*.

"Rae?"

John had followed her to the table. She slipped the used GSR container into the evidence bag Riyad had already prepared and sealed it, as well as the one containing the Glock, then turned to face both men. Prints on the 9mm, as well as the envelope and papers, would have to wait. Not to mention her pending call to the local morgue. "Sam, I need you to swap out your NCIS cap for that SEAL one. You know better than anyone here how Webber operates. I think we'll all be better off if you head back to the security office to assist Maddoc." Based on what they'd found in that desk, the RSO and his men would need new contingencies, and fast. "Major Garrison will be with me...and the Chaudhrys."

"Agreed." The spook peeled off his gloves and shoved the latex into his pocket as he headed for the door. "I'll keep you posted."

"Ditto." She turned to John. "You were there in that cave when it went down. Trust me, they're going to want to hear from you, too. Don't leave anything out. And don't try to be vague or use euphemisms to spare their feelings. When I call on you, tell them *exactly* what happened. They've already seen the worst of it: the photo of their daughter's mutilated corpse. If you try and tone it down, they'll know. And that risks them believing we're not being honest about the rest of it."

And *that* they could not afford.

Frankly, John's testimony and the files on her laptop were all they had to go on, quite possibly all that stood between this country and hers...and war.

John glanced at Crier's body, shifting as he turned back, deliberately using that massive torso of his to shield her from the death scene he'd realized was uncannily similar to her mother's the moment he'd entered the office.

His fingers came up to smooth a strand of hair that had slipped out of her braid, tucking it back under the *dupatta* she hadn't even realized she'd forgotten to remove upon her return to the embassy.

So much for claustrophobic.

As for the compassion that had begun to simmer within John's stare, however... "Are you okay?"

She shrugged. Really, what else could she do?

"I have to be."

The glower he'd worn upon entering returned. She knew he wanted to argue with her, but he didn't. Nor could he. Because he knew she was right.

"How bad is it outside the gates?"

His sigh was dark. "Bad. And it's getting worse."

Somehow, she managed a smile. But it was stunted, much like her dwindling hopes that she could pull this thing off. "So, no pressure then."

"You can do this, Rae."

She was grateful for his vote of confidence. Because at the moment, her own nerve was lodging an insistent, belligerent veto.

She corralled her doubts as best she could as she finished packing up the contents of her crime kit. She added in the items she'd taken into evidence, including the smooth envelope and its classified contents, then automatically secured the kit's barrel lock on a new number. Finished, she nodded toward the stainless-steel case, knowing John wouldn't let her carry it anyway. Not with the tremors beginning to work their way up her arm.

"That's ready to go. My laptop's still in the outer office."

John hefted the case and motioned her toward the door. "How do you plan on working this?"

The same way she always did. It was the only way she knew how. "Corporal Vetter?"

"Yes, ma'am?"

"I need access to a wireless printer and photographic paper, ASAP. I also want copies of all security footage that pertains to this office from this past week forwarded to my CID email." She definitely needed to know what Crier had been doing—and who he'd been doing it with. She motioned for John to pass her crime kit off to the corporal. "Have that case secured in the RSO's safe, and do not let it leave your side until it goes in. Finally, seal up this office and post a guard outside. Unless the chancery's on fire, the guard does not leave his post until I've had a chance to deal with the body."

God willing, her conditional wouldn't come to pass.

"Yes, ma'am. Corporal Swan will take you to the printer."

She and John followed a tall, black, sinewy Marine out of the secretary's office.

Twenty minutes later, freshly printed materials tucked beneath her non-trembling arm, John was escorting her down the corridor and into the conference room where Ambassador Linnet stood in the far-right corner, just beyond the end of the walnut table that dominated the space. Linnet was nodding her sleek, blond bob as she spoke quietly with a petite woman of roughly sixty years. Since Linnet's companion was the only female Pakistani in the room, she was most likely Mrs.

Chaudhry. And there was the evidence in the woman's face. The slightly reddened and puffy eyes. While Sitara Chaudhry had surely rivaled Inaya Sadat's beauty in her younger years, the plain burgundy of her silken *shalwar kameez* and *dupatta* suggested that the older woman preferred the more subdued end of the rainbow.

Either that, or Sitara had chosen the muted colors in honor of her daughter's passing.

Regan recognized the stocky white-haired and bearded, western-suited Pakistani male nearest the women from the news the year before: Chief Justice Chaudhry.

As for the taller, fiftyish, traditionally dressed Pakistani male engaged in a low, but politely heated conversation with Warren Jeffers in the opposite far corner, it appeared the country's prime minister had made an appearance as well.

Lovely. This was going to be hard enough without either of those blowhards chiming in.

Except, the look Jeffers shot her as he glanced up from his conversation with Prime Minister Bukhari hearkened more to his attitude toward the spook than it had during either of her previous conversations with the DCM.

Had she managed to knock the disdain and vitriol from the man when she'd shoved his bulk to the floor outside Crier's office following that gunshot?

If so, she could only hope she'd earned Jeffers' coming support, or at the very least, his silence. Though, in light of her previous intel on the man, she doubted it.

Jeffers headed toward her, his peppery curls and suit even more wilted and rumpled than they'd been at their last meeting. "Agent Chase, please, let me assist you with that."

She shook her head as he reached for the thick folder she'd just created. "Thank you, but I've got it."

Those overly generous lips flattened.

Scott and Aamer Sadat had been spot on, then.

Further proof arrived with the saccharine smile that resumed oozing as Jeffers turned toward the ambassador and her guests. The look he'd shot Regan upon her entrance had simply been a reflection of his need to keep up diplomatic appearances.

Good to know.

As John stopped at the head of the table to deposit her laptop beside the leading chair, she bypassed Jeffers and continued on toward the ambassador and the Chaudhrys. Though she hadn't yet met the former, she nodded as though she had.

The ambassador picked up on the cue and nodded back.

The thirty second crash course in Pakistan manners that John had given her in mind, she stopped in front of the chief justice and his wife and bowed her head to both. "Chief Justice Chaudhry, *Begum* Chaudhry, *As-Salaam-u-Alaikum*."

As she straightened, the errant strand of hair from Crier's office slipped free again. Her fingers shook as she smoothed it beneath the *dupatta*.

Given who she'd been about to meet and why, she'd decided against removing the head covering during John's customs lecture.

It was a good call.

Both Chaudhrys seemed pleasantly taken aback by the swath of black. Especially since it was clear she hadn't donned it simply to impress them, but had been wearing it a while. She'd caught her reflection in the sliver of glass embedded in the conference room door just before John had opened it.

Unlike the grieving mother's veil, the silk *dupatta* John had purchased at Al Dhafra was clearly crushed and limp from the day's use.

Even the prime minister appeared pleased with the tip

toward traditional, female Muslim modesty as Bukhari approached to let her know that his president was dealing with another crisis and would be arriving as soon as he was able.

Regan repeated the formal greeting to Bukhari that she'd offered the Chaudhrys and waited as Jeffers stepped up to encourage everyone to take their seats.

Though both the American and Pakistani contingents claimed chairs along the opposite side of the walnut table from her, she focused her attention solely on the grieving mother at the center of the grouping.

Her gut—and her quick googling of the woman while she and John had been waiting on the printer—had assured her that Mrs. Chaudhry was the key. Not only did the chief justice value his wife enough to bring her along and offer her the choice, center seat, ironically Mrs. Chaudhry was a practicing surgical nurse at the Shifa, of all hospitals. And, like her husband, the woman also spoke English.

If anyone would be able to study the evidence she'd printed and quickly zero in on the truth, it would be Sitara Chaudhry.

Despite that excellent grasp of English however, John had felt it best that, out of respect, he offer his statement to the Chaudhrys in their native tongue.

Regan had agreed. "Major?"

On cue, John departed the head of the table and moved down to her side. He took the seat to the right of her and waited.

"Chief Justice, *Begum* Chaudhry, I would like you to meet Major John Garrison, US Army Special Forces. Major Garrison led the mission into that cave where your daughter died. With your permission, I would like the major to begin with his account of what he and his men saw and did upon their arrival, and afterward. Please, feel free to stop Major Garrison at any point with questions—or...just to stop him."

John waited for Chaudhry's revealing, questioning glance in his wife's direction and the man's subsequent nod, then began.

As with the hospital interview with Inaya, Regan didn't understand a word of John's stream of gravelly Urdu. She didn't need to. The entire translation was right there, in Mrs. Chaudhry's face. In the emotions that took hold in the woman's reddened eyes and in those gently quivering lips. When John reached his hoarse, halting description of the mutilated bodies he and his men had found in the cave, and of the infants that had been cut free and dumped on their breasts, the woman's eyes turned even redder and filled with glistening tears.

As had John's.

Regan reached out without thinking and slipped her hand into his lap beneath the table to squeeze the taut fist his left hand had unconsciously made. As much as her heart ached for the Chaudhrys, it ached just as much for John. Yes, he'd encountered death in countless ways in his career—but he'd never had to describe it to a loved one before.

Not like this.

Though John promptly turned his fingers so that they engulfed hers, he continued to stare straight ahead as he held on tight, swallowing hard as the tears began to fall from both Mr. and Mrs. Chaudhry's eyes...and his own.

John finished speaking, cleared his throat and waited.

Evidently he'd offered enough—or perhaps too much—because the chief justice shook his head slightly. There would be no questions of John.

At least not tonight.

Her turn then.

Regan waited for Sitara Chaudhry to gather herself, or as best the woman appeared able, then slipped her fingers from John's and stood. She opened her folder and removed the copies she'd printed of the evidence reports and lab results that hadn't been leaked to the Pakistani media because they exculpated McCord. She slid a binder-clipped packet in front of the Chaudhrys, another in front of the prime minister, and a third between the ambassador and her deputy chief of mission to share.

Regan kept the fourth for herself as she returned to her seat, removing her black binder clip so she could hold up each item as she went through them. "The first few pages have already been released to the media, so you may have already seen them. And it is true, Captain Mark McCord's blood was found inside the cave on a shawl that had been draped over one of the babies, as well as on two women—one of whom...was your daughter. But Captain McCord's blood was planted."

Regan held up the second round of labs that had proven it. "These are the results of the tests that were run on the captain's blood. If you'll note the sections I've highlighted in yellow, you can see that the lab determined that plasma proteins were missing from the blood evidence that was found on the two women and the shawl. The absence of such proteins indicates that a quantity of the captain's blood was frozen sometime before the murders, and then thawed out and placed inside the cave."

She held up the next several pages. "You can read a description of the blood-washing process here, as well as a statement that proves that the machine vital to the process was purchased by a hospital in Tehran, and that the doctor who committed the murders attended a training session there. It's during this session that we believe the captain's blood was frozen. The technician who held the training picked Dr. Nabil Durrani's photo out of a lineup. Also, you'll find a statement by Dr. Soraya Medhi describing how she spotted Dr. Durrani leaving the pharmacy at the Joint Theatre Hospital on Bagram Airbase in the middle of the night on the twelfth of October of this past year—during a false bomb threat. The same night, a pint of McCord's blood was stolen. The pint had been donated during a blood drive. There are additional supporting documents in your papers as well. Along with a transcript of the initial statement of an Afghan translator by the name of Tamir Hachemi, admitting that he assisted Dr. Durrani with the murders, and even obtained knives belonging to Captain McCord. The knives that were used to commit the murders and remove the babies from their mothers' wombs. I'm ready to answer any and all questions regarding the contents of your packets. Finally—" She turned to the second to last sheet. "—I've included Captain McCord's statement. He admits he was having an affair with one of the victims and that the child *Begum* Khan carried was his. We believe this is why *Begum* Khan was targeted by Durrani. To more effectively set up the captain for the murders."

"And this?" Mrs. Chaudhry's voice whispered across the table. The woman's fingertips shook as she traced them over the final item in the Chaudhrys' stack.

It was one of the eight-by-ten-inch glossy photos Regan had printed in the office Corporal Swan had escorted them to half an hour earlier.

"That's Jameelah, the child who survived, *Begum* Chaudhry. Her doctors believe that the shawl that was meant to railroad her father into murder actually saved her life, as it allowed the infant to hold onto what little body heat she had until Major Garrison and his men arrived to rescue her. *Begum* Khan's husband does not know who fathered the child, but he has rejected her regardless, on the grounds that she's a girl and not worth the expense. As a result, Captain McCord applied for custody and has named his daughter after her mother. At the moment, the captain is with his daughter in Germany, in Landstuhl's neonatal intensive care. Jameelah has been growing stronger every day and is expected to be released from the hospital soon."

A fresh batch of tears welled up in Mrs. Chaudhry's eyes. Regan's began to burn too as the woman continued to trace her fingers over the photo of the thriving infant, swaddled in pink and lying in her plexiglass bassinet.

That slow, loving trace revealed so much.

Sitara Chaudhry was more than a grieving mother right now. She was also a not-quite-grandmother grieving what might have been.

But the child beneath her fingertips was also proof that Americans and Pakistanis *could* come together. Regan could see that in those tears and quivering lips as well.

For the first time in days, hope began to bud within her.

Until the prime minister coughed. Snorted really. "Agent Chase, you *say* a respected Afghan doctor killed these women. But there is no proof in the pages you provided. Just some American who claims the doctor purchased a machine to do this... washing of blood. Why would an honorable Muslim do this? Kill innocent Muslim mothers? Kill the precious flower of our chief justice?"

Regan pushed her temper down as she offered a respectful smile to the doubting ass who hadn't bothered to even glance through his own stack of papers, let alone study the highlighted sections that proved her case.

Fortunately, the chief justice and his wife had not only followed along with her commentary, they'd gone back to the beginning of their packet. Even now, both were carefully reading through each page before the chief justice turned to the next.

She left them to their personal horror and addressed Bukhari. "Yes, Prime Minister, Nabil Durrani was a doctor." Diplomatic meeting or not, she just couldn't refer to the bastard as respected or honorable. "But Durrani was obsessed with

Chief Justice and *Begum* Chaudhry's daughter. Durrani would not take no for an answer, much less leave her alone. During my discussions with the man, I came to believe Durrani even harassed the young woman to the point of her leaving her job."

Sitara Chaudhry perked up at that, shifting her focus across the table. Her husband might still be reading, but his wife wasn't.

Regan had the woman's complete attention.

And more.

She also had the blaring suspicion that Mrs. Chaudhry knew something. Quite possibly something she'd been told by her daughter. But Asma hadn't confided in her father, because Harun Chaudhry's expression hadn't changed.

He was also still reading.

Regan continued with what she did know, and suspected, hoping her facts and supposition would intersect with whatever secrets the mother had been privy to. "I think they worked together, but I'm not sure where. I know Durrani got his medical degree in the United States, at Harvard in Boston, Massachusetts. I also know that shortly before the murders, Durrani culled his remaining victims from the Malalie Maternity Hospital in Kabul, where he was volunteering and had recently been offered a full-time position. Before that, Durrani worked with a local Islamic charity that assisted in vaccinating women against polio and tetanus in your country's own Federally Administered Tribal Areas—"

Regan paused as the older woman sucked in her breath, then turned to her husband to speak softly, urgently, in Urdu.

Regan risked a glance at John.

He nodded.

Something she'd said had clicked with the mother.

She turned back to the prime minister, since technically she'd been addressing his concerns, but Bukhari was now ignoring her. He, too, was focused on the equally urgent comments that Harun Chaudhry was now offering his wife.

By the time both Chaudhrys had refocused on her, Regan knew she'd hit on the nexus between those two lives: Durrani's and Asma's.

She risked confirming it. "It's true, isn't it? Your daughter knew Dr. Durrani. He gave her reason to fear him...somehow."

The mother's eyes filled with fresh tears.

But it was the father who had the strength to nod. Speak. "Yes. She confided this, and more, to my wife. You are right. This man was unnaturally obsessed with her. She thought by leaving her job six months ago, and taking another, she would be safe. But she also believed in our tribal regions and its people. She suffered much pain and grief when she lost her beloved husband and her own unborn child. She wanted to remain there, working to improve their conditions. This is how he found her, yes?"

"I believe so." In an effort to give the father a moment to deal with the tears that had begun to tinge his eyes, turning them luminous and black, she busied herself with the papers that were now littering the table in front of her.

She gathered them together. After two failed attempts to reattach the binder clip, she gave up and set the papers down, laying the clip on top.

"Your hand. It shakes." The chief justice flipped through his stack once more until he'd located the medical assessment she'd included. The one that described her neurological fallout from that psycho-toxin, along with Sergeant Welch's and Staff Sergeant Hudson's. "It is a result of the chimera Dr. Durrani infected you with?"

"Yes."

"This damage may be permanent?"

The chief justice was asking for information she'd have

forced Durrani to barter his very life for. She gave it freely to this grieving father and his wife.

Nor did she mask her own pain. "Yes."

The admission caused her hand to shake harder. To her horror, the quivering hijacked her entire arm, as it had following Durrani's suicide.

She was mortified when the fingers of John's left hand came up to cover hers. To lightly stroke and soothe. Not because he'd done it.

Because it worked. In front of others.

But the Chaudhrys weren't staring at her hand; they were looking at John's. At the ring he, too, hadn't removed since the Serena. Both Chaudhrys' gazes shifted, almost in tandem, to her left hand. To the matching rings that were still there as well.

And then, something seemed to click in both husband and wife.

Again, it was Harun Chaudhry who acted on it. He stood. Bowed. "I thank you for the time you have taken to speak to my wife and myself." His attention shifted to John. "Major Garrison, I also sincerely thank you for your efforts, and those of your men, to save those precious lives. Asma's, as well as the others. I believe you both."

Regan was still stunned, attempting to put her gratitude in this man's trust into words, when the chief justice turned to the ambassador.

"Ambassador Linnet, I must do what I can to quell the unwarranted anger outside your gates. Perhaps a speech? Tonight. Before things grow worse. Televised, so that my fellow citizens can wake to the truth and not to lies. My wife will, of course, be at my side."

Bukhari stood then too. "As will I." The prime minister turned to stare down at Jeffers and the ambassador. "I will assist in the preparations."

Wow, that was quick.

And apparently definitive, because everyone else on the opposite side of the table had come to their feet and were now nodding their approval.

Regan came to her feet as well. She bowed her head to both Chaudhrys in turn. "Chief Justice, *Begum* Chaudhry, if you don't mind, I have one more thing. I would like to formally apologize for the leaking of the photo of your daughter. I cannot imagine your shared pain at losing a grown child, and I am truly sorry you both discovered it the way that you did. I don't yet know how the photo got out, but I will not rest until I find the leak. I promise you." And if it hadn't been Crier, she would plug it.

Permanently.

Regan bowed to the Chaudhrys again, then gathered up her papers and turned to head down the table for her laptop, leaving John behind.

As with Riyad, John's skills would be crucial to the security for the coming televised conference that Jeffers and the prime minister were already outlining.

One crisis had been successfully averted.

But there was another, potentially larger one looming on the horizon. From the comments she'd overheard, the prime minister was insisting—quite vocally—that the chief justice's speech take place outside the gates, off sovereign, American soil.

In front of that mob.

Harun Chaudhry appeared to believe that he could quell the anger of his fellow citizens before he even walked through the gates, by making a brief announcement via the embassy's loudspeaker. But even if that worked, it might not be enough.

Because that crowd wasn't their only concern.

According to Riyad's tip, Zakaria Webber had been in Islamabad for at least eight hours now. Given everything that had gone down around town tonight—events Webber himself had very likely set into motion—what were the odds that the rogue SEAL *wouldn't* be out there in that angry, overflowing crowd... waiting for Chaudhry?

And there was Bukhari's half-assed rebuttal to her evidence, not to mention the man's strangely swift capitulation to this entire, precarious scenario.

Why did she have the feeling this impromptu conference was playing into the prime minister's hands?

Unintentionally or not, had she just tagged Harun Chaudhry for death?

# 24

Harun Chaudhry had managed to calm the crowd, and he'd yet to make his appearance. At least in person.

Regan had to hand it to the spook; Riyad's assessment of Pakistan's love for their current Supreme Court chief justice was genuine and profound. All Chaudhry had needed to do was fire up the embassy's loudspeaker and begin speaking. The chief justice told his fellow citizens that he'd personally reviewed the evidence from the cave massacre, and that he had a statement to make. But he had his grieving wife with him. If the crowd did not quiet down and become orderly—and stay that way—he would not be bringing her out, nor would he be speaking himself and sharing what he knew.

In less than a minute, the unruly mob had shifted into a quietly grumbling press of people, almost polite in their eagerness to hear "the truth" firsthand.

But how long would the mood hold?

And why couldn't she seem to shake this sense of foreboding? The one that was buried deep in her gut?

Regan stared at the portrait of the commander-in-chief hanging in the RSO's office as she contemplated just how many ways the next hour could blow up in their faces—literally. And that didn't account for Webber's suspected attendance.

Already, there were signs that those gathered were growing restless. Worse, the numbers outside the front gate had begun to take on biblical proportions once the media had been informed that their presence had been requested en masse.

Fortunately, everything appeared to be a go. Like everyone else involved, she wanted this over with, and quickly.

"I heard you were in here."

*John.*

She turned around to find the dark gray suit he'd donned aboard the *Griffith* twenty hours earlier dominating the frame of the doorway. A moment later, he stepped all the way into the RSO's office, dominating the room.

Her nerves.

Once Pakistan's president arrived to complete the "united front" image, John would be walking out through the gates with the Pakistani and American contingents. Agent Riyad and Staff Sergeant Tulle would be in the crowd. She would be with Scott, already up on the hastily constructed, temporary platform designed to allow the crowd to see Harun and Sitara Chaudhry as the chief justice spoke.

With her hand still operating apart from the rest of her brain, she wouldn't be able to do much more than provide an extra set of eyes, continually scanning the crowd for a face that resembled the photos that Riyad had provided of Webber.

But she could at least do that.

And that scanning would be critical, since both Chaudhrys had refused to don bulletproof vests on the grounds that the coming event was one of mutual respect, leaving the remainder of the diplomatic contingents to decline as well.

"Rae? You okay?"

"Yeah. Just worried."

So much could go wrong.

John nodded. "Corporal Swan asked me to tell you that someone will be here shortly to open the safe for you."

"Thanks." Given the classified nature of over half the files on her laptop, she couldn't just leave it lying around, even now. Nor could she risk bringing it up onto that platform. That left her waiting in here for someone with the combination to the RSO's safe.

And quietly going nuts.

She just couldn't shake this sense of foreboding. It was buried too deeply in her gut. And, apparently, in her brain.

At least the portion that controlled her hand.

The tremors that had spread up her arm during her meeting with the Chaudhrys hadn't ebbed; they'd grown worse. A fact that hadn't escaped that steady stare of John's.

"We've got at least five minutes before tee off." His brow nudged up, then came down to frame a decidedly inappropriate twinkle. "I could always lock the door. Work my magic."

She couldn't help it; she laughed.

Damned if his dimple didn't fold in, warming her, and her mood, further. "What, no crack about my ego? Or has my arrogance finally dimmed?"

"Oh, it's there." But she was getting used to it. Among other things.

"Turn around."

She shook her head. They weren't in the privacy of some hotel room.

"Turn around, *Chief*." Dimple and twinkle had faded, leaving that irritatingly adamant stare behind. The unequivocal order issued from Army major to warrant.

One she had no choice but to obey.

She turned.

As his fingers came up to dig into her braid, ruthlessly

kneading the tension from the base of her skull, she was forced to admit that he was right.

It didn't matter where they were. Nor was this massage between the man and woman who'd shared a bed in the Serena's executive suit earlier that evening. This one was between two soldiers and based solely on unit readiness. Safety and mission might well be on the line within the next hour, and the major behind her, now relentlessly rubbing the day's incalculable stress and the night's lack of sleep from her neck and shoulders, was determined to make sure she was ready for whatever went down.

And bless him, it was working. Though not quite enough.

Unfortunately, it was going to have to suffice.

Major and warrant fell away as he finished and she turned around. For several taut, painful moments, man and woman assumed their place.

A strangely thick, acidic fear dripped through her, burning straight into her heart. She'd never felt it before.

But as she stared at John, she knew he was feeling it too.

"Major G? The Pak president's arrived." *Tulle.* The booming decibel of his voice suggested the staff sergeant was just outside the RSO's office.

John didn't respond to his soldier, nor did he turn to leave. His thumb came up instead, its calluses gently scraping along the curve of her cheek.

"I wish you weren't here."

She nodded slightly, and gave him the stark truth in return. "I'm glad you are."

His answering nod was equally slight. And then, one last scrape of his thumb, and he was gone.

"Agent Chase?"

She turned toward the door to find a thickly muscled,

Hispanic gunnery sergeant she didn't know hovering just inside. "Yes?"

"Swan said you needed to get into the safe?"

She nodded. "I need to stow my laptop."

"Yes, ma'am."

The gunny entered the room and made a beeline for the dial in question, spinning it several times. A sharp clunk followed.

He stepped back as she approached the oversized safe to tuck her laptop in next to the stainless-steel body of her crime kit. She was about to step back as well, when she spotted the numbers on the tumbler—and froze.

*What the hell*?

Someone had tried to tamper with her kit.

She could tell from the lack of jimmy marks that they hadn't been successful. But there was more. Based on the outdated set of numbers her barrel sported, there were only two people who could have touched her kit. And one had no reason to.

But the other?

That crisp brown envelope slipped into the forefront of her mind. The one she'd found in Crier's desk. The brass brad. She hadn't thought about it at the time, but the fastener had been as stiff and unyielding as that envelope's smooth flap. Unlike the worn pages within. Shouldn't the envelope have sported wear and tear as well?

Had Crier transferred the papers to a new sleeve? Or had someone else culled those papers from a larger stack of classified material and secreted them in a fresh envelope so that they could be planted inside that hidden drawer?

Had Crier been framed?

She stared at those outdated numbers on the barrel of her kit. Or had Crier been working with someone else? Someone *other* than Webber?

"Ma'am?"

Damn it, her nerves were shot. And she desperately needed sleep.

Evidence? Her arm for one. It was already returning to its pre-massage vibrating state. She'd been on edge given the nature of Crier's death, not to mention her pending meeting with the Chaudhrys. Hell, she'd probably reset that older number herself up in Crier's office without thinking. Either way, she had no time to delve into it now.

She could hear Scott speaking to another agent in the hallway, on his way to grab her for their joint assignment.

Tee off time had arrived.

She stepped back from the safe and nodded to the Marine gunny. "Go ahead and close it up."

"Yes, ma'am."

She waited until the gunny had shut the door to the safe and spun the dial, then headed into the hall. She found Scott, waiting as expected.

He held out a spare earpiece. "You ready to get this thing done?"

More than he'd ever know.

"Absolutely." She accepted the earpiece, donned it and gave it a quick test, then adjusted the *dupatta* to conceal its presence. "Let's go."

Fifteen minutes later, they were standing on the instant platform that several DSS agents had set up within yards of the floodlit embassy gates.

Regan continued to stare out at the crowd, constantly scanning the sector she'd been assigned. Considering. Rejecting. Moving on slightly to start over.

Again and again.

But for the additional floodlights that had been rigged, she wouldn't have had enough light to pick out a stray tank, let alone a sniper or a suicide bomber amid the thousands of faces that had gathered in the distant dark. Unfortunately, the chief justice was right. He might've managed to quell this mob, but the other demonstrations that had cropped up around the country had begun to strengthen. Closing in on five a.m. local time or not, they needed to get this done and on the news to combat what was already out there.

Moments later, the gates opened again. United front intact, the diplomatic contingent quickly streamed out and stepped up onto the platform.

The chief justice and his demurely veiled wife led the procession, along with John and a slightly less beefy DSS agent she didn't know. They came to a halt several feet down from her right, peripheral view. Following the couple and their walking American body armor were President Niazi, Ambassador Linnet, and Prime Minister Bukhari and their DSS agents, since they too had declined the wearable variety.

Warren Jeffers and his protection brought up the rear, in somewhat subdued diplomatic mode as the DCM bowed and scraped to a halt beside the others.

Clearly eager to get this finished so he could escort his wife off the stage and back home where she could grieve in private, Harun Chaudhry stepped up to the microphone and began to speak, first in Urdu, then in English.

Regan gritted her teeth at the succession of flashes that popped out among the crowd, intermittently interfering with and outright obscuring her view. Then again, the photos and instant phone videos would further their cause. Even better, she could see the sporadic nods in the crowd multiplying, feel the wave of compassion and support for both Chaudhrys as the chief justice offered a truncated, toned-down description of events, similar to the one she'd warned John against giving to him.

In short, his beloved daughter Asma had indeed been

murdered in that cave along with six pregnant women—but the women were *not* killed by an American soldier. They were slaughtered by an Afghan doctor who passed himself off as a devout Muslim. But no true Muslim would kill innocent women and unborn children. And as chief justice, he could not allow the falsehood to stand. In fact, another team of American soldiers entered the cave after the murders and tried to save the lives of those who were dying within. For almost all the souls in that cave, it was too late.

But one survived—because of the Americans.

As the chief justice moved on to his praise for President Niazi and the Pakistani president's patience in not jumping to conclusions as the investigation unfolded during the previous weeks, Regan shifted her focus to the far right of her zone in the crowd, once more considering. But, this time, there was no rejection.

Every other face was turned toward the chief justice, carrying varying degrees of horror, outrage and sympathy over the details that had been offered.

This man's face was anything but. His deep smile was almost rapturous...as if he'd made his peace with this world and was ready to meet his maker.

His focus? The ambassador.

Regan activated her mic as discreetly as she could.

"To the left of the justice, fifteen, twenty feet out and steadily moving up on Linnet. Male, local. Early twenties, bearded. On the tall side. Two, three inches over his surrounding companions. White, coarser traditional dress with matching *topi*, looks to be contrasting embroidering around the base of the hat."

What color, she couldn't be sure.

He was too far away and, even with the additional floods, too shadowed.

"Got him. Moving in." *Riyad.*

She caught sight of the NCIS agent moving rapidly within her forward vision, even as she spotted John and Scott moving closer to Harun Chaudhry in her peripheral view. The remaining DSS agents tightened in on their principals as well.

"Eight feet away, coming up on his rear." *Riyad.*

"I see you. That's him."

The spook was five feet and closing when she heard the RSO chime in. Maddoc's voice was immediately drowned out by a low, almost anti-climactic *pop*.

The target crumpled, disappearing into the crowd.

A second later, Riyad was on top of the spot, murmuring into his mic. "Suicide vest. Appears to have misfired—"

A man next to Riyad must've heard the spook, because he shouted something in Urdu. She lost the rest of Riyad's assessment as half the crowd bunched up, screaming and yelling as they moved as a solid wave of human flesh toward the platform. The rest of the crowd swept backward. Instinct had her shifting her vision to check the left side of her assigned sector. It, too, was moving en masse, the people within, pushing, pulling.

She caught the flash of a flailing reporter's light as it spun out of its owner's hand, glinting off the dusky face of another man in local garb before the light source arced toward the ground. Tinted wraparound sunglasses?

In the dark?

She dropped her gaze and caught a glimpse of the blackened barrel as it came up. No time for the mic, she shouted a warning as she automatically shoved her hand into her suit and drew her weapon. *Gun*!"

Worse, she'd swear his was a SIG Sauer P226, too. And it was sighting in on her right. *Harun Chaudhry.*

Her P228's forward sights were still an inch from lining up on her target—the shooter's head—when her hand and entire arm jolted, discharging her weapon prematurely.

A split second later, she caught another muzzle flash, this one from the shooter's 226, and its deafening retort.

The entire crowd shifted, turned frantic and ugly as it became every man for himself. Try as she might to locate the shooter, she'd lost him. She could only hope another agent had the bastard in his sights as she spun around to check on the Chaudhrys.

They were fine, if ignobly splayed out on the platform, the chief justice beneath Scott, his wife beneath another DSS agent.

Moments later, the agents were standing, hauling their assigned charges to their feet as well, as they half led, half carried them down the steps of the platform and into the waiting safety of the embassy gates—leaving John behind.

He was lying on the platform, face up, unconscious and bleeding.

He'd been hit.

Regan keyed her mic. "Man down; get a medic!"

She shoved her SIG into its holster as she vaulted to John's side to assess his condition, knowing damned well that there'd be no one to back her up until all the diplomats were behind the walls and safely accounted for. "*John*?"

*Nothing.*

Just that gush of blood that had soaked the front of his right trouser leg and his entire groin. It was pooling out around his midsection, spreading over the platform beneath. Worse, the scarlet geyser was jetting into her hands with each beat of his heart.

Artery.

She hooked her fingers into the hole in his trousers and tore them wide open to find the mangled furrow of flesh slashing across his groin, compliments of that bastard's glancing round. She pushed down above the furrow, directly over his right femoral, frantically trying to press the artery into the bone.

There was too goddamned much muscle beneath her hands. And the *blood*. Her hand shook as it slipped out of place.

More of that precious, scarlet fluid gushed out.

Unwilling to trust her right index finger, she shoved her left into the gaping furrow in his flesh and felt around. No metal, as expected—just far too much shredded muscle and all that terrifyingly hot, critically needed blood.

There appeared to be more outside his body than in.

Desperate, she shoved the tip of her finger deeper and up toward John's groin, relief searing in as the gush finally slowed to a trickle.

She pushed harder, and it stopped.

"Holy *fuck*, woman." *Riyad*.

Of course.

Yet, she'd never been so glad to see anyone in her life. Even this man, with that filthy scowl. "I can't move my finger. If I do—"

"I know. Hold on." A second later, the spook was on his mic, barking out orders. Whatever the man was saying blended in with the cacophony from the still frantic crowd. She was dimly aware of Scott showing up as well, but she refused to look up to acknowledge him. She was too terrified of losing her grip. The entire horrific experience with Durrani was slamming through her brain and her heart, taunting her.

*No*.

She would not lose this man. It had taken her too damned long to find him.

She would *not*.

She focused on John's groin and her hand, leaving everything else to Riyad.

She caught the blur of suits as more agents converged on the stage. She could even hear the Pakistani president over the loudspeaker, assuring the crowd, in Urdu and in English. Two men had attempted to silence the chief justice and the truth, but they would not let them. *Pakistan* would not let them. One man was already dead. The other was gone. People must *calm down*, because everyone was fine.

But everyone wasn't fine.

And then, bizarrely, the Chaudhrys were at her side, the wife kneeling down. Then again, it wasn't so odd. The woman was, after all, a surgical nurse. Sitara Chaudhry kept telling her over and over to keep her hand in place, to hold on. Assuring her that she was doing an excellent job—that the air ambulance was on its way. Everything was going to be okay, just as soon as they got her husband to the hospital.

Regan didn't bother telling the woman that she and John weren't married.

Not with those rings he'd given her swimming in his blood.

And then, the paramedics were there, working around her to heft John's mammoth, blood-soaked body onto a stretcher, even as they joined in with Sitara Chaudhry's gentle orders to keep her hand *exactly* where it was.

The rest was a blur.

She wasn't sure how she even got over to the chopper, much less inside it.

Her entire left hand and arm ached, this limb now trembling with exhaustion, too, even more than her right. Still, she pressed in.

Before she realized what had happened, the bird had landed at a hospital in the middle of a still darkened Islamabad, backlit by a glittering rainbow of city lights. Within seconds, and against her silently screaming will, her finger was sliding out of its desperate home as a doctor physically pulled her from John's side. And then, a dozen other white coats were rolling John away, leaving her alone in the dark.

Bereft of his warmth.

Wondering if she'd ever see him again.

For the second time in two days, Regan was standing in a shower, attempting to process the horror of what had happened as she stared at those surreal tendrils of red and pink slipping down her body to circle the drain before disappearing forever.

Only this time, she wasn't in a stateroom aboard the *Griffith*, she was in a bathroom attached to an empty hospital room at the Shifa...and those disappearing tendrils were the vestiges of John's blood.

Harun and Sitara Chaudhry had arrived at the hospital half an hour after the doctors had spirited John away. She'd been sitting right where John had been taken from her, still covered in his blood, in shock. But it wasn't the country's chief justice who'd taken charge, it was his soft-spoken wife. The woman had ordered her husband back to the embassy to deal with the fallout of the night's events, while she brought Regan inside the Shifa, where apparently Sitara Chaudhry wasn't simply a surgical nurse. She was the hospital's senior surgical nurse.

Like her husband, the woman had her own professional domain.

Regan had never been more grateful.

Fifteen minutes later, Sitara had been briefed on John's surgery—which appeared to be going well, but for the fact that it would take hours yet.

But there was hopeful news already. The round that had torn through the right side of John's groin had indeed punctured his right femoral artery, though oddly, above the section of shredded muscle. Which was why she'd had such a difficult time trying to clamp off his bleeding up on that platform. If things went well, John's surgeons should be able to repair the puncture without a graft, for which Regan was profoundly relieved on

John's behalf, since such a critical graft could make things difficult for his chosen career in Special Forces.

Personally, she didn't care if John sat behind a desk for the rest of his years, so long as he had those years. But she suspected he'd feel differently.

Once the woman's medical update had been delivered, Sitara—who had also firmly insisted that she be addressed by Regan as such—had led her to the executive patient room where John would be brought once he was out of surgery. There, Sitara had arranged for clean surgical scrubs as well as toiletries to be delivered.

Only then had the woman left her. Evidently, her intent was to scrub in on John's surgery. She would return with a full report, once it was finished.

Regan had the feeling that Sitara was using the situation, and her, to stave off the agony and acceptance of her daughter's loss, but she wouldn't judge her for it.

Lord knew, she'd deliberately sought out something to mute her own aching terror, or at least something to hold it at bay until John's surgery was over.

Her job.

Once she'd spotted those older numbers on the barrel of her crime kit, she'd known her search for the traitor wasn't over. But with everything that had happened, she'd had no way to proceed—until Tulle had phoned. John's staff sergeant had been frantic for news on his CO, and so he'd done the only thing he could think of.

Tulle had called her.

She'd shared what little she knew, and when Tulle had told her that he was on his way to the Shifa to wait with her, she'd asked him to stop by the RSO's office first to retrieve her laptop and kit.

He'd be happy to—once he phoned General Palisade, who

was also champing for an update. Grateful that Tulle would take care of that, she'd readily agreed.

With nothing else to do but stare at that tauntingly empty bed until the staff sergeant's arrival, she'd scooped up the toiletries with her good hand and escaped into the shower.

The blood was gone now. Even her hair was clean.

She knew she should take the rings off, so she could make sure there were no lingering traces of the most terrifying experience of her life clinging beneath the stone, but she couldn't. Not until she saw for herself that John was safe.

She needed to touch him. Make sure he was breathing.

In the end, she left the rings in place and settled for yet another thorough scrubbing with the soap and cloth Sitara and her fellow nurses had provided.

Regan turned off the water and departed the shower to scoop up her clothes and gear. Cramming her bloodied suit into the garbage bin in the bathroom, she carried her holstered SIG, cuffs, CID credentials, shoes and the *dupatta* into the hospital room.

She dumped the black scarf and her gear at the foot of the bed, and donned the waiting surgical scrubs and her shoes.

Her gear was a bit tougher.

She managed to wedge her phone, ID and cuffs into the pocket at the rear of the green medical trousers. Her shoulder holster, however, was not going to fly.

Not out in the open in a hospital.

She settled for removing her 9mm and tucking it out of sight at the small of her back beneath her borrowed smock. Her empty leather holster went into the drawer at the base of the small clothing cupboard to get it out of sight as well.

As dressed as she was going to get, she turned away from those crisp, white, *empty* sheets and used the comb from the toiletry kit to remove the snarls from her hair. As best she could, anyway. Her left-hand coordination might leave a lot to be desired, but her right was shaking so much, it was nearly useless.

Unwilling to offend those who were doing so much for John, she capped off her damp hair with the swath of silk he'd provided.

With nothing left to do, she headed across the antiseptic tiles to check the contents of the small refrigerator positioned next to a dark brown, utilitarian sleeper couch and matching coffee table in front of the room's curtained windows. The fridge was probably empty, but she hadn't eaten since their stopover at Al Dhafra the day before—or ingested caffeine. At this point, if she found a leftover can of cold-brewed coffee in there, she'd be willing to mainline it.

She was about to open the fridge when her phone rang.

Sighing, she reached into her rear pocket and worked the phone free. She didn't recognize the number on the screen. "Agent Chase."

"How's he doing?" *Riyad.*

Guilt cut in. The spook had moved heaven and earth to save John's life back on that platform and she'd hadn't even thought about updating him following her conversation with Sitara. "He's in surgery. His femoral was punctured. No word yet." And there wouldn't be for hours. "I'm sorry; I should've called."

Not that she'd had his number. But she could've tracked it down if she'd tried.

"No problem. You've had a bit on your mind. So have I."

"What happened?" Because something had. It was in his voice.

"There's been another Webber sighting. Solid source."

"Where?"

"Islamabad International Airport. Military ramp."

Well, "Shit."

"Yeah. I'm there now. Look, I'll be following this lead to the end, so I may be out of touch. Might even have to lose my phone for a while."

"Understood. If I have something, I'll call General Palisade." And he'd call Admiral Kettering. It was almost an amusing turnaround given that she and Riyad were the junior ones on the totem pole. Almost. "Good hunting."

"You, too."

He hung up.

She was about to make a second attempt at the fridge when a low, deep rap reverberated on the opposite side of the door behind her.

"Come on in."

The door swung wide. Staff Sergeant Tulle's still suited, though now rumpled, Nordic bulk entered the room, her laptop's strap slung over his left shoulder, her crime kit in the same hand. And in his right?

A gorgeous, oversized takeout cup of coffee...which he was extending to her.

"Oh, Lord, Tulle. I could kiss you."

The blond giant actually blushed, causing the scruff on his cheeks and jaw to appear burnished.

She met him at the foot of the empty bed to accept the cup with her steady hand and pop the lid. Not only was the coffee within still steaming, it was blacker than a brand new Humvee's tires. Despite everything that'd happened, and everything she was terrified might happen, she smiled and promptly gave credit where it was due.

"Outstanding instincts."

"Yeah, not really. The major might've mentioned your addiction in passing."

John had spoken about her?

For some reason, her heart clenched—painfully.

Tulle shifted her kit to his right hand. "Any news on his condition?"

She shook her head. "Not since we last spoke." She took a sip of the coffee, savoring the anticipatory rush that hit, then nodded to the small, makeshift sitting area. "You can set my gear down over there." It was where she'd be staying—and, hence, working—until further notice. "Any news on the mob?"

"It's over here, lined up outside the doors of the blood donation lab, down the hall and out of the hospital, wrapped halfway around the block. And it's still growing."

"What?" He was joking, right?

But the staff sergeant nodded, shrugging those massive shoulders that reminded her so much of John's. "We owe it all to Chaudhry, too. The chief justice stopped by the lab before he returned to the embassy. He donated a pint of his very own life's juice for the *brave and honorable* American major who took a bullet for him this morning—and he made sure everyone knew it. Before Chaudhry got to his car, folks were tweeting out what he'd done and calling the local stations with the tip. Pakistanis are driving across the city to donate blood as well. Heck, I heard they're even gathering in the mosques to pray for him."

The last warmed her more than the rest, especially since the hospital probably had plenty of blood. Naturally, Harun Chaudhry would've known that. But he'd also known that his symbolic act would speak volumes where even his voice couldn't.

And it had.

As for those prayers in the mosques, admittedly, she wasn't particularly religious. The raw end of her grandfather's belt had seen to that. But neither could she shake the belief that someone might be up there, looking down. And if they were, she darned sure wanted the celestial conversation bending in John's favor today of all days.

Especially since—

"No."

She stiffened. "What?" She hadn't—

"It's not your fault."

*Great.* Was Tulle's Rae-dar now in full-tune mode, too?

Or was it because of John? The terror and the guilt she couldn't quite seem to push to the back of her mind, much less off her face.

As deeply as she wanted to accept the staff sergeant's absolution, she couldn't. She shook her head. "I took the shot, Tulle. But it was early. My hand, it jolted. And I—"

"Saved his life." He nodded in the face of her disbelief. "I was there, Chief. I saw it go down, and clearly. I was fifteen feet behind that bastard and penned in by all those frantic, flailing bodies. I couldn't get to my mic, much less my weapons. I watched that fucker line up his shot. Your round went into his right shoulder, knocked off his aim at the last second. And this part I won't tell Chaudhry—or any of the Pakistanis, at least not today—but that bastard? He wasn't aiming for the chief justice. He had a hard on for the major. If you hadn't taken that shot —*however* it happened—when you did, his bullet would have punched clean through the major's skull." The staff sergeant's second, confirming nod was for her shock. "Yeah, that bastard was setting up a headshot."

But why?

It didn't make sense. "Why would Webber go to all that trouble to infiltrate that unruly mob to target John?"

Tulle shrugged. "Dunno. That's for you to figure out—and I'd really like you to do that, and soon. But there's more. Like everyone else, I lost that asshole in the moments that followed. The crush of bodies knocked me back. By the time I was able to right myself, he was gone. But I kept pushing forward, hoping I'd get another glimpse of him, or at least find that bullet of yours with some blood on it. There was no sign of it, so it's still in that fucker's shoulder. But I did find his shades. At least, I think I did. They were on the ground where he set up his kill shot. Must have got knocked off by someone during the panic. They were wraparounds, yellow tint."

*Yes*. "That's them."

Despite the loss of the round she'd fired, adrenaline surged. Because with those sunglasses came the same holy grail of forensic evidence that she'd have gotten from a bloodied bullet: DNA. Especially since they were all assuming Webber had taken that shot, but no one was certain. Even her. Despite all those floodlights, there had still been too many shadows flitting within that mass of bodies; the bastard's features obscured that much more by those wraparound lenses he'd been wearing.

But the odds were excellent that those glasses would contain epithelial cells, possibly even recoverable fingerprints.

"Don't get so excited. They're already gone. I gave the glasses to a gunnery sergeant in the RSO's office to put in the safe, so you could do your detective thing when you got back. But when the RSO opened the safe so I could grab your laptop and kit, they weren't in there. I tracked down the gunny. He swears he put them in the safe, but they're definitely gone now."

*Christ*.

Regan sank down onto the couch. What the devil was going on? If the shooter had been Webber, why would he want to kill John now? Even if Webber did want John dead, surely there would have been easier times and places to set up that shot?

"I got one more oddity—and this one's truly weird. It pertains to that suicide bomber."

"What about him? Did you manage to get an ID?"

Tulle shook head. "But we do know he was murdered. That vest—it was a dummy rig. But there was one live charge in it. The one over his heart. And, get this: it was rigged to blow *in*, not out, and not by much. It looks as though no one else was meant to be shredded during that speech, much less killed, 'cept the bastard who was eager to enter Paradise early and collect his seventy-two virgins."

She set the takeout cup on the coffee table and sank back into the couch as the confusion continued to rip in. None of this made sense.

Why would someone premeditate a murder so meticulous upon a would-be suicide bomber? Had the bomber simply been meant to serve as a distraction so that Webber could set up his kill shot on John? But why so elaborate? More importantly, was their murdered bomber—and that kill shot—connected to their search for the traitor?

The one still inside Embassy Islamabad?

Because she was more convinced than ever that Crier's death hadn't ended her quest.

She needed to view that security footage leading into Crier's office. She'd asked Corporal Vetter to have it sent to her CID email. Had the Marine even had the opportunity to get the footage downloaded from the embassy's system with everything that had gone on since she'd found Crier's body at his desk a mere six hours ago? Hell, she still hadn't had a chance to dust that Glock and envelope for prints.

She reached for her laptop bag.

"You got work to do, don't you?"

"I do." She tipped her head to the right. "But there's plenty of room on the other side of this couch. Have a seat."

He smiled. "Not for an ape my size, there isn't. But I appreciate the fib."

Her heart twisted at the ape comment. "I can request a chair."

If the locals were incredibly generous enough to donate blood on John's behalf, surely a spare seat wouldn't be too out of range, would it?

Tulle's light blue gaze darkened with the ghosts of too many soldiers who'd passed as it slipped to the center of the room. To those taunting, empty sheets.

Like most soldiers, she was all too familiar with that haunted stare. With the memories trapped within. She'd confronted too many hospital beds recently emptied by buddies to not be. Beds that hadn't been emptied in a good way.

"If you don't mind, ma'am, I'd rather walk the halls. If I eavesdrop enough, I just might polish my Urdu."

"Sounds good. Come back when you're bored. Meanwhile, I'll call if and when I hear something. But...stick close. I may need you professionally."

Exceptional SF soldier that he was, Tulle didn't question that final comment. He simply nodded.

She was already unzipping her laptop bag and dragging her computer out onto the low table as the door closed behind the staff sergeant.

She retrieved her CID credentials from the back pocket of her scrubs and slid her access card from its slot on the wallet side. Within minutes, she'd used it to assist in her push through the requisite security protocols and was skimming her overflowing email inbox. Fortunately, Corporal Vetter's email—and attached files—were near the top.

And there it was: the security footage she needed.

Even at a jacked-up viewing speed, it took a mind numbing ninety-four minutes to zero in on the sections of footage that she needed. The sections that would make her case—and ruin an embassy staffer's career.

Not to mention seal his pending conviction for treason.

She pushed through her fury and closed her laptop, swapping out the computer for her phone. Double confirmation was always a plus when it came to court-martials.

It took her a few minutes to phone Corporal Vetter at the

embassy and wait not-so-patiently while Vetter looked up Warren Jeffers' personal phone numbers.

Upon hanging up with the wonderfully chatty and informative Vetter, it took her mere seconds more to check her watch and calculate the time zone difference between Islamabad and Orlando, Florida, where Mrs. Bethany Jeffers' recent commercial flight had apparently landed while Mr. Jeffers had been up on that temporary platform in front of the embassy's gates.

From there, a brief introduction and several probing questions later, Regan had the confirmation she needed—and her traitor.

She shot off a quick text to Tulle to let him know she'd need his services. She was about to place a call to Scott when her phone rang.

Palisade.

*Damn*. The general needed a case update, yes. But he'd want a personal one regarding John, too. An update she didn't have. The lack of which she'd also desperately been trying to keep her mind from dwelling upon while she'd be studying two days' worth of security footage in fast forward. "Agent Chase."

"How's he doing?"

"I don't know." Nor could she keep the apprehension from her voice.

It had been two hours now since Sitara Chaudhry had left her in this room. Surely, there should have been an update by now?

Or was John experiencing complications?

*Focus*.

She got up from the couch to pace her way across the room as she worked to shove the ugly, thickening fear back down into her gut. "Sir, I haven't heard anything beyond what I was able to give Staff Sergeant Tulle earlier this morning."

The man's sigh filled the line. "Understood. I'll let you go, so you can—"

"General?"

"Yes, Chief?"

She turned around at the door and headed back toward the hospital bed bisecting the room. "I have another update. I've ID'd our traitor."

"I thought we already had him."

So had she. "Sir, Tom Crier was set up. He—"

"*Wrong.*"

She spun around, coming face to face with the one man she'd never expected to be paying a supportive sympathy visit. And definitely not to her. Then again, diplomacy was in his blood and, hence, faking it. The latter of which, this man was a master at.

"Sir, Deputy Chief of Mission Warren Jeffers has just arrived." Along with someone else. She nodded to Scott as he, too, entered the room. Either Jeffers had talked her old MP classmate into tagging along to help to perpetuate his faux sympathies, or Scott was here for another reason. Either way, "May I call you back?"

"I'll be waiting."

The moment Palisade severed the call, she tossed her phone onto the foot of the bed and rounded on Jeffers. "I don't appreciate you walking into my room unannounced, let alone interrupting my conversation with my boss."

"I don't give a shit what you appreciate. Especially since the information you were imparting was dead wrong—literally. Crier was guilty. From what Agent Riyad says, you yourself found that false bottom in the man's desk and the packet of classified information he'd secreted within. And there's the note. The bastard asked for forgiveness in own hand."

"Agreed." But was Crier asking for forgiveness because he'd committed treason, or was he sorry that he'd finally realized there was a traitor in the embassy? A traitor from whom Crier had failed to protect his own child?

"And those papers you found—"

"Were planted." She shrugged into the DCM's shock, stalking forward to where he and Scott were standing just inside the door. "And there's the timing of Crier's suicide."

Not to mention the timing of what she was about to do. She had the man she needed within arms' length. With all that had happened in this country, and still could, she couldn't afford to let him out of her sight. Not when he could easily disappear into Pakistan, never to be seen again...until the next terror plot was due to unfold.

But could she pull this off with her arm rattling around at her side?

She could wait for Tulle.

Except that risked this all going south before the side of beef made his appearance in time to balance things out. The hospital was even more massive than the staff sergeant's shoulders. There was no telling how far away Tulle was from this room.

She glanced at Scott as she stepped closer to him and Jeffers, hoping Scott would recognize her old look—and the intent behind it.

From the gleam in Scott's eyes, not to mention that ever-so-slight nod, he did.

She tipped her head toward the coffee table behind her. "Corporal Vetter was kind enough to email me the video surveillance for the corridor outside Crier's office prior to his suicide. I just finished it. Fascinating viewing. Not only does it show you, Mr. Jeffers, heading in to speak with Crier minutes before you came down to the lobby to find Agent Riyad conversing with me in the waiting area, but you were in Crier's office for a solid ten minutes. And when you came out, you were seriously pissed. Granted, that appears to be your natural state around your co-workers. But this time, your tantrum ended with Crier eating his gun. Just what did you two discuss?"

"Whatever it was, is none of your damned business—"

She stepped closer, until she was standing directly in front of Jeffers and Scott. "Oh, but it is. Especially since I also have it on good authority that you used that same desk of Crier's several years earlier when you served as political officer; the first, in fact, to occupy that particular office in the chancery. Hence, you knew about the false bottom in that drawer."

She slipped her right hand behind her back and wrapped her quaking fingers around the cuffs, praying she could pull this off as she tugged them from her pocket. She stepped sharply to the right, reaching out with her left hand to spin Scott's wiry frame around, slamming her old MP buddy's face into the wall to momentarily stun him as she simultaneously clipped one of the cuffs to his right wrist while jerking Scott's left across his back to secure the second.

Jeffers was still gaping at her as she reached around into Scott's suit jacket to remove the man's Glock 19 from his shoulder holster.

She was bending down to remove Scott's backup Glock 26 when Staff Sergeant Tulle pushed the door open and entered the room.

She tossed both 9mms onto the bed, then nodded to Tulle to take over the search for anything else that might be hidden within those gray pinstripes.

"What the *fuck* did you do that for? You can't disarm one of my DSS agents!" Evidently Jeffers had regained use of his tongue.

Scott, however, hadn't bothered to come to his own defense.

They both knew why.

Old friend or not, and as much as it pained her so profoundly to admit, "I can when that agent is a traitor."

# 25

"What gave me away, Prez?"

"Don't 'prez' me." That nickname was for friends alone, and damned good ones at that. A category to which Scott Walburn no longer belonged. As for that critical clue, "You reset the tumbler on my kit. Among other things."

"Yeah, so?"

"So I change it—every time I close it. And I'd closed it twice since that old number."

"*Christ*. I forgot about that idiot-savant skill of yours."

Yeah, well, he was the one in cuffs.

Who was the idiot now?

Though, granted, she still felt like one. She'd fallen for his *psst, Jeffers is an abuser and possibly more* bait. Despite the fact that offering that lie had been a solid, obscuring tactic, especially given how Scott had to have known that the DCM's filthy reputation would have come to her attention anyway. It had been a smart move, too, feeding her that obfuscating story while they'd been on their way to the Shifa—and she and her instincts had been distracted by the city's jockeying traffic and the dark.

And there'd been that clever, seemingly innocuous comment regarding Jeffers' previous stint as Embassy Islamabad's political officer and, hence, Jeffers presupposed use of and familiarity with that desk.

Plus, "I called Jeffers' wife. That was a nice touch, by the way. Accusing him of adultery—and implying the rest. Especially since you knew Bethany was already on her way out of Pakistan to visit her folks in the States."

She could hear Jeffers spluttering behind her. "You called my *wife*?"

She glanced back to see those meaty lips puckering down and white with fury. "Be grateful. The woman alibied you." God knew why, but Bethany Jeffers also appeared to genuinely love and admire the asshole.

It took all sorts, didn't it?

Bethany had also confessed that Warren Jeffers had bragged to anyone who'd listen about the hidden bottom in that drawer during his stint in the political office.

Meaning Webber probably knew about the drawer.

At the very least, Scott had.

"I thought you hadn't had a chance to dust the envelope for prints."

She hadn't. Nor would she. While she doubted she'd find any prints on it, much less on the papers within—despite their thumbed through appearance—it was probably best to box them up and ship them off to Forensic Documents at the CID lab at Fort Gillem. Given the critical nature of this mission—and the classified content of those pages—she'd prefer that the document experts at the lab did the honors. They'd have a much better shot than she would at culling any available clues from within.

Of course, that was going to take time.

Meanwhile, she'd head back to the embassy tomorrow to

dust Crier's Glock for prints and wrap up everything else related to the case, including her growing stack of pending reports.

"Damn it, Agent Chase. I will not just stand here and—"

"Oh, but you will." This time, she spun all the way around to stare the DCM down. "Make no mistake, Mr. Jeffers. One more word out of your mouth, and I'll arrest you too." Alibi or not. "So do just stand there—and *shut up*."

She ignored the flare of pure hatred she received in response and turned back to Scott. To the query he'd made regarding that envelope.

It was telling.

Scott wouldn't have had a lot of time to prepare those papers once he'd been tasked with picking her up at the airport—and realized why she was in Islamabad. Given the fear he'd let slip, there was an excellent chance Scott had screwed up and left his prints behind...or someone else's.

Webber's.

All the more reason to let the experts at Gillem take first crack.

Either way, "That's not where I got my confirmation. I lied earlier, Scott. I didn't just go back an hour on the video. I went back a lot further. I found you, going in and out of Crier's office, twice. Roughly twenty minutes before Jeffers arrived and, again, earlier in the day just after you brought me to the embassy and while Crier was still across town in his marathon meeting with locals." And during that first foray in the hours before, Scott'd had an envelope in hand. One that looked exactly like the one she'd pulled out of that hidden compartment in Crier's desk. "You really should've shoved that damning little Easter egg in a briefcase."

Scott just shrugged those wiry, pinstriped shoulders. "Hindsight's always twenty-twenty."

That, it was.

She could only assume Scott had intended to compromise the surveillance archive—and his suspicious appearances therein—later tonight while everyone was supposed to have been distracted by what he'd clearly hoped would be a full-blown Pakistani coup.

"That second foray into Crier's office?" The one Crier had actually attended. "You told the man the hospital called, didn't you? And that his son, Danyal, was dead." A death Scott had fully expected to occur within the next few days anyway, since he'd been the one to infect the boy simply to complete the frame he'd perpetuated on Crier.

"Yeah. But I added on the sweet piece he'd been screwing. I told him Inaya was so grief stricken that she threw herself out of the window before they could stop her. It was the best way to ensure he blew his brains out."

That would do it.

And, of course, Scott had known about Crier's 9mm since he'd been in there to plant that envelope. That said, Scott had only been at the embassy for two months. That wasn't long enough to have gathered all the intel he'd had on Tom Crier and put his plans into place. And there was Sergeant Brandt and his secrets. Not to mention obtaining the chimera, those crime scene photos and the McCord DNA report that had been leaked.

Scott had definitely had help.

Someone else had to have conducted the advanced reconnaissance. Especially since Scott had been at his desk at the embassy for the past two months, studiously working away on that human trafficking case that she now suspected he'd not only tipped the authorities off to, but had then volunteered to work. Whoever had done the recon had also been the one to go to Al Dhafra to pass off the strychnine to Brandt and infect the Marine with the chimera, thus preserving Scott's cover.

Hell, a tainted needle and a hearty smack on the back would've done the trick.

Again, Webber.

The rogue SEAL had attempted to stain John's loyalties back at Fort Bragg. He'd clearly succeeded with Scott. How many others had been targeted by Webber?

How many had he already turned?

And where around the world—or inside the United States—were *they* placed?

But first, she needed confirmation on this placement. "How long have you been working with Zakaria Webber?"

Her old friend pushed forth another wiry shrug. It didn't matter. His micro-expressions had given him away.

This was definitely Webber's party.

And that scared the shit out of her. Given that the man had been sighted at the airport hours ago—and that she'd yet to hear from Riyad—Webber was long gone.

God only knew where the bastard was headed. Nor did she think Webber would have entrusted his remaining plans to Scott. He hadn't with Durrani.

But Hachemi?

The translator must have known something.

Hachemi had worked with John and his men in Afghanistan. Had he worked with Webber and the SEALs, as well? Was that where they'd find the nexus between the two?

Because it did exist—somewhere. Why else had Webber gone to such lengths to murder the man once it looked as though Hachemi was willing to make a deal?

"As much fun as this has been, I'm done talking, Prez."

She nodded. This really wasn't the place for this anyway. Or the time.

She'd done her damned job. She could take a minute to sit down and curl up on that couch and stare at those empty sheets until they were filled with the only man she wanted to see right now. Yes, Webber was still out there.

But Riyad was on the hunt.

She'd have to leave it to him. At least for today. Especially since the AWOL senior chief was firmly within NCIS' jurisdiction, and not CID's—and hers.

"Staff Sergeant Tulle, switch the cuffs to Agent Walburn's front. Fold his suit jacket over his hands and get that bastard out of here—quietly." While she didn't give a buck private's ass about preserving Scott's dignity, "We don't need any more attention focused on the embassy or its employees today." She tipped her head toward the coffee table across the room. "I'd also appreciate it if you'd take my laptop and kit with you and hit up the RSO's hospitality one more time." Now that she'd closed her case, at least this part of it, "I'd rather they were locked up while I'm here...distracted."

She finally turned back around to address a surprisingly subdued Jeffers while Tulle followed through on her instructions. "You're driving them." Because he was not staying here with her.

For once, the asshole didn't argue.

Within minutes, save for her and her gnawing personal terror, the room was empty.

Desperate to kill the quiet that had set in, she returned her call to Palisade and filled the general in on Scott, then hung up and made several more calls to arrange for someone from the Shifa's morgue to pick up Tom Crier's body. Since the embassy had no way to store it, Crier would remain here in the basement of the hospital until Colonel Tarrington finished with his suicide in Bahrain and made his way to Islamabad.

Given everything else she had left to do to wrap things up, she'd still be around to view the postmortem.

The morgue tasking finally checked off, she phoned Fort

Campbell's Blanchfield Community Hospital next and spoke with Gil.

During this call, she discovered that although Fort Detrick's makeshift chimeral cure wasn't due to land at Islamabad International for hours yet, the baby upstairs in this very hospital was holding his own. Danyal had also already been given half of the treatment Gil had used on her, including the *varicella* vaccine and a course of acyclovir. Gil was hopeful. While Danyal was woefully young, the infant brain was more resilient in many ways than adult ones. All they could do was wait.

As for her, she needed to hang in there. Gil had spoken with the surgical section of the Shifa, too. John should be out of surgery soon.

She just needed to be patient.

The admonishment in mind, Regan severed her second call and sank onto the couch to endure the most painful wait of her life. Just when she was ready to venture out to find the surgical section of which Gil had spoken, there was a tap on her door.

"Come in!"

She sprang up from the couch and headed across the room, anxious to greet her visitor, only to realize it wasn't Sitara Chaudhry...it was her husband.

She returned the chief justice's traditional greeting, grateful she'd re-donned the now thoroughly crushed *dupatta* after her shower. This was one man who did not deserve slighting, however unintentionally. "Sir, I—"

"Harun, please. We are friends, no?"

That, they were. "Yes. Please call me Regan—or Rae."

Heck, this man and his wife could call her whatever they wanted. The two could also call on her for the rest of her life.

She'd be there, ready to assist, very few questions asked.

"My wife phoned me. Your husband's surgery is complete.

He is in recovery now, and they should be bringing him to your room shortly. All went very well. Most importantly, I am to tell you that a graft was not required."

Oh, thank God.

Both her hands trembled along with her entire body as the relief seared in. "Thank you so much for letting me know." But as to that misconception of his, the one she'd accidentally perpetuated with the rings she still bore, "I need to tell you, though. I'm not—that is...Major Garrison and I, we're not married." She held up her steadier hand. "These were necessary for our recent covers."

But Harun simply smiled and shook his head. "The formal ceremony will not be long in coming. For the major, he is already wed in his heart...as I suspect you are, as well. And from the brief exchanges my wife and I were honored to witness in your embassy conference room and after, there will be no going back, for either of you."

Yeah, she wasn't touching that one.

Not even with him.

But there was something else she needed to clear up. "I have another confession, too—well, a correction really. I've spoken with someone who saw the shot being set up. The one that injured John. The shooter, he wasn't aiming for you. I heard what you did for John and what you said this morning when you donated blood on his behalf. You deserve to know the truth."

This time the man shrugged. "Perhaps. But if this bullet had been fired at me, the major would have stepped in to shield me. So...no matter. We shall keep this to ourselves, yes?"

Leave it to a lawyer to split that hair.

This time, she smiled. Nodded. Because his assessment was the truth. "Yes, we'll keep it between us. And, yes, John definitely would have shielded you." It was one of the reasons why John had been up on that platform. And one of the so very many more reasons as to why the man had managed to invade her heart.

Harun was right about one thing. Now that John was firmly inside her heart, there was no getting him out. There was no point in even trying.

Not that she had any idea what she was going to do about that.

"I, too, have a confession."

Chaudhry had a confession? For her?

But, again, the man nodded. "It is the reason I told my wife that I would come here to tell you the news about the major. Our prime minister, he was given access to something that perhaps a man of his leanings should not have been given."

Oh, Lord. "My background investigation."

"Yes. He shared the contents with me while he was attempting to sway my opinion on...other matters. This was not right and, yet, perhaps Allah intended it. For having been privy to knowledge of your past that I should not have, I am able to come here to assure you that it does not matter. You are not the sins of your father. Some of my people might disagree, but I do not. His disgrace is not yours. You need not bow your head in shame. For through your relentless quest for the truth, no matter where it lies, you have restored your family's honor. Any man would be proud to call you daughter. I would be proud. I, as well as my wife, am also in your debt—as well as our country. Major Garrison's, too. Remember that. And now, my wife awaits. I must take her home, finally, so that she may begin to grieve."

"Sir?" She ignored his silent, frowning reminder to use his name. "If you've been briefed on my background, I'm sure you know the rest."

"Your mother?"

"Yes. I just wanted to tell you and your wife—that is, please hold fast to something as you both mourn your daughter. The pain? I can't lie; it doesn't ever really go away. Especially when you've seen that horror with your own eyes. But...it does lessen. Eventually. And you both will find joy again, I promise. Especially since you have each other, and Allah, to lean on."

He nodded once at that, and left.

She retrieved her phone as the door closed and quickly texted Tulle the outstanding news. She made yet another call to Palisade to update him on John's condition as well, then returned her phone to her pocket to resume the wait.

Less than five minutes later, John arrived as promised.

Unfortunately, he was fast asleep.

Two young men removed the empty bed from the room first, then rolled John's slightly wider one into the room, slotting it, and his IV stand and monitors, into place. Regan waited while a nurse adjusted the IV and those monitors on John's right then offered a soft invitation in English to press the call button if she needed anything.

And then the nurse, too, nodded politely and left.

Unable to return to the couch, she moved up the left side of John's body, near his head. She traced her fingers over his warm brow. She might as well have used her right, because her entire left hand was still trembling too, albeit with relief.

When her light touch failed to rouse him, she moved on to the growth on his jaw, savoring the texture. She didn't know if it was the lingering effects of the anesthesia or the more normal exhaustion his mind and body had suffered, given that neither of them had slept the previous night, but that soft touch failed to rouse John too.

Unwilling to head over to the couch to curl up alone, she slipped off her shoes and tucked them beneath the bed. Her *dupatta* went onto the small plastic set of drawers beside the headboard. Her 9mm and credentials, she slipped beneath John's pillow.

Only then, with her phone still in her back pocket, did she quietly slip herself up into the bed beside him. She lay on her right side, taking up as little room as possible at the very edge of the mattress. Satisfied she wouldn't injure him, she stretched up to kiss the side of his cheek, then moved on to his ear to whisper the one thing John had asked of her while they'd been in bed together at the Serena. The one thing he needed. Her assurance that she could get past what he'd flung at her all those months ago in that parking lot; that she already had.

*"I don't hate you."*

With that, she laid her head down onto the pillow beside his. He was last thing she saw as the exhaustion took over and the numbing darkness slipped in.

JOHN WOKE BEFORE HER—AND with that smile and that colossal ego of his firmly intact. She knew, because she could feel it swelling, even as she pushed through the layers of sleep that were clinging to her brain.

Regan opened her eyes anyway.

That deep, dimpled fold greeted her. "If I'd known what it took to keep you by my side while I slept, I'd have arranged to take that bullet sixteen months ago."

Her hand came up, instinctively covering his mouth. "Don't. Don't *ever* tease about something like that." Not after today.

His left arm, the one that had somehow made its way beneath her while she'd been sleeping, pulled her closer until she was lying atop the uninjured portion of his groin and his hospital-gown-clad chest. "All right. I promise."

While he was at it, she wondered if she could get him to ensure that he'd never get shot or seriously injured again. Because her nerves just couldn't take it.

Though, oddly, speaking of her nerves, the ones in her right hand and arm had quieted down significantly.

Because of her nap? Or because John had been holding her?

Though she suspected the credit lay in equal parts with both, there was no way she'd admit to it. The man's arrogance was inflated enough as it was.

"Did I dream it?"

She shook her head, not willing to tease him about something that was so close to his heart either. Arrogant or not, he deserved the truth.

"Would you tell me again, now that I'm completely awake?"

She reached up, just as she had earlier when she'd given in to temptation and the relief of finally having him in the room, warm and breathing. She traced her fingertips along his brow and through the cultivated thicket beneath, before she settled them into that mesmerizing fold. Only then did she lean closer, this time looking directly into his eyes as she said it again. "I don't hate you."

Like him, she'd tried, but failed...spectacularly.

His soft, slow sigh eased out, filling the air between them, and then that fold deepened.

"Although—" She glanced down at the rings he'd surreptitiously tucked into her palm when he'd assisted her from the car at the Serena. "—I should also tell you that, for a man who supposedly detests lies, you set up a whopper. And don't bother telling me it was merely a lie of omission. Because it still counts. And what the devil happened to taking it slow this time, and patience?"

"Ah."

"Don't *ah* me."

If anything, the crease that cut down into that thicket deepened that much more. "You're an outstanding detective. I knew you'd figure it out."

Oh, good Lord. "You are *such*—"

"An ass. Yeah, I know." That irritating twinkle entered the gray. "But I'm your ass. And, apparently, your gorilla. As for taking it slow and patience—what do you call sixteen months? I think I've been damned patient." He reached down to wrap his fingers around hers. He lifted her hand from his chest, tilting it so that the diamond gleamed as brightly as that warm, steady stare of his. "And I'd like to point out that you haven't taken these off. So, I should probably warn you...there's a ceremony that goes with these rings. One that'll involve both of us."

"I've heard that."

He let her fingers go and captured her chin, lifting it up so that she couldn't evade that now very serious gray, even if she'd wanted to. "Then, what do you say? I have my company chaplain on speed dial. There's no wait in Kentucky...I checked. We could head over to the post chapel when our flight lands. Grab two passing soldiers as witnesses and give Chaplain Ross an uplifting duty for a change. We've both even got a couple weeks of downtime coming so we can recuperate. We can call it a honeymoon. Unless you want a big thing with all the trimmings. I can wait for that if I have to."

She'd never wanted a big thing.

Heck, she'd never even thought she'd have this. *Him*. But now that she did, she did not want to lose him—ever. That bullet had made it excruciatingly clear to her. All she could do was pray that she didn't screw this up. Again.

"Rae?"

"Okay."

His brow hiked. "Okay?" His thumb scraped along her bottom lip. "Just to be clear—okay, you'll marry me? Or, okay we see the chaplain when we land?"

"Both."

This time, that mesmerizing fold cratered in as he pulled her even closer so he could slant his mouth down to capture hers in a brief, searing kiss. "Okay."

And that was that.

Her gaze drifted to the rolling hospital tray table on his right as he allowed her to settle back against his chest. Her phone lay on top. It had been in her back pocket when she'd fallen asleep. It must have rung, waking him.

"How much do you know?"

Her cheek lifted along with his chest as he shrugged. "Pretty much everything. You've been asleep for at least five hours."

She checked her watch.

Closer to seven.

Yikes. She could only imagine what the nurses had thought. "Why didn't anyone wake me and kick me down to the couch?"

"I wouldn't let them." He reached out to tap her phone briefly. "I should probably also confess that I've been fielding your calls all afternoon. Tulle and General Palisade filled me in on most of it."

If that was the case, he probably knew more than she did now. "Does Riyad know about Scott? And that he was working with Webber?"

"I don't know. Palisade hadn't heard back from Kettering when we spoke. But I also fielded a call from Fourche. He says the chimeral cure is already in the boy. Now it's wait and see over the next few days, but it's looking good so far."

Thank God.

"Also, Palisade had some interesting news. Jeffers has been removed from his post. Evidently when the ambassador found out why Jeffers was in Crier's office before he ate his gun, she had him fired on the spot. Seems Jeffers had placed the sole blame for yesterday on Crier's shoulders, screamed at him for not being able to prevent the leak of those photos and the cave info that led to the mobs around the country."

Jeffers had been fired? "Frankly, it couldn't have happened to a crappier guy." After all, if there were signs to miss, Jeffers had missed them too.

Even worse, she suspected that Jeffers had known all along that Crier had fathered the Sadats' son. Yet, he'd pounced anyway. His tantrum might not have caused Crier to commit suicide, but the stress had probably helped the decision along.

At least the boy had a chance at recovery now. That was something.

She reached up to trace her fingers along John's jaw, just because she could.

To her surprise, his smile turned sheepish as he scrubbed the opposite side of his face. "Yeah, I should probably shave this off when we get home."

She shook her head.

It was a mistake.

His brow rose as that fold, and that ego, slipped back in. "You like it."

Hell, yes.

"Maybe."

He laughed. "Oh, you definitely like it." His arm tightened briefly. "All right, I'll keep it. Though you're lucky I'm SF. Kind of a perk given some of the shitholes they end up sending us to. Hell, sometimes relaxed grooming standards are the *only* perk."

Oh, she was lucky, and about a lot more than just that cultivated scruff. But speaking of SF, "I need you to work with me when we get back. On the range."

His fingers came up, hooking beneath her chin once more, lifting it. "I told you I spoke to Tulle. You did *not* cause this. In fact, you saved my life. Twice."

"So he said." And, yes, she would be grateful to her rattling arm for the rest of her life. But if that rattle planned on coming and going when she was exhausted and/or under stress, she'd have to learn how to work around it. Immediately.

Because the next time, things might not turn out so well.

And that, she would not allow. "I need to qualify with my left hand—just in case."

He nodded. "The range it is. Though that's gotta be the strangest place to spend a honeymoon."

True. But they wouldn't be spending their nights there.

That thought had slipped through his mind too, as evidenced by his returning twinkle. He opened his mouth to say something when her phone rang.

John reached out and snagged the phone instead, passing it to her.

She didn't recognize the number. "Agent Chase."

"Hey, Prez."

*Jelly*? She knew all his numbers, including his wife's. Had he gotten a new phone? "Thanks for getting back to me, but I don't think—"

"You've got reason to be concerned."

"What?" About the spook? "Just a second." She glanced up at John. "You remember Agent Jelling from Hohenfels?"

John nodded.

"I texted him when you went to take a shower at the Serena. Asked him to poke around, see what Riyad was doing when we were in that parking lot." She shifted the phone back to her ear. "Jelly, I'm with Major Garrison. Can I put you on speaker?"

"Might as well. This concerns you both."

She clicked the phone over. "We're here."

"So, as I was saying. I think you both have reason to be concerned about Riyad. As requested, I did some digging as to the man's whereabouts on a certain date."

"Are you saying he was there?" In that parking lot, listening to them?

"No idea. All I know is Riyad was not stateside, because I tracked him leaving on an off-the-books flight out of Langley the day before. And get this: my poking raised a serious flag. As in, admiral level. I got a call a few minutes ago. The Big Bubble himself."

"Kettering called you? Why?"

"To tell me to stop poking around and to keep my fucking mouth shut about anything I might have come across during my initial search...up to and including chatting about the matter with General Palisade. Anyway, that's all I got. And all I'm likely to get. Sorry, but I got my wife and kid to consider."

"I know. For what it's worth, I'm sorry I asked."

"Don't be. You didn't know. But don't memorize this number, Prez. I'll be ditching this phone just as soon as I hang up. Bye."

She stared at her own phone as Jelly severed the call that had been made from what she now realized was a burner, then looked up at John.

Holy shit.

*Webber.*

The name ripped through her gut. Somehow, whatever Jelly had just accidentally stepped into on her behalf was connected to the former, dirty SEAL.

And Sam Riyad.

But there was more. There had to be. Why else was Admiral Kettering shutting everyone else out—*including* General Palisade?

"John, what the hell is going on?"

Both his arms came up, locking firmly around her, as if to protect her. Something that, given who appeared to be involved in all this, might not be possible. "I have no idea. But we will be finding out."

Damned straight they would.

The only question was, who would be left standing once they did?

*Are you ready for the next*
*Deception Point Military Thriller?*

CLICK HERE for more information on
*Choke Point*
Book 4 in the Deception Point
Military Thriller Series

## MEET THE AUTHOR

CANDACE IRVING is the daughter of a librarian and a retired US Navy chief. Candace grew up in the Philippines, Germany, and all over the United States. Her senior year of high school, she enlisted in the US Army. Following basic training, she transferred to the Navy's ROTC program at the University of Texas-Austin. While at UT, she spent a summer in Washington, DC, as a Congressional Intern. She also worked security for the UT Police.

BA in Political Science in hand, Candace was commissioned as an ensign in the US Navy and sent to Surface Warfare Officer's School to learn to drive warships. From there, she followed her father to sea.

Candace is married to her favorite soldier, a former US Army Combat Engineer. They live in the American Midwest, where the Army/Navy football game is avidly watched and argued over every year.

Go Navy; Beat Army!

Candace also writes military romantic suspense under the name Candace Irvin—without the "g"!

Email Candace at www.CandaceIrving.com

or connect via:

bookbub.com/profile/candace-irving
facebook.com/CandaceIrvingBooks
twitter.com/candace_irving
goodreads.com/Candace_Irving

## ALSO BY CANDACE IRVING

*Deception Point Military Thrillers:*

### AIMPOINT

Has an elite explosives expert turned terrorist? Army Detective Regan Chase is ordered to use her budding relationship with his housemate —John Garrison—to find out. But John is hiding something too. Has the war-weary Special Forces captain been turned as well? As Regan's investigation deepens, lines are crossed—personal and professional. Even if Regan succeeds in thwarting a horrific bombing on German soil, what will the fallout do to her career?

A Deception Point Military Thriller: Book 1

Free Download, Visit: candaceirvin.com/aimpoint

### BLIND EDGE

Army Detective Regan Chase responds to a series of murders and suicides brought on by the violent hallucinations plaguing a Special Forces A-Team—a team lead by Regan's ex, John Garrison. Regan quickly clashes with an unforgiving, uncooperative and dangerously secretive John—and an even more secretive US Army. What really happened during that Afghan cave mission? As Regan pushes for answers, the murders and suicides continue to mount. By the time Army comes clean, it may be too late. Regan's death warrant has already been signed—by John's hands.

A Deception Point Military Thriller: Book 2

### BACKBLAST

Army Detective Regan Chase just solved the most horrific case of her career. The terrorist responsible refuses to speak to anyone but her. The claim? There's a traitor in the Army. With the stakes critical, Regan heads for the government's newest classified interrogation site: A US Navy warship at sea. There, Regan uncovers a second, deadlier, terror plot that leads all the way to a US embassy—and beyond. Once again, Regan's on the verge of losing her life—and another far more valuable to her than her own...

A Deception Point Military Thriller: Book 3

More Deception Point Thrillers Coming Soon!

*Hidden Valor Military Suspense*

**THE GARBAGE MAN**

Former Army detective Kate Holland spent years hiding from the world—and herself. Now a small-town cop, the past catches up when a fellow vet is left along a backroad...in pieces. Years earlier, Kate spent eleven hours as a POW. Her Silver Star write-up says she killed eleven terrorists to avoid staying longer. But Kate has no memory of the deaths. And now, bizarre clues are cropping up. Is Kate finally losing her grip on reality? As the murders multiply, Kate must confront her demons...even as she finds herself in the killer's crosshairs.

A Hidden Valor Military Suspense: Book 1

**IN THE NAME OF**

*He'll do anything for his country...even murder.*

Kate Holland is back!

A Hidden Valor Military Suspense: Book 2

**Coming in 2021!**

More Hidden Valor Books Coming Soon!

## DEDICATION

For my brilliant & beautiful daughter Sarah,
who did so much to get Blind Edge Press
off the ground.

## ACKNOWLEDGMENTS

My ideas tend to fall well outside the range of my expertise. I'd like to thank the following folks for loaning me theirs. The cool stuff belongs to them; the mistakes are all mine.

My very special thanks to Father Bob Popichak & Don Curtis. I leaned heavily on their expertise & amazing friendships while writing this one.

My deepest gratitude also goes to the following folks for helping with information & plot threads that are woven throughout the Deception Point series:
Retired NCIS Special Agent Mike Keleher
Dr. Henry C. Lee, Ph.D.
Lt. Col. J.D. Whitlock, USAF, Retired
Dr. John "Jack" Shroder, Ph.D.
Lt. Cdr. Michael J. Walsh, USN, Retired

I'd also like to thank my critique partners CJ Chase & Amy McKinley, as well as Judi Shaw & the awesome members of the

Goat Locker. And, of course, my wonderful husband, David. I appreciate the input, support & sanity more than you can know.

As always, my deepest thanks to my editor, Sue Davison, for her uncanny talent for tracking facts & figures, and of course, her truly brilliant editing. Sue, your brain is phenomenal!

Finally, a huge thanks to Ivan Zanchetta for another gorgeous cover. I envy your talents!

You're all incredible!

# COPYRIGHT

eBook ISBN: 978-1-952413-20-9

Paperback ISBN: 978-1-952413-23-0

BACKBLAST



This first edition was published by Blind Edge Press in 2021.



This is a work of fiction. The characters in this book do not exist outside the author's imagination. Any resemblance to actual persons, living or dead, is purely coincidental. All incidents in this book were invented by the author for the sole purpose of entertainment.

Printed in Great Britain
by Amazon